A Long Way from Home

Brian W. Caves

DEDICATION

This novel is for my daughter, Hilary.
I love her with my heart, my soul. She
is the very essence of my being.

Every man's life ends the same way.
It is only the details of how he lived
and how he died that distinguish
one man from another.

~ Ernest Hemingway

A Long Way from Home

CHICAGO

August 1955

Thursday afternoon, the eve of my thirty-third birthday. It has been another bitch of a hot day and I am driving home from work. Art Tatum's version of "Tiger Rag" is on the radio. The windows are down and I can smell exhaust fumes and the hot tar from the sunbaked streets. I am completely bushed after a ten-day straight run on duty.

My head is aching and my throat desperate for a cold one. But I am going home and looking forward to a long weekend with Jenny, my wife. No getting up for work. No clipping on my detective shield or my gun holster for three whole days. Days spent lazing around, looking up at the blue sky, romantic meals, making love, and just being together.

A perfect, happy, long weekend

At 6.30 I pull up outside our house, kill the radio and close the windows. The engine skips a beat as I turn off the ignition. I make a mental note to get that looked at over the weekend.

Peeling myself out of the driver's seat, I reach back for my jacket and lock the doors and smile as I take the steps up to the front door two at a time. I hesitate before inserting the key. Beyond that door is everything I ever wanted. The job is the job and something I love doing. But beyond that door is my life.

Tiger Rag is still playing in my head as I insert the key and turn the lock.

The instant I step into the house, I feel the hairs on the back of my head bristle.

Something is most definitely wrong; I can feel it. The atmosphere is compressing, stifling. All the windows are closed, and the air conditioning unit is off.

I call out. *Jenny! It's me...Jenny*!

No response.

I search through the lounge and into the kitchen. Nothing out of place. Out in the backyard, I call her name again. Still no response. Back inside, my heart thrumming in my chest, I climb the stairs. No sign of her anywhere.

Jenny is a creature of habit. Everything planned, organized, one of the qualities that makes our relationship work, and for her not to be here when she promised without calling me at work or leaving a note on the pad by the phone...it just never happens.

There is no note.

I run up the stairs again, calling out. Something is most definitely wrong. The hairs on my neck feel like thorns, my blood feels like water. I search every room again, then hurtle back down, taking three stairs at a time. I check the small notepad on the kitchen counter again for messages. It's routine, habit, something we do all the time to let each other know where we were and about how long we'd be.

Nothing.

And then the telephone rings.

I stop dead and stare at it, letting it ring four times before I dare make a move. Maybe it's Jenny calling from a phone booth, maybe her car has broken down or she's got a flat? It could be as simple as that couldn't it, I told myself. Couldn't it?

Six steps all in a slow-motion haze and I lift the receiver off its cradle, put the phone to my ear. My voice is shaking. "Yes...? Jenny? Jenny...is that you...?"

It's not Jenny. I listen, drop the phone and run to my car. I ignore every stop sign and commit every traffic violation on the books.

When I get to the hospital Jenny is being wheeled into the operating theatre. Around her doctors and nurses move quickly, orders are barked out, rubber soles squeak on the linoleum floor. They won't let me see her. I'm pushed out of the way and ordered to wait.

The corridor is crowded, and I stand there for what seems like a lifetime before one of the doctors comes to see me. He talks at me, explains how badly hurt she is: shattered knees, broken legs and arms, pelvis, facial and head injuries, internal life-threatening injuries. The surgical team is doing all they can.

The information comes at me like a spray of bullets from a Gatling gun and when the doctor is finished, I collapse onto a plastic bench, my heart a cold stone, my blood ice. I sit there staring at the pale green linoleum floor while everything moves in a blur around me, and the smell of hospital antiseptic is the only thing reminding me of where I am.

When the surgeon enters the corridor, way he pauses in the doorway, way he pulls down his mask, way his brow knits together; I knew what message he brought for me.

PART ONE

Six Years Later

CHAPTER 1

Little Joe Williams was a big man, a contradiction of terms. Six four in his stockinged feet with a chest and shoulders the width of a barn door; skin the color of used motor oil, pale-yellow eyes and a wide, bright smile that could light up a darkened room so you didn't need a lamp. You'd have thought him a boxer with his flattened nose and hands the size of shovels, but it was ivory that Joe laid his hands on for a living, not human flesh. He was a great piano player. He'd played all the clubs and juke joints down south by the time he was twenty-two and then made his way north, migrating to the Chicago blues scene along with a host of others after the Second World War.

Joe played with the best of them: McKinley Morganfield, Willie Dixon, and Chester Burnett. But while their fame grew after signing to the newly formed Chess record label, Joe's own career would see him remain forever as a sideman to the main draw. And that was on account of the knife wound he received while saving my worthless ass.

I was being turned over by a gang one night down an alley on Chicago's South Side, only three blocks from my apartment, when Joe happened to be passing. As I lay semi-conscious, blood streaming from nose, mouth, and a deep cut above my right eye, Joe hauled the men off me and got stabbed for his trouble, but not before he busted a couple of jaws first.

We got patched up at the local charity hospital, but the wound to Joe's shoulder was serious. The knife blade had caused extensive nerve damage, so much so that when he got back to serious piano playing the muscles in his right arm and hand would occasionally spasm and he would lose all functionality. But the measure of the man was such that he bore me no ill-will. As far as he was concerned, we were all brothers. I told him anything he needed, any time, I'd be there for him. Wrote it on the back of a business card and handed it over. The card looked no bigger than a snowflake in his huge hand.

They never caught the hit-and-run driver who took Jenny's life, and since the day I stood in that hospital corridor and was dealt the crushing blow that ripped my world apart, I'd been to hell and back and Joe was one of only half-a-dozen people who helped pull me out from a long black tunnel with no light at its end.

I couldn't go back working for the Chicago Police Force, so I became a licensed Private Investigator. I worked the odd missing person case, insurance scams, cheating husbands; nothing too dangerous, and it kept a roof over my head, the refrigerator stocked, and a full tank of gas in my car.

Last time I met up with Joe was on a chilly night in April. The Russians had sent Yuri Gagarin into space and the Bay of Pigs fiasco was just a few days behind us. We were halfway down a bottle of Johnnie Walker and trading jokes at Kennedy's expense when Joe's right hand suddenly grabbed at his chest and that big smile he had twisted into a grimace of pain. At first, I thought it was one of those all-too-frequent spasms causing his hand to flutter like a bird on the wing, but when he collapsed over the beer-stained counter, I realized it was something much worse. Despite Joe having a body builder's physique, he also had a heart condition. A condition not served well by the amount of whiskey he drank, although I had never once seen him incapacitated. He always said, 'You wanna play good, then you can't play drunk'.

Between his family down south and his Chicago musician friends, we rallied around for a decent oak coffin and paid to have his body sent home. I gave what I could. It was the very least I could do. I'd lost one of the few people I could truly count as a friend, and suddenly my world was less complete. I mourned his passing, missed his stories of life back in Georgia; missed his piano playing and that big, bright smile.

About six weeks later, I got a call from Little Joe's sister, Ellie-Mae Jackson. The conversation was brief and to the point, and hearing the fear and anguish in her voice I didn't need any further persuasion to head south. I'd made a promise and I owed a debt to her brother.

It took me a day to get my things together and check over the Dodge ready for the journey. I drove a straight eight hours down I-65 and stopped overnight in a sparsely furnished motel in Nashville. I rose early the next day, back aching, sun low and bright. I grabbed a coffee and two cinnamon doughnuts, estimated another straight eight to Paradise Creek, Georgia.

I picked up the I-75 at Chattanooga, through Atlanta, and onward to Tifton. By the time I was headed east on Highway 82, my cheap gray shirt was sticking to my sweat-soaked skin like a shammy leather on a wet hood, and my hands were skidding around the steering wheel. I'd had Marty Robbins on the radio when I entered Nashville, but now the radio was off, my left elbow was hung out the driver's window and the wind blew through my hair.

There was little traffic on the highway and the scenery was just mile after mile of flat land interspersed with steaming creeks, the occasional gas station, and dilapidated roadside food joints with tin roofs and boarded-up windows. Most of the tarpaper shanties dotted here and there had been abandoned like the farms, the small mom and pop concerns with a few head of cattle taken over by the multinationals.

I found the Paradise Creek Motel a couple of miles outside town. There were a dozen cabins built in a straight line, each with a veranda out front and a single allocated parking space. The place looked as if it hadn't been painted in ten years or more; the paint, blistered and brittled by sun was peeling away from the wood it was designed to protect. As long as the shower worked, the room and sheets were clean, I didn't really care much about the outer appearance. It was just a place to rest my head for a few days. I parked up and headed for the manager's office.

The door creaked when I opened it. There was nobody in the office, so I stepped over to the desk and rang the bell. I looked around while I waited. There was a message board screwed to the left wall with some brochures pinned to it and a set of house rules, a copy of which, a sticker informed me, could be found in each of the cabins. I made a mental note to hunt it down later and take in some light bedtime reading. Behind the desk was a cheap reproduction print of a seascape in a yellowing frame, which I guessed had been white when it was new, but over the years had taken on the color of tobacco smoke. Next to this, a framed photograph of an angular-faced man, unsmiling, holding up a large fish in both hands. The label underneath said, 'Hubert Trenton, Bowfin 1952'.

I rang the bell again and after a few seconds heard footsteps and a tall, bony man with greased back dark hair and shifting dark eyes appeared in the doorway to the room beyond the desk. He had a beak for a nose and lips so thin it looked as if a pencil line had been drawn across his face. Not someone you felt you could trust, just a man with a lot of secrets. I looked up at the framed photograph again and sure enough the man standing in front of me was Trenton, nine years on.

"Help you?" he said in a voice as thin as the pencil line on his face. He studied me with suspicious eyes. I wondered if he greeted every paying customer in the same way, and if he did, how much repeat business he got.

I gave him a practiced smile. "I'd like a room, please?"

He twisted the register around so I could write down my details. "Sure, we got cabin six free," he said. "That'll be ten dollar a night. How long you need it for?"

I jotted down my name and address, using a ballpoint attached by a silver-colored chain to a small wooden block that appeared to be glued to the desk. I gave the pen a sharp tug just to test it and the block held fast. "A week," I said, maintaining a smile. "Perhaps two."

He turned the register back so he could read my details. "Chicago, huh? Long way from home. What brings you down here?"

"Business."

He reached under the desk and produced a key. It was on a metal ring looped through a hole in a polished wooden fob. He handed it over. "What kind of business you in?"

I said the first thing that came into my head. "Financial." There wasn't a chance in hell I was going to give away what I came to do.

His eyes grew sharper. "What…like insurance?"

"Something like that," I said, and before he could interrogate me further, I asked for directions to Cotton Cut Road.

You would have thought I'd just given him a sour lemon to suck on his faced screwed up so much.

"That's where the black aspect live," he said in a voice edged with disgust and surprise all at the same time.

"Yes, that's correct," I said politely.

"What business you got down there, one of them niggers renege on a debt?" I didn't say anything, but after a moment those dark eyes narrowed even more and he gave me a twisted smile, as if he'd suddenly made a connection. "Oh, I get it," he said. "Financial problems…insurance. Their kind always gambling, borrowing money, and not honoring payments. Yeah, yeah, I get it. You come to collect on a debt. Must be a big one for you to come all this way?"

I forced a smile and said nothing. I withdrew my wallet and counted out seventy dollars to cover the week. "I'll let you know in a few days if I need to stay any longer."

"Sure," he said, nodding slowly, flicking each note between thumb and forefinger and then placing them in a drawer beneath the desk. He had a smug expression on his face, thinking he'd got the measure of me, and almost as if the idea of me collecting a debt from a black man amused him in some way.

He gave me directions and there we left it. I got my suitcase out of the trunk of my Dodge, went over to the cabin, and dumped the case on the bed. I didn't even look at the room. I had more urgent things to attend to.

CHAPTER 2

I followed the Georgia-Pacific rail track as instructed and headed west of the town boundary by about two miles until I reached a point where a rusting disused water tower stood beside a large freight warehouse and three silos. It was here that I had to turn south while the railroad continued.

After about ten minutes, the road lost what little evenness it possessed, and the Dodge was bouncing in and out of deep ruts that felt more like ravines. I had to slow down for fear of losing a wheel or wrecking the axle. To either side of me, tin-roofed houses appeared. The houses rested on cinder blocks and railway sleepers, and dogs lay panting in the shade of porches while children dressed in little more than rags played in their front yards among the chickens that scratched around in the red dirt.

I rounded a bend and came across a small girl with skin so black it was almost purple. She stood at the side of the road, a battered doll crooked in her right arm. As I got closer to her, she instinctively clutched the doll to her chest, almost as if she were afraid I would suddenly leap from the car and snatch it away from her. The fear in her dark eyes told me everything I needed to know. That doll was everything to her and probably the only thing she'd ever had other than the rags on her back and the timber house behind her.

A large black woman burst through the screen door of the house like a tidal wave. Everything about her was big: hair, face, body, ankles. She had on a stained housecoat which billowed around her as she rushed toward the girl, hooked her up under an arm as if she were no more than a small bundle of sticks, and carried her back through the screen door into the house.

I was a white man, and I wasn't welcome.

I continued along Cotton Cut Road to where a junked, rusted out old army Jeep peered bug-eyed out from tall, dry grass and thicket. Beyond the Jeep, a haphazard line of broken-down houses and trailers began. Gardens had run to riot and wrecked appliances had been dumped, now used either as makeshift card tables or had been stripped out and had garbage burned in them. Ellie-Mae's house was the last one on the left. I parked up under a live oak draped in Spanish Moss, got out, and crossed the road, kicking up dust and disturbing chickens as I went.

The house was flat roofed with windows either side of the door and a large porch with railings you could reach climbing four wooden steps. I knocked on the screen door, waited, swatting flies, wiping sweat from around my neck and forehead. The door opened and a tall young Negro boy of around sixteen stood there. He had half his crumpled white shirt hanging out of a pair of khaki pants and no shoes. He examined me with wary brown eyes.

"Help you?" he said.

"Name's Tom Bale," I said. "Here about Alice."

"You the detective Mama called?"

"Yes, son, that would be me."

He gave me a contemptuous look and went back into the house, leaving the door open. "I ain't your son."

A woman's voice rose from somewhere close. "You watch your mouth, Moses. Pay some respect." Then, "Come in, Mr. Bale. Come in."

I stepped into a gloomy hallway that ran front to back of the house. The walls that separated the rooms coming off the hall were no more than unevenly placed boards so you could see through the gaps from one room to the next.

Ellie-Mae was sitting on a busted sofa in a twelve square room to my left. In front of her was a wicker basket. She'd been stripping corn husks. She stood to greet me, wiping her hands clean of corn strands on her apron.

She was a small woman, barely five feet in height, trim and firm bodied with curly graying hair, sad dark eyes, and a wide flattened nose. Her skin showed every one of her fifty years and was etched with darker lines where the creases formed around her eyes and mouth. She had on a gray calf-length skirt with the apron tied over and a pale-yellow blouse. She shook my outstretched hand with a surprising firmness and motioned for me to sit in the armchair opposite. She thanked me for coming and asked if I wanted something to drink.

"Don't keep no liquor in the house. There's coffee, juice, water, iced tea. You want something to eat?"

I hadn't eaten since breakfast, but I wasn't going to take advantage of her hospitality. "Just coffee would be fine, ma'am."

She turned and called out to her son. "Moses. Bring Mr. Bale a cup of coffee."

I was in a sparsely furnished room with a bare wooden floor. A three-legged dog of mixed heritage hobbled into the room, came over to me and sniffed at my crotch. I tickled its ears, which it seemed to appreciate.

"That's Deefa," Ellie-Mae said.

The dog lay down at my feet and went to sleep. "Unusual name, Deefa."

"Happened upon us one day. Came from nowhere and ended up staying. Didn't know what to call it, so I chose Deefa. D for dog."

I surveyed the room once more. It was clean, spotless even. Ellie-Mae didn't have much, but what she did have she took pride in. Moses brought a pot of coffee and a single tin cup on a tray and set it down on an occasional table. He barely acknowledged me and went away without saying a word.

"You'll have to excuse Moses," Ellie-Mae said. "He just full of the usual teenage moods. Older brother was the just same. Part of the problem growing up. I do the best I can on my own."

I said, "I heard from Little Joe your husband was killed several years back. I'm sorry for your loss. Must be tough losing a husband and then a brother. Kids suffer bad."

She huffed. "That no good husband. He was a drunk and a gambler, best he gone. As for Joe, he was different…gracious, kind, and now the Lord watching over him."

I couldn't agree more about Joe and owed it to him that I visit his grave. "Where's Joe buried, ma'am? I'd like to pay my respects."

Ellie-Mae threw me a dark look. "Will you stop with the ma'am business? Makes me uncomfortable. Joe buried at the chapel. You go on past the Jeep about a mile, you see it."

I poured myself a coffee. It was rich and strong tasting, best coffee I'd ever had, and I said so.

"Secret is to keeping the beans airtight and out of the sun. And you got to be careful when you grind them. Too fine will make it bitter and too coarse will make it watery."

"I'll be sure to remember that," I said. Then, "So you found my business card in Joe's things?"

She reached over to the side cabinet, pulled open a drawer, and handed me one of my business cards without saying a word. I turned it over and sure enough it was the one I'd given Joe all those months ago back in Chicago. I had written 'call me anytime' on the reverse side. I handed it back and she placed it on the arm of the settee.

Ellie-Mae's daughter, Alice, had gone missing. She was fourteen and last seen walking along Cotton Cut Road. Ellie-Mae had asked most people in the Bottoms, but nobody had seen her after that. There was mention of a black car seen around the same time, but again, nothing more; no make, model, or plate. Time about four-thirty in the afternoon.

"How long has it been now?" I asked.

"Two weeks and two days."

"And the sheriff hasn't made any progress at all?"

She let out a bitter little laugh. "Progress? No. The sheriff hasn't made any progress. One of his deputies took the details, had me fill out a missing person form, and that was it. Heard nothing since. I don't think the sheriff counts the disappearance of a young black girl high on his priority of urgent things to attend to."

"I'm sure they're doing what they can..."

"No, Mr. Bale," she said firmly. "I don't think they are."

"Why do you say that?"

"There's been a number of girls gone missing over the years. Not one of them found. I don't think the sheriff even tries...not with colored girls, anyhow. She was a sweet teenager from the white part of town, sheriff and his deputies would be out night and day looking for her."

I tried to sound sympathetic. "Surely that's not the case? I'm certain they're going through the usual procedures. It's just that so far nothing has turned up. Chicago...it's a common thing for young people to up and leave, and..."

"Not Alice," she interrupted, her eyes fixed firmly on mine. "She wouldn't do that...up and leave? She's only fourteen. No...not my Alice."

By the time she was done telling me everything she could, the sadness in her eyes had deepened and worry lines furrowed her brow. Moisture had formed in her eyes.

"Mind if I ask you something personal, Mr. Bale?"

"Sure." I smiled at her. "Can't promise I'll answer though."

She didn't return the smile. "You ever lost someone close?"

I focused on a point in the room, seeing nothing, saying nothing.

"Mr. Bale...?"

I came back to the moment.

Ellie-Mae was staring at me, a deep, troubled frown creasing her forehead.

Took me a few seconds to respond. "My wife..." I began to say, but had to stop and clear my throat.

"How was she taken from you?"

She waited for me to continue, but I just stared back at her for a while, letting her know that it was a subject I didn't care to talk about.

Ellie-Mae got the message. She understood perfectly. "So you know what it's like to have unresolved issues?"

I nodded; the memory too painful to put into words.

"Alice, she my baby and..." Her eyes welled with tears as she fought to control her emotions. "I need you to find her, Mr. Bale. You promise me you'll find her."

I didn't want to raise false hopes, but Ellie-Mae needed more from me at that moment. Against my better judgment, I lied. I leaned forward, held her tiny, calloused hands in mine, stared her straight in the eyes, and told her I would find her daughter. She half-smiled, wiped away the tears with a handkerchief from her apron pocket and thanked me. From the same pocket she pulled out a small photograph.

"Got this picture of Alice, figured you'd need it."

It was shot from the waist up. Alice was a very pretty young girl, with lovely almond-shaped brown eyes and high cheekbones. Looked an easy two or three years older than her actual age. "Beautiful girl," I said and tucked the photo into my wallet.

"You'll do whatever you can?" Ellie-Mae said, her eyes searching into mine. "Won't you, Mr. Bale?"

"I will," I said.

When I got outside, dusk was heavy in the sky and the crickets were having a conversation, trying to drown out the cicadas. Moses was waiting for me on the porch steps. He was scratching some kind of design into the red dirt with a stick. He stopped when he heard me come out.

"You going to find my sister?" he said.

I sat next to him, stared at the shapes he'd etched. "Going to be hard," I said. "Don't know this town, this county, or the people in it."

"Don't think you going to find her."

"Promised your mother I would."

He shook his head, and I saw beads of sweat threading through his pitch-black hair. "It's a false promise. Ain't nobody going to help you around here. They don't know nothing. Wasting your time."

"What makes you say that?"

He turned to me and his dark brown eyes grew hard. "Cos that's the way it is. You can't trust nobody. Nobody from town, anyways. They don't care for us out here."

"Where's your brother at? Might be useful for me to have a talk with him."

"He don't know nothin' either. He tell you same as me. Alice, she gone, ain't never coming back, not alive."

"You don't know that."

"Said, you wasting your time. Alice ain't the first and she won't be the last."

And with that, he got up, threw his stick to one side, and went back up the steps. "Brother's out, but he works up at the mill you want to speak to him."

I thanked him and asked what the shapes were.

"None of your business."

He went in the house, slamming the screen door.

I drove on past the bug-eyed Jeep and broken-down houses until I saw a white clapboard Baptist chapel with a short central spire set back about a hundred yards from the road on my left. A stone pathway led to the entrance. Dense woodland of pines flanked the sides and back of the church and out front to either side of the stone path there were graves set into yellowed sunbaked grass. Night was descending fast, but there was still just enough light to make out the graves, and the more I looked and walked around the more I could see graves extending beyond what at first appeared to be a natural boundary and into the woods.

I discovered at least thirty abandoned, overgrown plots, many unmarked and some inaccessible in the thick undergrowth. I assumed slaves were buried here, maybe even before the chapel had been built. No names, no identity, nobody taking ownership. Their lives, their stories faded over time and forever lost amid the forgotten souls. The more recent plots mostly had markers that included only a name and dates of birth and death.

I found Joe's, the most recent, a small bunch of summer flowers maybe only a day or two old placed in a stoneware jar. The inscription read: 'At Rest With The Lord Joseph Abraham Williams: Jan. 4, 1923 April 27, 1961'. Joe was thirty-eight, same age as me. I'd assumed he was older. I also discovered he had a middle name. You think you know someone. I said what I had to say to him, apologized for not being better prepared, and promised I'd bring flowers next time.

I got back to the Paradise Creek Motel around nine, a heart full of melancholy and a body desperate for sleep. There was a blue Chevy BelAir with white walls to the right of my cabin and a '52 Allstate Sedan to the left. I had neighbors. I hoped they'd be quiet.

I let myself in, switched on the light and overhead fan. There was a double bed freshly made up, a side cabinet, a small desk with a TV on it, a single chair, closet, and a door through to the bathroom. The carpet was worn but clean. It was all I needed. I stripped, went through to the bathroom, and turned on the overhead shower. Fresh towels and soap had been laid out for me. After, I lay back naked on the bed, closed my eyes. Two people, a man and a woman, began shouting at one another in the next room.

"I told you before we left Jacksonville to bring it!"

"I forgot it for chrissake, let it go!"

"You moron. How many times did I remind you?"

"Don't call me a fucking moron, bitch!"

And then the sound of a slap.

"You bastard!"

A door slammed and a moment later a car started, accelerated across the dirt and gravel, and was gone. Then, for the next hour, just the TV turned way too loud. I thought about getting up and going next door to complain, but my eyes started to flicker and I eventually fell asleep listening to the *Jack Paar Show*.

CHAPTER 3

I was rudely awakened from a dreamless sleep by a telephone ringing and at first, I was disorientated, unsure of where I was. Then I recognized the motel room, rubbed sleep from my eyes, propped myself up on one elbow, and reached for the phone on the nightstand.

"Yes?"

"Morning, Mr. Bale."

It was the motel owner, Hubert Trenton. "Morning, Mr. Trenton. What can I do for you?"

"Forgot to mention that we have a small diner located next to the office where you can have breakfast if it takes your fancy. Breakfast ain't included in the price. Pay as you go. We close it at ten."

I hadn't yet properly woken up and my stomach wasn't ready for it, despite me having eaten virtually nothing the day before. "Thanks for letting me know," I said, "but I'll pass this morning. Maybe tomorrow."

"No need to book a table. Just come over when you feel inclined."

I put down the receiver, sat on the edge of the bed, twisting my head and shoulders this way and that to ease the tension in my joints from yesterday's long drive and sleeping on a strange mattress.

Twenty minutes later I'd showered, put on a fresh shirt and my light-gray suit. It was 9:45 a.m. according to my watch. Stood under the ceiling fan, I felt ready to face the day, so I decided to walk into town, find me a place to grab a coffee and by then my stomach would have roused itself to the idea of breakfast.

Outside it was hot and still, the sky blue and cloudless. The Chevy BelAir was still in its bay, but the Sedan hadn't returned, so I guessed the moron had slapped the bitch a little too hard.

By the time I got to Main my shirt was sticking to my body it was so hot and I had my jacket hooked over one arm. I sat in the shade outside Benson's grocery store, wiped my sweat ringed neck with my handkerchief. I could hear someone busy on the phone inside. When they came free, I'd get me a cold Coca-Cola. Up and down the street there wasn't much going on, so I settled back and waited. I wanted to speak to Benson anyway on account of the fact he was one of the last people to see Alice Jackson alive.

Perhaps a couple of minutes had passed when an old black man dressed in crumpled khaki pants held up by suspenders, and an off-white shirt that had seen far better days came shuffling along toward me, walking stick clacking with each step. I could hear him wheezing from twenty feet away, and when he got up close, he stopped, eased his geriatric frame onto the bench beside me, and rested the walking stick between his legs. He removed his soiled gray hat, waved it across his face a couple of times then set it on the bench close to my jacket. Across the street, two young boys were strolling along, fishing rods slung over their shoulders like carbines. They were like ghostly apparitions through the vaporous swirling heat lifting off the sidewalk. Their laughter greeted us and put a smile on the old man's face. When he finally spoke, his words sounded like river water rushing over pebbles.

"Hot," he said by way of introduction.

"Indeed," I said.

"Lucas James."

"Tom Bale."

We shook hands. He nodded toward the two boys.

"You ever been fishing?"

"Long time ago."

"With your daddy?"

"Yeah."

"He teach you much?"

"Not really."

"Didn't take to it?"

"No. He went to war, never came back."

Silence for a moment. Reflection. A long time ago. Then the old man started up again.

"Used to wade up to my knees in that cool river water. Sun filtering through the trees, dappling the surface. Brown trout twitching this way and that on the line. And when I didn't got no line used to try catch 'em with my hands. Weren't no good at that though. You ever done that?"

"With my hands?"

"Yeah."

"Never tried."

And that was our conversation done about fishing.

He shifted his body with that awkwardness old people have, found a comfortable position against the wooden slats. A breeze stroked our faces. Put another smile on his as he closed his eyes.

I remembered fishing the Calumet River as a young boy. The Calumet was mostly industrial waste and pollution, diverted from its original course and interrupted by canals and feeders to support the onslaught of steel mills and heavy industry. There were some pleasant spots along its banks if you knew where to find them, but the fishing was mostly for carp, which, for some reason beyond my thinking, seemed immune to the chemicals being dumped. Later, I dated a pretty girl in high school, and turned from boy to man in one of those private spots. We imagined that only the river knew our secret, drew it down into the eddies and then carried it away through Cook County.

Then there was the fight I'd had with my father. Teenage angst, that difficult period in life when most teenagers rebel against everything: parents, school, their peers, authority. I recalled seeing my parents' faces, despair etched forever in their eyes as the police came to arrest me for breaking and entering a neighbor's house; trashing the place while out of my skull on booze. Weeks after, the authorities done with me and the fine paid, my father took me down to the river to fish and to talk through what had happened. Tempers flared, and I punched him hard on the jaw. My father didn't even flinch. He showed no surprise, for he'd come to expect that kind of behavior from his only son. All I saw was the dimly remaining light finally die in his eyes. A month later, war claimed my father and never gave him back, lost in action. Two years after that my mother, still recovering from the loss, got the cancer and it took her slow. It ate away inside her until her flesh was like tissue paper to the touch and she breathed in shallow gasps. I held her, counting each frail breath until the last.

Thinking back through that time, I hoped that in some way my behavior had been compensated for by my return to decency, my studies, and my eventual enrolment to the Chicago Police Department. But in truth, I had lost something forever and my achievements hadn't compensated in any way for that period of my life. I always believed however, that somehow things could be undone, wrongs could be righted.

Someone big and blocky filled the doorway to my right. Benson.

"Hey, Lucas. How you doing?" he said.

Lucas flicked his eyes open at the sound of his name, shifted in his seat again, and blinked a couple of times as if pulling everything into perspective.

"Sure, Mr. Benson. Just taking a rest from the heat."

"It's damn hot out there," Benson said. "Can I get you a drink or something? Got a full refrigerator back o' the store."

"Sure, sure, I'll have one of them Dr. Peppers, if you got a cold one. I like those Dr. Peppers. Always gives me a funny tingle back of my nose."

Benson nodded toward me. "How about you, fella?"

"Coke if you've got one?"

He smiled. "Be right back."

The old man leaned forward, rested both arms on his knees, and clasped his hands together. He pressed two calloused thumbs against his forehead and stared down at the wooden boarding beneath his feet. I heard the breath straining in his chest.

A discarded chewing gum wrapper lay by his battered right shoe. He studied it for a while. "See, Mr. Bale," he said. "Me and that wrapper, we is just the same."

"How so?" I asked, not seeing at all.

"Well, take a long look. What d'you see?"

I did as instructed, said the obvious. "Creases, folds, shiny, silver?"

"Exactly. Except I ain't shiny silver no more."

I got it and we laughed at that.

A sudden puff of wind lifted the wrapper away from his shoe. It pitched and yawed, did a little dance for us a couple of feet off the sidewalk. Then the wind died and released it back to the heat-cracked street.

"I can't dance no more either," he said, flashing me a toothy smile.

He ran his right hand slowly over his bald head as if squeezing the sweat out from his pores, then stared across at the storefronts opposite. The two boys were long gone, but there was still the faint sound of their laughter in the distance.

"So, where you from, Mr. Bale? Not around here, that's for sure."

"Chicago."

He raised his eyebrows. "So you're the fella Ellie-Mae got looking for young Alice?"

"Yeah, you know about that?"

"Certainly do. Live in the Bottoms. Ellie-Mae she went around asking everyone if they'd seen Alice. Think you'll find her?"

"I really don't know. I promised Ellie-Mae I would, but I'm a stranger in a strange land down here. Back home, if a case like this came up, I could go to contacts, call in favors, speak off the record to my old buddies in the police department. There would always be someone who knew somebody who could lead me somewhere. Down here, I got to start cold."

I heard the sound of a refrigerator door open and close, the chink of glass, and the rattle of two steel caps as they were dropped into a metal bin. Benson stepped out from the store.

"Here you go, fellas," he said, holding out the bottles. As I was closest to him, I took both and passed the Dr. Pepper to Lucas.

"I got you a couple of real cold ones," Benson said.

I raised the Coke in a *thank you* gesture.

"Why thank you, Mr. Benson," Lucas said. "Mighty kind."

"No problem, Lucas. And please, call me Dan."

Lucas held the bottle for a moment and transferred it to his other hand in one long, thoughtful movement. Without taking a sip, he set it down on the bench between his hat and my jacket.

"Damn thing so cold made my hand ache," he said.

"Known Lucas here forty years," Benson said. "Still won't call me by my first name."

I asked why and Lucas gave me the answer I should have already guessed, had I really thought about it.

"Eight generations my family been here, Mr. Bale. All of them working the fields. You owned by a white cotton farmer you showed him respect."

"But that was then," I said. "Slavery's been abolished for almost a century."

"Yeah, but we had to endure two hundred and forty-six years of it before the 13th Amendment was ratified." He looked at me side on. "You know when that was?"

I thought for a moment, scraping up memories of history lessons at school. "January 1863?"

He huffed. "Most get it wrong. January '63 was when Lincoln issued his Proclamation and in areas controlled by the Confederacy slaves were freed. But Union held areas and states kept slaves in bondage because Lincoln couldn't control those. Total slavery ended in December 1865. That was final ratification."

A lesson learned. "But you can call white people by their first name."

"Maybe so, but that don't make it no different. I saw the whip marks on my granddaddy's back once and when I asked why he told me it was cos he didn't call the farmer sir. Put the terror into me knowing you get whipped for that and I guess it just stuck."

Benson said, "But you're a free man, Lucas. You don't owe nothing to nobody."

The old man shook his head. "These are still intolerant times. But maybe that Martin Luther King fella bring some change about."

"Times have changed," I said.

He smiled at me then, in that way older people do when trying to educate the naïve. "You a Chicago man, Mr. Bale. Chicago got its problems but you in the South now, and don't you forget it. Things work a little different." He paused and drew in a breath. "You ever heard about the Georgia lynchings of 46?"

I thought for a moment, but nothing came to me. "No," I said, shaking my head.

"Happened in July, up in Walton County, east of Atlanta. White farmer hired four young African sharecroppers, couples they were. One of the women was expecting a child. She was about seven months gone. That same month, one of the men—husband of the pregnant woman—allegedly stabbed a white man and was arrested. Don't know why he stabbed him, and even if he ever did, it's just how the story goes. The white farmer, a decent man by all accounts, drove the other couple and the pregnant woman in his car to county jail and he posted the six-hundred dollar bail for the husband, got the man freed, and was heading back to his farm when a lynch mob stopped them—maybe a couple of dozen men. The mob dragged the two black couples out of the car, strung them up, and shot them. Coroner estimated sixty shots fired at close range. White farmer couldn't do a thing. You know what the mob did then?"

I couldn't imagine.

"They cut out the pregnant woman's fetus."

"Jesus," I said, revulsion spreading and turning over my stomach as I imagined the scene. "What happened to the farmer and the mob?"

"Farmer was threatened and told to keep quiet for fear of his life and life of his family. FBI was all over it like baby chiggers on flesh. Short answer…nothing. You have anything like that in Chicago?"

"No," I said quietly. "Riots, murders, but nothing like that, not that I know of. That's barbaric."

"As I said, things done differently down here. We still got segregation, denied rights, although some establishments will tolerate black folk. Good old 'Jim Crow Law'."

"What's 'Jim Crow Law'?" I asked, confused.

"Comes from a fella known as Jump Jim Crow. He was a song-and-dance man back in the early 1800s. White man, forget his real name, used to black up his face and tell tales of how black folk were treated, slavery, that kind of thing. Jim Crow became a pejorative expression, meaning Negro. When southern legislatures passed segregation laws, they became known as Jim Crow Laws."

And there we left it; the weight of the stories as heavy as the heat pressing down on us.

Benson broke it. "You that Chicago detective Ellie-Mae called?"

"Yes, sir," I said, turning to shake the outstretched hand. If ever there were two opposites. Lucas James's handshake was no more than a delicate brush of fingertips, frail, breakable. Whereas Dan Benson's hand was big and strong, like being gripped by a vise.

"Pleased to make your acquaintance, Mr. Bale."

"Same here."

"Call me Dan," he said nodding at Lucas.

I tried to laugh, but the image I'd conjured in my head of the lynchings refused to shake off its grip. "OK, Dan. I'm Tom." I sipped at the Coke. It felt like an appropriate time to start asking questions. "Is there anything either of you can tell me about Alice and the day she disappeared?"

"Couldn't say, Mr. Bale," Lucas said. "Didn't see her that day. Like I said, Ellie-Mae already asked."

I looked up at Benson. "How about you, Dan? Have you spoken to the sheriff? Is there anything at all you might have thought strange? Alice's behavior, did she seem worried about anything…or…"

"No. Nothing. She came into the store like she often did to grab a couple of things, and that was it. She was here no more than a couple of minutes. Just her usual self. Bright, happy, not a care in the world. As for the sheriff, I've not seen him or his deputies. Nothing I could tell them, anyway."

Given that Benson had seen Alice on the day she disappeared, even if it was only a couple of minutes, then surely the sheriff would want to confirm? I decided to park that question for the sheriff himself.

"Long walk from Cotton Cut Road to here," I said.

"Way things are," Benson said. "No buses or trams like in the big cities take you one place or another."

"No, I guess not," I said. Then I thought about Lucas James. No way he could have walked that distance.

"In case you're wondering," Benson said, as if reading my thoughts. "Lucas here gets a lift. Drops in to see me then heads off to the library. He likes his history does Lucas. Young man name of Corey Peters takes him here and there."

"Corey's a good kid," Lucas said. "Had it tough since his mother died and his dad ain't up to much, but Corey he got a kind soul."

Library. So Lucas James was a well-read man. That explained the lesson a moment ago. I smiled to myself. You can't underestimate anybody.

"This Corey Peters," I said. "He live in the Bottoms?"

"No," Benson said. "He and his dad got a trailer halfway between Cotton Cut and town, about a quarter mile off the blacktop. It's surrounded by junked cars, and they got a repair shop where they patch up beaten wrecks and do tire changes. Basic stuff. They survive."

"Corey's a friend of Alice's then?" I asked.

"Sure," Benson said. "But he's a bit older, too old to have any close involvement."

"How old?"

"Got to be twenty-one or two I guess," Benson said. "That be about right, Lucas?"

"About that. Brings Alice into town from time-to-time…well…until she went missing."

I made a mental note to go pay Corey Peters a visit. When it came to abduction, if indeed that's what had happened to Alice, age didn't come into it. When I was a cop, I became all-too familiar with the fevered and unquenchable desires of adult males and their preference for young girls; girls sometimes no older than ten, abused, raped, murdered and then dumped like trash. I dismissed the thought and took a different line.

"This the only grocery store in town?" I asked.

"Only private one," Benson said. "There's a community convenience store other side of Main about a quarter mile from here."

"You do a lot of business?"

"Good and bad days. Why?"

"So, you must get to know everyone, hear gossip, rumors."

"Some. But nothing to do with Alice."

"You know Alice not the only one gone missing?" Lucas said.

I nodded. "Yeah, Ellie-Mae and her son, Moses, said as much. What can you tell me about those?"

"It's a damn mystery is what it is," Benson said. "Nobody heard or seen anything. It gets reported, sheriff does his thing for a few days I guess, then that's it. Gives up. No sign, no trace." Lucas shrugged.

"Same thing. Over the years, they just upped and gone. Never seen again. Thinking the same has happened to Alice."

His words hung in the air for a moment until the bright trill of a telephone from deep in the store blew them away. A truck rumbled past. Dust circled and settled. Benson apologized, went back in the store to take the call.

"There a place around here I can get coffee and breakfast?" I asked.

"There's a diner a couple of hundred yards up the street. Mabel Watts runs it."

"Thanks. Go there yourself?"

"Now and then. Not really a place for us folks from the Bottoms. We get served, but Mabel would rather we didn't go in there. But you'll do OK. Got the correct skin color."

We sat in silence for a minute, sipping our drinks, staring at nothing.

"I guess I should go speak to the sheriff," I said. "Just as a matter of courtesy. Let him know I'm in town and what I'm up to."

The old man's breathing was becoming labored as he spoke. "You might as well…talk to this chair…the good it will do you." A series of racking coughs escaped his throat, and he bent over, both hands gripping his cane, fighting for breath.

Concerned, I knelt down, one hand on his shoulder. "You OK, Lucas…can I get you something? You need the doc?"

He waved me away as the coughing subsided. He drew in a deep breath, straightened up, grabbed the Dr. Pepper, and drank a quarter of it.

"It's OK," he said. "No need to concern yourself. I got this problem with my chest…and it's going to kill me one day." A smile faltered on his lips, then he wiped the spittle from his mouth with his shirtsleeve. "But not today."

I stood up. "You sure I can't get you anything?"

"I'm sure," he said. "Now you go do what you got to do. Find Alice."

"You want breakfast? My treat."

He shook his head, stuck his hat back on, rested his head back on the store window, and closed his eyes.

"Kind of you, but no thanks. Just going to sit here and rest awhile."

And there we left it.

CHAPTER 4

The heat was relentless.

When I reached the town square, I stopped for another breather under the glistening, freshly painted bandstand, appreciating the shade and to be out of the unforgiving sun. I sat there nursing an unlit cigarette, unsure about whether I should make myself known to the sheriff or quietly go about my business. The sheriff might be cooperative. There was always that chance, but more than likely not. He wouldn't take kindly to me tramping all over his territory where my PI license wasn't worth a dime.

Across the square, the courthouse stood majestic and righteous. Paradise Creek was the county seat, but even so, the red brick building was far and away grander than I'd expected. It had six Doric columns supporting an imposing capital and an ornate entablature carved with scenes from the civil war. It was impressive. I'd seen lesser civil buildings in Chicago.

I slipped the cigarette back into its pack, flapped my shirt to circulate the air around my body and set off again. By the time I'd crossed the square and reached Mabel Watt's diner I had dabbed at my neck and forehead so much that my handkerchief was soaked in sweat and my shirt needed to be put through a wringer.

A bell above the door announced my entrance. It was a light, smart, clean place with a couple of dozen tables decked out with green and white checkered cloths, each with a set of condiments carefully placed in the center. The service counter was edged with chrome strips and had a green top dotted with menu cards.

There was a woman behind the counter, who I took to be Mabel. She was about fifty years old, heavily made up and with hair done in the latest Jackie Kennedy style, like about ten million other women. She was sitting behind the counter, flipping magazine pages, sipping coffee, and drawing on a cigarette. I occupied the stool opposite, felt my stomach groan and glanced at my watch. It was close to midday. Little wonder my stomach was protesting. I ordered coffee and asked if the peach pie was good. I suddenly had this urge for something sweet and sticky.

"Best in the state," she said. "It's what we're famous for."

"Sounds good. Does it come with cream?"

She smiled at me then said, "Comes with whatever you want it to, hon."

"I'll just take the cream," I said, smiling back.

A minute later, I had the coffee and the pie. The pie looked good. "Quiet," I observed.

"Busy as it's been all day."

The coffee wasn't as rich and flavorsome as Ellie-Mae's, but it hit the spot all the same. "Heat keeps people away, I guess."

40

"Tell me about it. Only person in today is that guy." She nodded over at the far corner.

I glanced over my right shoulder to a table where a guy around mid-thirties was reading a newspaper. He wore a tight blue T-shirt that strained against his muscular torso. Hard, angular face, brown hair, and what looked like a thin white scar stretching from just under his left eye, across his cheek and down to his jaw line. He reached for his coffee and caught us staring at him. He held our gaze for a moment with cold, unsettling eyes and Mabel offered him a smile to cover her embarrassment. But there was no acknowledgement. He just turned away from us and went back to his newspaper.

I dug into the pie. It was good, and I said so. "Delicious."

"As I said, best in the state."

I licked my lips, then used a napkin to wipe away the cream that had escaped down my chin.

"I assume," I said, "your name is Mabel?"

"What it says on the sign outside." She sat back on the stool, lit up another cigarette. "You ain't from around here, though."

I swallowed another mouthful. "No. Chicago."

She blew smoke out of the corner of her mouth, away from me. "Really?" she said, sounding surprised. "What brings you to Paradise Creek?"

I finished the pie, wiped my chin again and was tempted to ask for a second serving, but elected not to. Instead, I asked, "You know an Ellie-Mae Jackson?"

She shook her head, tapped ash. "Can't say I do, no. Why?"

"Lives over Cotton Cut Road. Her young daughter, Alice, is missing. Two weeks now."

She shrugged. "Don't know nothing about that. We don't see many of their kind in here."

"Many of whose kind?" I knew from what Lucas James had told me, but I wanted to hear her say it.

She stared at me as if I was stupid. "Blacks, Negros. What did you think I meant?"

As distasteful as it was for me to hear racism declared so matter-of-factly, my job was to find Alice and if that meant I had to play along, then play along I would. I smiled. "Sorry, wasn't thinking. Of course."

The sound of a newspaper rustling loudly behind us and chair legs being scraped across the floor caused us to turn toward to the man in the corner as he rose to his full six feet and threw some coins down on the table. He glanced briefly at us and went out into the afternoon sun.

"What the hell is wrong with him?" I asked.

"Beats me," Mabel said. "He's been in now and then. Sometimes don't see him for months, then he turns up, orders, and goes sit in the corner. That's about as much as I get out of him."

She topped up my coffee.

"Thanks," I said. I withdrew my wallet and placed more than enough in bills to cover the coffee and pie down on the counter.

"What's it to you anyway, this girl gone missing? You a detective?"

I drained the coffee, got down from the stool. "Family friend," I said, thinking that should stir up some gossip.

The bell tinkled as I left the diner and walked into a wall of heat. It almost took my breath away. I stood there for a moment shielding my eyes against the sun and watched the man from the diner head across the street and get into his car, a red Chevy BelAir with white walls.

CHAPTER 5

I decided to pay the sheriff's office a visit. Seemed the right thing to do, despite my reluctance. I was bound to get the brush off, but courtesy dictated, and you never knew when you might need their cooperation.

There were a couple of black and white Plymouths parked at an angle outside a municipal building adjacent to the courthouse. I pushed through the double doors and entered a long wooden floored corridor, grateful again for the relative coolness against the heat and humidity of the day. There were a bunch of offices left and right and I made my way along until I found one with SHERIFF'S OFFICE painted in gold and black letters on the frosted glass.

Inside, a deputy was searching around in the top drawer of a file cabinet. He turned, affected a smile, and his eyes narrowed suspiciously. "Deputy Swales," he said guardedly. "What can I do for you?"

"Tom Bale," I said and held up my PI license. "Down here from Chicago. Looking into a missing person's case. Is the sheriff around?"

He came over, took the license off me, and cast his shifty eyes over it.

"Chicago, huh?" He ignored my outstretched hand and dropped the license on his desk, made his way around back of it, and sat down. He slipped a pack of Strikes from his uniform breast pocket and lit up, grinned at me, and blew smoke. "We ain't got no missing person."

I expected a little hostility and was prepared for it. I held my patience and continued with the polite, professional approach. "Alice Jackson," I said. "Went missing just over two weeks ago. You should have her name on file."

"Jackson you say?" he said, shaking his head. "Don't know nobody of that name."

"Her mother, Ellie-Mae Jackson, reported her missing. Her maiden name would have been Williams, if it helps any. Filled out the form…maybe its best if I speak to the sheriff."

I retrieved the license from his desk, put it back in my wallet. I didn't care much for Swales or his attitude; an arrogant, rude, rat-like little man with a snappy, energetic way about him, furtive eyes and brown hair slung over to one side.

"He's out back," Swales said. "Reckon on him being another ten minutes at least. Likes to take in some reading material when he's on the john."

"I'll wait."

"Ain't nothing I can't deal with in his absence."

"I'm sure, but best if I speak to him. I'm not here officially. I'm a friend of the family, just helping out. Thought it would be the right thing to do, let the sheriff know I was down on his turf."

Again, that infuriating damn grin. "Suit yourself. He'll be a while. Might want to come back some other time. But as I say, we ain't got no missing person called Alice Jackson. Sheriff'll tell you the same."

"I'll take my chances."

There was a stack of buff-colored folders on his desk and the deputy busied himself shuffling through one of them. I wondered if it was just for effect as I watched him study the information and make notes on his pad. He was focused, running a finger back and forth along the lines of text, concentrating on the detail, tip of his tongue poking out the side of his mouth.

I sat in one of the visitors' plain wooden chairs, which creaked every time I moved and studied the office. There were three desks, a row of filing cabinets stacked against a far wall, on top of which stood an ailing house plant and a couple of metal file trays. On another wall hung several black and white photographs of perpetrators taken at the point of their arrest and a couple of wanted posters dated from two years back. A rear window allowed a minimum of natural light to spill through, but it did little to lift the overall aged gloomy atmosphere. Further back was the sheriff's own office and a corridor, which I presumed led to the bathroom. Overhead, the ceiling fan was set to slow rotate. It needed a little oil.

After five minutes or so, I heard the flush of a toilet, a door slamming, then heavy footsteps, and the rustling of paper. Then a heavy-set man, fiftyish, tough looking, appeared at the mouth of the corridor, newspaper in hand. His uniform was rumpled, and he wore a Colt .38 with a checkered grip in a holster slung to his right. Most police forces were switching to the Smith and Wesson on account of it being cheaper. The sheriff was obviously a traditionalist.

"Afternoon," he said, surprised.

"This here is Sheriff Alban Somers," Swales said, without looking up.

Somers was someone who, along with many men of his age, was predisposed to the comforts of home and the occasional beer and had put on a few inches, yet still wore the same sized pants so his belly hung over the top of his waistline. He wasn't an obese man, but vanity overshadowed the reality that he'd put on weight and his shirt stretched tight over his gut, so the buttons were straining. His thinning light-brown hair was combed straight back, and his face was starting to thicken under chin and jowl.

"Tom Bale," I said, standing.

Somers dumped the newspaper on Swales' desk. "What can I do for you, Mr. Bale?"

"Reckons we got a missing person situation," Swales said, this time looking up from his pad, grinning.

"Really? Now that's the first I heard of it. What's your interest?"

I fished out my PI license again, handed it over. "I've been asked by a local woman to look into the disappearance of her daughter. Been gone a little over two weeks now. She says she reported it to you and filled out the form, but your deputy here says you have no record of it."

Somers handed back the license. "You know this license ain't worth shit in the state of Georgia."

"Yes, I'm aware of that, Sheriff, but I thought it a matter of courtesy to let you know I'm here, not officially, just for a friend."

"OK. Appreciate you taking the time to let us know, but if Larry here says we have no record of this missing person, then we ain't got one. I certainly don't recall anyone in the past couple of weeks filing an official report."

"Woman's name is Ellie-Mae Jackson, lives over on Cotton Cut Road. Alice is her daughter."

He leaned forward then, hands on hips. "Cotton Cut you say? That's the Bottoms where all the negras live." He waved a thick arm in the air. "Those folks go missing all the time. They migrate from family to family or go looking for work. It's what they do. Once they gone missing, they stay missing."

I pulled out the photo of Alice and handed it over. Swales got up, glanced at it, and hesitated. It was only a split second, but I saw something shift in his eyes. Recognition maybe, but I couldn't be sure. Or he could have just been reacting to how pretty she was. "She's barely fourteen, Sheriff. I doubt very much she'd be out looking for work."

"Pretty girl, looks older" Somers said. "You seen her, Larry?"

Swales shook his head and went back to his desk. "Nope, can't say I have, Sheriff."

I rubbed my forehead, took back the photo. "Then why would Mrs. Jackson tell me she'd reported it to this office and filled out the misper form?"

"Beats me," Somers said, turning to one of the file cabinets. "But let's take a look anyhow." He pulled out a drawer and thumbed through a series of file tabs. "So, where you from, Mr. Bale?"

"Chicago."

"That's a fuck of a long way from Paradise Creek," he said, his back to me. There was a dark line of sweat showing clearly through his khaki shirt. It ran down the center of his back from collar to belt and no doubt beyond.

"Ellie-Mae's brother was a piano player up in Chicago," I said. "He and I were good friends, so I'm doing this as a favor."

"Helluva big favor come all the way down here."

"Owed him. He saved my life one night."

Somers was either not listening or didn't care one jot about what had happened to me up in Chicago. He was just politely going through the motions. Instead, he turned to me, file in hand.

"Here we go," he said. "Missing person file." He opened it up, spread the contents on the deputy's desk. There were three separate reports, and he ran a thick forefinger over the names and dates. "Nothing here for Jackson and the most recent is dated over a year ago."

"That's it?" I said.

"'Fraid so. Sorry, can't help you. Seems like you came all this way for nothing. Unless…your friend is lying for some reason."

"She wouldn't do that," I said. "She'd have no reason to."

He held up his hands. "Just putting it out there, fella, not saying it is the case. But as you can see, we got nothing about any Alice Jackson."

"Told you," Swales said, sporting that shit-eating grin again.

"Perhaps you misunderstood, Mr. Bale," the sheriff said. "Perhaps this Mrs. Jackson said she was *going to* report it, not that she had."

That got me thinking. Had I misunderstood? I didn't think so, but then something else came to mind.

"I'm led to understand," I said, "that other girls have gone missing over the years. Any of those files pertaining to them?"

"Nope."

"Can I see what you have?"

Somers gathered up the papers and replaced the file in the drawer. "You'll have to take my word for it, Mr. Bale. These are official police files."

I expected him to say that, but thought I'd ask anyway. So had I misheard or misunderstood Ellie-Mae? Could be. I was exhausted at the time from the long drive and the heat and thinking about Jenny. Maybe I wasn't as focused as I should have been, and it would explain why Benson hadn't heard from the sheriff. I was sure I'd heard Ellie-Mae correctly. Still, the doubt was now running around in my head, so I had to make certain before I did anything else. Time to go.

"Thanks, Sheriff," I said, extending my hand, which he took in a firm grip. "Sorry to trouble you."

"No problem," he said. "If we can be of any further assistance, just come right on in. Be happy to help." He gave me a big broad smile, which I felt was genuine enough.

"Bye now," Swales said in an over affected lighthearted tone.

I let myself out, went back down the hallway, and out into the sun. I had to go see Ellie-Mae again. Had to be sure.

It took me almost an hour to walk back to the motel, and the sweat was flowing down my spine like a river. The Chevy BelAir was nowhere to be seen, but there was a '57 Olds Super 88 parked outside cabin three.

I went into my cabin. The room had been cleaned, and the bed made up with fresh sheets and pillowcases which surprised me. Trenton didn't strike me as a man who cared much about customer satisfaction, and I hadn't expected him to bother for a couple more days at least. I stripped and got in the shower.

A half hour later I was driving back over to Ellie-Mae's house thinking about the sheriff and his deputy. The sheriff seemed genuine enough when he confirmed they had no file on Alice, and I didn't have a reason to doubt him. But there was definitely something in the deputy's eyes when he saw Alice's photograph, and I felt certain it was recognition.

Ellie-Mae greeted me at the screen door when I knocked and invited me in. "I won't take up your time," I said. "I just need to confirm something."

"Sure," she said.

51

"You told me you reported Alice's disappearance to the sheriff's office, is that correct?"

"Correct."

"When was that?"

"Two days after Alice gone missing."

"And you filled out a missing person form?"

"Yes…" Her eyes grew hard then and deep furrows creased her forehead. "What's this about? I already told you. Someone saying I didn't?"

"I went to see the sheriff, asked him about it and he had no knowledge of Alice and no report filed. He double-checked."

She got angry. "That's impossible. I got somebody to take me into town, went to the sheriff's office and filled out a report. Didn't speak to the sheriff, but I told one of his deputies. Sheriff don't know what's going on in his own office?"

"Which deputy did you report it to?"

"Oh, I don't know…fella called…"

"Swales?" I suggested.

She shook her head. "No, no, no…it was a tall guy, red hair…Car…Caro…Carson. That's it, Deputy Carson."

"You sure?"

Her eyes grew sharp. "You calling me a liar, Mr. Bale?"

"Absolutely not," I said. "I'm just getting all the facts before I go see the sheriff again. Don't worry, there's obviously been some kind of mistake, Alice's file lost or something like that. I will find her, I promise you."

I left Ellie-Mae at the door and made my way back to the Dodge. I turned over the engine, looked back at the house and she had gone inside. Night was beginning to close in and I saw a light come on in the front room. There was no power out here, save for those who could afford a generator, so it must have been a hurricane lamp.

The sheriff's office could wait until tomorrow. Instead, I elected to do some more asking around and I remembered seeing a bar on Main. If I recalled correctly, it was stuck between a used car lot and a bait shop right on the edge of town. And where there was a bar, there would be people, and people like to talk.

CHAPTER 6

Nat's Bar was a long, narrow establishment with not much in terms of lighting which gave it a subdued atmosphere. There was a place at the back where four guys were playing pool, a small stage, and a demarcated area with a dozen dining tables, only one of which was occupied by a middle-aged couple sitting in silence while they ate dinner. A menu board advertised the house special, an indulgence consisting of sausage and shrimp fried in bacon fat with beans, fried tomatoes and greens all mixed together in a kind of gumbo with a rich sauce that would have my gut groaning from regret the following morning. I was feeling hungry but decided to pass on the special. When it was time, I'd take a roast beef sandwich to go. Safety in simplicity.

At the end of the bar closest to me, sitting alone, was a chubby man with his head low and his right hand wrapped around a whiskey glass and his left around a bottle of Pabst. A cigarette lay dying in an ashtray to his right. I went over and hauled up on the stool next to him. He gave me a cursory glance and slugged back his beer.

"Evening," I said.

"Hot," he said, lighting up a fresh cigarette and tossing the match toward the ashtray. It missed. He pulled on the cigarette, coughed and stubbed it out, turned to me. "Got this damn cold. Throat's on fire."

"You have my sympathies," I said. "I can handle a cold, but sore throats, they keep you up all night coughing. No sleep makes you feel a damn sight worse."

"Ain't that the fucking truth?" He coughed into his hands.

The bartender approached with a fresh beer and a bottle of Kentucky Straight. He set the beer down, flipped the top and then refilled the glass with the whiskey.

"You sure don't look well, Coop," the bartender observed, voice booming around the bar, cutting through a scratchy tune playing on the jukebox.

Christ, I thought, the guy's only sitting three feet away from you.

Coop grabbed the cold beer and drew long from the bottle. "Feel like shit," he said, placing the bottle on the counter then scooping up the whiskey and finishing it in one take.

The bartender cupped a hand over his left ear. "Watcha say?"

Coop used the stool's footrest to push himself up across the counter. He raised his voice a notch. "I said I feel like shit."

The bartender nodded. "You look it."

Coop sat back down. "Thanks, I feel a whole lot better you saying that."

The bartender smiled at him, not really having heard a single word. "You're welcome," he said. Then, turning to me. "What can I get you, mister?"

I was about to ask for a cold Coke when Coop interrupted. "He'll have the same as me," he said loudly.

I started to protest, but the bartender didn't hear and the next thing I knew a bottle of Pabst and two fingers of whiskey sat before me. In for a penny, I thought, threw back the whiskey then pulled on the beer. It tasted good.

Coop turned and officially introduced himself, sticking out a hand for me to shake. "Sam Cooper's the name. Coop for short."

"Tom Bale," I said, shaking the outstretched paw. I noticed cuts and grazes in the flesh and dirt under the fingernails, a workman's hand. I made a mental note to scrub my own clean of his flu germs as soon as I could.

"Pleased to meet you, Tom," he croaked, and coughed into his hands again. At least he wasn't spreading germs by coughing openly over the bar. He made a circular motion over our drinks, indicating to the bartender that another round was in order. No sooner had I finished the beer than another was on the counter with two more fingers of whiskey by its side.

"This here," Coop said, nodding at the bartender, "is Nathan Vandiver, Nat to his friends. Owns the bar."

I stretched a hand across the counter. Perhaps I could transfer all the germs, or at the very least share them, maybe lessen the impact. "Good to meet you, Nathan."

"Meetcha," he shouted.

"Nat. Meet Tom Bale," Coop said.

Nat cupped his left ear again. "Watcha say, Coop?"

56

"Jesus H, Nat," Coop shouted back. "Tom Bale. Get yourself a goddamn hearing aid."

Nat went off to serve a customer, waving a hand as if dismissing Coop's suggestion.

Sudden realization. Nat had the same surname as the Governor of Georgia. I turned to Coop. "He related to the governor?"

Cooper chuckled. "Everyone asks him that, but he's no relation."

Nathan Vandiver was mid to late forties. Just an average man with sad gray eyes, salt and pepper hair combed over to one side and a pleasant way about him. I asked Coop how long he'd owned the bar.

"It was real seedy fifteen years back, stank of stale beer and mildew with a floor so sticky you felt like you were walking through mud. Windows so caked in grime the sun struggled to come through. No ladies allowed, just a place full of macho bullshit. Eventually fell to rack and ruin, got boarded up and left for dead until Nat decided to invest his hard-earned dollar." He looked around nodding appreciatively. "Now it's pretty decent and the food's OK, but I'd avoid the gumbo. Plays hell with your gut."

"Appreciate the advice," I said, having already come to that decision.

He raised a bottle, tipped it toward me. "You're welcome. Hearing damage came from his time in Korea and then working as a supervisor up at the mill. Bombs and the constant whine of the steel cutters. He retired early and chose to open a bar. Keep telling him to get fitted up for a hearing aid, but he's a stubborn bastard."

"How about you, Coop?" I said. "What's your story?"

He shrugged and swayed a little unsteadily on his stool. "Not much to tell. Born and raised here. Work up at the mill."

"Wife? Kids?"

"Never had kids. Wife upped and left four years ago. Been jumping off the deep end ever since and climbing back up, just to jump off again. And when you're down there, shit just seems to keep falling on top of you. So, I come to this bar most evenings just to take my mind off it."

I knew exactly what he meant. I'd been there a dozen times. So low sometimes that I felt it would be better for me and everyone around me if I never came up again. "Know that feeling too well," I said.

He swallowed the rest of his beer, finished his whiskey, and promptly poured four fingers into his glass, some of which sloshed over the side. He held the bottle up to me, but I stuck a hand over my glass. Wouldn't be good for me to get drunk. I needed to keep a clear head. "Not for me, Coop," I said. "Can't take it like I used to."

"Suit yourself," he said, voice starting to slur just a little. "So, Tom Bale, where you from? What's your story? You lost a woman too?"

Jenny. My beautiful Jenny. "Wife," I said. "Six years back."

"Oh man, that's a real fucker. I'm sorry to hear it. Another guy, was it? Usually is. You do everything, think you've got it right. Hold down a job, roof over your heads, food on the table. Sure, you go through a few hardships along the way—what couple doesn't—but you come out the other side, together…"

He tailed off, lost in the alcohol induced fog of his own memories.

"And then…and then she ups and leaves for the vacuum cleaner salesman. You know those fuckers from Kirby, they go door-to-door. Flash suits and nice cars. Well…fuck 'em." He clapped me on the shoulder. "Hang in there, buddy. Someone will come along, you'll see."

We touched glasses. "Thanks," I said. "To health and happiness."

Coop swallowed, huffed, sniffed. "I could sure do with both at the moment," he said. "Now tell me, what brings Tom Bale to the sleepy town of Paradise Creek?"

I gave him the short version while studying his face for signs of recognition. Nothing.

"Damn," he said after I'd finished. "All the way from Chicago. Sorry I can't help."

"You must know the Jacksons' oldest boy, Leroy? Works at the mill."

"Oh, sure, sure, I know Leroy. He never mentioned anything about his sister, though."

"Really? He didn't say anything?"

"Uh-huh," he said, shaking his head. "Keeps himself to himself. People from the Bottoms don't usually mix with townsfolk. We see them in town from time to time, but mostly it's only for hardware and groceries. The white folk here ain't quite caught up with the times and don't tolerate them too well. Negros don't bother me none, I just don't get to hang out with them. Only other person I know from the Bottoms is Carl Robard. He's a millworker too and like Leroy, just gets on with the job. Both are OK guys, though."

59

"I heard the name, Robard," I said. "Mrs. Jackson mentioned it, said Alice used to play with Carl's two sisters. Similar ages."

"Don't know anything about that."

"You working tomorrow?"

"Saturday? Nope, not my turn. Leroy and Carl will be there, though."

I took out my wallet, withdrew Alice's picture. "You sure you haven't seen this girl?"

Coop swayed some more, blinked a few times and got the picture into focus. "Damn, she's a pretty thing. I'd seen her I would have remembered. How old: seventeen, eighteen?"

"Fourteen," I said.

He looked at me, frowning. "You're kidding me, right?"

"No. She's fourteen and missing almost three weeks. And you've never seen her in town or around anywhere?"

"No, no, no. Never. As I say...had I, I would've remembered. Fuck. Fourteen."

Nat came over, see if we needed anything. I raised my voice so he could hear and ordered a roast beef sandwich to go. I showed him the photo of Alice and very briefly explained. He got it but didn't know her or her family. "What about the guys playing pool and that couple eating? Would they know?"

Nat turned away and asked the question at such volume I thought the windows were going to shatter.

"ANYONE KNOW AN ALICE JACKSON?" Six heads turned to him, all shaking at once. He turned back to me, shrugged, and announced in slightly less megaphonic tones that he would get my sandwich.

I stared at mine and Coop's reflections in the mirrored glass behind the bar. I passed as reasonably respectable: suit not too crumpled, only a day's growth on my face, less dark under the eyes than I used to be when I was hitting the bottle hard; dark brown hair still thick with a few whips of gray at the temples. I looked my age, I thought. But Coop was an easy decade or more over me. In reality, I guessed he was early forties. The rings under his eyes made him look like a panda; thinning, lifeless hair, and capillaries threading across his nose and cheeks, way he was going with the booze I doubted he would make it beyond fifty.

He suddenly leaned in closer to me, breath reeking of cigarettes and alcohol. I doubted my own smelled any sweeter. He coughed again, this time openly over me and our drinks. Maybe I should go to the hospital, get a shot or antibiotics just to be sure. Another long slug from his beer and he was ready. His voice lowered like he was sharing a secret. "I tell you something, Tom."

I waited.

"A man could be forgiven for going after young girls."

At first, I thought I hadn't heard him correctly. "What?" I said, slightly taken aback.

"You know, young girls, way they look, their bodies."

I stared at him, incredulous. I'd thought him just a sad, lonely guy who drank too much to make the pain go away. Just an ordinary Joe slipping through middle age without direction; just a job and booze. Harmless enough. Now I had an entirely different opinion.

"How so?" I said, not giving anything away.

"You know. Young girls…all those pouty lips and big titties. Like that photo you just showed me. Fuck, I would never have guessed she was fourteen. See, that's what I mean. She looks a lot older, and a man could be forgiven for trying to get it on with her. Like that Caitlin Dexter, oh man she's something else."

"Who's Caitlin Dexter?" I asked.

"Oh boy, she's sweet. She got blond hair, big tits, and that come-on look some girls have. Hangs out with another girl. She's not so hot. I see them sometimes walking around, and I think I would love to fuck her. She's a little older than Alice, about seventeen I guess, but she dresses and acts like twenty."

This was most definitely not the man I thought I was having a friendly drink with. Was he my guy? Did he abduct Alice or any of the other girls?

"Sounds like she's way too young for you, Coop."

He leaned closer, voice almost a whisper. "I know. But these girls…looking like that…how can you resist?"

Any decent man could, I thought.

Nat brought over my sandwich. It was wrapped in a greaseproof napkin and housed in a brown paper bag. I thanked him and decided to get out of there. I'd had enough of Coop and wanted to collect my thoughts. If I needed to, I could always find him again.

I fished some notes out of my wallet and left them on the counter, along with my unfinished beer and a finger of whiskey.

"Got to go," I said to Coop. "See you again." Most definitely. I waved a goodbye at Nat.

"You too, Tom," Coop said, placing a finger against his lips and winking at me as if we shared a secret.

Outside, the stars were pin spotting the night sky and the sweet smell of spring blooms rode on the air.

There was a light on in the manager's office when I got back to the motel and I could see Trenton behind the desk. Other than that, the place was devoid of life. No cars and only a single pale light spilling out from behind the blinds in the cabin next to mine. The one where the Allstate Sedan was parked before the bitch got slapped and took off.

I let myself in to my cabin and the first thing I did was strip down to my jockeys. I had a whole bunch of jockeys which I purchased from Marshall Field's department store on State Street in downtown Chicago. You could never have too many jockeys in my opinion.

Relaxed on the bed with the fan thrumming overhead, and no beer to fill my belly, I realized just how hungry I was. I devoured the roast beef sandwich. It was surprisingly good, and I could easily have eaten another. Five minutes passed, and I heard the crunch of tires on dirt and gravel outside, then a car door slamming. The cabin door to my right opened and closed and I could make out a woman's voice, and then a few moments later the sound of a man and woman having real noisy sex. I guessed the Allstate Sedan was back, and the bitch had forgiven him.

I got up and turned on the TV, loud enough to drown out their lovemaking. The *Donna Reed Show* was on, so I flipped the dial and caught *Perry Mason*. I let it play and went back to bed, picking up my pen and notebook off the nightstand as I lay back against the pillows. I stuck a cigarette in my mouth, toyed with it.

Whenever I was on a case of any significance, I had a habit of developing a timeline, a way to collect my thoughts and get them down on paper in order to try to make sense of what had occurred. So far I had very little, but I had to make a start.

May 1, Mon—Alice goes missing.

May 3, Wed—Ellie-Mae reports it to sheriff's office and fills out missper form with Deputy Carson.

May 15, Mon—Get call from Ellie-Mae.

May 18, Thurs—Arrive in Paradise Creek. Speak to Ellie-Mae and Moses. Both state other girls have gone missing over several years. Is Alice linked to this?

May 19, Fri—Speak to Lucas James (nothing)

Speak to Dan Benson (nothing)

Speak to Mabel Watts (nothing)

Speak to sheriff (no record of any missper report). Contradiction to Ellie-Mae. Report misfiled maybe?

Speak to Deputy Carson. Unsure of Larry Swales—did he lie about not knowing Alice?

Nat's Bar (nothing) apart from…Coop—habitual drinker, loner, works at mill with Leroy Jackson and Carl Robard. LIKES YOUNG GIRLS, TEENAGE GIRLS—was that just the drink talking and a fantasy, or something much more—need to watch him/question again

I put down the pen and studied the timeline. There wasn't much. In truth, I didn't expect there to be in the first twenty-four hours, but at least I could clear certain things out of my head and concentrate only on that which was relevant.

There was always a danger of overthinking things, so I decided to get some rest and take a fresh perspective in the morning. At least I had it all down on paper so could refer back when I needed to. And there was one thing for sure; the timeline would grow. And grow considerably.

I'd sat through almost all of *Perry Mason* without once glancing at the TV. I got up, turned it off, and was pleased to hear a soundless cabin next door.

Sleep came easy. It would be the last time.

CHAPTER 7

The next morning, I showered quickly, wiped the steam off the mirror, and started to shave. I was tapping the razor on the edge of the washbasin, my whiskers peppering the yellowed ceramic, and thinking on something I'd missed, something I'd forgotten to include in the timeline. I thought hard as I shaved, but it wouldn't come to me. Done, I wiped the soap off my face with a fresh towel and got dressed.

I crossed the carpark and went over to the diner. Like the cabins, it was a tired, sad establishment but the tables, cutlery, and cloths were all clean and neatly laid out. The service was surprisingly attentive. Trenton's wife busied herself around and made sure I was topped up with coffee. The sole diner, I feasted on pancakes, crispy bacon, and maple syrup. They hit the spot.

Mrs. Trenton was a plump woman with wispy gray hair tied up in a bun, a pair of butterfly framed glasses perched on a tiny nose, eyes set too close together, and an overly fussy way about her that irritated more than pleased.

"Coffee?" she asked, her tone light and a little singsong.

"No more thanks," I said. "I'm going to be awake until Sunday at this rate. That was a great breakfast, thank you."

A big smile broke out on her chubby face. "It's my pleasure, Mr. Bale. And how is your room?"

"Comfortable, clean, fresh towels. Couldn't ask for more."

"We aim to please." She angled the coffee pot, raised her eyebrows to an alarming height. "You sure you won't have another cup?"

"Really, no. Thank you. I've had three, and that's plenty."

"Well, if you're sure."

She returned the coffeepot to the hot plate and busied herself wiping down the dresser on top of which sat the cutlery basket, cruet sets, napkins, and plates. Over her shoulder, she said, "What you up to today? Going to be another hot one, but I reckon storms will come early next week. Mr. Trenton tells me you're from Chicago, down here on financial business."

I chose to ignore the question and noted that she hadn't mentioned the Bottoms. Undoubtedly, Trenton would have told her I had business over there. Instead, I asked her if she knew Ellie-Mae Jackson.

"No," she said, her back to me. "Don't recognize that name. Is she from around here?"

"Cotton Cut Road," I said and waited for the reaction.

She stopped what she was doing, turned to me, her face serious, concerned, worried even. She played with her cleaning cloth in a nervous, twitchy way. Seemed like she was struggling to find the words.

"Oh, no…err…we don't tend…err…to…err…associate ourselves with those…err…people." She turned away again and hid her

67

embarrassment by loudly stacking plates in the cupboards under the dresser drawers.

I smiled to myself, amused by her unease, but then I thought about how black people were still being treated. Men and women persecuted purely on the grounds of color. Lucas James's story about the lynching of those two couples came to mind. It truly was a barbaric act. Essentially, two dozen men—white men—had gotten away with murder.

It was an unsettling thought, but I could not allow myself to be diverted by sentiment. I was down here to get a job done, not try to change century's old mentality.

"By the way," I said. "Didn't expect fresh sheets on the bed when I got back yesterday. Expected a change after three or four days."

Mrs. Trenton turned again, frowning. "Fresh sheets, you say?"

"Yes. I was really, and pleasantly surprised," I said, beaming. "Most motels I've ever stayed in, you wouldn't even see a maid for a week."

She looked troubled, a natural worrier. "But we only change them once a week, or before if a guest specifically asks. Did you request a change?"

"No," I said.

"Oh, that's OK," she said, waving a hand at me, smiling. "Maybe Mr. Trenton got confused about the cabin numbers."

"That must be it," I said. "Still, it was much appreciated." I bade her good morning and was halfway out the door when I stopped and asked how to get to the sawmill. She was surprised at first, but offered the directions with a smile and those eyebrows raised so high it was almost cartoonish. I thanked her again and headed to my car. Mrs. Trenton was right about one thing. It was another hot one. The interior of my car was like an oven already. A turkey would have feared for its life.

I drove through town with my window down, heading for the mill. People were going about their business, and I caught sight of Larry Swales standing outside Mabel Watt's diner with a doughnut in his hand. He had his hat pulled low over his sunglasses. I eased the Dodge to a stop next to him and he bent down, checking who it was. He greeted me with a mouthful of doughnut and sugar dotted around his lips.

"Well...good...morning," he said between chomps on his doughnut. "And what pray, can I do for you today?" He finished the doughnut, licked his fingers, and wiped his mouth.

"Morning, Deputy Swales," I said. "Deputy Carson in today?"

He looked up and down the street, then back at me, placed a hand on each knee. "Now what would you be wanting with Frank?"

"He's the one Mrs. Jackson filed the missing person report with."

He pushed his sunglasses up his nose a little more. "Thought we already told you we ain't got no report."

"Yes, you did. But I wondered if Deputy Carson might have forgotten to file it or had perhaps misfiled it. If that was the case, you and the sheriff might not be aware."

Swales thought about that for a moment. "Can't be," he said.

"Any reason why not?"

"Frank's taken a leave of absence and handed all his work to me. If he had that report, and I mean, if, then I would know about it. Personally, I think you and your Mrs. Jackson are confused. Just like the sheriff said yesterday."

I chose not to mention that I had gone back to see Ellie-Mae yesterday, and that she had confirmed a report was filed with Deputy Carson. There was no confusion at all. "OK," I said. "I guess that's it. Thanks again for your help."

"That's no problem," he said, giving me a stupid grin and a lazy salute. I pulled away from the sidewalk and waved back, making sure that my middle finger was prominently displayed. My rear-view mirror caught him staring at me as I drove past the courthouse.

I'd met guys like him before, full of their own self-importance and cocky show but gutless wonders underneath. Back in Chicago, when I was a rookie cop, I was assigned to such a guy. He'd been in the force eight years and loved to regale me with stories of his encounters with criminals, his gun skills, bravery and how many women he'd bedded. Each day dragged out to an eternity as we drove the neighborhood, stopped for coffee, breakfast, lunch, and did nothing more than pull over errant drivers for minor traffic offenses, deal with family disputes or stolen cars. I couldn't wait for my shifts to finish. How he was still employed as an officer was beyond me. It was chalk and cheese sitting in a black and white and doing nothing to improve the lives of the people we served.

Donnelly was about 210 pounds, five-nine, thirty-four, and had breath that could strip varnish. One afternoon—me with a coffee, him with a coffee and burger, the grease spotting his shirt where his belly sat—we got a call from dispatch. Disturbance. My partner, although I hated to think of him as such, carried on stuffing his face while we drove at the same steady pace to the address. When I questioned him about it, he just said that by the time we got there it would have sorted itself. Probably just some guy having a beef with his girlfriend or wife.

He had finished his burger and slurped the rest of his coffee by the time we drove the fifteen blocks to an area where the streets were full of potholes, garbage bags, junked cars and torn down wire fences. The houses were just painted cinder block with rotten doors and windows, and yards like jungles. We got out opposite number 32. Donnelly dumped his burger wrap and coffee on the street. I left my coffee in the car. He elected to take the front door and indicated that I should go around back.

I heard the front door open, voices, and then the door closing. Out back there was a powerful, broad-chested dog of mixed heritage chained to a stake in the ground, and it didn't like the look of me one bit. It lunged, snarling with vicious intent. I took several steps back, but the chain held it in check, giving me a clear six feet of breathing space. The speed and the power of its lunge would have easily pulled the stake from the ground had it not been cemented in.

Then, in a matter of a few seconds, it all went down. Through the kitchen window, I saw Donnelly fall to the floor and a white guy standing over him. I drew my service revolver and kicked in the rear door. The dog was snarling and barking as the rotting wood splintered like matchsticks. The man turned to run, a bloodied knife in his right hand. I ordered him to stop. He didn't. I shot him in the upper thigh, and he dropped by the front door, howling out in pain.

Donnelly lay there, hand clutching his wounded stomach, blood seeping through his fingers. He was groaning and blubbering like a baby. I went to check on the man I'd shot. He was muscular, tattooed, scarred, broken nose, and calling me all kinds. One hand pressed against the bullet wound, the other holding the knife. I aimed the gun at him, advised him to drop the knife. He thought about it for a second and took the wisest decision he'd probably ever made in his life up to that point. He dropped it. I pulled out a handkerchief, used it to pick up the knife so my prints weren't all over it, then ran across the street to the patrol car and radioed it in.

Back in the house, I cuffed the white guy's free hand to a radiator then tended to Donnelly's wound as best I could. He'd stopped crying and his wound wasn't that serious. The knife had sliced his skin rather than punctured it. I pressed a towel I found draped over a chair against it, told him to put his hand there while I cleared the rest of the house. There wasn't much, torn sofa, stinking bathroom, frayed carpet a few boxes here and there, and in one of the bedrooms, cowering in the corner, a young black woman around eighteen-nineteen. Her left arm lay uselessly at her side. One of the bones—radius or ulna, I couldn't tell which—jutted through her skin. She would have been in tremendous pain but couldn't utter more than a series of grunts and could not see who I was her face had been so badly beaten. I gave her my name; told her I was a police officer, and that help was on its way.

The guy with the knife had obviously dropped his weapon of choice when Donnelly knocked the door, choosing instead something more discreet should he have to deal with any kind of threat. I picked up the discarded baseball bat and went back downstairs to the hall, intent on doing real damage.

I stood over him, blood racing through my veins like a thoroughbred. How I stopped myself from beating him to within an inch of his life, I'll never know. I still had the bat over my right shoulder, wavering, ready to strike when another squad car and the medics arrived. An officer had to physically pry the bat from my fingers, such was the visceral rage I felt.

CHAPTER 8

I continued five miles east of town, up Towers Hill Road, until I saw the sign on my left for Towers Lumber Co., just as Mrs. Trenton had said.

I turned left through the double gates onto a wide road flanked by pine trees and more used to logging trucks negotiating its deep ruts than my Dodge. I arrived at the mill a half mile on in a swirl of dust and heat.

The mill lay idle in about three acres of parched, dry grass. Against a stand of lush, green pine wood, it sat there like a ponderous, dark monolith as a thickening haze lifted off its blackened roof and sides, and a long shadow fell behind it at a forty-five-degree angle. Over to one side was a large storage shed, again with blackened roof and sides. To the left of the shed were a couple of old pickups, a '49 Ford F3 and a battered and bruised Chevy 3600. Occupying space to the right was a pyramid of logs, already limbered, stacked twenty feet high ready to be debarked, planed, and decked. Next to this, were an ancient crane and two tractors fitted with logging grapples. I walked to the far end of the mill where various lengths of timber were stacked ready for shipment. It wasn't a huge mill by any stretch of the imagination, but big enough for a family concern.

Beyond the mill, a wide creek came off the Marston County River and became lost in the cypress groves. The cloying smell of pine and gum lay so thick in the air that I could taste it at the back of my throat.

I made my way back around to the shed and noticed an external wooden staircase leading up and over the entrance to the mill where the logs would be loaded. There was a half-glazed door at the top of the staircase. The whole place appeared deserted, which seemed odd because of what Coop had told me. But someone must be around because of the trucks, unless they'd been abandoned. Apart from numerous dents and patches of rust, they appeared roadworthy enough. I started up the stairs.

At the top, I had a wonderful view of the river, hundreds of acres of pine forest and the town way over in the distant east. It all looked peaceful, idyllic, a place a man might want to retire to.

The door had *Towers Lumber Co.* painted on the window in a straight line of black letters and underneath that, Office. I tried the door, it was open and made no sound as I pushed it. I stepped in, immediately having to adjust my eyes to the gloom. I found myself on a mezzanine floor with a couple of empty desks and file cabinets to my right, and an office to my left. There were typewriters on the desks and wire trays filled with various paperwork, I assumed shipment dockets and orders. From the mezzanine, I could see over into the mill itself. Huge logs lay on runners ready for cutting, and there was an overhead pulley on rails and a gantry running the length of the mill.

There were islands of sawdust covering the concrete floor, some with boot prints threading through, and others like a deserted sandy beach. I went over to the office door and knocked on the mottled glass. A gasp of surprise came from behind the door, some shuffling around, a desk drawer slamming, and a rasping voice said. "Just a minute."

I waited.

Thirty-seconds later the door opened, and I was facing a plump man of around thirty, medium height, light brown hair razored to the sides, and almost mop-like on top. He wore jeans held up by suspenders and a plaid shirt. "Yes," he said, sounding irritated and nervous at the same time. I noted his upper body was crooked to one side. "Help you?"

"Name's Tom Bale," I said. "Sorry to call on you unexpected, but I was hoping to catch a word with Leroy Jackson. However, the mill looks to be closed today. I assumed it would be working on a Saturday."

His tongue played at the corners of his mouth. "I see, I see," he said, almost a whisper. He stared down at the floor as if something had suddenly caught his attention. When he looked up again, his eyes were flicking around in their sockets, and he was frowning. "Mill is closed today for...err...maintenance. There's nobody here. Is there something I can help with?"

He had a hurried way about him and in his speech, slightly nervous, almost embarrassed. "Maintenance you say? Don't see any engineers around."

A pretend smile, tongue playing. "Been and gone."

I didn't believe that for one minute. "I assume you're the manager?" I said.

He nodded. "Yes. Tibbett's the name, Floyd Tibbett."

"I expect Leroy will be at home then."

"Yes, yes. I assume so. Leroy's not in trouble, is he?"

"No," I said. "Not at all. Just wanted to ask him some questions about his sister. She's missing. I'm investigating her disappearance. Well...I say investigating. What I mean is, I'm a family friend just looking into it."

"Missing you say?"

"Yes, you know Alice Jackson?"

"Oh no, no, no," he said quickly. "Don't know Alice." Then he seemed to hesitate, as if wondering what to do or say next. "Why don't you step into my office, take a seat, and tell me what's going on?"

He held the door for me, and I went inside, sat in a metal framed chair opposite his desk. The desktop was strewn with paperwork and had an angle poise lamp to one side. He leaned over as he walked and had a slight limp. He dropped into his chair, squeezing his eyes shut as he did so, as if in pain. "Sorry," he said. "Accident a few years ago. Back has never recovered. Hurts sometimes."

I chose not to comment.

There was a heavy scent of stale body odor in the air, and something more that I couldn't quite make out. A low wattage light bulb hung from the ceiling in the center of the room. Two filing cabinets stood in the far corner and, leaning next to these were several well-thumbed files and box folders. Behind his head a wall chart with

77

names scrawled on it and various colored circles and crosses, and over on the right wall was a rectangular wooden board with a dozen metal hooks. Each hook had a small chrome plated key dangling from it. Locker keys, I thought. The whole office felt oppressive, stale. It was untidy and more than a little seedy.

"Leroy ever mention his family?" I asked. "He said anything about his sister, Alice? She's been missing a while. Any light you can throw on it would be appreciated."

Tibbett had this habit of staring at the floor when considering what answer to give. I'd met a lot of people who did that in my time as a cop, trying to avoid your eyes, giving themselves time to come up with some bullshit answer.

"Are you a private investigator, Mr. Bale?"

"Yes, up in Chicago where I'm from. But as I said, I'm down here as a family friend. My license does not permit me to act officially in the state of Georgia, so I've got to be extra respectful of peoples' time and privacy."

"Hmmm," he said, but didn't question it. Instead, "Leroy is a good worker. He's been here three years now. Never had any problems with him, but he don't talk much, just gets on with the job. I don't know anything about his sister." Then his eyes grew keen. "You talked to anyone else, anybody helpful?"

You're hiding something, I thought. Wonder what it is. "Yes," I said. "I heard that Alice was last seen along Cotton Cut Road." And then it came to me, the information I couldn't remember earlier.

"Somebody mentioned seeing a black car around the same time. But that's it so far. Not very much, I'm afraid to say."

"A black car, you say?"

"Yeah, but no make or number I can trace."

"Ah, probably just a coincidence."

Did I detect a sense of relief in his voice? "Met another one of your guys at Nat's Bar last night."

"Oh, who might that be?"

"Sam Cooper. He was a little drunk, couldn't add anything, and just said that Leroy and a friend of his, Carl Robard, worked here."

"Cooper, yes. He's OK, not so reliable. Has plenty of time off, but I think that's more down to excesses of drink."

"He had a bad cold last night. Seemed real sick."

Tibbett tried to force a smile, but it failed. "First time for everything."

I wasn't going to get anything more out of Tibbett; no sense in flogging a dead horse, so I made my excuses and thanked him for his time. "Best be on my way. I'm sure you've got plenty to be getting on with." What though, I wondered? Why would anyone be sitting alone in their stuffy, sweaty little office on a glorious Saturday morning? When I first knocked on his door, there was hurried movement from inside, the kind of movement you hear when someone is trying to hide whatever it was they were doing. "Don't suppose you could point me in the direction of anyone who might be able to help?"

"The sheriff?"

"Been there, spoke to Deputy Swales and the sheriff. Can't help. Don't know anything about it."

"Oh," he said, feigning surprise. "Didn't the family file a missing person report?"

I didn't let on. "Apparently not," I said.

I got up, shook a sweaty hand, and thanked him again.

Outside, the sun was glinting so hard off chrome bumpers, it could blind you. I shielded my eyes and glanced up to the door at the top of the staircase. Floyd Tibbett suddenly jerked back from the window, caught in a moment of duplicity.

I found Corey Peters easier than I thought I would. He was literally halfway between the highway and Cotton Cut Road, down a long winding track that opened out to a yard full of junked cars and pickups, mounds of worn tires, oil drums, and engine blocks all divided over two sides; like Moses parting the Red Sea. At the end of this channel was a workshop and a man bent under the hood of a flatbed truck. Further back and over to the right by a bank of pines stood a silver-hulled trailer that had seen better days.

I got out. A young man who I guessed was Corey Peters headed in my direction, wiping his hands on a rag. His dark-blue overalls were open to the waist, revealing a muscular torso. The overalls were worn at the knees and oil stained. Steel capped work boots kicked up red dust and grit as he came toward me. I checked my watch.

"Hot afternoon," I said.

"Storm coming," he countered.

He was a pleasant young man, early twenties with neatly barbered blonde hair. Maybe an inch shorter than me in height but broad, powerful, and I guessed a lot fitter than I used to be at his age.

I looked up at the bright blue cloudless sky. Storm? "Don't see it," I said.

"It's there," he said. "Waiting. Maybe tonight."

"Tom Bale," I said, extending a hand and looking up again at the Robin's egg sky. Couldn't see a trace of a potential storm.

He held up his right hand. "Sorry," he said. "I'd shake, but I guess you don't want oil and grease over yours."

He was certainly polite. "That's fine," I said.

He nodded toward my Dodge. "Problems?"

"No," I said. "She's running OK. You must be Corey Peters."

"That's me. Do I know you?"

"No. I was speaking to Dan Benson and Lucas James yesterday and they mentioned your name, said you sometimes help people in the Bottoms."

His expression suddenly changed from open and welcoming to one of doubt and suspicion. "Yeah?" he said, dragging out the word.

I needed to put him at ease. People are far more likely to offer up information when they feel safe and not under threat. "I'm down here from Chicago, a friend of Ellie-Mae Jackson. It's about her daughter's disappearance. I was asking Dan and Lucas about it." Using first names gave the impression that I was a good deal more of a friend than I actually was. An old trick designed to make me less of an outsider and that I had gained trust and acceptance. "They couldn't help much

81

with what happened to Alice, but said that you gave her lifts into town now and then. Anything you can tell me might help."

His expression eased a little, and he scratched his head, leaving black smudges in his blonde hair. "Yeah, I know about it, but I wasn't around that day." He motioned with his head back towards the man still bent under the hood of the flatbed. "Took my dad to see his sister over in Valdosta. Dad can't legally drive because he's partially deaf, and got a cataract in his left eye."

That would explain why he was still under that hood. He hadn't heard my car. And there would be no point in trying to question his dad either if both of them were away.

"Did Alice walk into town much? It's some distance."

"Oh yeah, many times. People from the Bottoms ain't afraid of walking a few miles."

"So how would she know when you could give her a lift?"

"We got a routine worked out, twice a week, and I would let her know in advance if I couldn't, like on that Monday. Same with Mr. James. Neither can afford a car, and I guess Mr. James is too old now anyway."

Seemed logical enough to me. Strange though, that a young man in his early twenties would be friends with a fourteen-year-old girl.

"So how come you know people in the Bottoms? From what I gather so far, most of the town doesn't take to them very well."

"Way it is," he said, sighing. "Black and white don't seem to go together. Don't understand it myself, where all the bad feeling comes from, but I ain't got no issues. Mrs. Jackson was real supportive when my mom died. Most of the people from the Bottoms were real kind. Dad didn't cope so well, but they would come up with pots of stew for us, sit in the Airstream, talking, having dinner, playing cards. Helped us through a very bad time. So, in turn, we fix their trucks, generators, give them lifts if they need it, and help where we can."

Sounded to me like the whole world needed a lesson from this young man. "Sorry to hear about your mom," I said.

"That's OK, been a time ago now. Dad and me, we got through it."

I wondered if he knew about Ellie-Mae reporting Alice's disappearance to the sheriff. Was he the person gave her a lift into town? "You give Mrs. Jackson a lift into town so she could report it to the sheriff?"

He shook his head. "Nope. That was someone from the Bottoms, I guess. I know Mrs. Jackson reported it…"

"For certain?"

"Well, I can't say for certain, but Leroy told me she had."

"Sheriff or one of his deputies been out to see you?"

"No. Ain't seen the sheriff or any of his deputies for a while. A month maybe?"

"Someone said they saw a black car on Cotton Cut Road about the same time Alice went missing. You ever seen a black car cruising around, looking like it don't belong?"

He shrugged. "I've seen a thousand cars around. Some end up here, some just passing. All colors, all makes, all models. Who can tell?"

"Did you help look for her?"

"Yeah, a whole group of us from the Bottoms, we looked everywhere we could. Three days and nothing."

Damn, this was getting frustrating. Somebody, somewhere, must know something. "You say you've already searched for her, but is there any place around here where someone could literally vanish, or hide away for a while? Anything like that?"

"There's a thousand places in the swamps. And we got the biggest in the country, the Okefenokee."

"The what?"

"Okefenokee. Almost six hundred square miles of cypress forest, marsh, lakes, and islands filled with alligators, water moccasins, snapping turtles, diamond back rattlers, copperheads, and black bear."

"Sounds like a friendly place," I said

"Land of the Trembling Earth the Indians called it."

"I don't understand," I said. "Trembling earth, what does that mean?"

"Peat deposits. It's a very shallow wetland and if you stand on the peat mounds they tremble."

You live and you learn, I thought. "So, could Alice have gone into the swamp?"

He shook his head again. "Nah, not the kind of place Alice would go on her own. But if I wanted to disappear, that's the place I'd choose. It's a protected reserve now, but there are still many areas tourists ain't allowed to go. Dangerous areas, full of ancient and rusting logging machinery, tractors, and shacks left deserted from the old settlements, animal traps, and some very nasty wildlife. They say black panthers roam the swamp but, I ain't ever seen one."

I very much doubted Alice would have ventured into such a vast and dangerous area on her own. Why would she? From all accounts she had a happy home, friends; no reason for her to leave. Seemed pointless running that possibility around in my head, as she'd been missing almost three weeks, and every element of rational thought convinced me she'd been abducted and was probably dead. But I had to cover all angles, improbable or otherwise.

"How far is the reserve from here?" I asked.

"There's areas of swamp, lakes, ponds, and creeks all over, but the official northern boundary of the reserve is about twenty miles. There's places all around the reserve you can hire canoes or small boats with outboards. Camp sites, official trails, you name it. In fact, we got an old aluminum two-man with a Johnson outboard over in the workshop. It don't look much cause it's battered to shit, but motor works fine. You can borrow it if you want."

It was just too improbable to contemplate at this point. "I don't think it'll come to that, but thanks, Corey, that's good of you. In any case, I don't have any means of getting it to the reserve."

"I can take you down there, show you where to go and what to look out for. Go fishing sometimes with Carl Robard and his dad. Supposed to have a license, but there are hundreds of places you can go undetected. Fish for brim, pickerel, bluegill, bowfin. Help you look if you want. Hate to think Alice might be out there."

"That's kind of you. I'll pass for now. But would appreciate any help if you hear or see anything that might just point me in the right direction. By the way, how does Leroy get to the mill?"

"Grabs a lift with Carl. Got an old Ford. Ain't up to much, but I keep it going for him."

Corey smiled then, and the warmth spread across his face and into his pale-blue eyes. I had one last question for him. "You ever heard anything about other black girls gone missing?"

He shrugged. "Some," he said. "Rumors. Nothing for certain. My dad told me once that spirits from dead Indians roam the swamp and if you go in alone, you never come out again."

"A little far-fetched," I said, smiling at him.

He laughed. "Yeah, I guess. But a lot of what you see around here is ancient burial ground. And I guess the spirits don't like it much, that we took it away from them. At least, that's what my dad says."

Put like that I thought, he was probably correct. Wouldn't want anyone fucking with my grave after I was gone. Make me really angry that nobody gave a damn or showed any respect. I do me some serious haunting.

"All right, Corey," I said. "I got to go, but you and your dad take care now. If you think of anything at all, I'm staying at the Paradise Creek Motel. Cabin number six. Just come knock on my door, leave a message with the manager, Hubert Trenton, if I'm not around."

"I will," he said. "Sorry I can't be of any help, but I hope you find Alice. I really do. She's a sweet kid."

"Going to do whatever it takes," I said, and held out my hand.

"You sure?" he said, holding up his right hand again.

"I'm sure," I said, smiling.

He gave his hand another wipe with the rag, studied it. His grip was firm, honest, and I didn't care about the oil and grease. Corey Peters presented himself as a good, generous-hearted young man, and I felt encouraged knowing there was at least one white person of his age growing up not blighted by bigotry and intolerance.

Maybe this world of ours had a chance after all.

The sun, high and mighty, had bleached the sky to a blue so faint it was almost white. No way could I see a storm coming.

Driving back toward town, I was thinking how ridiculous the idea of Alice hiding out in the swamps was. She would have no reason to. What would she be hiding from all this time? I doubt she'd been scared by anything, and even if she did feel threatened in any way, she certainly wouldn't walk twenty miles. As Corey said, there must be thousands of places much closer to home.

No. Why in God's name was I even giving it consideration? I'd already told myself once not to waste precious time on it. I was clutching at straws already and it had only been two days. Come Monday, Alice would have been missing three weeks.

I knew the answer. I had already argued with myself about that, but I didn't want it to be so. Not for Alice, not for Ellie-Mae, and not for Little Joe. But sometimes you just had to accept what your head told you to be true and not what your heart told you to hang on to; that single gossamer thread of hope, when there was no hope to be had.

Three weeks and nothing. Alice had to be dead. I dreaded the thought of delivering the truth to Ellie-Mae and her sons.

I thumped the steering wheel in frustration and swore at the windshield. "Fuck, fuck, fuck."

What the hell was wrong with me? Two days, that's all I'd had so far. I usually had to be a week into something and getting nowhere before frustration kicked in. So why was this case getting to me so much?

Truth of it was, I knew the reason. Didn't want to admit it, but I knew, I knew damn well.

CHAPTER 9

Nat's Bar on a late Saturday afternoon would be a good place to reflect. Maybe get something to eat, have a couple of beers and who knows it being a weekend, might get a few more people in there later on. More people, more opportunity to ask questions. Throw enough shit at the wall, some had to stick.

Nat's neon sign was on so I pulled in to the lot, parked up and got out. As I closed the driver's door, a sudden gust of wind blew up, throwing grit and dust into the air. I looked up, shading my eyes. The sky above was still a hot, whitish blue but south west had darkened to a cold and heartless slate gray. Some birds passed overhead, their cries shrill and broken, as if giving a warning of the storm to come. I shook my head. Never would have thought it.

Inside, the bar was empty. I pulled up on a stool, had a shouting match with Nat, got my beer, and my order in for burger and fries. I went over to the jukebox, a '58 Rockola. I stuck in a dime, looked through the listings, chose "Mack the Knife", Bobby Darin's version.

Back at my stool I heard the clacking from the selector arm and the 45 being placed on the turntable, then a few scratches as the needle caught the outer edge, and finally the hiss before the music started.

Bobby Darin had a number one hit when it was released in '59, but "Mack the Knife" had a long history and as far as my memory could recall was adapted from stories called murder ballads regaled by strolling minstrels back in medieval times. Then, in the eighteenth century, those ballads became *The Beggar's Opera* and were further adapted in the twenties to *The Threepenny Opera* featuring stories about murder, rape, robbery, and arson; "Ballad of Mack the Knife". Funny what you remember.

The burger and fries came, and they were good. I hummed along to the tune and wondered if anyone else was going to walk through Nat's door.

Several minutes passed, the meal finished, the music over. Just the soft whirr of overhead fans and the sound of Nat busying himself in the back room. And I began to wonder what in hell I was doing almost a thousand miles from home chasing something that couldn't be found; like all the hours, days, months I'd spent chasing every lead I could back in Chicago that had even the most tenuous link to Jenny and the day she was taken from me. A day I'll never forget. Jenny was my heart, my soul, the very essence of my being.

Nat was shouting, asking if I wanted another beer. I nodded and looked up as the door opened. I recognized the newcomer immediately, the man with the Chevy BelAir. He surveyed the room, looked at me and I saw a fleeting note of recognition on his face, then he walked straight past me and stood at the far end of the bar, having not said a word. Nat brought me my third beer and grabbed another from the cooler, flipped off the cap, took it to the end of the bar, and placed it on the counter in front of the guy. No shouting needed. A regular? But why stay in the motel? Occasional business perhaps?

I picked up my beer and went over to him.

"Hi," I said. "I see we're staying at the same motel. You own a Chevy BelAir, right?"

Without looking at me he said, "So?" His voice was hard, unfriendly.

"Seen you around a couple of times, and as we're temporary neighbors just thought I'd say hello. You here on business?"

Still no eye contact. I sipped my beer. He slugged his back in three Adam's apple bobbing swallows. As soon as he'd finished, Nat had put a fresh one in front of him.

"You must be a regular," I said. Then trying to make light of the situation. "Saves having to shout at Nat."

I saw the tension grow in him and the muscles bunching in his throat. His skin reddened, accentuating the long white scar. He grabbed his bottle off the counter, went and took a seat over in the corner. I guessed that was our conversation done.

"OK," I said and went back to my stool.

People behave in all kinds of different and weird ways, and his was typical of those who had something to hide.

A minute later, the door opened again, and a couple came in. Both in their mid to late thirties, she an attractive blonde dressed in denims and boots, he a wiry, angular-faced guy with long dark hair parted in the middle and dressed in the same manner. They came up to the counter. She stood closest to me. She turned and gave me a smile. I smiled back. She was good looking in a worn kind of way, like she'd seen everything the world could throw at her and she was still beating it off, waiting for the day her luck would change.

Again, without any exchange between them, Nat produced a beer for him and a Dr. Pepper for her. They took their drinks over to Scarface in the corner. Clearly, Nat knew who they were, but asking him was out of the question. Trying to have a private conversation with Nat would be impossible, might as well announce it on TV. I motioned him over and indicated with both hands I needed something to write on. He went off into the back room and returned with a pencil and a small notepad. I put a forefinger to my lips to indicate I wanted to be quiet and wrote, *do you know them?* I turned the pad around for him to read. He nodded, took the pencil, wrote for a minute then turned the pad back to me.

Yes, meet here every few months, stay at motel, don't know names.

I thought for a moment, then, *over how long? They meet anyone else?*

Nat read, then wrote. *Two years. Nobody else.*

I mouthed a "thank you" to Nat and returned his pad after tearing out the page and slipping it in my jacket pocket.

"You're welcome," he boomed at me. I sensed heads turning over in the corner, but didn't look. Jesus, Nat, I thought. I considered putting another tune on the Rockola, but the three in the corner intrigued me and I wanted to know more, so I sat in silence and couldn't hear a damn thing. They were talking so quietly. I glanced over a few times at the occasional giggle from the woman, but with

92

the wind blowing up outside, I gave up after half an hour. I threw a twenty on the counter, more than enough to cover the beers and food.

It was dark outside, the stars hidden by rolling thunderheads blacker than coal. The wind howled and bowed the pines, threw trash down the road.

There were three cars in the lot other than mine, one of them I expected: the Chevy BelAir. But the other surprised me. It was the Allstate Sedan. So, the good-looking bitch that got slapped and her lover were friends of Scarface. That made perfect sense with what Nat had said about them staying at the motel.

The other car was parked right at the back of the lot out of the way under some trees where it was really dark. I thought nothing of it and got in the Dodge. I flipped on the radio, found a station playing country music and sang along to Don Gibson's "Oh Lonesome Me".

As I pulled out, I saw a flicker of yellow in my rear-view mirror and a tiny red dot appear. Someone was inside that vehicle and that someone had lit up a cigarette.

I chose not to return to the motel and instead drove into town and turned left onto Cumberland Avenue. It was madness, really. The wind was bending trees, bucking the car, and it was so dark it felt as though I was driving through a tunnel. I'd gone maybe four miles, past large antebellum houses on both sides, before I decided to turn around and head back. It was crazy in this weather, but sometimes driving around allowed me to think in different ways.

As I was maneuvering the car around, another came up the road and passed me, then was gone around a bend up ahead. I straightened up, drove about a half mile then pulled over again, thoughts running through my head. I turned on the overhead light, dug around in the glovebox for a pen, and took the piece of paper Nat and I had written on out of my pocket.

The three of them arrive at the motel around the same time, stay for a few days maybe, and depart. The bitch and her lover I assumed were from Jacksonville Florida, given what she had screamed at him on Thursday night when I had first arrived. Scarface from somewhere else? Clearly, Paradise Creek was their meeting point. What was it Nat had written, every few months over two years? I wrote, WHY.

I put the piece of paper on the dash, rummaged in the glovebox for a notepad, and started furiously writing down everything that came into my head and in no particular order. I ripped off a page, placed it on the dash, and started on a fresh sheet. Thoughts were rushing, jumbled, incoherent, and before I knew it, I had a dozen pages. I stopped suddenly, sat back and realized I'd been holding my breath all the time I'd been writing. I breathed in deep, closed my eyes and eventually steadied myself.

I remembered a writer guy I once knew. I'd asked him how he could put a hundred thousand words down on paper and turn it into a story. Seemed like an impossible task. Like many writers, apparently, the trick was to write it all down, get everything on paper whether it made sense or not. Finish the story, leave it for a while—in his case a month—then reread it and edit like your life depended on it. Sometimes the words had come together and made perfect sense. Other times they were a nonsense. There would be occasions to back up an idea by researching and amending where necessary, and other occasions where apparently unrelated sections would suddenly come together, fused as if by magic and give you that eureka moment.

And so that's what I did sometimes, just made notes as they came to me. Got everything down and then later tried to make sense of it all. It worked most of the time.

I opened my eyes, glanced into my driver's mirror, and saw two men coming up alongside the Dodge, both wearing Klan masks. One of them had what looked like a length of thick pipe in his left hand.

I threw the notepad and pen to one side and just got the Dodge fired up when there was a loud explosion and my driver's window blew inwards. I was showered in a million fragments of glass as the wind tore through the car, throwing loose papers around like a tornado. The man with the pipe leaned in, grabbed at my hair, but I managed to pull away. He screamed into my ear.

"Time you headed the fuck back to Chicago, you hear me?"

I rammed the gearshift into drive and floored the accelerator, but not before he caught me on the side of the head with that pipe. Thankfully, his swing was restricted on account of his position, but as I took off, sparks danced around in my head and my vision blurred for a second.

The force of my acceleration threw him back on the road and as I looked in the rear-view mirror, I saw him get up and hurl the lead pipe after me. It bounced once, and I heard a metallic clang as it caught my rear fender.

Twenty minutes later I was back at the motel, holding a towel soaked in cold water against my head and pouring four fingers of bourbon into a glass. I drank half of it, topped it up, went back into the bathroom, and surveyed the damage in the mirror. I was surprised to see that my head didn't look too bad. There was an ugly gash where the pipe had landed and it was starting to swell, but apart from that, it was nowhere near as bad as it could have been.

I reasoned that the two hooded men had been in the car that went past me on Cumberland Avenue. They must have turned around and come back slowly, to avoid being seen, and then pulled over a ways back of me when they saw my car parked up. With it being so dark and the wind raging, I wouldn't have heard or seen them creeping along the side of the Dodge until the very last moment. And if my senses hadn't alerted me to movement, then who knows what might have happened.

I drank some more bourbon, leaned in closer to the mirror, and dabbed at the blood with some toilet paper. The overhead light seemed to be glinting off my hair. Window fragments. Carefully, I ruffled my hair and several tiny pieces of glass fell into the washbasin, tinkling and throwing up pin spots of light like a bunch of diamonds. I grabbed more toilet paper and carefully scooped up the pieces then wrapped them up and threw them into the wastebasket under the basin. I rinsed my face with warm water, then dried myself with a fresh towel. Studying myself in the mirror again, I saw that the bleeding had stopped, but the swelling had increased. There would be a significant bruise by morning.

I stripped down to my undershorts, then went over to the window and opened the blinds. The Chevy BelAir was back, as was the Allstate Sedan. Dust blew around the lot as the wind moaned and howled. There were no other cars that I could see, so I shut the blinds, double-checked the door lock, stuck a chair at an angle under the doorknob, and retrieved the Smith and Wesson from my suitcase. I refilled the glass tumbler with bourbon, transferred the glass, bottle, gun, and me to bed. It was almost midnight.

CHAPTER 10

Following morning I rose with an aching head, a bruise the size of a golf ball at my temple, and a mouth as dry as desert sand from an overindulgence of bourbon. I'd updated the timeline while keeping an eye on the door and my gun real close. I must have finally dozed off around 3 a.m. with the storm thundering outside.

Six hours later, I had already been out to survey the damage. Small tree branches everywhere, trash, and no sign of the Chevy or the Sedan. Must have left early. The sky was still weighted with storm clouds, rain had temporarily ceased, but wind was gusting, although much lighter than the previous night.

I'd patched up the driver's window as best I could with some duct tape I got from Trenton and had swept out most of the glass. The car's interior was a mess. All the notes I'd written were beyond salvation. The overnight rain had saturated the paper so much that when I tried to pick up the sheets, they just fell apart in my hands. I could remember bits and pieces, but most of what I'd written was gone from my head.

There was a repair shop not far from Nat's, so I'd get a new window installed later if they were open. If not, I'd go see Corey. He was bound to have a window somewhere amongst all those wrecks.

I had been threatened and received a warning to back off. At least one of the people I'd spoken to in the past two days felt I was getting close enough to make them nervous and had taken action. Alternatively, any one of those people could have mentioned me in casual and innocent conversation with others, and the grapevine would have taken over. Gossip would spread like wildfire in a town like this. But my money was on the former, and I had a good idea of who it might be. Now I had to work out exactly how I was going to take it from here on in without alerting even more attention. I only hoped I wouldn't be chasing something for nothing. I also had a desire to find the guys who attacked me last night, because it certainly would not have been the person I thought was behind it. And what would I do when I found the guy who hit me with that pipe?

Break his fucking arms.

The sky was a mix of gray and black, bold thunderheads looking ominous as I drove toward the repair shop. Storm damage was everywhere, and the townsfolk were out doing what they could to repair roofs, shingle, fences, and clear the streets. I noticed a couple of cars had suffered the same damage as me, windows smashed, dents in bodywork, all from falling branches caused by the storm, but not from a lead pipe. Funny, I thought. I'd created a little storm myself and suffered the consequences.

Frank Carson's repair shop was indeed open. I eased the Chevy onto the lot and parked in front of one of the two up and over workshop doors. There was another car up on ramps in the next bay and a mechanic with a torch underneath, who appeared to be checking the exhaust system. I got out and went over to the office.

The door opened before I got to it and a large ruddy-faced man about sixty, with cropped red hair came out holding up a worksheet. Like Corey, his overalls were stained and worn from years spent under hoods, his life ingrained under the fingernails and across his skin. He looked at me, then the car. Face broke into a wide grin.

"You're the third this morning," he said.

"No surprises there," I said. "Can you fix it?"

"Sure. Be about an hour." He nodded over to the car up on the ramps. "Just got to fix the exhaust on that one and we'll get your window sorted for you."

"Thanks, appreciate it."

"Wouldn't usually be open on a Sunday, but after last night's storm I figured folks might need some repair work doing."

I smiled at him. "Very enterprising," I said.

"Got to earn the dollar. Business to run, mouths to feed."

"I'm with you on that one. Way things are out there, you're going to be busy next twenty-four hours."

"Maybe he will," Carson said, nodding over at the mechanic. "Me. I'm taking a lie-in tomorrow." He chuckled at the thought.

"What time you open?"

"Seven, Monday through Friday. You can go wait in the office if you want. There's a pot of coffee on the plate, and a tray of doughnuts on the desk. Help yourself."

Coffee and doughnuts sounded good. "Thanks," I said again.

"Welcome."

He caught sight of the bump at my left temple. He frowned, sucked in his breath. "Nasty," he said. "What the hell happened there?"

I made something up. "Bumped my head on the bathroom cabinet door this morning. Wasn't looking, stupid thing to do."

He tilted his head slightly to one side, studied the bump, looked at me as if he didn't believe that story for one minute. Probably thought I'd been in a fight, which I had, more or less.

"There's some Tylenol on the desk, if you need it."

He was about to walk away when I stopped him. "You wouldn't know an Ellie-Mae Jackson, by any chance?"

He thought for a moment, head bowed to the floor, scratching three-day-old stubble. "Name's familiar," he said. "Can't think why, though."

"Lives over in the Bottoms. Her daughter is missing."

"Don't know nothing about that, don't tend to deal much with the people out there, but I've heard the name mentioned."

"Any idea who by?"

He thought some more, shook his head. "No, sorry, it's not coming to me." He looked up. "What's your interest?"

"Family friend. I'm from Chicago, trying to help find her daughter."

He didn't question that I had come all the way down here or that I was a friend of someone from the Bottoms. He just accepted it. I liked him already.

"Sure hope you find her. Easy to get lost around these parts, swamps, creeks, marsh. And it's a few miles away but go into the Okefenokee on your own and not know what you're doing, then don't be thinking you're coming out."

"I'd heard that," I said.

"Well, you go have yourself a doughnut and coffee, and we'll let you know when your window's fixed."

Office door closed, I settled into a vacant chair, the smell of sugared doughnuts and coffee wafting up my nose, my stomach hurrying me along, in need of sustenance.

It was a typical workshop office; untidy, beat-up desk, oil-stained paperwork, calendar on the wall alongside pictures of cars and trucks, hand tools on a rack, auto magazines, and engine parts lying here and there. There was a cork board on one wall, notes and photos pinned to it. Underlying the heady scent of coffee and doughnuts was the ever-present mechanical scent of grease and oil, a scent that could stay with you forever once it had burned its way into your senses.

I looked for the cleanest of the chipped, coffee-stained mugs, filled one from the pot, and selected a doughnut from the open tray on the desk. Both were gone in half a minute. My stomach thanked me.

I selected an outdated and well-thumbed copy of *Sports Car Illustrated* and flipped through the pages while I waited. Even though I kept abreast of car makes and models, I was not an enthusiast by any stretch of the imagination.

Perhaps ten minutes had passed when the office door opened and the mechanic who I saw fixing the exhaust stepped in. He greeted me with a smile as warm as Alaska in midwinter and let me know that he was about to start on my window. I thanked him as politely as I could and as he stretched over the desk to deposit a sheet of pink colored paper in the wire tray, the left sleeve of his overall exposed about three or four inches of his lower arm. There was a tattoo, a dagger with a snake coiled around it, tip of the dagger pointing to his wrist.

He was out of the office in less than four-seconds, and I was sitting there as if jolted by a bolt of lightning. That tattoo meant something profound to me and an image flashed through my brain a few times like a camera shutter. And then it was gone.

The office door opened again, shattering my concentration, and Frank Carson came in and sat behind the desk, his chair protesting under his weight. He started searching for something on his desk.

"You helped yourself to coffee and doughnuts?" he asked.

"I did," I said. "Just what I needed."

"Have as many as you want. We can't eat them all."

"I might just do that."

My mind drifted again, back to that tattoo. Why did it have such meaning? I thought for a moment, but it wouldn't come.

Carson found what he was looking for, a photograph hidden under some paperwork. He held it up, a proud smile creasing his face. "Meant to put this up when I came in," he said. "Repairs got in the way."

He handed me the photo. It was a professional shot taken in a studio, and I saw a happy, smiling family. There was Carson, and a woman about the same age I took to be his wife. They were standing on either side of a younger man and woman, both in their late twenties. The younger man was straight out of the Frank Carson mould. The younger woman was good looking, dark hair, slim, and had clearly applied make-up before the shot. However, the telltale lack of sleep signs were still there under her eyes. All four of them stood proud as the younger woman cradled a baby in her arms.

"That's a great photograph," I said. "How old?"

"Ain't it just. Girl. Two weeks. I'm a very proud granddaddy. She's going to get spoilt rotten." He thought for a second. "Maybe best get a frame before I hang it." A look of shock took over his face when he realized how he'd phrased that last sentence. "Err…the photograph I mean…hang the photograph."

"It's OK, I got it," I said, smiling. I looked a little closer this time at what everyone was wearing instead of their faces and the baby, and I noticed that Carson junior was dressed in his official deputy uniform.

"Your son a deputy?" I asked.

"Damn right he is," Carson said, pride filling his face. "That's William Carson standing right there with his lovely wife, Susan, and his mother. Couldn't wish for more."

So that was the Deputy Carson Ellie-Mae filed a report with. And with the baby being only two weeks old that fitted precisely with Carson taking time off, just as Larry Swales had told me. At least Swales was telling the truth about that, but it still didn't explain the absence of the missing report.

I handed the photo back and Carson beamed at it once more before placing it out of harm's way in the desk drawer.

"That missing person case I mentioned earlier," I said.

"Oh yeah? What about it?"

"Ellie-Mae…Mrs. Jackson, she told me she filed a missing person report with your son. Must have been the same day he had to take leave. Did he mention it to you by any chance? Is that why the name was familiar to you?"

"Don't think so," he said, scratching his stubble again. "My son and his wife have their own house, so his mother and I we don't get to hear as much as we used to. Not that we heard much before he moved out. My son's not the type to discuss police business outside of the office, not even with his family. No, I heard that name somewhere else."

"Do you think it'd be OK if I paid your son a visit? I really need to get to the bottom of this and so far, it's going nowhere."

"Ordinarily I'd say yes, but you'd have a fuck of a long way to go. They took off to San Antonio, Texas yesterday. That's where Susan's parents live. Back next weekend."

Another corner turned, another dead end. Next weekend. That would make it four weeks since Alice went missing. Short of beating it out of Larry Swales, it looked like I'd never find her. I was sure Swales knew something, and I was sure he got those two guys to threaten me last night. But, and it was a perfectly logical but, Carson could have misfiled or just not done anything with that report. If he got a call to say his wife was about to go into labor, his concentration would have not been on a missing person that was more likely to either come home from their own volition or would be gone forever. That was perfectly logical.

No. Swales knew something. His body language, general attitude, and that shifty way about him told me he was a man I could not trust.

Fifteen minutes later my window was fixed, good as new. I thanked Carson and paid up. I was going to tip his mechanic but there was no sign of him, so I gave Carson an extra five dollars and asked him to pass it on. He said he would.

"May be a dumb question," I said, "but you have any Klan activity out here?"

He laughed out loud. "Klan? No, sir, not in Paradise Creek. Mississippi maybe, but not out here. Why, you thinking of joining up?"

"No, no," I said, trying to laugh with him without it sounding flat. "Just something I read about a long time ago." I got in the Dodge, wound down the window to test it. It ran smoother that it did when it was new.

"No pointy hats around here, fella," Carson said. "Too quiet and peaceful. Not much happens that's exciting more than a couple of times a year;: beer and cider festivals, July 4th parade, that sort of thing."

"OK," I said. "Thanks again."

He tapped the roof of the Dodge a couple of times. "You go steady now."

As I reversed out of the bay and onto Main, I noticed the mechanic outside, leaning against the office wall smoking. So that's where he'd disappeared to. He was literally no more than twenty feet away. I waved at him as I drove past. He nodded back.

As I drove, I thought about those Klan hats the two men were wearing and that dagger tattoo with the coiled snake. If there wasn't Klan activity in the area, the threat had no substance. I figured those masks were worn to scare me and hide the identity of my attackers. Nothing more. At least one of those was true. But that tattoo kept coming back. As for the sheriff, Alban Somers, he wasn't high on my list of potential kidnappers. But I couldn't dismiss him either. So many things going around in my head, and no matter which way I looked at them, I couldn't make anything fit.

I didn't want to question Larry Swales any more. It would just add fuel to the fire.

Floyd Tibbett interested me, interested me a lot. The mill was bound to be closed on a Sunday, a perfect opportunity to do some quiet snooping around. What was I hoping to find? God only knew.

CHAPTER 11

The mill gates were locked, so I drove on another quarter mile and tucked the Dodge into a gap in the trees, got out and proceeded on foot through the woods. It was surprisingly easy going and within a few minutes I came up to a ten-foot-high wire fence with a 'NO TRESPASSING' sign hanging at a forty-five-degree angle. I walked along the fence a little ways until I found what I was looking for, a small opening where the wire had been cut. Every fence has a gap in it somewhere, usually made by kids just wanting to get in, explore, and make mischief.

I gave the fence a few hefty kicks to widen the gap. My jacket snagged on a piece of wire, and I lost a button, but I managed to pull myself through. The mill wasn't too far away and under the storm clouds it looked even more dark and ominous.

I approached cautiously and stood by the storage shed. One of the pickups was gone, the Chevy. The Ford sat there growing old and absent of any grace. I guessed the Chevy was Tibbett's, but couldn't take any chances. He might be up there in his office doing whatever he does on his own, whatever he's trying to hide.

Keeping this side of the shed meant that if Tibbett was up there, he couldn't see me from any of the windows. No locks on the shed door, so maybe someone was here after all. But I slipped inside anyway. The door hinges silent, well maintained.

The only source of light, apart from the two naked bulbs overhead, was from a small window to my right. I wasn't going to risk turning on the lights, so allowed my eyes to focus with what little the window had to offer. From what I could see, there was nothing of any relevance: tins of paint, steel cutters, rope, buckets, wide-mouthed wrenches propped in one corner, sheets of tarpaulin. I rummaged around for a minute, not knowing what I hoped to find and found nothing.

I let myself out and crouched behind the Ford. Directly in front of me was the staircase leading up to the office door. At least I couldn't be seen from the upper window to the right of the office. A tentative look and no face at the office door window. I ran across to the staircase, stopped at the foot of it to compose myself. I took each step up as quietly as I could, held my breath and looked through the window. No sign of activity, just gloom. Tried the door handle. Open. Either Tibbett was around somewhere on site, or security wasn't uppermost his mind.

A silent entry onto the mezzanine floor. Quiet. Eerily quiet. I went over to Tibbett's office, listened at the door for any sounds. Again, nothing. Tried the door handle. Locked. I guess I couldn't expect everything to go my way. Strange that his office was windowless, but if you've got something to hide then you wouldn't want people taking a peek. Wonder how that worked with his staff and the secretaries on this floor. They must think it a little odd. Still, not my concern.

The lock could be easily manipulated. All I needed was something to lever against the doorframe and pull it away. I looked around and found a screwdriver. Perfect. I pushed the tip between the door and the frame, pulled back and sure enough it worked, but not without damage to the frame and a lot of noise. I didn't care. When Tibbett returned, he'd see the damage right away, but wouldn't know it was me.

Inside the office, there was that same stink of sleaze and body odor. Tibbett had clearly become oblivious to the smell over the years. Not something his secretaries would have thought pleasant to walk into.

I looked in the file cabinets first, again with no clue as to what I was looking for. A quick scan through some of the folders revealed exactly what I expected them to; paperwork related to the business. A lot were on headed paper, Towers Lumber Co. And there were some actually mentioning a Henry Towers as the owner.

I closed the cabinets and went to Tibbett's desk. The central drawer and the two drawers to the left were unlocked and like everything else, revealed nothing of any significance. Top right drawer the same. And then I tried the bottom right. Locked. I felt a tingle up my spine, the expectation of what I might find. I inserted the screwdriver between drawer and frame and pushed downwards. No splintered wood this time and minimal noise, but I found his secret. So that's what you were doing when I knocked on your door. That explained the noise and sounds of hurried movement. Sleazy little fuck, I thought.

Porno magazines, a half-dozen of them, all well-known publications featuring women in various stages of undress. Nothing wrong with that, each to their own, but in your office?

I closed the drawer, managing to ease the lock back into position using the screwdriver again. The wood was a little bruised from the pressure I applied to it, and maybe Tibbett wouldn't notice. Did I care if he did? No, I didn't give a damn. I was just angry with myself for wasting time on a hunch that he was hiding something of importance. Sure, he was hiding something: porn.

I levered the office door back into position, but you couldn't fail to notice the damage I'd caused. To make it a little less obvious, I picked up the wood splinters and dumped them in a waste bin next to one of the desks. It was then I heard the sound of a car.

I took a quick look through the office door window and my heart jumped a few beats. A black and white Plymouth was coming to a stop outside. Jesus, how in hell did they know I was here? Did someone see me in the woods and report me? Was there anyone on site? I didn't think so. I'd been careful enough. I waited to see who got out and, much to my surprise, it was Larry Swales and Floyd Tibbett. That I hadn't expected.

There was no rush in their movement. They stood chatting by the Plymouth for a minute, smoking. That meant they had no idea I was upstairs. Nowhere to hide up here, so I had to get out and quick. I looked around, trying to find a way down into the mill itself. Partially obscured by the file cabinets was another staircase over the far side of the mezzanine floor. I took a few steps down, then bent over and looked toward the loading area. I could just make out the two men by the Plymouth. I waited, breathed deep, trying to hone in on their conversation, but they were too far away.

I took another couple of steps, wooden boards creaking under my weight, looked again. They were gone. My heart jumped another couple of beats. My guess was they were going up the outer staircase to the office, but I couldn't be certain. I listened out for conversation. Nothing at all, so I carried on to the mill floor as quickly as I could and hid behind machinery. I wasn't so much in fear of confrontation. With Tibbett's back problem and Swale's slight frame, I could easily handle myself. But what I didn't need was to be arrested for breaking and entering. That just would not do. It would mean an end to my investigation, and I would be letting Alice and Ellie-Mae down, and that couldn't happen. Not for anything.

I moved in a crouched position alongside the beds where tomorrow more logs would be loaded and planed. And that's when I heard Tibbett say, "What the fuck?" He'd seen the damage to his office door. I took off, dodging around machinery and a line of gray metal lockers, and was out the far end of the mill in four seconds.

I ran in a straight line and dived into the woods as fast as I could. I was at least a half-mile away from the gap in the fence, but I carried on, ducking under branches and being whipped in the face by spring saplings. I got to the *no trespassing* sign and was through the fence in an instant. Then I stopped, sucking in air like my life depended on it.

A quick look back and no sign of anyone. My car was only a couple of minutes away and although I didn't run, I made quick progress.

It was getting very dark when I fired up the Dodge and accelerated hard onto the blacktop. The clouds looked as though they were about to unload their heavy cargo at any moment.

As I drove, I took out my frustration on the steering wheel again. Fucking porno. What a fucking waste of time. Stupidity, sheer stupidity. But something had made me go there, mostly Tibbett's behavior, and now I'd seen him with Larry Swales in the patrol car. Was there something more? Or were they just good friends sneaking up to the office to look through Tibbett's stash of magazines?

Still, that missing report had Swales's name all over it.

"Jesus," I shouted at the windshield.

CHAPTER 12

When the storm came again, it made the previous night seem like gentle spring rain. TV news reported flash floods, hundred-year-old trees ripped out the ground, trailers and tin-roofed shacks broken apart.

I stood on the veranda outside my cabin and watched lightning cracking the night sky at various points in the distance and listened to the thunder as it boomed and echoed across town. The rain came down in sheets for three solid hours, hitting the cabin roofs like rapid machine gun fire. Hell had broken loose on Marston County.

The storm raged until 2 a.m. Then quiet descended on the town, just the wind dying down to nothing, like a whispering ghost until it was gone. I'd updated my timeline again and fallen asleep.

I was in a recurring nightmare where my head was being smashed to a pulp by an unknown assailant with a heavy pipe. The scene kept repeating and each time I miraculously came out of it alive. In the final recurring scene, I saw something else for the first time and it shocked me into full and breathless consciousness, sweat pouring down my face, heart pounding, eyes blinking rapidly.

I got out of bed, didn't bother to shower or shave, just threw on some clothes, went outside, and fired up the Dodge. It was seven-thirty and people were already out removing debris from the road. Overhead it was still pretty dark on account of the storm clouds, but I could see they were weakening, moving on to allow the sunshine its rightful place.

I parked up about two hundred yards from where I needed to be, opened the trunk, and grabbed the wheel brace. I hefted it in my hand. Heavy enough to do damage, small enough to be concealed up my sleeve. I closed the trunk and felt the adrenalin begin to thread its way through me. By the time I got to my destination, the black poison that lay dormant was ready to corrupt my heart and head.

"Hey, you," I shouted at the man I'd come to see.

He turned to me, surprised to see me again, and more than a little wary. "Do for ya?" he said guardedly. "Something not right with the window?"

I strode toward him. "Window's fine," I said.

And that's when I let the wheel brace slip down my sleeve until I had the metal shank tight in my right hand. I got to within a couple of yards and swung it at him with everything I had. The look on my face told him everything he needed to know, and he started to move, but not before I'd connected with my intended target, his left arm.

He screamed out and before he could do anything else, I was on him and smashed the wheel brace into his arm again. He screamed some more and then I punched him full in the face and he went down hard, banging his left shoulder against a heavy tool chest. Blood gushed from his nose. I knelt next to him, the tapered end of the wheel brace touching his left cheek, just under his eye. He was in serious pain and terrified all at the same time. Blood bubbled in his nostrils.

"You…broke my fucking…arm," he blurted out.

"Report this to the sheriff and make no mistake I'll come for you again." I pressed the wheel brace into his cheek and his eyes widened.

"No…no…don't do it," he begged.

"I'll fucking tear your goddamn heart out. I see you within fifty feet of me. You understand?"

He nodded. "My arm," he pleaded. "I need the hospital."

"You can go when I say so," I said. "My head hurts pretty bad too, you know. Now, who put you up to it?"

A brief shake of the head.

"Was it Swales, Tibbett, someone else? Who, you fucker?"

He shook his head again.

"Tell me about Alice Jackson?"

"Don't know nothing about an Alice Jackson."

"You shitting me? 'Cause if you are, some serious damage is going to happen."

"I…I swear, I don't know nothing about any Alice Jackson."

I looked into his gray eyes and saw he wasn't lying. I pressed the wheel brace a little more and it cut into his flesh. He winced. I tried one more time. "Who made you put on those stupid pointy fucking hats and come after me?"

More shaking of the head. He was more terrified of revealing that piece of information than me threatening to take out his eye. It was no use pushing him for more, I thought. He wasn't going to tell. I stood up, and he relaxed a little, relief flowing into his face.

"You ought to think about that tattoo," I said. "It's a giveaway."

I walked out of the workshop, wheel brace concealed, got to my car, dumped it on the passenger seat, and drove off back to the motel for a shower and change. Slowly, the poison ebbed, settled, and became dormant once more.

I figured it wouldn't be long before it erupted again.

CHAPTER 13

By midday, the storm clouds had rolled away as if pushed by a giant hand and the sun returned, bathing everything in hot yellow light.

My general countenance didn't look especially good and raised a couple of eyebrows when I got to Mabel's diner. The swelling to my temple had eased a little, but there were a few cuts to my face where tree branches had whipped me while I was running through the woods the previous afternoon.

Mabel wanted to know what happened to me and before I could reply with some lame-assed story, two women stepped into the diner, flushed with heat and giggling like schoolgirls. They sat on stools at the end of the counter about ten feet away from me and exchanged greetings with Mabel while she prepared two ice cream sodas. One of the women was around early thirties and the other closer to Mabel's age. The younger one had a hospital uniform on. Mabel asked what they were laughing at.

The older woman looked up at the ceiling fans. "Hon," she said. "Can't you get those things to turn any faster? I feel like I'm going to expire."

"Just got the one speed," Mabel said, placing the sodas on the counter. "Salon closed up for the day?"

"Yeah. Karen was my last appointment."

Karen twisted her head this way, and that, fluffed her hair up with her fingers.

"Looks nice," Mabel said.

Karen and the hairdresser shared a quick conspiratorial glance, and they both giggled again. They leaned over the counter some more. The hairdresser lowered her voice, thinking I couldn't hear, but I got the gist of it.

It was something about a Clayton Burke having an affair with his secretary, Donna Benjamin. Apparently, his secretary had dropped by the salon earlier and took the hairdresser into her confidence. I focused my attention on the conversation, keen to know more, but all I got was a graphic description about how cute they thought his tush was and Mabel keen to know if Donna had gone into detail about the size of his manhood.

"Donna didn't say nothing about that," the hairdresser said.

"Clayton Burke and Donna Benjamin," Mabel said. Who would have thought it? Papers would make a field day out of that. Doubt Mrs. Burke would like to read that headline.

I had been attacking peach pie again, it was that good. I finished the pie and went over to join the conversation. Gossip. The life blood of every small town.

"Afternoon, ladies," I said. "Mind if I join you?"

Karen and the hairdresser looked me up and down and seemed to like what they saw because they said yes instead of telling me to get lost. I thanked them and complimented Mabel again on her peach pie.

She smiled. "Anytime, sugar. Plenty more where that came from."

Karen and the hairdresser sniggered, and Mabel introduced us. The hairdresser's name was Betty, and she held on to my hand just a little longer than was necessary.

"You look like you could do with a little trim here and there, Mr. Bale. Betty's Beauty Parlor, just up Main a little ways, other side of the street. We don't usually do men, but I could make an exception."

"Tom," I said amid the giggles. "Kind of you to offer, Betty, but I think I'll pass. Just down here for a few days."

"Looks like you got caught up with something already while you been here. You had a fight?"

"No," I said. "Walking through the woods." I touched the bruise at my temple. "Tree branches. Nothing more exciting than that."

Mabel explained where I was from and the reason for my visit.

"Don't know the name," Betty said, meaning Alice Jackson.

"Me either," said Karen.

"As I told you the other day," Mabel said. "We don't tend to get involved with the black aspect. Town's divided that way, and it works fine."

No point in pursuing this any further, I thought.

"So, you work at the county hospital, Karen?" I asked. She was a fair bit younger than I had first thought; late twenties, perhaps. Light

120

blond hair trimmed only an hour before into a tasteful bob, pale blue eyes, and a slight dusting of freckles across her forehead and nose.

"Nurse," she said.

"Town's quiet," I said. "Can't be many emergencies to deal with. Apart from the past couple of days maybe because of the storm."

"We get our fair share," she said lightly. "Just this morning, we had the mechanic come in from Frank Carson's repair shop. Broken arm and nose. Said he'd had an accident in the shop, fell over and banged his face on something. Looked more like he'd been in a fight."

That he had, I thought. At least he'd said what I asked him to.

"Probably," Betty said. "That Weaver fella always up to no good."

Changing the subject, Mabel had further news. Karen skewed around on her stool, crossed her legs, and bounced her right foot up and down in the shadow under the counter.

"Do tell, hon," Betty said.

"Night before the storm," Mabel said. "Around midnight, my David got up on account that he couldn't sleep in all this heat. Told me he was gonna take a walk. Went over and sat under the bandstand for a smoke. All of a sudden, this police cruiser pulls into the square, moving real slow and quiet-like." Mabel reached for her cigarettes, touched a lighter to one, and inhaled deeply.

"So?" Betty asked.

Mabel tapped ash into a foil tray. "The cruiser stops right outside that Julias Cranver's office. Deputy Swales and Floyd Tibbett gets out, looks around see if anyone is watching—they didn't see David in the dark, of course, and then they went inside."

Mabel took another draw on her cigarette while Karen continued to bounce her plimsoll.

"And...?" Betty whined. "Don't keep us in suspense."

"This is the best part," Mabel said. Karen's foot stopped. "According to David, they came out five minutes later holding Cranver up under the arms 'cause he's as drunk as a skunk and shouting out all kinds of stuff."

"Like what?" Karen said.

"David said it was really weird, crazy stuff, like how he's gotta get out of this shitty life and he's gonna go to church and pay a visit to God. Lots of religious mumbo jumbo."

Swales and Tibbett again. Now why would Floyd Tibbett be involved with a police matter? I wanted to interrupt, but chose to bide my time. The information would come my way when it needed to.

"Who's Cranver?" I asked.

"Local defense attorney," Mabel said.

"Been practicing long?"

"Fifteen-twenty years thereabouts," Betty said. "Father was a lawyer way back before he passed on. Cranver lives on his own now in the family home on Cumberland. Big old place, tumble down, seen better days."

Cumberland. That's where I was attacked. "Bit of a drinking man," I said.

Mabel huffed. "More drunk than sober. No surprise he don't win many cases."

"Not when he's up against our local stud Clayton Burke," Betty added and set the three women giggling again.

"I assume," I said, "this Clayton Burke is on the opposite side of the fence? Prosecutor?"

All three women nodded at once.

"His wife," Betty said, "she's a handsome woman. Comes from good stock. Wealthy. They live in a big mansion house out on Jacob's Point, overlooking the river."

"Second biggest house around here for miles," Mabel added.

"So, whose is the biggest?" I asked.

"Henry Towers," Betty said. "Our mayor and soon to be Georgia's newest governor."

"Ambitious," I said. "He own Towers Lumber?"

"That's him," Betty said. "As well as many other things. He's got so many business deals going on, they don't make enough pies for his fingers."

I laughed at that. "Bit unusual for a small-town mayor to be so wealthy."

"His family go way back," Mabel said. "Built most of this town more than a hundred years ago. Before that they had cotton farms, slaves, you name it. What they call old money."

"The lumber yard," I said. "Went out there on Saturday to see the brother of that girl who's missing. He wasn't working that day, but I had a chat with Floyd Tibbett, the manager."

Karen shuddered. "Gives me the creeps," she said, screwing up her face.

"Seemed OK to me when I spoke to him," I lied. "Got a problem with his back."

"Yeah," Karen said. "Has to come to county now and then for treatment. Spine's a little twisted. He's all touchy-feely." She shuddered again.

"He's a weird one all right," Mabel said.

When an opportunity arises, if you don't take it, you regret it. "Excuse me for asking," I said, "but a few minutes ago, Mabel, you said Deputy Swales and Floyd Tibbett were helping this Cranver guy out of his office because he was drunk. Why would Floyd be involved in a police matter? Surely that's the sheriff's responsibility?"

"Larry and Floyd are always together," Mabel said. "Cousins. And, believe it or not, both related to Henry Towers. He's their uncle. Towers family stretches wide and far in this county and beyond."

When it comes, it comes. Answered a few questions I had floating around in my head. Things were starting to make sense. I paid for the coffee and pie, bade the three women good afternoon, and slipped down off my stool. I'd just got to the door when Betty made a final comment.

"Your tush ain't too bad either, Mr. Bale."

I stuck a hand up on my way out and let the bell hide the giggles.

CHAPTER 14

The destruction caused by the storm down in the Bottoms had been epic. The whole community was out repairing neighbors' homes, boarding up windows, removing debris from the street. I couldn't get my car through. There were so many trees across Cotton Cut Road. I got out and walked, helping to clear what I could. Corey Peters and his dad were each using pickups with towlines to haul trees out the way and clear a path. I waved to Corey, got a smile and a wave back.

I saw a man struggling with a large sheet of corrugated tin that had blown off someone's roof and went over to help him. We got it off the street, carried it to the house in question. With the help of another man, we got it back on the roof and secured.

After, we stood there for a moment, wiping sweat from our faces and gulping down homemade lemonade like our lives depended on it. We shook hands and introduced ourselves.

"Jason Robards," the first man said. "And this is my son, Carl."

"Tom Bale," I said.

We slurped lemonade some more. "Good stuff," I said.

"Wife makes it," Jason said.

"Well, you tell her from me, she's got it just right."

We laughed together.

Jason and Carl were definitely cut from the same block. Broad shouldered, tall, strong, muscular. Only difference was age, Jason's white hair, and goatee beard. Carl's hair was glossily dark with tight curls, and he was clean shaven.

Jason's voice was deep and authoritative when he spoke. "You come to see Ellie-Mae? Got any news for her?"

I shook my head. "Not so far. Questioned a lot of people. Seems like nobody saw or heard anything."

A sadness came over him then. "That's a shame," he said. "Breaking her heart."

"I'm sure," I said. "But I don't know where to go next. I'm kind of stuck, out of my depth down here. You'd think a person would be harder to find in a big city with millions of people and buildings crowding in around you, but down here is different. Seems like the wider the space the easier it is to lose yourself."

"Yeah," Jason said. "And Alice ain't the first."

"I know. I heard the same from a number of people."

"Been five including Alice," Carl said, kicking the ground with his boots, dried clay spurting up in little bursts.

"That's right," said Jason. "Over maybe a dozen years or more."

"All of them just vanished?" I asked.

"Correct," Jason said. "And nobody knows a thing. Each time everyone comes together at the chapel where I hold prayers for the safe return…"

"You the minister?" I interrupted.

"Did Ellie-Mae not tell you?"

"No. Not something that came up." I imagined Jason's voice, urging people to unite together, and not one of them faltering under his command.

"Yes, I am the minister. As I said, we'd hold prayers, then form search parties, go out into the woods and swamps, three-four days, just like we did for Alice." He leaned toward me then, looked me straight in the eyes. "We find nothing."

I almost took a step back for fear that God was going to strike me dead through Jason's dark and penetrating eyes. "Sheriff's Office get involved?" I managed to say.

Carl kicked the ground even harder. "Sheriff don't do a damn thing," he said almost spitting the words out.

Jason turned to his son and, with the same vigor he'd demonstrated to me, said, "Carl. Watch your mouth."

Carl attempted to shrug off his embarrassment. "Just that the sheriff don't help us folks out here."

"Either of you ever seen a black car around this area?" I asked.

"You got a make and model?" Jason asked.

"No. Just something Ellie-Mae mentioned. Someone told her they'd seen a black car around about the same time Alice disappeared."

"Well, there's any number of cars come through here, black and otherwise. No make and model, I couldn't tell you specifically if I saw it."

"OK," I said. I turned to Carl. "Met up with a work buddy of yours at Nat's Bar Friday night. Sam Cooper."

"Yeah, Coop. Was he drunk?"

"He was getting there. Said he worked with you and Leroy up at the mill, so I took a drive over there on Saturday. Place was deserted, but the manager was around. Thought the mill might be operating on a Saturday."

"Floyd, he's a strange guy. Friday night said not to come in the following day. No reason, just said come back Monday. There was still a ton of logs to get through, made no sense. Leroy's up there now, but I chose to stay down here and help. Mrs. Jackson, she ain't got much, needs the money."

"I asked Floyd about Alice, said he didn't know anything. Coop said the same. Leroy hasn't mentioned it to anyone?"

"Only me and Leroy talk about it, so I doubt Coop knows anything. Maybe he heard a little, but would have forgotten after a few beers. Floyd though, he knows more than he lets on. Keeps his ear to the ground. Sits in that office all day, occasionally walks around the mill checking things but he don't miss much. Listens to gossip, rumor, anything he can pick up on. Seems like he gets some kind of kick out of it."

I bet he does, I thought. "You think Leroy could add anything that might help me?"

"No," Carl said. "We talked it through a lot, but there's nothing we can think of. Nothing at all."

Needle in a damn haystack.

"How long you think you'll be staying, Tom?" Jason asked.

"Long as I have to, Jason. Made a promise. I'll do everything I can."

"I'm sure you will," he said, clapping me on the shoulder. "We best be getting on with it. You staying to help?"

"I was going to update Ellie-Mae. See how she is."

"She's over at ours. Her house didn't suffer too much in the storm, but there's some repair work we got to do before nightfall. As you'd expect, she's not taking things too well and if I were you, I'd come back when you got some solid news, good or bad. At least that way there is closure. Carl and me, we'll let her know you came around."

"Thanks, Jason," I said. "You too, Carl." We shook hands, and I headed back to my car. Corey and his dad had made good progress clearing the road.

Driving back to town, all I could think about was Coop, who got the two men to warn me off, Tibbett and Swales. Everything else was just peripheral noise at best. Coop was the most obvious because of what he'd revealed Friday night, but Swales and Tibbett were definitely hiding something: their actions, body language spoke volumes. Why would Tibbett be involved with the removal of a drunk lawyer from his office in the middle of the night? Swales and another deputy, or the sheriff, yes. Get Cranver in the drunk tank for the night, sleep it off. And it mattered nothing that Tibbett and Swales were related. So what? Tibbett was a civilian, not a town official, and had no business getting involved with police work. Could be that no other deputy was available; the sheriff's office would be closed at that time.

No twenty-four-hour watch needed in this sleepy town. And what about the time? Midnight, and how did they know Cranver was drunk in his office? It just didn't make any sense at all. The only absolute and relevant people I had making a storm in my head were Coop and the guys who attacked me. If I could somehow discover who was behind that, I would have answers that meant something.

I didn't take it out on my steering wheel this time. I just drove with my elbow crooked out the window and my head resting in my hand.

I did thump the door a couple of times.

CHAPTER 15

Tuesday morning, I had just stepped out of the shower when I noticed a folded piece of paper had been slipped under my cabin door. My first reaction was to check outside. Not surprisingly, there was no sign of life. Whoever had slipped that note under my door was long gone.

I sat on the edge of the bed, water soaking into the sheets and dripping on to the threadbare carpet, and read the note:

She's in the swamp
Look for the old hunter's shack
Make it quick

Underneath this was a crudely drawn map, indicating the spot.

Could have been a hoax, a cruel joke, or someone leading me into danger, but I had to check it out. I knew I should go report this to the sheriff but doubted how much credence would be given. No name, no link to Alice. I got dressed and went out to my car, the Georgia sun beating down hard on my head.

Driving over to Corey's place I debated whether to involve him in this, get him to drive me to the spot and help me find Alice. However, if this was just a hoax to get me out there and it turned nasty, it wouldn't be right to put his life in danger. This was my mission, and mine alone.

Corey was out front of the workshop fixing a wheel onto a pickup when I got there. No sign of his dad. We exchanged pleasantries, talked about the work he and his dad were doing yesterday.

"I need to borrow that boat you mentioned," I said.

"Sure, no problem. I guess you're looking for Alice?"

I nodded. "Figured I'd take a look, probably clutching at straws, but I have to cover all options no matter how improbable."

"OK, but you'll need a guide. I told you, Okefenokee is a big place…"

I stopped him. "I appreciate it, Corey, I really do. I need to do this alone, and lord knows I could use your help, but this is my headache, not yours." He started to protest, but I held up a hand. "No. Thank you, but no. All I need at the moment is the boat, the outboard, and a vehicle to transport it. I'll hire them, pay for all the fuel. No worries on that score. And I need guidance to help me get to somewhere specific."

He slapped the side of the pickup he'd just fixed a new wheel to. "Old Bessie here. She's seen everything and been everywhere, but she's got a good engine and will get you where you need to go. Pulls a little to the left and no matter how many times I adjust the tracking rods it don't make any difference. Seems to have her own mind, so watch out for that."

"Fine," I said.

He smiled. "She ain't got power steering like you're used to. You'll need to hang on to her."

I helped him fetch the aluminum boat and the outboard and he showed me how to secure the motor to the back, how to start it, and operate the accelerator and rudder. The boat was lighter than I thought it would be, and Corey was right about one thing: it was battered to shit.

Back in the motel, I had redrawn the map on paper from my notepad. I didn't want to risk Corey seeing the message on the original. I showed him the copy I'd made, and he scratched his head.

"Yeah, yeah," he said. "Think I know where that is. One of them out-of-bounds areas. You'll need to be watching for everything in there and you ain't gonna get to it from the highway. I'd go Route 23, then come off west onto the Swamp Road. It's marked. This will take you to the perimeter roads and to the official north entrance. You don't want to go that far. There'll be a ton of tracks leading off the Swamp Road through the woods and close to the water itself. But you gotta be careful, go too far and you'll be stuck, so stay on solid ground and walk in. It'll mean dragging the boat with you, but it's doable. I can't tell you where that exact spot is, so you'll have to take a real good look around."

"OK, I got it," I said.

"And don't think about staying out there overnight. I want to see you back here before nightfall, so I know you're safe."

What a stand-up young man, I thought. We need more like you, Corey. Teach the rest of us a thing or two. "I'll be sure to," I said.

133

He looked me up and down, smiled again. "And don't be thinking your shoes and clothes are gonna survive this. For one day, maybe, but if you gotta go back again, I'd suggest a good pair of jeans and gumboots or work boots at the very least. You're gonna get wet, stung, covered in mud."

Man-oh-man, was I getting into something. "I'll take the hit this time, then do what you say."

"Just hang on a minute," he said and hurried off to the Airstream. Five minutes later he returned with a backpack over his left shoulder.

"What's this?" I asked.

"Bet you ain't prepared for this, are you? There's water bottles, couple of cheese sandwiches, and a small first aid kit in there."

I was so far out of my depth, so ill prepared, so amateurish it scared the life out of me. "Thank you, Corey," I said. "I really appreciate this. You don't know how much."

"That's OK, Mr. Bale. You go look for Alice and remember, I'm here, you just gotta say. Keys are in Bessie, plenty of gas in the tank, plus there's a full can in the back for the outboard. Take it steady, be careful and good luck."

I got into Bessie, fired her up, and headed out of the yard. No power steering felt like I was trying to steer a tank.

So many lessons learned from that young man. Made me feel like I needed to take stock of my life.

I crossed town and headed south on Route 35. Old Bessie was a nightmare for steering. Felt like my arms were going to drop off. She was so heavy. I saw the sign for Swamp Road and rolled along that for a while, the sun flashing through the oaks and pines. I heaved the steering wheel left down a suitable red-clay track into a half-light with the pines tall and erect, and then onwards into darkness where trees crowded over us and vines hung loose, scraping across Bessie's roof like witches' fingernails.

Bessie bounced this way and that and the steering wheel was wrenched out of my hands several times as her wheels caught in ruts and rode over exposed tree roots, and finally we got on even ground and emerged into a clearing with an old, abandoned hunter's shack; roof caved in and half of one wall rotted through. The air was thick and rank with the smell of dead fish and swamp water.

About thirty feet away, partially obscured by tall reeds and overhanging branches, the remains of a wooden jetty lay half-drowned in the water. I got out and went over to it. Dragonflies hung motionless in the air near the water's edge. The swamp water was dark brown on account of the tannic acid released from the peat beds. It created a kind of mirror effect on the surface, so much so that when sunlight bounced off it, I had to shield my eyes against the glare.

The jetty was of no use, but the ground seemed firm enough where I was stood, so I guessed I could wade out a few feet and launch the boat from here. The water was shallow enough.

I dragged the boat and the outboard from the back of the pickup, fixed the motor in place like Corey had shown me, and then topped it up from the gas can. Then I fetched the backpack off the passenger seat, dumped that and the gas can in the boat, and dragged it all down to the water.

If anyone had been watching me getting the boat in the water and trying to clamber into it, they'd have thought it was part of a circus act. But get in it, I did, shoes and socks soaked, pants wet up to my knees, and sweat hanging off my forehead in ribbons.

I took me several attempts and playing around with the choke to get the outboard started, and when it finally spluttered into life, I felt a quiet sense of satisfaction. I eased the throttle and steered away from the bank. And then I looked at the vast swamp in front of me and thought, oh my Jesus.

As I navigated the waters, I soon learned that you could easily be fooled into a false sense of security watching the alligators sunning themselves on the banks. You thought you knew where they were. What you had to really watch for was the dense green duckweed floating near the banks, with the alligators waiting patiently underneath. The gators were mostly around six or seven feet in length, but there was the occasional big guy who put the fear of god into me.

I covered a fair-sized area that first day, stopping every so often to investigate old tarpaper shacks long since left to the forces of nature. There must have been a dozen landing points hidden away among reeds, arching tree branches and giant exposed tupelo roots. Anyone who knew the swamp could come and go as they pleased completely undetected. Wildlife scurried, birds chatted and sang, woodpeckers rat-tat-tatted against trees. Clumps of Spanish moss hung like witches' hair from the live oaks, and with the sun filtering through, they turned into fine gossamer wings. The swamp had a breathtaking beauty and power all of its own making. But it didn't reveal Alice to me that first day. The swamp was not ready to give her up just yet.

By the time the pale blue sky started to turn into those deeper hues that come before dusk takes hold, I had managed to find my way back to the broken jetty, had hauled everything out of the water and onto the pickup and was ready to head back to Corey's.

And the very next day, I rose early and did it all over again.

CHAPTER 16

I was at the end of my third day in the swamp; a day of heat and sweat and a thousand insect bites when I cut the Johnson outboard down to idle and looked all around me, wondered at the sheer futility of what I was doing. The sun was beginning to slip behind the oaks and cypress trees, pale slashes of ochre, red, and orange on the horizon. Egrets had fled to the treetops, their slender form in relief against the fading sky. And then I saw it, just as I fired up the spluttering outboard and pushed on the tiller to steer the boat around; some kind of wooden structure about two hundred yards to my left and partially obscured by giant tupelo. Blinked and I would have missed it. And as if someone had flicked a switch and killed the light, the sky grew dark. I looked up at the gun-metal clouds, felt the first spot of rain on my cheek, and heard the distant roll of thunder. The air felt charged, as if lightning had struck.

I needed to head for shelter real quick and steered towards the wooden structure I'd seen. As I got closer, it turned out to be another hunter's shack on a small island and raised up on cinder blocks. I managed to secure the boat to the makeshift jetty just as the clouds released their payload. In an instant the red earth became a mud slide and as I jumped out, shoes digging into a carpet of leaves, I had to grab an overhanging vine to stop myself slipping back into the swamp. I pulled myself up the rain slicked bank, covered in mud, and ran for the cabin. I pounded up a creaking porch then stood there for a minute, taking in my surroundings. The tree branches were darker in the rain and every color, sound, and smell intensified: mulched rotting leaves, peat mounds, and bullfrogs singing in their guttural tones, the staccato hammering of woodpeckers. The noise was deafening.

There was a line strung between two trees with a couple of dozen small rusty hooks running along it, and under this a tree stump about two feet in diameter stained black with blood. I guessed the stump was used to gut fish and other animals before they were hung up to dry.

Then, as suddenly as it had come, the rain ceased. Just one of those freak bursts, and seconds later the sky was streaked with color. I stood on the porch fanning away midges, my shirt and pants clinging to me like they would never let go and feeling heavy from the mud slicked over them. It struck me then. Something wasn't right.

For three days I'd been surrounded by noise, but now the air felt dead, heavy with humidity and the silence was so absolute that it screamed in my head. The sounds of the swamp had shut down. My skin began to crawl, and I knew I'd found her. I pulled open the shack door. It came away with a screech that pierced the silence and sent birds broiling up into the sky.

A sour, malodorous smell greeted me and caught in the back of my throat. Coughing, I cupped a handkerchief over my nose and mouth and stepped inside. The room was quite dark on account of the overhanging trees blocking what little light there was left, but it was enough to make out a square wooden table, two rickety chairs and an old potbelly stove, all coated in dust, not used in years.

Another door led to a back room and as I got closer to it, the bad smell intensified. I tied the handkerchief across my face, grasped the handle and stopped, suddenly afraid of what I might find. The hairs on my back and neck bristled. I turned the handle and pulled.

The smell hit me like an express train going on full tilt. I turned away gagging, staggered through the front room onto the porch, and threw up over the railing until there was nothing left. It took me a good while to recover.

I had found Alice Jackson.

Her arms were raised above her head, hands tied to a steel shackle which itself was bolted to the wall of the cabin. She was sitting on a filthy mattress, feet splayed out. The dress she'd been wearing at the time of her disappearance had been ripped open, exposing her young body. Or more to the point, what was left of it. Her skin had gone through the early stages of death and was beginning to blister, which told me that death had occurred some eight to ten days before. The body had bloated from gases released by the internal organs and the tongue had swollen out of the mouth. Alice's once beautiful brown eyes were bulging from their sockets.

Blowflies landed, investigated, took off again.

Wasn't difficult to make sense of what had occurred. She'd been kept tied up in the stinking, filthy room at the rear of the shack, no doubt repeatedly raped and then discarded when he, or they, had had their fill of her.

I sat down, back against the far wall, withdrew a pack of cigarettes from my coat pocket, and shook one out. How does a person do this, I wondered? What turns a man into a monster? An innocent girl walking home from the store, she's happy, it's a beautiful day, nothing is wrong in her world. And then suddenly she is hurtled into a terrifying ordeal, her young body subjected to the most horrific torture and pain. The extent of man's cruelty to his own kind, whether driven to it by twisted desire, drink, drugs, or a combination of all three, never ceased to shock, sadden, and anger me to the point that sometimes, particularly when it came to the abuse of children, it fueled so much anger in me that all I could think about was exacting revenge in the most foul and painful way possible. I felt as though I could easily be driven to torture. To make them suffer in the way they had made others. Thankfully, the sane part of my conscience told me that I would, in turn, be no better than them.

Alice had been dead a couple of days longer than I'd been in Paradise Creek. So close. So damn close.

It weighed down on me like a curse.

CHAPTER 17

I didn't envy the medical examiner's job or the sheriff's, for that matter. Between them, they would have to remove the body to the town morgue and attempt to find some evidence of who had done this. I didn't hold out much hope they would find anything. I tugged the unlit cigarette from my lips, slipped it back into the pack to snuggle with the others.

Looking around the cabin, I found some old corn sacks. I waved away the flies and covered Alice as best I could. I figured she was too far gone for the sacks to disturb any real evidence and felt that I owed it to her, offer some dignity even though there was none to be had. I even apologized to her before leaving. I decided to speak to Ellie-Mae before I went to see the sheriff.

I got back to Corey's place, but neither he nor his father were around, so I left Bessie by the side of their workshop, keys under the driver's seat, got in my Dodge and steeled myself for what I had to do.

Dusk had taken hold and night was just waiting patiently for its turn, and by the time I got to Ellie-Mae's, the stars were coming out one by one.

As a homicide detective back in Chicago, I'd had to break bad news more times than I cared to think about. To watch a parent, a wife, husband, or family receive the news that their world had suddenly come apart through some senseless killing, and that their lives had changed immeasurably in the blink of an eye, was something I never got used to. Seeing them go through the initial stages of shock and disbelief, tears mixed with anger while they were sitting down and taken through the details, only half listening to what was being said. And then hanging on to that spider thread of hope that the person lying in the morgue was someone else and a terrible mistake had been made. Then the reality and the crushing, agonizing grief that followed. And days later, a slow-motion drift through a fog in a kind of limbo. Seeing, but not seeing anything at all, just a world of gray.

I sat roasting in the Dodge, covered in dried mud, staring at Ellie-Mae's screen door from a hundred yards away, trying to summon up the courage. Officially, this was the sheriff's job, but he could wait. This was my personal mission. Ellie-Mae had called in a debt I owed to her brother, and eight days ago I had given her my word.

I got out, my legs feeling like mud was sucking at my every step such was my reluctance to do this final thing. I'm not a religious man by any means, but I looked up to the darkening sky and prayed for guidance. Eyes watched me from the shadows on the raised porches. I got to within thirty feet of Ellie-Mae's house and realized a small crowd of people had begun to gather. I stopped and turned, saw some faces I knew, people I'd already talked to. They all sensed what I was about to do. The messenger from hell had entered their world.

143

Jason Robard came up to me, laid a hand on my shoulder.

"I don't know how to tell her," I said. "Or what to tell her."

"Whatever you think she can take. Truth is best."

I couldn't rid myself of the lump in my throat and the heaviness in my heart.

The screen door opened, and Ellie-Mae stood there, the look on her face a mix of expectation and fear. Moses and Leroy stood behind her. She came down the steps toward me and mouthed the words, 'You found her?' I nodded.

She looked me up and down, guessed where I'd been.

"Swamp?"

I nodded again.

"And?"

I couldn't say it, so I just shook my head.

A trembling hand flew to her mouth.

"Was…was it an…accident?"

I didn't move, didn't speak, but it was enough. She saw it in my eyes.

It was almost as if someone had punched her in the stomach, hard, because she suddenly doubled over, and an agonizing wail escaped her throat. She collapsed onto her knees in the dirt, groaning, hugging herself. She looked so small, little more than a tiny bird. I knelt down and laid a hand on her shoulder to offer some kind of solace but realized its effect would be nothing more than a single snowflake in a blizzard, and feeling awkward I removed my hand for fear that Ellie-Mae might see it only as some arbitrary gesture. Two women rushed forward from behind me and somehow managed to get her to her feet, but she shrugged them off and looked directly at me, anger suddenly flaring in her eyes, mouth quivering, tears tracking down her face. I knew what was coming next, and I'd already made the promise to myself when I stood in that hunter's shack.

Her voice was low, almost guttural. She stammered when she spoke. "You f…find w…whoever did…did t…this. You find h…him and c…cut out his heart."

I nodded again; my mouth dry as dust.

"You p…prom…promise me, Mr. Bale."

"Yes." It was all I could say.

She turned at that point and was helped back into her house by the two women. Moses and Leroy stayed at the door, looking at me, anger on their faces as if I had caused their sister's death. Maybe it would have been better if I hadn't found her, if I hadn't received that note under my door. Jason gripped my arm, guided me away.

"We'll take care of Ellie-Mae now, Mr. Bale," he said. "You gone done what you could. I expect you'll be needing to speak to the sheriff."

I managed to draw some saliva into my mouth, but still it was an effort to speak. "Yeah."

"Where'd you find her?"

"Okefenokee."

"Carl and me we go fishing there from time to time. It's a big place. Man get lost if he ain't careful. What made you go there?"

The how and why would remain with me, so I lied. "Tried everywhere else. It was the only place left. I rented a boat, found her in an old hunter's shack."

"There must be hundreds of old shacks and settlements, a lot of them cleared now since it became a protected reserve, but who knows what's still hidden and waiting to be discovered."

"Took me three days. I was about to give up, found the cabin deep in the swamp. Guess I just got lucky."

"How was she…how did she look?"

"Bad," I said. "Very, very bad. Tied up, beaten, undoubtedly raped. Been dead several days."

He too raised his head to the stars. "Oh, my Lord. Oh, my good Lord."

Breaking the news to Ellie-Mae had been close to the hardest thing I'd ever done.

I clapped him on the shoulder, turned away, and caught sight of Carl standing at the back of the crowd, staring directly at me. I thought nothing of it and walked back to the Dodge, but with every step I could feel his eyes burning into my back. I turned again when I reached the car. Most of the people had returned to their houses, but Carl was still there, looking in my direction. He hadn't moved.

CHAPTER 18

I explained how I found her to the sheriff, same lie I told to Jason. He questioned me for a while and seemed satisfied. Two days later, Alice was buried in a pine coffin next to Little Joe. I left flowers at both graves. I went to see Corey, told him that I'd decided to leave him out of it. The sheriff didn't need to know. I thanked him for all he'd done and offered to pay, but he refused to take my money. The light shining in his eyes had died a little, and he was genuinely sad about Alice. He never questioned me about why I wanted to investigate that particular part of the swamp. He just accepted that I was doing something to find Alice, no matter how random my choice of where to look might seem.

The sheriff began his investigation. There was still the missing person report, which I pushed the sheriff about. Not that it made any difference now Alice had been found, but I needed to know. I went to see Frank Carson and found out that his son and his daughter-in-law had elected to stay over at her parents a few more days with their new baby. I got the number where his son could be reached. I even got the sheriff to call his deputy, and Carson did indeed confirm that Ellie-Mae filed a misper report with him, but a short while after she left the office, he got the call from the hospital to say his wife had been admitted and the baby was on the way. He owned up to the fact that he couldn't be sure whether he filed the report or not, his mind being on his wife at the time. While on the phone, the sheriff told him his presence was needed back at the office to help with the investigation into Alice's murder. The sheriff and two of his deputies, Martin Torrance and Larry Swales, conducted a thorough search, and that report could not be found. Swales was telling the truth after all he just had an infuriating way of dealing with people.

And I still had that piece of paper with the note and map scrawled on it. Whoever put that note under my door was determined to remain anonymous. Who and why? I kept asking myself those same questions over and over.

I looked, snooped, asked more questions, got hassled by the sheriff. I got threatened and threatened some people in return. I made no friends, pissed everyone off, and got nothing for all my efforts. Most I could hope for was another note under my cabin door with the killer's name on it. I had to admit that I was beaten. There was nothing left for me to try. When all's said and done, I couldn't really see either Coop or Tibbett guilty of murder. Coop was just a drunk, his head full of fantasy born out of loneliness. As for Tibbett? He was a sleazy little bastard right enough, but like Coop I very much doubted he would go that far.

I went and paid my respects to Ellie-Mae, sat opposite her in the half-light on those beaten-up chairs in that twelve-by-twelve room devoid of life and replete with the heartbreak and despair of death. Her eyes bore the tragedy that she would live with for the rest of her life.

I'd done all I could and would have to leave it to the sheriff. I was sorry I couldn't do more. I felt wretched telling her that, but she seemed to understand and thanked me.

Eight days after I found Alice I was back in Chicago, checking my messaging service, feet up at their usual position on the window ledge, sipping bourbon, toying with an unlit cigarette, and watching the traffic three floors below me. Hoping, always hoping, praying that there would be a message waiting for me from the Chicago Police saying they'd arrested the driver of the hit-and-run vehicle that killed Jenny.

Little had changed in Chicago. But a lot had changed in me.

I was back in my own apartment; the services having been completely restored while I'd been away. In my bedroom I lay awake for several nights after, eyes fixed on a patch in the ceiling that I'd painted after the guy in the apartment above me had allowed his bath water to run over. The water stain had annoyed me for two years and each time I looked at it I promised myself that I would repaint the whole thing to get an even color. In the end, I just painted over the stain. The color was a little off and came to annoy me even more than the stain left by the water. But I was more annoyed with myself for not doing a good enough job in the first place.

Now, the patch was a focus for thought, Alice Jackson. Had I really done all I could to find her killer? Had I ever really done enough?

I tried to convince myself that it was Alban Somer's responsibility to find the killer, not mine. I'd done what was asked of me, I'd found Alice. I was an investigator, not a cop anymore. However, my conscience told me the short answer. No. I hadn't done enough. Not enough for Little Joe, not enough for Ellie-Mae, not enough for Jenny, and not enough for Alice. I closed my eyes, saw her lying on that stinking mattress and prayed for morning.

I got lucky with a couple of good jobs, which paid enough for me to go a month ahead on the office rent and head south.

I had to go back.

PART TWO

Late July

CHAPTER 19

I threw whatever I could find into a suitcase; clothes, gun, bottle of Johnnie Walker Red, spare shoes, the file containing my notes, and the timeline I'd created. I drove overnight and most of the next day, arriving at the Paradise Creek Motel late on a Thursday evening. Hubert Trenton checked me in, his eyes even darker in the gloom.

"Expect you'd be wanting the same room. Most people do if they comes back, gives them a sense of familiarity. They knows what to expect."

"Are the rooms all different then?" I asked, not giving a damn which room I had. I just needed a shower and sleep.

"No, they's all the same. Curtains, sheets, color scheme. Only thing that's different is the picture hanging on the wall. Why you ask, you not satisfied with the room you had?"

His eyes had grown a little more intense, almost as if he were daring me to complain. I could neither find the energy nor patience to explain that by his statement he'd suggested the rooms were indeed different. I just took the key.

"No," I said. "Perfectly fine. In fact, I was surprised at how many times during my stay the sheets were changed and the room cleaned. Very rare to find that kind of service, I was most impressed."

His eyes lost some of their intensity, but nervously flicked from side to side. "So, what brings you back down to Paradise Creek?" he said, completely ignoring my compliment.

"Unfinished business."

He tilted his head some. "I know you ain't no insurance guy or debt collector like you told me. You still got interest in that young negra girl you found?"

"Some," I said.

His eyes narrowed. "Ain't nothing going on down here you should be concerning yourself with, Mr. Bale. Sheriff's perfectly capable."

"Maybe so. Got to check for myself."

"Ain't your business anymore. Sheriff's got the matter in hand."

I leveled my eyes with his. "I always make it my business to see justice done." And with that I left the office and headed to bungalow six.

I fell asleep with the file of notes on my lap and slept the sleep of the dead. Next morning, I took a shower, put on clean clothes, and went out to my car. The heat back in May had nothing on this. This was midsummer killer heat and humidity.

I parked on Main and once again found myself outside Dan Benson's store, sipping cold Coke and part of a three-way conversation between myself, Lucas James, and Benson. As before,

Lucas had placed his bottle of Dr. Pepper on the bench between us. Felt like life had turned full circle.

"So how come you're back down here, Tom?" Benson asked.

"Thought I might poke around a little more, wasn't happy with the way things were left about Alice. Bet the sheriff's no closer to finding her killer than he was back in May."

Lucas huffed. "I know why you here. Ellie-Mae called you, didn't she? Told you they'd caught the man responsible. You didn't get closure for Alice when you was down before. Now they got young Carl Robard on trial for murdering that white girl, and they're saying he's the man done those terrible things to Alice too. That gonna ease your conscience?"

I wondered if I'd heard the old man correctly. "Did you say Carl Robard is on trial?"

He stared at me surprised. "Ellie-Mae done told you, didn't she?"

"No. I haven't spoken to her since I was last down here. What's going on? Carl Robards…murder, surely there's been some mistake?"

Benson said, "What they say. Can you believe it? Carl Robard. As God is my witness, I can't believe that boy is guilty of such a thing."

"But the Robard family live across the road from the Jacksons," I said. "There is no way Carl would have done those things to Alice."

"Sheriff got all kinds of evidence," Benson said. "They say Clayton Burke gonna be asking for the chair."

"Jesus." Was all I could think of to say.

"Yep, that poor boy gonna be facing the death penalty," Lucas said. "Parents are out of their minds. And Ellie-Mae can't believe it either. But it's an odd thing, this trial."

"Odd? How d'you mean?" I asked.

The old man leaned forward again, placed both hands on his knees as if he were struggling to hold his body upright.

"This white girl was found about ten days ago, molested, strangled."

"Caitlin Dexter," Benson said.

"That's her. Damn pretty thing she was, a real looker. I remember seeing her with her boyfriend and I knew he didn't come from these parts. Not from Paradise Creek, anyways."

"Caitlin Dexter?" I said, wondering why that name was familiar to me.

He hesitated for a moment, removed his hat, wiped away a line of sweat with a crumpled shirt sleeve. "We was—Corey and me that is—we was headed back from Waresboro in that old truck of his, Bessie I think he calls it. He'd took me to see a cousin of mine over there. Couple of miles from town, young Corey needs to relieve himself so bad he pulls over, jumps out and does his business right by the truck. That's when I sees this girl up ahead, sitting on the opposite side of the road on her own, and I got to thinking that maybe we should go ask and see if she needs help or something. Well, just as Corey is done and getting back in the cab, this young fella come out from behind the trees tugging on his zipper. Figured he needed it bad too. He was young, maybe twenty. The girl just stood up and they started heading toward town, holding hands."

I could hear his breath coming in snatches, as if the telling of the story had depleted all his remaining strength. He reached for his hat and sat it back on his shiny head. Clearing his throat, he prepared to finish.

"Damn fool Corey just got a new radio fixed in the pickup and had that Presley guy from Memphis on so loud it hurt my ears. As we started up again, Corey was singing along, slamming his hands on the dash, I don't think he even noticed those two kids. And that's the last I of saw of them. Well, until I noticed her picture in the paper. No mention about the boy, though."

Then it came to me. Caitlin Dexter. She was the girl Coop had mentioned that night at Nat's. "Caitlin Dexter," I repeated. "Carl Robard raped and strangled Caitlin Dexter, and they're pinning Alice's murder on him, too. That can't be right."

"Watertight case apparently," Benson said. "Trial's about to close, been running all week."

"Carl got that no good Julias Cranver defending him," Lucas said, shaking his head. "Court appointed."

A car drove past and a piece of silver colored paper flipped onto the sidewalk in its wake, landed close to my shoes. Gum wrapper. Wondered if it was some kind of message, like they say about a bird feather landing on you is an angel in disguise. I stared at it and thought about what Lucas said all those weeks before when the very same thing happened. 'I can't dance no more.' And then it was gone, doing a little jumping jive for us aided by a swift gust of hot air.

Someone stepped into the store and Benson went to serve them. Didn't notice who it was, didn't care, just a brief shadow. Too occupied. "You take it easy now, Lucas," Benson said. "You too, Tom."

Had he heard the old man's reply, I think it would have pleased him.

"Sure thing, Dan," Lucas said. "Sure thing."

An almost unearthly quiet seemed to descend upon us at that moment.

Nothing moved.

Absolute still, like the town had sucked in and was holding its hot breath.

Lucas closed his eyes and rested his head back against the store window. At his side, the frost on the Dr. Pepper bottle had melted in the heat and left a trail of water around his handprint. A dark circle had formed underneath the bottle on the bench slats. Having lost a degree or two of its icy bite, the Dr. Pepper would be about ready for Lucas to take a drink.

In the distance, the town hall clock struck the half-hour. Seemed like an appropriate time to leave, head for the courthouse.

I bade Lucas good day but got no answer. I crossed the street, opened my car door, stopped, turned back. The old man hadn't moved.

The words, *Benson's Store*, were painted on the window in an arc of white, eight-inch-high letters, emphasized by black shadow lines.

From a distance, they looked like part of an inscribed halo above the old man's hat, like he was some kind of holy person.

Or an angel.

CHAPTER 20

I drove to the center of town, parked at an angle in one of the bays next to the leafy square where some folk had gathered in the shade, seeking relief from the penetrating sunlight, and made my way across to the courthouse. I climbed the steps, pushing my way through a crowd of people and reporters.

Two enormous oak doors led me into a marble hall with staircases on either side running to the first floor, which I assumed led to the public galleries. There were two courtrooms, both accessed through more oak doors at the far end of the hall with the administration and law clerk offices left and right. I asked one of the court officials how the trial was progressing and was told that the jury were about to return from their deliberations and sentencing would begin at any moment. He blocked my path to the courtroom, saying that it was already full to bursting, and advised that I head upstairs to the gallery. I took the stairs two at a time, almost burst through the door, and managed to squeeze my way to the front, but I had to stand in the aisle as all the seats had been taken.

Court One had four tall, wide rectangular windows that faced due south. Way the windows were positioned waves of natural light flooded in over the judge's bench. I guessed this natural backlighting was to give them a more imposing presence.

Ellie-Mae and her two sons were seated along the front row of the gallery, and I caught their attention. Leroy and Moses seemed to resent my being there, and I guessed in some way I could understand that. But Ellie-Mae gave me a half-smile and then averted her eyes.

The County Court Judge swept, as much as a man of barely five-eight could sweep, out of his chambers and climbed the steps to his bench. The bailiff asked the court to rise.

The judge, white-haired, mid-sixties, slight of build, positioned himself upright in his chair, a look of inflexible resolve on his face. His rigid posture was one that suggested a man of determined means.

"The Superior Court for Marston County is now in session, the Honorable Theobald Manning, Judge Presiding. Draw close and give your attention and you shall be heard. The People versus Carl J. Robard." The bailiff returned to his seat.

Judge Manning banged his gavel to kill the verbal hum that had swelled in the room and to indicate that the court should be seated. While the room began to settle, I looked down at the defense table, saw Carl and a huge, obese man dressed in a crumpled, off-white suit, padding at his face with a handkerchief. This, I assumed was Julius Cranver.

Carl's family was sitting in the row immediately behind him, his mother already dabbing a white handkerchief to her eyes, matching purse resting on her lap. Jason looking down, a small bible clutched in his hands, mouthing words in silent prayer. Carl turned to his parents and the fear in his eyes was so palpable I could almost feel it.

Brightly colored fans flapped across faces, while up in the gallery newspapers instead of silk and ivory batted back and forth. Ceiling fans circled uselessly overhead.

The judge motioned to the bailiff.

The bailiff, a tall middle-aged man with sad gray eyes and a world-weary expression, turned and disappeared through a door to the left of the jury bench. It opened a half minute later, and the selected twelve—eleven white, one black, nine men and three women; the women were white—filed into the courtroom ready to declare the outcome of The People vs. Carl J. Robard. Such was the way things seemed to be manipulated down here. Just the one token black person.

I still had a lot to learn.

Cranver was shuffling papers as the jurors settled. Carl had his eyes locked on the jury, his large hands placed firmly on the polished oak desk in front of him; palms down and with such pressure that they shook. Even from my position up in the gallery I could see the sweat dripping down his face, soaking into the collar of his gray shirt. The pulse in his muscular neck beat furiously.

I'd spent time in prison, bathed in that jailhouse stink sitting toe-to-toe with rapists, murderers, men serving life sentences. But mine was a purely professional curiosity. Strange thing to want to do I'll grant you, but I had a fixation with knowing how people's lives had been affected, even the criminals'.

One man, a death row prisoner, had no qualms about admitting to his crimes, but it was the way he described his time in prison that will forever remain in my memory. His only knowledge of what was going on outside of the eight by ten enclosure with its single bunk, cracked basin, and open toilet, came from visitors and lawyers. He'd forgotten what it felt like to be free and have the sun on his face, or a warm breeze lick his skin. With only the sound of a distant clock ticking, measuring his existence, setting parameters on each breath or blink of an eye, he had somehow become a dead person, anyway. The cell, unlike the house in which he had lived with his parents and younger brother, was not a living thing. There was no laughter, no cooking smells, no color, no nothing; just gray bars. He would lay awake most nights he told me, stagnating, desolate, listening to that ticking, and inside he would die a slow, agonizing death. His fear was not of the guards or other inmates, it was fear of time and of those dark things that dwelt in the untapped corners of the mind.

In the early stages of his confinement, his parents had visited every day they could, but he soon began to wish they would stay away. The constant tears, the never-ending proclamations of his innocence, the fear of what was going to happen permanently etched on their terrified faces; it had all become too much for him to cope with. He'd even begun to tire of seeing his attorney, the one appointed to him by the court, sitting there across from him in that tiny interview room; another dead room with the same monochrome color scheme as everything else. Even his attorney's gray suit blended well with that room, blended well with the dead. As each morning greeted him in

162

that final week before his execution, another piece of his soul had been taken until all that remained on the final day was a giant chaotic pile of snapshot images randomly assembled in his head; images that had once been his life.

Way he described it, I felt sure I would kill myself rather than go through that.

I tried to read the faces in the jury, but by the sudden hush that descended over the courtroom we all knew in an instant what the verdict would be. Carl knew by the way his mother's voice cracked behind him and the words, "Oh my, Jesus," escaped from her mouth in one long trembling sob.

Judge Manning banged his gavel, bringing silence to the room once more. He asked council and the defendant to rise.

Carl was supported by his attorney as he stood, his whole-body trembling. I'd seen men in his position before, black and white, young and old. When standing in front of judge and jury, they either had their heads bowed in remorse, wide-eyed disbelief or some shit-kicking grin on their faces that said, 'yeah, and I'd fucking do it again.' Carl, way his eyes danced around, looked like he couldn't understand what he was doing there. Got me thinking some more about what Daniel Benson had said.

Carl's father turned to the jury. Apart from the foreman, they all averted their eyes. Some studied their shoes, while others found refuge within the faces of the spectators.

The judge was speaking. "Will the foreman of the jury please rise and offer your verdict to the court."

The foreman rose from his seat, hard chiseled features set in a grim intransigent expression as if he were eager to pronounce the verdict. He was dressed conspicuously better than the other male jurors in a beige-colored summer suit and pale-blue tie. And, unlike the others, he preserved a proud, defiant stance against the accused father's gaze. He was not afraid to look a Negro in the eye.

Justice in the South.

Judge Manning clasped his hands and leaned across the bench. "Mr. Foreman. Have you reached a verdict, sir?"

"We have, your Honor."

The foreman gave a folded slip of paper to the bailiff who transported it over to the judge. Manning flipped it open, gave it a cursory glance, and smiled. He looked up at the foreman again. "Is the verdict made by you all?"

"Yes, your Honor."

"Very well then. What say you, sir?"

Silence for an interminable moment.

"Guilty, your Honor."

The courtroom erupted. Carl collapsed against the desk. Papers scattered across the floor and there was a loud thump as the attorney's briefcase landed among them. Cries of, "fry the nigger!" and "kill the black bastard" bounced off the walls.

Around me, people just sat there, eyes closed, mouthing words of prayer. Others shook their heads. No way, they seemed to say in silent contradiction to the verdict. No way.

Pandemonium reigned, and the courtroom walls seemed to swell with the uproar. Judge Manning just sat back in his chair and watched the spectacle, almost like he was enjoying a theatre show. Two deputies came forward to help Cranver pull Carl to his feet, but with Carl's big, powerful frame even the three of them struggled. Eventually, Judge Manning brought the court to order with several rapid strokes of his gavel. Carl's attorney hurriedly snatched up the papers and his briefcase and laid them in a disorganized heap on the table. He mopped his face with the handkerchief and raked pudgy fingers through his sweat-greased hair.

"Before I pass sentence," Judge Manning began, "does the defendant have any last words to offer the court?" His thin, reedy voice seemed to float lazily through the air, the words spoken with such matter-of-factness that they almost seemed to dance above the suppressed sobbing, sniffles, and mumbled prayer. After a few brief seconds, he leaned across the desk again and spread his small hands. "Well, Mr. Cranver?"

Cranver looked at Carl and then to the judge. "Your Honor, my client is obviously too distressed to speak. However, I would beg the court to show leniency. My client is a young man, your Honor, smitten in the prime of his…"

The judge shook his head and held up both hands. "Counsellor, I've heard enough." There was anger in his voice now. "Don't be telling me about how young your client is. Your client has committed the most heinous of crimes, and sentencing will reflect that."

The prosecuting attorney leaned back in his chair with the smooth grace of an athlete and smiled. Hands reached forward from the row of white folk seated directly behind him. Congratulatory pats rained on his shoulders. A hushed, "damn fine job, Clayton," filtered through the rows of seats and he turned around, his handsome features broadening into a gleaming smile of appreciation. He nodded in thanks then stood up, buttoning his suit jacket in preparation for the judge's next question.

So that was the famous Clayton Burke.

Judge Manning asked, "Does the prosecuting attorney's office seek the ultimate penalty?"

The country's chief prosecutor cleared his throat before speaking. "It does, your Honor. We feel that given the severity of the crimes, full justice should be served."

"Very well, sir. Court reporter, can you please note that the prosecutor's office has asked for and been granted their request."

Judge Manning turned to Carl. "Carl J. Robard," he announced in a suddenly affected authoritarian tone, "you have been found guilty of murder in the first degree. Mr. Cranver there"—he nodded briefly at Carl's attorney—"was about to launch into some tedious diatribe about you being a young man and not quite in the prime of life." The judge pointed his gavel at Carl. "But let me remind you of the two young lives that were so suddenly and horribly taken by your hand. One, a teenage girl, a beautiful teenage white girl, and the other from the black persuasion…" He paused to let the significance of this sink in. Carl moved to say something, but the judge cut him off.

"No, you've had your chance to speak. There is nothing now that you can say to this court. If it wasn't for the generosity of our Mayor and the Reverend Alvin, two upstanding men held in high esteem in this county, then that poor white girl could be rotting in some pauper's grave next to Alice Jackson in another part of this town."

Cranver tried to interrupt, but Manning just leveled his eyes, furious. He slammed both hands down on the bench. "I said, no, Mr. Cranver." The judge turned back to Carl. "Carl J. Robard. You will be taken from this place and incarcerated at the Georgia State Penitentiary in Atlanta where it will be decided, after an appropriate period of time, on the date when you will receive the ultimate punishment for your crime. During this period of incarceration, I can only hope that you repent your sins and may God have mercy—"

There was a sudden muted cry from somewhere behind Carl, followed by a shuffling sound. We all turned to see Carl's mother staggering toward the judge's bench, tears streaming down her face.

"No, no, not my son. He didn't, couldn't do it. Please have mercy." She collapsed to her knees, shaking her head. "No, no, no. Please, no."

The courtroom started to rumble again. Judge Manning looked over to the deputies stood to one side of the courtroom.

"Restrain this woman," he barked. Moments later, two deputies were pulling Carl's mother to her feet. She still had her white handkerchief and matching bag gripped tightly in her right hand, but her Sunday-best hat had tumbled to the floor. It sat in a pool of burning yellow sunlight at the foot of the judge's bench and she tried to reach for it, but the deputies held her back, showing a needless amount of restraint.

Something inside of Carl snapped. That black poison, so familiar to me, must have also risen from deep within him. Maybe it was how the two deputies were treating his mother. He shoved his attorney to one side, sending the obese man sprawling across the aisle into the laps of two middle-aged ladies. Jason could see what was about to happen and began to push through the crowd gathered in the aisle. He screamed out a warning, but his son was oblivious.

Carl strode forward and in two seconds had his arms clamped around Deputy Torrence's throat. "Let go of my mother," he screamed, hauling the man backwards.

The deputy instantly released his hold and grabbed at Carl's thick, powerful forearms while the other held on to Carl's mother. Carl screamed at him again. "I said, let her go. Allow her some dignity." He jerked the deputy's head back again clearly unaware of the force he was using, and we heard a sickening crunch, like someone had just cracked their knuckles. Deputy Torrence gave out a thin, choking gasp and his body went limp, dead before he hit the floor. His head lolled grotesquely to one side, thumped against the judge's bench then flipped back to rest against Carl's mother's Sunday-best hat. Carl just stood there, open mouthed in disbelief, his arms spread wide over the body.

For several long moments, there was a stunned silence in the courtroom. Every breath, every heartbeat, every pulse seemed to hang in a kind of momentary limbo. Then war broke out. Screams and shouts came from the gallery. The judge called for order and banged his gavel several times to no effect. Half-a-dozen armed deputies rushed into the courtroom and fought their way through the heaving mass of spectators. Jason Robard tripped and fell over Cranver's legs as the attorney struggled to get to his feet.

I stood there watching Carl, every sinew in my body taut, my heart thumping crazily in my chest, people jostling me from both sides. Something bad was about to happen and I could do nothing to stop it. Carl slowly lifted his gaze from the dead officer and over to the judge. The other deputy was unclipping his holster, drawing his weapon, flicking off the safety catch.

Time began to escape.

Carl reached down and wrenched the revolver out of the Torrence's holster. He swung it up, placed it against the side of his head, and pulled the trigger. Nothing happened. He pulled it again and again, still nothing. I realized that probably in his ignorance of such things; he hadn't considered the safety catch. He cried out in frustration, lowered the gun so that it was pointing directly at the judge. I could see it wasn't an intentional action, but Judge Manning seemed to freeze in his chair, totally misreading the situation.

Jason Robard was back on his feet, fighting through the crowd. He got to within a yard of his son when the onrushing deputies raised their weapons and three loud cracks of gunfire came in rapid succession, splitting through the turmoil in the courtroom. The first bullet hit Carl in the side of the neck, sending a spray of arterial blood high in the air.

169

The second bullet blew away half his father's face, and the third hit Carl center chest. He stood there swaying for a long moment, then his knees buckled, and he sank to the floor.

He fell to one side, and the screaming began.

CHAPTER 21

The courthouse steps were crowded with townsfolk and reporters; camera bulbs popped, notepads flapped. With the bodies removed, the grieving families and courtroom cleared, calm restored, I watched Clayton Burke and the town's mayor, Henry Towers, standing side by side among the heaving mass of people, arms raised in a victory salute. More accurately, the mayor holding up Clayton's right arm in a victory salute. Not much of a victory: three men dead, heartbroken families, lives destroyed forever. Still, the broad smiles creasing the faces of Paradise Creek's two most prominent officials made you think that all was rosy in the garden. The mayor in particular seemed to be relishing the attention, but when I studied the face of the county's chief prosecutor, it looked like he didn't seem as thrilled to be there, his smile strained, reluctant.

Several heads turned at a car engine sounding as though it was catching its last breath, and I caught a heavy-set man in a battered Chevy slowing for the townsfolk spilling out onto the street. He brought the Chevy to a stop, blue smoke coughing from its exhaust, took a long pull on his cigarette then tossed it out the driver's window.

He stared up at the courthouse steps for several moments, shaking his head. I recognized him. It was Coop.

The crowd began to thin, and he powered up the engine, continued on past the square, but not before releasing a huge wad of phlegm onto the sidewalk. Nice. He drove along Main and then onward to Towers Hill. As I watched him, I had this awful feeling of unease creep into my stomach. I turned to one of the bystanders, a middle-aged man with a whippet face and three front teeth missing, pretended I didn't know who the driver was.

The man's tongue worked the gap in his teeth. "Sam Cooper."

I shrugged. "Don't know him," I said.

"Works up at the mill."

"He get around much?"

"Not that I know of."

"Bit of a loner, maybe?"

"Lives over on Dale Street. Wife left him a few years back. Likes to get drunk over at Nat's Bar when he ain't working. Sheriff's had him overnight in jail a few times. Heard tell he's got an eye for the girls."

"Don't strike me as the type to make the ladies' hearts beat fast," I said.

He worked the gap with his tongue again. "Wouldn't know 'bout that, but I do hear he likes 'em young. Younger the better."

I left it at that. No point in pushing people. Makes them suspicious the more questions you ask. Had enough doors shut in my face last time. I wondered how far Coop's liking for young girls and drink took him as far as rape and murder when he got juiced up? Had I been wrong about him after all? Could he be the killer? Maybe I'd pay him a visit tomorrow. Should be easy enough to spot the buckled Chevy.

The show over, reporters gone, people started to scatter, and Paradise Creek was almost a ghost town by midday. Much of its business had been conducted and concluded, and now the townsfolk rested on their porches in the shade, hid behind window blinds or opened refrigerator doors and stuck their dripping faces into the cool vapor. Apart from a few restless souls, errands still to run, the town shrank back from the uncompromising heat and humidity like it was some malevolent thing sent in punishment by the Devil.

I was sitting under the bandstand again, unlit cigarette dangling from my lips and trying to understand the travesty of justice I had witnessed that morning. The judge appeared to relish the fact that a black man had been found guilty of murder. Carl's defense lawyer, Julias Cranver, had been nothing short of useless. All those lives pointlessly wasted. I just couldn't get my head around it. And Sam Cooper, questioned by the sheriff after I found Alice. Questioned and cleared. And now he was back under my radar.

I walked over to Mabel Watt's diner thinking I would grab some lunch, let my head settle. But in truth, I had little appetite for food after what had taken place in that courtroom. Maybe just a cup of coffee for now and later I'd try to get some time with Clayton Burke. An ambitious notion, but I had something on my mind, an opinion formed by what I'd witnessed in that courtroom, and I wasn't about to let it go.

Most of the tables were occupied, the diner filled with chatter about the trial. I went up to the counter, sat on an empty stool.

"Well, well, well," Mabel said, stubbing out her cigarette and offering me a smile. "Look who's back in town."

"Afternoon, Mabel," I said, attempting to return the smile, but my heart just wasn't in it.

"You come down for the trial?"

"Not intentionally," I said. "Had some unfinished business. Didn't know about the trial until this morning. Pure coincidence."

She poured me a cup of coffee, asked if I wanted some of her peach pie. I refused politely. "Tempting," I said. "But not today, thanks." I slapped my stomach. "Got to watch the waistline."

She raised her eyebrows, looked at me. "From where I'm standing, you got nothing to worry about."

She busied herself topping up coffee for the man and woman seated at the far end of the counter, then returned and leaned closer to me. "Must have been awful for you finding the body like that."

I nodded. The sight of Alice tied up in that cabin jumped into my head. After a very long moment, I said, "Yes, it was."

"Heard it was messed up bad."

"It wasn't pretty," I said.

"Still, at least they found the killer. That poor Caitlin Dexter, she was a pretty girl, and that Carl Robard did those things to her. Well, he got what was coming to him, if you ask me. Shame about Deputy Torrence, though."

174

I looked Mabel straight in the eye not caring for her offhand attitude and although what happened to Caitlin Dexter was nothing short of inhumane, to show such disregard for Alice notched up the temperature of my blood. I managed to keep my voice low, mainly out of respect for those sitting close to me.

"Alice Jackson had been tied up like an animal, raped several times, savagely beaten, and left for dead. Her tongue had been partially torn out, her eyes were almost out of their sockets, and her belly had been ripped open on account of the swamp animals getting a taste for human flesh." I watched Betty's face grow pale, and she placed a hand to her mouth like she was going to be sick.

She hurried off to clear a table and returned a minute later, cutlery and plates in hand, color back in her face. She placed the items on the counter at the back, turned and lit up another cigarette, drew the smoke in deep and held it there before releasing it through her nose.

The death of Deputy Torrence was not, as Betty described, 'a shame,' it was damn tragedy. She'd obviously heard about the trial from her diners, but had made no mention about Carl's father.

"I got to see the verdict in court this morning. Shame about Carl Robard's father. He was a church minister down in the Bottoms."

Betty shook her head. Not one hair of her Jackie Kennedy hairstyle moving on account of how much hairspray held it together. Her tone was more defensive when she spoke, the semi-flirtatious southern drawl gone. I didn't give a damn.

"You still got a lot to learn about the South, Mr. Bale. Take my word for it that you don't want to be supporting the black aspect too much. They don't need encouragement. We've got more trouble from them than we can handle in this county already, and God knows that Luther King fella is causing enough problems as it is. Those two men got shot cause they brought it on themselves. That black boy raped and murdered a white girl and God has passed judgment on them both for their sins."

My blood temperature came up a few more degrees. Dismissing the lives of two people so matter-of-factly, just because the color of their skin didn't fit. "What do you mean, they both sinned?" I asked. Not that I believed for one minute that Carl was guilty, but he had been tried and convicted on apparently strong, substantiated evidence. "Carl's father committed no crime."

"He was the boy's father," Mabel said. "He was the one brung him up, didn't have to do nothing more than that."

I had never struck a woman in my life, it was not part of my creed, but at that very moment I bunched my fists and pushed them hard into the wooden paneling under the counter to stop myself from lashing out. Mabel must have sensed it because she backed away from the counter, alarmed. I counted in my head, trying to suppress the anger, and wasn't even aware of Karen's presence until she spoke.

"Seems like we had a day for dying," she said.

She hitched up onto the stool next to me as I unclenched my fists and greeted Karen with a smile. Mabel looked relieved.

"Oh, hi there, Mr....?"

"Tom," I reminded her.

"Coffee?" Mabel asked.

"Yeah and keep it coming. Have I had a morning."

She reached over and took a cigarette out of Mabel's pack of Slims, lit up, sucked, and blew. She was still in her hospital uniform, bounced her right foot under the counter. Things really don't change much down here, I thought. Just an endless cycle of repeats, progress creeping along in all but attitude and conscience. Russian technology had sent a man into space, nuclear missiles had been developed, agriculture had changed, automobiles were becoming more stylized and powerful; so much was going on around our heads. Yet, the plight of the black communities remained a constant. True, in their marches and preaching, most conveniently forgot that it was their own kind who sold them into slavery hundreds and thousands of years before the first slave ships came to America. They had their own to blame for that. But still, the ridicule, punishment, treatment of them by the white community, was none of their doing. They did not ask for it. And what saddened me most, is that I could never see it changing.

"Tragic what happened today at the courthouse," I said, bringing myself out of my brief melancholic stupor.

She took a mouthful of coffee. "Oh my Lord," she said. "Never thought it was gonna end. That black minister, he was alive when they brought him in, but we couldn't save him."

Mabel huffed, looked at me, challenging and nervous at the same time. "Don't mean nothin' to me, sugar, ain't no loss."

I checked myself, breathed deep.

"The old man, Lucas James. He was first in this morning," Karen said. "But he was real old."

"What about him?" I asked, concerned.

"Went and died right outside Benson's grocery store."

I felt a rush of sadness sweep over me. Must have happened right after I left him. But I wasn't surprised way the old man was breathing. Old age is a terrible thing. I pictured him as he was when I looked back from across the street. Silent. At peace, head resting back against the store window. I made a mental note to visit Daniel Benson. What I had to share with him would put a smile on his face. A smile amongst all this tragedy and heartache.

I felt my time in the diner had come to an end. Mabel was clearly agitated by my behavior and didn't look comfortable with my presence. I doubted very much whether I'd ever set foot in there again. Pity, as the peach pie was something else.

The relief on Mabel's face when I paid for the coffee and left a generous tip was something to behold.

CHAPTER 22

I went back to the motel, showered, and changed. I seemed to be forever showering and putting on fresh clothes in this heat. The room had been made up again in my absence. Fresh sheets, pillowcases. Hubert Trenton didn't come across as a particularly sociable person, but he went to a lot of trouble to keep his guests happy. How many times had he made up my room when I was down here last? Four at least, maybe as many as six times. Couldn't say for sure, just got used to it every time I returned after a long day out.

I went to Nat's, ate steak and salad, washed it down with a beer. I was there no more than forty-five minutes. Nobody in there I recognized and when I left there were no suspicious looking cars waiting in the dark under the trees.

The shadows had lengthened as I drove through the town; dark fingers trailing behind the trees and the bandstand. The breeze, such as it was, had settled, and the streets were completely clear of people.

The town hall clock struck the hour at seven as I drove north east toward the Satilla River and Clayton Burke's house up on Jacob's Point.

The drive took no more than twenty minutes and I cruised along Braintree, gradually rising up a long gradient and passing mansion houses at least a quarter mile distance from each other, until I came upon Clayton Burke's house before Braintree dipped again and turned right, following the path of the river.

I slowed and turned left between two stone pillars with wrought-iron gates that were open and found myself on a large, in-out driveway bordering a lawn with immaculate flower beds and mature trees. Even at night, you could see the garden was a riot of summer colors.

The house was white antebellum situated in three or four acres of land bordered by pine, cypress, red maple, and pecan. Magnolia and yellow jasmine were in full bloom, their scent hanging densely in the thick weight of the summer heat wave. A balcony, supported by sixteen white columns, ran around the whole of the second floor. Most of the houses I'd passed were of similar grandeur although not so big, and I wondered how it was that a state attorney could afford such a place. Then I remembered Mrs. Burke's extremely wealthy family.

I parked up, got out. There was an old Ford pickup, looking completely out of place within its surroundings, parked way back along the side of the house to my left. Lights were on in the rooms either side of the grand entrance door. I went up the six steps up to the door, grasped the heavy iron knocker with the lion's head.

A few moments later, one half of the double door opened, and the housekeeper greeted me with a stare that could have slain a hundred men from fifty yards. She was a large black woman, late fifties to mid-sixties with a thick mop of curly gray-black hair, a big round face, intense almond-shaped eyes, and a pugnacious attitude. I was considering making a run for it before she could strike me down with her eyes and that attitude when she asked my business.

"Is Mr. Burke in?" I asked.

"No. He's late…as usual."

Sounded more like she came from Chicago with that attitude. Never would have expected a housekeeper in a southern town put down her boss to a stranger.

"When are you expecting him?"

"Any time now." Then she added, "Hopefully. Never home on time. Dinner's almost ready and I don't intend to waste it again."

She was about to ask my name when she squeezed her eyebrows together and furrows deep as a ploughed field rippled across her forehead. "Wait a minute. You that private detective fella found Alice Jackson?"

"Yes, ma'am, that's correct."

She stood back, chin on her chest, arms folded across her ample bosom. "Hmmm, polite young fella, ain't we?"

At that moment, twin beams fanned like searchlights across the front of the house, and I turned to see the attorney coming up the drive in his shiny black Lincoln Convertible. He came to a stop directly in front of us, got out, and then reached back for his briefcase and jacket. He mounted the steps and greeted the housekeeper who nodded stiffly.

Clayton Burke was about the same age as me, a couple of years lighter, maybe. He was my height, a little over six feet, and we matched each other in weight at about two hundred pounds but his jaw was a little leaner than mine and the way his shirt formed around his torso he looked like a guy who kept in shape.

"Dinner will be at eight, Mr. Burke," the housekeeper said in a tone more suited to some schoolchild being reprimanded for errant behavior. She turned and marched off down the hallway, muttering about the lateness of his arrival.

Burke finally turned to me, startled, almost like he'd not seen me standing right next to him or my car parked a few yards from his very own.

"May I help you?" he said.

"Name's Tom Bale, Mr. Burke. Realize turning up unexpected at this hour is probably not convenient, but wondered if I might have a moment of your time?"

He looked a little put out, but Southern politeness shone through. "Well, as much as I'd like the pleasure of your company, as you heard I am about to sit down to dinner. Perhaps you could contact my secretary tomorrow morning, make an appointment." He leaned in close, whispered. "Pays not to upset Ms. Nesbitt. She can be a difficult woman at times."

"Tomorrow's Saturday, Mr. Burke."

"Ah, so it is. Monday then."

At that moment, a mulatto woman in her late twenties or thirty, maybe, dressed in a flower print summer dress came down the long hallway and relieved the prosecutor of his jacket, car keys, and briefcase.

"Thank you, Charlotte," Burke said. "How are you today?"

"Very well, Mr. Burke, and you?" Her voice was husky and smooth, made me think of melting chocolate.

I wondered how he would answer that question, given what had taken place in the courtroom earlier.

"It's been a tough one to deal with," he said with sincerity. "I'm sure you heard of the events in the courthouse. They were not pleasant at all."

"No, sir."

And with that, she turned and left us, but not before offering me a nice smile. At that moment, a part of me left with her. I watched her disappear into a room at the end of the hallway and my stomach did flips.

Clayton Burke dragged me back to reality. "So, Mr....what was your name again?"

"Err...Bale. Tom Bale."

He frowned. "Rings a bell. Where have I heard that name before?" I moved to explain, but he cut me off and waggled a thick forefinger at my chest. "Yes, you're a reporter for *The Tribune*." A smile spread across his face revealing perfect white teeth. "Yes, of course, always got time for you fellas. Come on in. That was one hell of a trial, wasn't it?"

He slapped me once on the shoulder and was through the door and halfway down the hall before I had a chance to tell him that he'd gotten me mixed up with someone else. But I followed him anyway. I'd heard that he liked to see his picture in the papers, and if he wanted to think

I was a reporter and it got me where I wanted to be, then that was just fine.

He mounted the sweeping staircase with ease and grace, two at a time. "Just gonna freshen up," he said, "Won't be a minute." He pointed toward the living room. "Help yourself to a drink."

I glanced around the grand hall, taking in my surroundings but really hoping to catch Charlotte again. Those dark eyes and that mane of thick wavy hair. She certainly was striking to look at. Not pretty in the traditional sense, but very attractive...beautiful even.

I heard the chink of glass and followed the sound through to the living room. A woman who I assumed was Mrs. Burke lay stretched out along a red, velvet covered Davenport, her head buried in a late edition newspaper. A tall drink, gin by the smell, sat on a small round table next to her. A cigarette smoldered in a white marble ashtray.

"Good evening," I said, eyes sweeping around the expensively furnished room, admiring the rich drapes, the heavy antique furniture. Opulent. Not my taste at all, but oh boy, to have this kind of money.

The woman's head stayed buried in the news. Instead, a slender tanned arm jangling with bright, gold bracelets appeared from behind the paper and waved five slim and expertly manicured fingers in the general direction of the drinks cabinet. "Drinks are over there."

I stared at her long legs, appreciating how their shape was accentuated by the soft, cream-colored silk lounge pants.

The fingers ceased waggling and automatically picked up the cigarette. It disappeared for a second behind the newspaper, then reappeared and was returned to the marble ashtray. I watched the plume of gray smoke weave and dance above the *County Tribune*.

"Did you hear about the trial?" she said dryly. "Seems we lost some people. Shocking."

I didn't care much for her off-hand tone so changed the subject while helping myself to two fingers of bourbon. "Lovely house, Mrs. Burke," I said.

"Yes, isn't it."

"Lived here long?"

"Five years. A gift from my father after Mr. Burke made chief prosecutor."

"Some gift," I said.

The newspaper rustled as she turned a page. "Yes, my father is a very generous man."

"What line of business is he in?"

"Agriculture."

I was about to ask in what line of agriculture, when Clayton Burke entered the room. He'd changed out of his formal suit into lightweight slacks and a loose white shirt. "So, Mr. Bale, I see you've got yourself a drink."

"Yes, sir, thank you." I lifted the glass as a gesture of thanks.

"I'll get one myself. What are you drinking?"

"Bourbon."

"Good choice. We'll go through to the study, I can give you five minutes."

"That's it," his wife snapped from behind the newspaper. "Go on, go hide in the study. Don't worry about me. I just sit around all day getting bored and waiting for you to appear so I can have some decent conversation. And all you want to do when you get home is ignore me."

"Maryanne," Burke said, face breaking into a forced grin. "I hardly think this is the time. We have a guest."

"No doubt another reporter?"

Burke ignored her. Instead, he placed a hand on my shoulder and guided me out of the living room and across the hallway.

Maryanne Burke's voice followed us. "We haven't had a decent conversation in over a year!"

Burke stopped at the door to his study, looked at me, and tried to hide his embarrassment. "Perhaps we should take our drinks outside. It's a fine evening."

We sat down on the veranda stretched out our legs and leaned back against the steps, the smooth worn-down wood pressing a line into our backs. Sunset was a slash of red and violet disappearing behind the treetops. I could just make out where the end of the garden sloped down to the sand bar and the river. We listened to bullfrogs and crickets for about half a minute before he spoke. He leaned forward, rested both elbows on his knees, glass of bourbon held in two hands straight out in front. Some of the enthusiasm had gone out of his voice.

"I apologize for my wife's behavior," he said. "She gets a little lonely and I always seem to be at the office."

"No apology necessary," I said. The rumor I'd heard about his affair with a secretary might well be true after all.

He sat back again, sipped his bourbon. "So what can I do for you, Mr. Bale, need something for your paper?"

Time for some honest talking. "I'm not a reporter. I'm kind of unofficial investigator."

He turned to me, surprise evident on his face. "Well, now, ain't that something? Could've sworn you were a newspaperman. So how come I recognize your name?"

I told the story, left out the part about my view on Carl Robard's conviction. When I was done telling it, he just shook his head. "Can't imagine what it must have been like to find Alice Jackson like that. I saw enough horrors in Korea: men, women, children. Bodies ripped apart from mines or burned beyond recognition. No matter how many times you see it, it don't get any easier. Poor girl. You a forces man, Mr. Bale?"

"No. Chicago Police Department until about six years ago."

"Still, you must have seen plenty of action in the city."

"Enough," I said, pushing away the image of Jenny lying on that operating table, bones and body crushed, her once beautiful face almost pulped beyond recognition. I threw back the remaining finger of bourbon.

"Not like our quiet little town, huh?"

"Don't seem so quiet at the moment."

"Yeah," he said reflectively. "A real, real tragedy what happened today." He reached over and took my empty glass. "Let me freshen that for you."

He got up and went back into the house. I heard raised voices, angry voices, and the sound of glass breaking. Then Mrs. Burke's house slippers clacking on the wooden floor in the hallway and Burke shouting after her.

"That's it. Go off and sulk in your bedroom. Better still, why don't you invite all your socialite friends over for another round of drinks and chew the fat over how goddamn bored ya'll are."

The housekeeper's voice cut through the argument. "I guess," she said in that frosty tone of hers, "that you and Mrs. Burke won't be seated for dinner tonight?"

"Damn right," Burke snapped.

"I don't know why I trouble with it. Waste of time me cooking anything. Guess the pigs over at the farm got another fancy takeout."

A minute later, he was passing over my glass. I noticed he'd poured about two fingers for me and about four for himself. I guess he felt as though he needed it. He also had a ripe red apple in his hand.

"Dinner," he said, holding up the apple. "Sorry, do you want one? Very juicy and sweet."

"No thanks," I said.

He put down his drink and fished a small knife, no more than two and a half inches long, out of his back pocket. Opened it up and started peeling back the apple skin.

"Fearsome weapon," I said, joking.

He stopped, turned it over in his hand. I could see an intricate engraving along the blade.

"Fruit knife. My great grandfather's. Attractive little thing, isn't it?"

"Yes, is it silver?"

"It is. See those hallmarks along the top of the blade? Finest quality. Pearl handled. Made in 1873. Passed down to me. My father used to keep it in his back pocket, and I do just the same. Take it everywhere. Never know when you might need it."

The sultry Georgia night lay heavy, and we sat there batting midges while Clayton munched on his apple. When he was done, he wiped the knife blade with his handkerchief and tucked back into his pocket.

"None of my business, but you and Mrs. Burke don't seem to be getting along too well."

He huffed. "That obvious, huh? We got married for all the right reasons, seven years now, but the last two have been a little…shall we say…fractious."

"Happens. But you can work through it."

"You sound like a man who's been there."

"Can't say personally, but I have friends who've been through some pretty difficult times and come out the other side." Jenny and I seemed to have an idyllic relationship compared to others. God, how I missed her. How I missed her touch, her smell, and totally uncomplicated generosity of her being.

"Never married then?"

A conversation for another time. "Are we on first-name terms yet?"

He looked at me strangely. "Wow. That was a little left field. But sure, you can call me Clayton."

"Tom," I said, and we shook hands for the second time.

I weighed up the potential consequences of what I wanted to say, considered my armament and chose the bomb. "I don't believe Carl Robard was guilty of murdering Caitlin Dexter or Alice Jackson."

He let out a nervous little laugh. "Wow again. That's left field and beyond." He swallowed bourbon. "Where'd you get that notion from?"

And that's where my argument fell down. I had nothing concrete other than what I saw in the courthouse, my experience as a police officer and detective dealing with the guilty and the innocent every day for fifteen years, what I had learned the last time I was in Paradise Creek, and my limited knowledge of Carl and his family. Present that in court as part of Carl's defense and Clayton Burke would tear it to shreds and the judge would quite rightly laugh it out the door. But I had nothing else and sometimes you just had to lay it out how you saw it, right or wrong. So I told him and he laughed. Or at least he pretended to laugh. He had that same forced smile on his face that I saw on the courthouse steps when the mayor was holding up his arm in a victory salute. He wasn't comfortable, not comfortable at all.

"Tom," he said. "You're a long way from home and a little out of your depth down here. We may have a major problem with our divided community and Martin Luther King is not making matters any easier…" I moved to interrupt him, but he held up a hand before I could comment further. "Let me finish. Now, before you say anything I want you to know that I don't necessarily subscribe to the way colored people are treated and I do think they need a strong voice, someone like King to take their message forward, to be heard. But it does upset the balance. It fuels the fire in the colored community and enrages the white. It's like a box of old dynamite just waiting to be shook. But you can't let the plight of the colored man cloud your vision to what's right and wrong. I'm a fair man and believe that I considered all the evidence in Carl's case very carefully. It was tight and irrefutable. I don't have to justify my actions to you, Tom, and what I'm about to tell you is already open to the public, but I feel, given that you were not in court for the whole trial, I should at least inform you of the following: that Carl's crucifix was found on Caitlin Dexter's body, we got fingerprints, we matched Carl's blood, we got witnesses testified under oath that Carl was seen in the vicinity of where her body was found. The girl's scarf was found in his locker at work, like he'd taken some kind of trophy. The defense can't argue against all of that."

Sounded like a tight argument to me. "Talking about the defense," I said. "Seems to me that Julias Cranver didn't do much for his client. Carl was facing a death sentence, and he hardly said a word. While it's true I wasn't in court all week and therefore have no idea what went before, but today he might as well not have been there."

I heard an engine start, sounded like the pickup. Crunch of tires on gravel then listened to it accelerate along Braintree until the sound of its old engine faded in the distance.

Burke finished his drink and set the glass down on the step, spread his hands. "OK, Cranver has a tendency to like the drink a bit too much at times, but he's an experienced defense lawyer. Tried hundreds of cases over the years, won some and lost some. This time, given the evidence and witness testimony, there wasn't much he could do."

"What about Judge Manning?"

"What about him?"

"From where I sat, he appeared to be relishing the idea that a black man was going to the chair."

Burke considered for a moment before speaking, like he was trying to find the most tactful way to answer my accusation of the judge's obvious racism, a district court judge who'd served the county for better than thirty years.

"Manning is part of the old school. I'll grant you. His mind's still sharp as a razor, though. He comes across all fire and brimstone, but he'd be the same if it were a white man convicted of murder."

Burke had put up a good case and in theory it busted apart my argument. Still, I was going to see this through until I was absolutely certain. It was time to go and leave him to deal with his angry wife and housekeeper. I hoped for the chance to see Charlotte again before I left. He walked me back through the house to the front door and we shook hands.

"I can understand how you feel, Tom," Burke said. "You wanted some closure on Alice Jackson. That's natural. You've got suspicions, things didn't seem to go the way you thought they should and you're right to ask questions. It all ended horribly, but it's done and now best left. I firmly believe the conviction was sound."

I looked him straight in the eye. "You sincerely believe that, Clayton?"

He hesitated again, and it was enough to tell me he didn't, or at least wasn't sure. "Yes...yes, Tom...I do."

"OK then. But let me just say one thing before I go."

"Sure," he said, a little nervous.

I smiled. "Great bourbon."

"What?"

That threw him, but he quickly recovered and relaxed. Either that or was relieved. He laughed. "Yeah, Bourbon Supreme. Made for sipping, not slugging."

He was still chuckling when I said, "Another thing..."

"Yes?"

"I doubt I could ever beat you across the table in a court of law, but I'm damn fucking good at reading people, and I know when someone is speaking words that their conscience doesn't believe."

I bade him goodnight, left him standing there, shocked and troubled.

Never got to see what Maryanne Burke looked like, and I didn't really care, but I hoped I'd get the chance to see Charlotte again.

CHAPTER 23

I swept out of the driveway and drove back the way I came. The road was deserted, and I'd driven about five miles when I saw an old pickup hauled over to the side of the blacktop close to some trees at a forty-five-degree angle. I pulled up. It was the old Ford I'd seen at Clayton Burke's house. It had been abandoned, probably broken down. I drove on another mile and then saw someone up ahead on the opposite side walking in the same direction. As I drew closer, I realized it was a woman, so I slowed to see if I could offer a lift.

I pulled over on to the soft verge, leaned over, and wound down my window. She stopped, turned toward me. It was Charlotte. What the hell was she doing out here on her own?

"Hey, Charlotte, can I offer you a lift?"

"Oh, hello," she said, recognizing me from earlier.

"Where you headed, I could drop you off."

She checked the road both ways then crossed over to me. She had on a light-weight summer coat with the collar up and her hair tucked inside otherwise I'd have recognized her from behind. She bent down so her face was level with the window and even in the dim lights from the dashboard she looked lovely, radiant even. A knot formed in my stomach.

"That your truck back there?" I asked.

"Yeah. Stupid me, I forgot to fill it up. Out of gas."

"It's no problem at all," I said quickly. "I was just heading back to the motel anyway, so get in. I'd be happy to take you home. Come back tomorrow with a can. Will it be OK out here all night, or shall we drive into town, get some gas now?"

She screwed up her face. "Not at this time of night. Everything's shut. It'll be fine where it is." I saw laughter lines at the corners of her eyes. Maybe she was a little older than I first thought. Thirty-two or three, perhaps? I liked the laughter lines, made her seem even more real.

"I'll take you home then. I can come by in the morning with a gas can, take you back and get you started."

"I'm not so sure. It's off this main road into the country a ways."

She was uncertain about me. Who could blame her? She didn't know me from Adam. "Look," I said, giving her my friendliest smile. "It's really no bother. Just tell me where to go."

She stood there a moment, head angled, making up her mind, then went around the Dodge, and got in.

We drove a couple of miles in silence before she indicated a turning to the right. "Down this track about two miles and you'll see it."

"You were going to walk all this way on your own?" I asked. "Heck of a risk."

We plunged into complete darkness. Trees arched over us, felt like we were driving through a tunnel. The road was a little uneven, with loose stones spitting up from my tires and clanking under the bodywork.

"I can look after myself," she said.

"But aren't you in the least bit concerned? You know about the trial. Two girls murdered. You can't take risks." In Chicago, she wouldn't have lasted more than a week on her own.

I could feel her staring at me as I concentrated on keeping the Dodge from veering into the trees.

"The dark doesn't scare me."

"I would think twice before walking on my own. By the way, name's Tom Bale."

"I need money, so I asked Viola if there was any extra work and she got me this job at the Burke's residence. You do what you have to do. If I have to walk, I walk."

"Who's Viola?"

"Ms. Nesbitt the housekeeper."

"Oh, right, the one with the unfriendly bark."

She laughed and it was the sweetest sound I'd heard in years. "She can be a little bullish at times, but she's harmless enough."

"I was surprised at how she spoke to Clayton Burke, she being a Neg…the housekeeper." Instantly, I wished my brain had engaged before I'd spoken. "I mean…it's not the usual way someone speaks to their boss."

Her voice got as hard as glass. "You mean a Negro. It's not right for a Negro woman to speak to her boss that way."

"No. What I meant was that down here that's the way things seem to work, or at least that's how I perceive it. It's your history, it's the South it's the way things are. Down here, white people still treat the black community like slaves it would seem. I mean no disrespect, but personally I think you need more people like Ms. Nesbitt instead of relying on one man do all your talking for you."

"You're referring to Martin Luther King?"

"Yeah. Why does it take someone like him to shout for the rights of the black population?"

"I'm not going to lecture you on history, Mr. Bale. Suffice to say that you are so wrong and so out of your depth, it would take a year to educate you. Now the turning to my place is about two hundred yards on your left."

It came upon me faster than I imagined. One minute it was pitch black and the next an opening in the trees led into a clearing ringed by live oaks draped in Spanish moss. I saw a large timber house with a porch across the front and a glider to one side of the door. As I came to a stop, I noticed something else. A small tree with completely bare branches except about thirty or so colored bottles of varying shapes and sizes stuck over the ends.

"You live on your own, then?" I asked, already having assumed, hoped that she did.

"I do, so what?"

"Nothing," I said, hesitating and a little lost for words. "I…just…assumed. I was planning on seeing Mr. Burke again tomorrow, so I could come by with the gas. Go get your truck started. You working tomorrow?"

There was a smile playing around her mouth. She knew where I was headed with this conversation. "Well…OK," she said. "I'm due to be there at eight. See you at seven-thirty."

"Great," I said. "And maybe tomorrow evening I can bring you home again. You really shouldn't be walking alone in the dark."

She closed the door, bent down at the window. "See that tree, Mr. Bale." She pointed to the dead tree with the bottles.

"Yeah, sure, meant to ask you about that."

"That's what us Negros call a bottle tree. It's a crepe myrtle. You know what it's for?"

"I…have no idea."

"The bottles are placed on the tree to capture the evil spirits. When the wind blows it's the spirits howling and moaning. Once in the bottles, they can't get out. So you see, Mr. Bale. I got no problem walking on my own in the dark. Ain't nothing going to touch me." She said goodnight, started to turn away then stopped. "By the way?"

"Yes?" I said a little too eagerly.

"Tomorrow night, I'll have my truck and won't be needing a lift." She walked away from me, laughing, and went up the porch steps. I sat there for a full two minutes, waited for her to go inside and feeling foolish.

Lamps came on one by one, and I watched her slender form move with a lithe grace from window to window, closing curtains. She hesitated at one of the windows and stared out directly at me. Then she was gone.

Driving back to the motel, a song came into my head, "Georgia on My Mind". It was written by Hoagy Carmichael and Stuart Gorrell back in the thirties and a lot of singers had covered it but my favorite version was released only the year before by Ray Charles. I bought the album it came off, *Genius Hits the Road*. Wasn't so sure about Georgia, but I certainly had Charlotte on my mind all the way back to the motel.

I must have turned this way and that a thousand times until I finally lifted my head off the pillow, opened my eyes and propped myself up on elbows. I'd forgotten to close the blinds and a pale, vaporous silver-gray moon lit the bedroom. Shadows crept deep into corners. I reached over to the bedside cabinet and checked my watch. It was one forty-five.

I lay back down, unable to shake away the past hours, thinking how one single event could alter the course of your life.

There were times when everything seemed as though it was coming apart, like pulling at a loose thread and watching the seam gradually open up to reveal a gaping hole, the edge of which was a ragged mess of loose ends. And then there were those events which were sudden and brutal, like the deaths of Alice Jackson, Caitlin Dexter, and those three men in the courtroom; sudden and brutal.

I thought about their families and how their lives had been torn apart, how in the space of just a few seconds their worlds had come to such an abrupt end. No loose ends, just an absolute.

I got up, closed the blinds, crossed the bedroom, and poured myself a large shot of Johnnie Walker. I drank it straight back, enjoyed the burn in my throat and chest. Reaching into my jacket, I took out the pack of cigarettes, stuck one of them between my lips. Propped up on pillows, I sat the bottle and glass on my stomach and moved the unlit cigarette back and forth using my lips and tongue, a trick I saw my father do and couldn't wait for him to teach me. I tried to reason with myself, told myself to walk away. Every sane voice in my head urged me not to pull at that thread, to pack my things and get out of there. But I was already too involved. The mere fact that I had driven all the way back down here told me that. And now I had that loose thread between my fingers I knew I couldn't let go. But this unsettling feeling crept into the pit of my stomach and somehow whatever I discovered while pulling at that thread, it was going to change the course of my life forever. I just didn't know how.

I filled the glass again and thought about Charlotte.

About 3 a.m. sleep finally came to me.

My nightmare was filled with bottle trees, dead bodies, and blood. Lots of blood.

CHAPTER 24

I came awake suddenly, bathed in sweat. There was a sickly sweet, pungent odor in the air. I tried to sit up and the dizziness overwhelmed me, paralyzing my efforts. My head fell back on the pillows and it was like a hammer blow. I lay there for a minute, totally incapacitated, waiting for the pain to ease off.

The smell was from the whiskey. It had soaked into the blankets and dried like some sticky goo on my chest. I reached out and found the glass and bottle on the bed. I needed water, lots of it. Slowly, inch by inch, I managed to raise my head off the pillows without feeling like Thor was seeking revenge on me. I sat there breathing deep, trying to control the lurching sickness in my stomach.

I got up and blundered across to the bathroom, ran the cold faucet, cupped my hands, and swallowed water like my life depended on it. I stared into the mirror above the washbasin and what I saw didn't look good. I was thirty-eight going on sixty-five. Last time I looked like this was after Jenny was killed and I went on a downward spiral I never thought I'd recover from.

I threw water over my face and stood there feeling like death had finally come for me. One of those days I could easily shy away from my duties, just take the day off, curl up in bed, and sleep. But that would not do. That was not me.

I let the shower run to ice cold and almost screamed out when the water hit me. I let the spray numb my body then gradually brought the temperature back to something more bearable. I bowed my head and a large globule of water dropped off the end of my nose. I watched it in a kind of cinematic slow motion as it fell and exploded on impact with the bath.

Fifteen minutes later I was dressed. I drew back the curtains and opened the window. The fog was heavy that morning, and it hung over the parking lot in a dense pearl-gray blanket; so thick that I could barely make out the darker outline of the neon sign.

Summer smells were greatly enhanced in the fog, and I could feel the warm air against my face. A tiny dot of silver-yellow sun was beginning to burn its way through. It would be clear by nine and hotter than hell. I would go see Coop this morning and then base my next move on what I got from him. But then I remembered Charlotte and our arrangement. I was going to be late. Coop would have to wait.

A quarter mile on from the motel was a three-pump Gulf looking worn down and lifeless in the fog. But it was open, and an old man with a salt and pepper beard, wearing a baseball cap and faded blue dungarees, refueled the Dodge and sold me a five-gallon army-green steel Jerry Can. From there I drove east across the outskirts of town on Montague Avenue, and then onto Charlotte's, hoping I could find the farm track leading to her cabin.

As it happened, I didn't have to worry about finding her place. She was standing under the shade of a live oak, just off the blacktop at the entrance to the farm track, waiting for me.

She was dressed in tight-fitting denims cut just above the ankle, a white T-shirt, and white pumps. Her hair was glistening in the dappled sunlight, and she looked radiant, not angry, which was surprising given that I was forty minutes late. She picked up the bag at her side, got in the Dodge, and we drove off.

"Are you always this late?" she said, staring straight ahead.

"Sorry," I said. "I slept in."

"Heard of alarm clocks?"

"Don't usually need them. Rare for me to be late."

"I thought, given the time and that you might have difficulty in finding my place, I would wait for you where you could see me."

I kept glancing at her profile. She really was lovely. "You didn't need to, I would have found you."

She looked at me then, stern. "I thought it would save time." She emphasized the last word, making a point.

I glanced at her again, ready to apologize once more, and she quickly turned her head away, attempting to hide a smile, her cover broken. We laughed together, and it was the warmest and most comfortable, easy moment I'd had in a very long time.

The fog was finally lifting, and we found her pickup exactly where she'd left it, lonely and thankfully unharmed under the trees. First few attempts, the engine struggled but we got it going again. Charlotte turned the old Ford F1 around, stopped, wound down the window, and thanked me. I was about to ask if we could perhaps meet up for a drink and dinner, when she said, "Louis Shine's Juke Joint in the Bottoms. Tonight at nine."

And with that, she headed off, leaving me standing at the roadside thinking of nothing but her.

CHAPTER 25

By the time I found Cooper's house on Dale Street, the air was so hot and thick I could see it wavering ten feet off the blacktop. I got out of the Dodge, closed the door, and looked up and down the street. Three houses away I heard spluttering coming from a lawn sprinkler. Water pulsed out in a counter-clockwise spray, offering little hope to a patch of yellow grass. Across from me, an old couple sat in a rocker on their porch. They nodded, and I nodded back. Somewhere in the distance, a dog barked. I glanced at my watch; eleven o'clock on a peaceful, hot Saturday morning.

I walked up the driveway, passed the buckled Chevy, and felt heat radiating off metal. I climbed the porch steps, rapped the screen door and waited. No answer so I rapped again, gave it twenty seconds this time. Still nothing. I tried once more, gave it another twenty seconds and was about to walk away when suddenly the inner door opened and Coop stood there, a week's growth on his chin and his belly hanging over his light-brown pants.

"Hey, Tom Bale," he said, his voice heavy with the aftereffects of an evening at Nat's. He coughed a wad of phlegm onto a patch of dead grass and sniffed.

Charming.

"How's it going, Coop?"

"Same."

"Wondered if I might have a few moments of your time?"

"Was trying to get some sleep."

"Won't take a minute."

Reluctantly, he invited me in. "How come you're back down here?"

"Lot of unfinished business with Alice Jackson," I said, closing the door behind me.

He looked at me quizzically. "You found her, didn't you? Wasn't that what you was asked to do?" He motioned for me to sit at his breakfast table, which I did, careful not to get my shirt sleeves dirty from all the detritus spread over the melamine top.

"It was, but there's still the matter of her killer."

"Carl been tried and convicted for that."

"Yes, I know. I was in court yesterday. I came back not knowing another girl had been murdered, and that Carl had been arrested."

"Sad what happened in court, real shitter. Feel sorry for Mrs. Robard now Carl and Jason are gone. Gotta bring the twins up on her own."

His words seemed heartfelt enough. So was I chasing the wrong guy, again? "I got some questions about Carl, too."

A half-smile. "With what's happened, I guess all the questions have been asked about Carl," he said.

The late morning sun pushed through the windows, hot on my back. There was that morning's edition of the *County Tribune*, a cold beer and half-finished bowl of Frosty O's and milk on the table. Plus dots of dried gravy, breadcrumbs, and a TV dinner tray with spots of mold growing around the edges of each compartment. Alcohol sweat dropped off every inch of his body. He coughed again, reached for the beer, and swallowed. I looked around. The kitchen was a mess, the man sat in front of me was a mess. I couldn't judge him as I'd been exactly where he was. But I still didn't completely know who I was dealing with. Caitlin Dexter had been murdered. Had Coop gotten away with it, had he somehow planted evidence; was he that clever, or desperate?

"What made you go looking in the swamp?" he asked, staring at me with weary, bloodshot eyes.

Didn't see that coming. "I'd just about looked everywhere else."

"Swamp's a big place."

"I got lucky." He was drawing me into a conversation I didn't want to have. Not yet. "So, about Carl and Caitlin Dexter, I seem to recall we had a conversation about her at Nat's one night."

Coop was having none of it and pressed me some more. "How long you take to find her?"

"A few days."

"You musta got lucky. I've been fishing the Okefenokee more than twenty years and I still don't know half of what's out there."

So Coop knows the swamp and has a liking for young girls; had a liking for Caitlin Dexter. Could he really have killed Alice as well and hidden her body in the swamp? Was I sitting opposite her killer? But why would he put a note under my door telling me where to find her, and then not try to hide Caitlin's body? Was Caitlin just a matter of risky opportunity and the chances of him being seen so much greater, so he left her there in the grass, planted evidence? And then there was the matter of the black car seen when Alice disappeared. Coop had a brown Chevy Impala. Didn't make sense.

"I went all the places you're not supposed to go until I found her," I said. "I would still be looking if I hadn't."

He shrugged. "Guess if someone's paying you by the hour or the day, don't matter to you how long it takes."

"I didn't earn a dime out of it."

He looked surprised.

"You came all the way from Chicago to help out a negra family for nothing? You jerking me off, right?"

I gave him a hard stare just to let him know that the subject was done. He took the hint.

"Do you believe Carl murdered Alice Jackson and Caitlin Dexter?" I asked.

"I don't know," he said. "Carl seemed a decent enough guy. Can't see him doing it, but who knows?"

I studied his reaction, see if I could detect a killer's conscience in his eyes or body language, but if there was something there, he didn't give it away. Instead, he leaned forward, placed the bottle on the table, and twisted it around with his fingers. He eyed me carefully, measuring me. He spoke quietly. "I was stood right beside Carl when

208

the sheriff and three of his deputies came to arrest him. Right at the start of our shift, we hadn't even got our overalls on."

"And?" I said as Coop's eyes wandered, losing concentration.

"Demanded he opened his locker. Had a search warrant."

Coop got up, stretched, bones cracking along his spine. He reached for the refrigerator. "You want a beer?"

I held up a hand, my head still suffering from the bourbon. "I'll pass, but you go ahead."

He came back to the table, twisted off the top and swallowed deep. "Jesus that's better. I'm dying here." He belched. "'Scuse me."

All I needed, a fog of foul breath. Happy Saturdays. He settled himself and continued.

"Carl opened up his locker. Guess what they found?"

I knew but wasn't going to let on. "Tell me."

"Caitlin Dexter's scarf."

"Her scarf?"

"Yep. Like he'd taken it as some kind of trophy. Had her smell on it. At least that's what I heard. Carl looked as surprised as you do right at this moment."

He finished his beer, got up, and grabbed another from the refrigerator, sat back down, glanced at the open newspaper, and did a double take.

"That ain't right," he said.

"What isn't?"

He scanned the paper again, shaking his head, then swiveled it around so I could read the column where his finger was pointing. The

County Tribune had printed a full account of what had happened the night Caitlin Dexter had been murdered, and also the evidence that led to Carl's arrest. It was the part about Carl's gold crucifix being found tangled in the girl's hair. "That ain't right," he repeated to the newspaper, prodding the article with a thick finger.

"What isn't right?"

"I know that ain't right."

"Tell me," I said, voice rising a notch or two. God, the man could be infuriating.

"Carl told me he'd lost that crucifix the day before." He stared at the shocked expression on my face. "Yeah, and I got something else to tell you as well. Two things first, though."

I spread my hands.

"You gonna be at Nat's tonight? It's Saturday and I'm heading over there early. And you sure you don't want a beer right now? Refrigerator's stocked."

CHAPTER 26

I came away from Coop's feeling that first prickle of excitement begin to thread its way through my stomach. He might have been bullshitting me, but he seemed genuine enough. I had to pay Burke another visit, get him to check the evidence and how it was obtained. He would be home it being a Saturday. I would get to see Charlotte. But first I needed to head over to the Bottoms, pay my respects to Ellie-Mae and Mrs. Robard.

Fifteen minutes later I turned into Cotton Cut Road, so called, Lucas James had told me, because generations before the slave workers would march along this route during harvest time to work an eighteen-hour day in the fields. From first light until it was too dark to see, backs bent, muscle and sinew screaming, they would pick cotton. The women worked the same hours as the men and pregnant women were expected to work until the child was born. After the birth, a woman was expected to work the field with the child on her back. At the end of a day, driven hard by a white overseer with a whip, the slaves got in a line to have their cotton weighed and receive their daily food ration. The minimum amount of cotton to be picked in one day was 200 pounds. All the workers lived in tiny huts with dirt floors. The huts offered no protection against the cold winter winds and their only source of heat and light was from old kerosene lamps. At least that much had changed.

A few people in this part of the Bottoms had attempted to keep their homes decent and well maintained. One of them had been Lucas James. But now, in the space of twenty-four hours since his passing, the starving wolves had ransacked the place. Windows had been smashed and the screen door hung pathetically by a single hinge in its frame. Unwanted clothes, tins of food, and furniture had been tumbled out onto the porch. It was funny how the poor could be so particular at times in their choice of what to steal. I felt angered by this violation of the old man's home, but knew well enough that folks needed to survive somehow. This was their way of doing it. It wasn''t right, but often when you had nothing, you had no other choice.

I was passing Donald 'Duck' Averly's place and noticed since I last came through, he'd fixed another roll of barbed wire around his front yard. I decided to pull over.

I knew a little about Donald, but had never met him. He was the only white resident in Cotton Cut Road and had been retired from the army after doctors were forced to remove a large, jagged piece of shrapnel that had embedded itself in his right buttock during a mortar attack in Korea. The botched surgery and extensive amount of scar tissue had stiffened up the muscles so much that to walk with any degree of comfort, he had to swish his rear from side-to-side, waddling like a duck. Donald's other handicap in life, was that by the time he'd reached fifty his sane mind had left him, and standing in his front yard he took it upon himself to drop his pants and ask any lady who would be passing, their opinion on the size of his manhood, which, if you believed the local stories, was considerable. Two years on from his time in the state mental hospital, and cured of his desire to display his genitalia to the public, he now threatened to shoot anyone on sight if they dared to step foot onto his property. By ten every morning, he would be sitting in his striped deck chair out among the weeds, surrounded by sandbags and barbed wire. Dressed in army fatigues with a .3 M-1 carbine resting on his knees, sweat bristling on his scalp, and a manic stare on his craggy face, he would slug at the bottle of bourbon cooling in an old army helmet filled with ice next to his chair and scream at the kids as they ran past, laughing and making loud quacking sounds.

Donald was sitting in his deck chair, just as I had seen him on a couple of occasions in the past. I reversed and pulled up along the barbed wire fencing. I didn't think he'd have much to offer in terms of information, but I wasn't exactly spoilt with the number of options coming my way. He eyed me suspiciously as I got out of the Dodge. I stood by the fence as Donald got up from his chair and approached me.

"You out on maneuvers soldier?" he asked, cradling his rifle over both arms and shifting his eyes nervously from side-to-side.

Just go along with it, I thought. You never know. "Sure, Donald," I said, humoring him.

He edged closer to the fence. His combat uniform wet up to the knees, his blackened face streaked with sweat. Tiny pinpricks of blood

213

dotted his cheeks. His breath reeked of bourbon. His eyes twitched up and down the road again. "Just got back myself," he hissed.

"Where from?"

"Been all over this morning."

"On maneuvers yourself?"

"Damn right. You come across any of 'em?"

"Who, Donald?"

"Commies?"

"Can't say as I've seen any this morning."

"Hmmm, they can be sly little fuckers."

This was going to be impossible. The old man was completely deranged. Why the hell did I bother to stop? I started to leave. "Good talking to you, Donald."

He looked me up and down, running a critical eye over my crumpled suit. "Being a trifle hasty ain't you, soldier?"

I hesitated, sighed. Another minute. "You see any this morning?"

He leaned over the barbed wire. "Damn right I did," he whispered.

"Really?" I said, trying to suppress a smile.

"Yeah. Found the little fucker over at the creek." The old man's eyes grew as wide as an owl's. "Underneath that overhang of rocks."

I stared at him for a long time. Was there something back of what he was saying? "You shoot him, Donald?"

He shook his head. "Nope. Little fucker was already dead."

I felt my heart begin to pump just a little faster. "Where did you say you found him?"

"Creek. About a half-mile from the mill. Wouldn't have seen him if the water wasn't so low. No rain, you see. Waded in up to my knees, then found him where the creek bed rises up out of the water. Found lots a junk too. Commies are untidy bastards."

"So what did you do with him?" I said.

"Left the little bastard where he was, couldn't stand the smell."

"What'd he look like?"

He squeezed his eyebrows until they were no more than slits. "You shitting me boy, what kind of fool question is that?"

"What'd he look like? How was he dressed?"

"You sure you're a soldier? A soldier would know what a commie looks like."

I cursed myself for asking the question. Now he was doubting me, and I had to keep him going on this. I gave out a laugh that was none too convincing. "Sure I'm a soldier, Donald. A soldier just like you."

He stared at me through those thin slits a while more. "The fuck you are," he said and marched off back to his trailer.

I sat in the car for a while, debating whether I should go see Ellie-Mae and Mrs. Robard, or leave it for a more appropriate time. I didn't want to intrude on their grief, especially not Mrs. Robard having just lost her husband and son. Might be better to wait until I had something other than bad news to share.

I was greeted at the door to Clayton Burke's house by Ms. Nesbitt, who informed me that Mr. Burke had gone to his office. When I asked if that was his usual habit on a weekend I received a straight, no. I asked if Charlotte was there. She leveled her eyes at me, gave me a look that said, you lay a single finger on that girl you'll have me to deal with. I thanked her and scooted down the steps toward the safety of my car before her eyes could strike me down dead.

CHAPTER 27

The Office of the Marston County Prosecuting Attorney was officially opened on April 10, 1861, two days before cannon fire at Fort Sumter plunged the Confederacy into war with the Union. Then, the building was known as the Town Hall, and the design, although not as grand as the courthouse, still smacked of old money.

The ground floor was empty except for a Negro man about mid-sixties, hair turning to white, who was sweeping the floor when I walked in. He stopped sweeping, leant on the broom handle, and looked up at me.

"Help you, sir?"

"I need to see Mr. Burke, understand he's at his office today."

"Yes, sir. Up those stairs, second floor."

I thanked him and he went back to his sweeping, started whistling a tune that was familiar, but it wouldn't come to me.

Clayton Burke was indeed in his office, window open and the overhead fan on full power. I caught him sitting back in his swivel chair, tapping a pencil against his chin, staring out the window. I stood in the doorway watching him. Burke was a decorated soldier, something which, he never failed to remind the newspapers, was a 'humbling experience'.

A year after finishing his law degree he'd signed up for Korea, and it was during the Battle of the Pusan Perimeter that he risked his own life under heavy enemy fire and pulled a wounded senior officer back across a hundred yards of exposed battle zone to safety. And now the country was at war with Vietnam. I wondered at how many men would return, broken, physically and mentally damaged beyond repair. How many would return only to be forgotten? Burke had been one of the lucky few.

He put the pencil down on his desk, pressed his fingertips together, as if in prayer. What are you thinking? I wondered. The trial? Carl Robard? Did you feel the same connection to Carl that I did? It was certainly more real to me than imagined. Isn't it more real to you than the reporters and newspaper stories, the pats on the back, the congratulations from the Mayor, the framed certificates that hang on your office wall? I felt it during that moment of stillness in the courtroom, the moment when Carl Robard realized that something had separated and fallen away. Did you feel it too?

"Good afternoon, Mr. Bale."

That caught me off guard, but I recovered enough.

"Tom," I said.

He continued to stare out the window. "Right, we agreed first name terms."

"Didn't realize you knew I was here."

He pointed a finger at the window. "Your reflection."

He swung around, smiled, indicated that I should take a seat, so I did.

"So what brings you to my office on a hot Saturday afternoon?" he said.

I noticed the tiredness in his eyes. Their gray-green sparkle had all but disappeared. "I was going to ask you the same question," I said. "I drove out to your house and Ms. Nesbitt said you were at the office."

"I came here to think, too much noise at home."

I guessed he and Mrs. Clayton had drawn swords and continued battle this morning. "What about?"

"This and that."

I couldn't blame him for being deliberately evasive. After all, if Carl hadn't been shot and killed, he would have gone to the chair. To have second thoughts about the credibility of the trial wouldn't be something anyone would want to admit to. Still, the trial, what I saw of it, was a joke. I decided to approach it from a different angle, throw him a little and see if the rumor about him and his secretary were correct.

"You and Mrs. Burke seem at odds quite a bit."

He shrugged. "Couples have their spats. We're no different."

Fact of life. Jenny and me had a few, just minor stuff, but in the main we were truly happy with our lives. "Sure it happens, but you and Mrs. Burke…well it seemed like it had been going on some time. Wasn't a one-off."

He leant forward on his big oak desk, sighed, looked at me, and nodded. "When I got the chief prosecuting attorney's job, Maryanne's

219

father gave us the house, I won a few cases, got my face in the papers, and then it all started to turn a little sour. Everyone suddenly wanted a piece of my time: reporters, mayor, governor, businessmen, you name it. I'm out more than at home. Maryanne accompanies me to the charity balls and functions, but it's the lack of home life that gets to her."

"Your wife's father sounds like a very generous man."

"Oh, he is. Generous and very, very wealthy. That house and most of the furniture in it is all his. And to be honest, it's not really me. Maryanne's different. She's used to mixing with the social elite. Me? I'm just an ordinary Joe who's made a name for himself through study, hard work, and an absolute belief in what I do. Trouble is, I always feel I'm on the outside looking in."

"You don't seem to fit."

"Not at all. On the surface, yes, but it's all gloss. The mayor pats me on the back. We get our picture taken, but it just doesn't seem enough for Maryanne. Can't work out what she wants."

"Sorry if this seems a little flippant, but have you asked her?"

He fell back in his chair. "Sure I've asked her. Says she just wants me home more but I'm sure there's something else. She doesn't understand that to be someone in this town, this county, this state, you've got to be seen, heard, and successful." Then he looked at me rather sheepishly. "I'm thinking about running for governor in a couple of years. Vandiver will be coming to the end of his term. Got to do my share of palm pressing."

And there was my opportunity. "That's quite a calling," I said. "With you out so much you sure she doesn't suspect you of having an affair?"

He huffed, threw his hands in the air. "Jesus, I don't know. She's never said anything. In any case, she has nothing to worry about on that score. I don't play around. Heck, you've seen her. She's a fine-looking woman, why would I want to?"

I hadn't actually seen her face on account of the newspaper being stuck in front of it, but if the figure was anything to go by, she had it all. There was sincerity in Burke's voice and in his eyes, but he could be hiding something. Though why would his secretary make it up?

I noticed a file open on his desk. Reading upside down I saw the name Frank Delaney. It was dated five years earlier, and I asked him what he might be doing reviewing old case files.

"I got to thinking about what you said last night, Tom. Spent half the night pacing around, couldn't sleep, kept going over the trial in my head. Had I made a mistake, was there something I'd missed? Came here this morning, went through it all again and I have to say the prosecution side is watertight. Started going back through previous trials...just an innocent conscience feeling guilty I guess."

I thought about what I'd learned from Sam Cooper. Should I throw it out on the table or keep it to myself for now? Burke had been up half the night and spent the whole morning reviewing the trial. But was it to make sure he'd conducted his part of the trial correctly, or to cover up any mistakes, deliberate or otherwise? Despite all his posturing,

Burke seemed a decent enough man, and I doubted there would be anything untoward in the way he handled things.

"I've got something for you to think about."

He raised his eyes. "About the trial?"

I nodded. "Went to see a man called Sam Cooper this morning."

He shook his head trying to recall the name. "Cooper...Cooper...nothing comes to mind."

"I doubt you'd know him. Lives over on Dale Street, used to work with Carl Robard up at the mill."

"What of it?"

"In yesterday's *Tribune* they printed a full account of the trial, Carl's arrest, details about the evidence, and so on. Cooper tells it different."

He screwed his face up. "In what way different?"

"You know that crucifix found tangled in the victim's hair?"

"Yeah, so?"

"Cooper says there's no way that could have happened because Carl was paranoid about safety and would always remove it every morning and hang it in his locker. It was on a long chain and he was worried that it might get tangled in the machinery. The night before he was supposed to have raped and murdered Caitlin Dexter, he went to his locker at the end of his shift and his crucifix wasn't there. Told Cooper about it, asked him if he'd seen it, maybe dropped it on the floor. The two of them looked around, couldn't find it. In the end, Carl figured he must have lost it somewhere, or it got cleaned up with all the sawdust. He was real upset about it too on account that it was a gift from his mother."

Clayton reached over to a bundle of files on the left corner of his desk. He untied the retaining cord, flipped a file open, and sifted through papers. He pulled one out, laid it on the desk and with brow deeply furrowed, traced down the page with his right forefinger. His finger stopped.

"Here it is," he said. "List of evidence found at the scene. Gold crucifix found tangled in the victim's hair, identified by defendant as belonging to him, tested and found positive for his fingerprints. Defendant claimed he'd lost it the day before, as you say." He turned the page to me. "There it is, Tom. Plain as day."

"Well, either Sam Cooper is lying, or you got your facts wrong."

He stood up suddenly, face lightly flushed with anger. "You accusing me of something, Tom?"

I held up both hands in a gesture of peace. "I'm not accusing you of anything, Clayton, so calm down and just take it for what it is." His face lost a little of its color, and he began pacing behind his desk. "I'm only passing on what someone said. Up to you what weight you want to give it. Personally, I think Cooper was genuinely surprised to read that report in the paper."

Clayton stopped, wheeled round to me. "If that's the case, then why didn't he come forward as a witness?"

"Said he did. Told the sheriff and Cranver, apparently. Cranver said he would call him as a defense witness if required."

Clayton leafed through the file again. "Nothing," he said, throwing his hands in the air. "No mention of Cooper as a potential witness for the defense at all. His name doesn't appear anywhere."

"Maybe it was missed?"

"Yeah, and maybe Cranver investigated, found the statement inconclusive, and decided not to bring it to court. There's nothing more damaging than having testimony ripped apart during cross-examination."

"I get that," I said, having learned that valuable lesson a long time ago.

Hands stuffed into the pockets of his pants, suspenders stretched taut over his shoulders and chest, Clayton stared out the window at Julias Cranver's office across the town square. "It's funny," he said quietly. "Throughout the trial I did wonder about Cranver. I've known him to be a pretty sharp defense lawyer. But at other times, he seems lost."

"Could it be the drinking?" I asked.

"Could be?"

"Or something more?"

"Sometimes he seems troubled, overly nervous."

I asked him what he meant by that, see if it confirmed my feelings about Cranver's apparent total incompetence, but he chose to ignore it. Instead, he went over to a side table that was standing next to a floor to ceiling bookcase filled to bursting and picked up a newspaper. He flipped it open to page four, folded the paper in half, and laid it on his desk in front of me. A column had been circled in red pen.

"Take a read of that," he said.

So I did. It only took a minute or so, and I could see why it had him rattled. Staff reporter Cornell Tate had interviewed local grocery store owner Daniel Benson. Benson had a lot to say about the justice system and how the black community suffered because of its undeniably prejudiced leanings toward the protection of the white community's rights. He'd stated that it was unconstitutionally biased. What amazed me was how an article like that had come to be written in the first place, given how the South viewed its black population. I were a Southern man I'd be donning a pointy hat, rallying the clan, sticking burning crosses in the ground, and have Daniel Benson, Cornell Tate, and the editor of the newspaper hanging from the nearest tree by now. The article definitely came down on the plight of the black community, but I had to hand it to Tate because at least he dared to show a different side.

"I can see why this doesn't sit well with you."

"Doesn't sit well? The article practically accuses the system and me of racial prejudice and holding an unfair trial, goddammit."

"As I said last night, from where I sat it seemed like a done deal before the verdict was announced. I mean, apart from one token black person, how was that jury selected? If he were able, the jury foreman would have taken Carl to the electric chair himself." I held up a hand before Clayton could launch his next assault. It stopped him, but he was ready to go. "And before you say anything I don't mean you. I think you did your job, but I think other forces beyond your control conspired to make the outcome what it was."

"That's ridiculous. I would have known. You are directly accusing Judge Manning of…"

"No, I'm not. I heard what you said last night about the judge. It's not the judge."

"Who then?"

"Cranver. I think there's more to his so-called incompetence than meets the eye. I think it's more deliberate."

He sat down again, stared out the window some more. "But why," he said.

"As yet, I don't know. All I've got to go on is what I saw in that courtroom, Sam Cooper's story, and a twisting feeling in my gut. And I aim to get to the bottom of it. I could be wrong, but I don't think so. I just need to get people to open up a little so I can start digging into his background some more."

"Well, I think you're wrong. I think it is just a matter of drink which occasionally fails him. Carl Robard was guilty, and that's it."

"Then why have you been pacing around all night arguing with your conscience and spending all morning going through previous trials? You know something's not right, you're just trying to convince yourself that it isn't possible. You're too close to see through the fog and bullshit, see things for what they really are. But I tell you what, if I can't come up with something over the next few days, I'll call it quits and head back to Chicago. How does that sound?"

He took a long time before answering. "Fair enough, I guess."

"OK. We've got ourselves a deal. So, why don't you help me get to that point by telling me about that trial folder sitting on your desk?"

"How's that going to help?"

I smiled. "You wouldn't be going over it if Cranver wasn't involved."

"OK, OK. A few days, right. You find no evidence of anything remotely clandestine, and we're done?"

"You have my word."

A heavy sigh. "If it gets out that we've spoken about this, I'll be finished in this county. You do realize that don't you?"

I looked at him hard, so he was left in no doubt about my intent. "I'm a good investigator, Clayton. You have no need to concern yourself over my discretion."

Another sigh and then he began.

"A ten-year-old black girl was reported missing, and Sheriff Somers subsequently arrested a man by the name of Frank Delaney on suspicion of her abduction. Delaney lived alone in a big tumbledown farmhouse three-four miles out of town, an inheritance after his father died back in the spring of 48. Judge Manning issued the warrants for Delaney's arrest and for the search of his house. Delaney was a hoarder: books, newspapers, toys, clothes, cheap jewelry, junked items he found in the street. Almost anything that took his fancy ended up as part of his collection. Among the squalor, the police discovered crucial evidence of the girl having been there: a ring, a button from her dress, and a pink satin bow she had worn in her hair on the day of her disappearance, all identified by her mother.

"Delaney flatly denied having anything to do with the abduction, despite an intensive six-hour interrogation by Sheriff Somers and two of his deputies. Delaney shunned the opportunity of having a lawyer present, and that was duly noted on record. He was also noted as stating that, 'an innocent man don't need no lawyer'. He couldn't understand how those items had gotten into his house, and assumed that he must have picked them up at some point during his travels around the town and surrounding countryside. I mean, his house was stacked with stuff. The sheriff pushed hard, but Delaney denied everything."

"I'm guessing they didn't find the body?"

"Correct. With no body the sheriff had nothing."

"I'm also guessing that Delaney was eventually tried and convicted?"

"Yes. The sheriff conducted another more exhaustive search of his house. They lifted prints off everything, compared them to other prints taken from items in the girl's bedroom. None matched. The sheriff went back a third time, convinced that Delaney was their man, and then Deputy Swales discovered the young girl's right little finger in an old cantilever toolbox in the basement. The tiny scar on the underside of the finger was again identified by the girl's mother."

"What about the body?"

"It all seemed to hang together, but with the absence of a body, we thought conviction would be impossible. Still, we developed a case based on the discovered evidence, the type of character Delaney was, his mental state, his previous two convictions; one for theft and another for child molestation—an offense he'd committed fifteen years previous as a seventeen-year-old on a girl five years younger, and the finger, which we understood to be one of his trophies, part of his collection. But with no body, no matching fingerprints, and no witnesses, any judge could legitimately throw the case out of court."

"So, how did you manage to obtain a conviction?"

"We buried ourselves in research and eventually unearthed an almost identical case whereby the defendant, a middle-aged man from Rock Hill, South Carolina, had been successfully tried and convicted of the abduction and murder of a ten-year-old white boy a decade before, even though the body was never found."

"And so Frank Delaney was convicted and sentenced to death."

Clayton nodded.

"Who was the defense lawyer?" I asked, already knowing the answer.

"Julias Cranver. Court appointed."

"The judge?"

Clayton hesitated, reluctant. He closed the file, sighed heavily. "Manning," he said finally.

Swales discovered the finger. Cranver was the court appointed defense lawyer. Manning was the trial judge. Coincidence? I didn't think so. The look on Clayton's face spoke volumes, and I didn't need to tell him what was running through my head at that moment. He was thinking the exact same thing.

"Any other cases involving missing girls since then?"

"A couple. Nina Brown and Jessie Dubois."

"Black?"

"As I recall. Is that of significance?"

"Either girl found?"

"No. Nobody arrested either. Where you headed with this, Tom? People from the black community go missing all the time. Family members migrate between one another. Hard to keep track."

"But you know about those two girls."

"Only because they were reported missing. Most of the time, nobody says anything."

"Alice's mother reported her missing, and Deputy Carson helped her fill out the missper report. But then Carson got a call from county to say his wife had been taken in and was about to give birth. Carson went straight to the hospital and can't remember what he did with the report. When I checked back in May, Larry Swales and the sheriff swore blind they didn't know anything about it."

"And that leads you to think…what exactly?"

"Well, it does explain why the sheriff didn't start an investigation the moment Ellie-Mae reported it, but even though that may have been a genuine mistake, it kind of falls into line with all the other misinformation."

Clayton crooked his head to one side. "If indeed there is any," he said, slightly accusatory. I got up, extended a hand, and thanked him. "I'll be back," I said.

"I don't doubt it," Clayton said as I left his office.

The old man was still sweeping the floor when I got down the stairs. He stopped sweeping and leant on the broom handle, a position he seemed to favor when the moment took him to break from his duties. We nodded to each other, and I felt his eyes on me as I left the building. He started up whistling the same tune. Bugged me that I couldn't put a name to it.

I had to go see Dan Benson. There was a lot of anger and frustration in those remarks quoted in the newspaper. Was there more to tell?

CHAPTER 28

I found the front door to his store locked. I knocked a couple of times, cupped my hands around my face to shield my eyes from the sun's glare, and peered through the window for signs of life. Nothing. I stepped back, surveyed the building for an open window or any indication that he was at home.

I continued along the sidewalk until I came to where Johnson intersected with Main and turned left. Twenty yards along I found a back alley, turned down it and saw rear access doors, presumably used for deliveries. I counted down the doors in the cool shade of the alley until I found the one I wanted. It was propped open.

Daniel Benson was on the telephone when I rapped on the door. He was hunched over an old roll-top desk with the phone clutched in his right hand, shuffling through papers as he spoke. He looked up at the tapping sound and saw who it was standing in the doorway. He replaced the receiver, stood up.

I was suddenly very aware of the man's size. A little taller than me at about six-three, but much broader and muscular, with big hands and thick forearms. Not a man to mess with. I could see his eyes were bloodshot, either from the lack of sleep or maybe alcohol induced. The plaid shirt and pants were creased like he'd spent a restless night in a chair. He gestured for me to step inside and sat back down.

I was in a small room, about twelve-by-ten with a wooden floor coated in a light film of dust and grit. A steel cabinet stood next to the roll-top and there was a rack of shelving on the wall to his left filled with alphabetically ordered box files. A framed black-and-white photograph hung on the wall to the right of the shelving. It was a grainy image, with the exposure just off the mark of Benson standing in the center of a boxing ring holding aloft a silver trophy. I read the inscription at the bottom of the photo. *'Daniel Benson, Southern Gloves Champion 1938'*. He caught me looking at it. "I was twenty-eight back then," he said. "Two years later I went to war." I nodded, impressed. "Please, Tom, take a seat."

He pointed to an old, winged button-back chair stuck in a vacant corner of the office. The chair was at least half a century older than its owner and over the years the texture and color of the leather had turned from a taut, rich burgundy to an aged, creased peach skin. I eased into it and briefly closed my eyes. There was an immediate sense of history in that chair; of roaring fires in winter, of cigars being smoked after dinner, of newspapers being read, and cards being shuffled. I felt as though I could stay there forever.

"Feels good, don't it?" he said.

I caressed the faded leather arms. "It's like stepping back in time."

"My father used to say the very same thing and I feel the same way every time I sit in it."

"There's history in this chair," I said and crossed my legs.

We stared at each other in silence for several beats. I saw a man with quiet confidence and a moral conviction that made me feel at ease in his presence.

"So what brings you here, Tom?"

Little point in preamble. Get right to it. "I read the article in the *Tribune*. You've got a lot to say about the justice system, Dan."

He gave me a thin smile. "And I guess you feel that I should explain myself?"

"You don't have to explain yourself to me, but I am curious to know why."

He took his time to answer. "Known the Robard family for better than twenty years," he said finally. "Good people. Jason and Carl worked hard, took pride in what they did and how they conducted themselves. Carl Robard was no more a killer than my Rosie there." He pointed a thick finger at the eight by ten framed picture sat on his desk.

I stared at a head and shoulders shot of a fresh-faced looking woman with fluffy, light-brown hair, kind eyes and skin the color of porcelain. She looked to be around thirty-eight to forty and had a smile so natural that a genuine warmth and love of life seemed to radiate right out of the picture.

"Your wife?"

For several moments, he appeared to become lost in the image. Memories.

"Yeah," he said quietly. "She left me about six years back."

Divorced; not an easy thing to live with. "I'm sorry," I said, meaning it.

The big man sighed. "Life takes all sorts of twists and turns. Sometimes it can be very cruel."

I thought about Jenny. Cruel didn't even come close. "If you don't mind me saying, it seemed you were blaming Clayton Burke for what happened in the courtroom yesterday?"

"No. I said it's the justice system. That's what I said to the reporter." He leaned forward, eyes hardening. "And Clayton Burke is part of that system."

"He don't make the rules," I said, wondering why I was suddenly defending a man I didn't yet completely trust.

"Maybe not, but he don't play fair by them either."

I sat forward, spread my hands. I chose not to let on that I had been to see Clayton Burke. "Burke is a much-respected lawyer in this county and beyond from what I can gather. I don't think he'd take too kindly to that accusation."

"Don't you now?" Benson said, leaning into the challenge, eyes gaining intensity.

This was not turning out how I'd planned, but I wasn't going to give up just yet. If anything could be said about me, it was that I always saw both corners of an argument. "He's doing what the justice system requires of him. To a great degree his hands are tied. If the defense can't pull together a strong enough case, then the prosecutor isn't to blame."

Benson sat back in his chair, turned his big hands palms upwards. "Then we ain't got much to say to each other. You know, when I first met you, I considered you a decent man with morals and a high sense of what's right and wrong. You came down here at your own expense to find Alice Jackson and I thought that was a real decent thing to do. But now I'm so sure that the man sitting in front of me measures up to my first reckoning of him. So, I bid you good day, Tom."

And with that, he turned his attention back to the papers on his desk.

I rubbed my forehead, frustration and anger at myself for getting us started on the wrong foot. It sat there, simmering just below my temper threshold.

"Look," I said. "I didn't come here spoiling for a fight. I want to know the reasons behind what you said."

Benson concentrated on the papers. "Not just me. Most folks who know the Robard family are of similar mind."

"Yeah, that may be. But you're the only one to put it in writing."

He stared at the photograph of his wife and some of the fire in him seem to die. "Maybe I shouldn't have said what I did. Maybe it was the drink talking?" He paused, reflecting. "I'm not much of a drinking man, Tom. Only two times in my life when I've let the bottle touch my lips more than it should have. Once was the day my Josie passed away and the other time was yesterday. It just got too much and so I walked to Nathan's and had a few too many."

So his wife had died. That's what he meant when he said she'd left him. Assumption, I thought. It was never good to assume anything. "And Cornell Tate... just happened to be there?"

"That's correct. He was outside when I left, hustling folks for their comments. Caught me at just the right moment."

"So, you spoke up about truth and justice. That's fine, but what was the reasoning behind it?"

He shrugged. "I'm a friend, that's all. And I know Carl could not have done those things he was found guilty of."

"That's it?" I asked, incredulous. "There's got to be more of a reason for you to say what you did, something more to it than just being a friend."

He eyed me suspiciously. "You searching for something, Tom? You didn't just come here to find out about my thoughts on the legal system, did you? What's back of all this?"

"Have you been to court at all this week?"

"When I could. Got a business to run. Times are hard enough as it is. I did think about going yesterday, but you know Lucas passed away?"

"I heard. Want to know what he said after you went to serve that customer?"

Benson shrugged those big shoulders. "Doubt it'd make much difference now."

"You told him to take care of himself. And you know what he said? 'Sure thing...Dan'."

"Well, wouldn't you know it," he said, smiling. "After all these years he finally calls me by my first name, and I wasn't there to hear it."

"Guess he knew his time was up."

"Guess he did at that."

"So, how did you get to hear about the verdict, then?" I said, pulling us back on track. "What prompted you to head up to Nathan's bar?"

"Deputy Larry Swales," Benson said in a single heaving breath. "Walked right into the store, had that stupid grin on his face. He knew I was a friend of the family, and it was like he couldn't wait to break the news." Benson lowered his voice and his eyes turned to stone. "One of these days I'm gonna tear that stupid shit-kicking grin right off his face."

I wondered if Daniel had eyed his opponents in the boxing ring with that very same look, and if it had chilled them as much as it did me at that moment. I glanced at my watch and rose to leave. I held out a hand. "I've got to be someplace else now, Dan. Thanks for your time."

He seemed to loom over me as he shook my hand, dwarfing it in his own. "I'm not sure we resolved anything, Tom, but thank you for coming to see me. The fact that you had the decency to at least ask the questions tells me the measure of you."

"For what it's worth, I don't think Carl murdered those girls, either."

He nodded his big silver-gray head. "Now I got the real reason why you came to see me. You're investigating Caitlin Dexter's murder, too."

"And I don't intend to let it go."

"Well, as you've already experienced, there's not too many people forthcoming with information in this town."

"Ain't that the truth?"

"Small town. Folks are very protective of each other. You start casting doubt over how the case was handled, might cause upset. Some people got a lot to lose."

I knew who he meant but chose not to acknowledge it.

"I'm staying over at the motel," I said. "Think of anything, let me know." I bid him good day and was about to leave when he stopped me.

"Oh, and there was something else."

I felt the rush of energy into my stomach again. "What?"

"Lucas. He said something about that Caitlin girl."

"What about her?"

He thought for a moment, squeezing his bushy eyebrows together, shook his head. "Damn, it just won't come to me. But I'm sure there was something back of it."

Try as I might, I couldn't recall the conversation. A lot had happened since we spoke yesterday morning, easy for the mind to become fogged. "If it comes to you let me know, could be important."

"I'll be sure to."

"You like your music, Tom?"

A little strange but I went with it. "Sure, jazz, blues, swing. Got my favorites, but I'll listen to most stuff if it's good. Why?"

"Just thinking you might want to pay a visit to Louis Shine's Juke Joint down in the Bottoms tonight. They got a fine blues band on. Do you some good to mix with the folks. Get to know them a little better. There'll be people from neighboring towns, who knows what you might find out."

"Thanks, I might just do that," I said, leaving out that Charlotte had already invited me.

"Might help you get where you need to be."

Strange thing to say. "In what way do you mean?"

"Just go. You'll like it. Great music, great people. Louis Shine's quite a character."

I stepped out into the cool shade of the alleyway, mind churning thoughts and ideas. When I got out of the alley, the full force of the late afternoon sun hit me square between the eyes like a battering ram.

Time for a shower. Time to think.

CHAPTER 29

I lay back on my bed head, propped up against pillows, a position I seemed to have found myself in on many occasions since I first came down to Paradise Creek. Almost like a second home. I had a towel around my waist and was turning an unlit cigarette around in my fingers, and occasionally popping it between my lips just to remove it again a few moments later. There wasn't any whiskey on my bedside table or any balancing on my chest.

Not this time.

More than a whole day and a half had passed since Carl Robard stood to face the judge and be told that his life was going to end in some chair up at the state penitentiary. Doused in water, a wet sponge and leather cap strapped to his head, the executioner's hand ready on the switch, and that agonizing few minutes while the prison chaplain recited the words that no man ever thought he would hear.

And then the nod.

And then the switch.

Witnesses: the men and women required to be at such executions, would sit patiently, some smoking, some chatting, some sitting in quiet reflection, and most, in their own way, thinking of themselves as

241

superior over the man sat only a few feet away. They were good, and he was evil. But when that switch was thrown, and they saw the physical reaction of the man arching up in the chair against the leather straps, white foam spewing between clenched teeth, veins standing out on his neck and on the back of his hands and arms like ropes, then some would look away horrified while others squirmed but couldn't take their eyes off the spectacle. And then there were those witnesses who relished, salivated over what they saw.

Especially if the man was a Negro.

Adding more to the timeline, I went back over it, asking myself what I really had, what was significant, what could I make of everything I'd come to learn over this past day or so. Sam Cooper had been insistent that Carl had lost his crucifix before he left the mill the evening before Caitlin Dexter's murder, a story clearly disputed by the fact that it was found tangled in her hair. Carl's blood had been found on the victim's body and clothing. Timing matched as well. Carl would have left work and be on his way home about the same time Caitlin was murdered, her body discovered in the long grass just a little ways off the path he'd taken. Witnesses testified under oath they saw him walking that way home. Coop had told me Carl's pickup was over at Corey Peters' being fixed, so he would have had to walk home. Leroy, his usual companion, was off that day.

Cooper also told me that Floyd Tibbett had asked Carl to fetch two new cutters that same morning from the storage barn behind the mill and replace the worn ones on his machine. Carl had cut his hand badly on the teeth when he was removing the old blades, had to have his hand bandaged up. That, of course, would account for Carl's blood being on the victim.

It did, if you ignored Cooper's story about the crucifix, all make perfect sense. A young male in his early twenties sees a pretty white girl walking along on her own. It's a gathering dusk, there's no one around, it's hot, he's frustrated, and he takes his chance. Maybe he tries to talk to her first, and she refuses him. Inside, he's boiling up and ready. Things get out of hand. She struggles and screams maybe. He grabs her by the throat, squeezes until she can't make a sound, leaves traces of blood from his cut hand on her skin. After he's done, he panics, doesn't think about the crucifix which she has ripped from his neck during the struggle, and which gets tangled in her hair.

Yeah, it all made sense.

But it didn't at all. Could Carl really have raped and murdered Alice Jackson and Caitlin Dexter, and perhaps the three missing girls as well?

And what about Frank Delaney: watertight evidence, Cranver as his defense lawyer, and Judge Manning presiding. Three times Delaney's house was searched, and finally the crucial piece of evidence was discovered by Larry Swales.

My watch told me it was 6 p.m. Saturday night, and I had a little time to visit Nat's Bar, to see what gossip I could stumble into before meeting Charlotte at Louis Shine's place. I couldn't wait to see her.

Sure enough, Coop was propped up on a stool by the bar, head bowed low, with a bottle of Wild Turkey, a glass tumbler, and a beer in front of him. It was still early evening, but he was already displaying signs of inebriation, probably helped by the number of beers he'd put away earlier when I was at his house. I joined him, unscrewed the cap off the bourbon, and poured him another two fingers and myself a single. The jukebox was playing Hank Locklin's "Please Help Me I'm Falling". There were a number of people occupying tables, playing pool, and talk was casual, inconsequential.

"Been thinking over that conversation we had earlier," I said.

"What of it?"

"Couple of things still a bit fuzzy in my head and I need some perspective."

"Nah, you're better to leave well alone. What's done is done, told you that? Ain't nothin' you can do."

"That's what everyone keeps telling me. Everyone that is, except the questions running around in my head."

"There's no more I can tell you. You got all I know. Some odd things happened when Carl got arrested. He got put on trial, found guilty, and now he's dead. Story over."

Time passed without another word being spoken. The juke box played "Billy Bayou" by Jim Reeves. Nat left the bourbon for us to help ourselves and a half-hour later it was down by a third.

I paid a visit to the men's room and on my return saw Coop throw some notes and loose change on the counter. He waved at Nat and slipped off his bar stool, cigarettes tucked into his shirt pocket, the bottle of Wild Turkey crooked in his left arm.

"You drive safely now," Nat shouted across the room.

"Be fine," Coop said, flipping a hand in the air. I watched him walk unsteadily to the door and let himself out. I couldn't let him drive in that condition, so I too left some money on the counter and stepped out to watch the sun's boiling copper-red flame disappearing into a gathering twilight.

Coop was swaying against the driver's door of his Chevy Impala, fumbling with the keys which he dropped, cursed, then went down on one knee and scratched around in the dust and shingle until he found them. He rested his head against the door for a moment. He really was in no fit state, so I did the honorable thing. Getting him into the front seat of the Dodge was no mean feat. Coop was a heavy man and by the time I got him buckled in I was ready for another shower and change. I laid the bottle of Wild Turkey on the rear seat and decided that after I got him settled, I would go back to the motel for a change of shirt before heading over to Louis Shine's.

I hadn't been driving for more than a couple of minutes when a truck seemed to come out of nowhere. It overtook and then slewed real close in front. So close I had to brake hard for fear of hitting the rear fender. The bottle of Wild Turkey shot forward from the back straight between mine and the passenger seat where Coop, just a dead weight, strained against the seat belt, his head jerking forward and then back. He grunted, licked his lips, and continued to snore. The bottle, no seatbelt to halt its trajectory, smashed into a thousand fragments against the dash. Bourbon sprayed everywhere, and the smell blew up into my nostrils. I uselessly screamed obscenities through my windshield at the truck, but it didn't stop and within a few seconds had crossed the Georgia railroad tracks, turned a bend in the road and was lost in the night.

I cleaned up with spit and a handkerchief, then picked up as much of the glass as I could see and dumped it on the grass verge.

I had all four windows down as I drove Coop back to Dale Street. The smell of bourbon was strong, sickly, but thankfully the night air circulating through the car took some of it away. It would be a while before the smell left entirely, if it ever did.

I got Coop through the front door of his bungalow settled him safely on his bed, removed his shoes, and shut the blinds. I found paper and a pen in the kitchen, wrote him a note, which I left with his keys on the kitchen table.

Getting into my car, a feeling of intense unease suddenly crawled over me. I looked up and down the street expecting to see the truck bearing down on me, but it was empty, silent.

Back at the motel I tried to clean up the car some more, then changed out of my clothes. It was just gone nine by the time I got to Louis Shine's Juke Joint.

CHAPTER 30

The Juke Joint sat on a flat bed of red clay at the end of a long, tree-shrouded, winding dirt road. It wasn't a big place, L-shaped and about forty feet at its longest point. The building was a ramshackle affair built out of timber and tin, with a blackened smokestack sticking out of the upper left wall at an angle. Above the entrance door were a few tinplate advertising signs for Coca-Cola, Pabst Blue Ribbon, and Lucky Strike, and above those was a hoarding proudly displaying the Juke Joint owner's name. You couldn't fail to miss it. Louis Shine's name lit up in eighteen-inch-high italics. Several cars were parked outside; a couple of Fords, an old tan Buick, a smart new Chrysler, and a year-old Plymouth with huge stabilizer fins at the rear. I wondered how anyone from the Bottoms could afford to purchase such an automobile. All I'd ever seen around these parts were a couple of old pickups and a flatbed truck.

I parked away from the rest over by a bank of trees, keeping the car in shadow. Staring across at the building, I heard the sound of laughter through the timber walls, saw pin spots of light poking through the knot holes, and began to doubt the wisdom of me coming here, a white man from Chicago. Yeah, I'd fit right in.

247

A group of black men who I didn't recognize were smoking outside the entrance. Must have been from a different town, certainly not from around here. They fell silent as I approached. Uniformly dressed in gray and tan suits, shirts opened to mid-chest, and scuffed shoes spotted with dust, one of them, a tall hard-looking man moved to block my path.

"Looking for something?" he said, his voice thick and deep with a low-down power that vibrated in your chest.

I stared into his eyes. They were like blackened steel pins under the moon. I'm not going to be welcome here, I thought. Not at all. But I stood my ground, measuring myself against him, reading the hostility in his eyes. I said nothing. He moved to one side after a long moment and let me pass. I climbed the steps to the entrance door, hesitated, then pushed. Sudden laughter from the group of men died as the door closed behind me.

The atmosphere inside was dingy, the air thick with cigarette smoke. Through the gloom, I could see a makeshift stage situated over in the far-right corner, illuminated by a few colored spots. The stage was raised up off the floor about two feet. A small set of drums sat center stage and there were a couple of guitar combos to either side, flaps of black and brown vinyl hanging off them, a testament to their life on the road.

In front of the stage was an area for dancing and filling the gap between that and the entrance were rows of wooden chairs and beer ringed tables, most of them occupied. To the left was a small counter with a couple of shelves behind it stacked full of liquor bottles and beyond that a black door with a silver star painted on it, which I took to be the dressing room. I let out a small laugh at the ridiculous idea of having a dressing room in such an establishment.

There was a sudden shift in the atmosphere. Eyes turned toward me, and silence gathered in the room. I felt every muscle in my body tighten. Sweat beaded on my forehead, the palms of my hands got clammy. A man's voice pushed through the tension.

"Took your time getting here, Chicago Man?"

I was expected. I turned toward the direction of the voice and my eyes rested on an old man of medium height with a bald head, deep, sunken eyes, prominent cheekbones, and a row of teeth made you think you were looking at a skull with a piano keyboard for a mouth. I guessed his age at about seventy. He wore a black T-shirt with the inscription, 'It's Always Time to Shine' printed across the front in white letters. The lettering had to be set in two lines because the man's chest was so narrow, crafted more like a bird's.

"I came here looking for Charlotte," I said.

From a table over near the rear wall, a voice I recognized said, "It's OK, Louis, we'll take it from here."

Viola Nesbitt stood up, and I felt relieved as the room erupted with talk and laughter again. A tall man dressed in a brown pin-stripe stood up next to Viola. Underneath the porkpie hat I saw handsome features and kind eyes. They came over to me and Viola introduced me to her husband, Amory.

"Glad you could make it, Mr. Bale," Viola said. "Amory got some things you might want to hear."

I said nothing.

Amory shook my hand. "Mr. Bale," he said, voice sounding like he had swallowed a sack full of marbles. "At last we meet."

"I'll leave you gentlemen to talk," Viola said and wandered back to her table.

Confused, I asked what it was he had to tell me.

Amory put an arm around my shoulders and guided me to the far end of the room and around the corner into the foot of the L-shape. The old man with the T-shirt went to the bar and brought over two bottles of beer.

"It's quieter here," Amory said. We sat at a vacant table and the bottles were placed in front of us. "This here's Louis Shine, Mr. Bale. He's the owner of this establishment."

I held out a hand, but it was ignored. Instead, Louis Shine said, "He going to see Miss Veronique, Amory?"

"Uh-huh."

"Good." And with that, he turned away and went back to the bar.

"Who the hell is Miss Veronique?" I asked, wondering how it was I hadn't already met these people and what in hell was going on.

Amory smiled and his dark eyes danced. "Oh, you'll find out soon enough. She got a way to make you see things a little clearer."

I sat back, frowning. "What does that mean?"

"I said you'll find out. Now, I need to tell you something that's been bothering me since early this morning."

"I actually came here to see Charlotte."

"Heard you was taking an interest. But all in good time. She's around somewhere."

Amory sipped his beer, placed the bottle back on the table, turned it with his fingers, wiped the condensation off the label with a large thumb.

"There's a guy lives round here, an ex-Korean vet by the name of Donald Averly. He's a little off the wall." Amory circled a finger at the side of his head. "But he's harmless enough. Thinks he's still in the jungle hunting down commies. Every so often, he takes to the booze and goes out into the swamp—on maneuvers as he likes to call it—well, he was telling Viola that he found a dead body, a commie he suspected, under that big rocky overhang at the creek."

I knew all this from my own audience with Donald Averly. "Yeah, spoke to him earlier today, told me the same thing."

"Is that right?"

"Yeah. He'd just got back he told me. Pants were still wet from the creek."

"He didn't say nothing to me. Anyway, you can't always rely on what's factual and what's not, after all he is a little gone in the head but way he described it to Viola kind of made me think it was for real."

I coughed as cigarette smoke steeled its way down my throat. "Have you reported it to the sheriff?"

Amory shook his head. "No, sir. I been chewing on it all day, but the missus, she went and told Daniel Benson this morning. And he had something to share with her too."

"What was that?"

"About the missing boy nobody seems to know anything about."

And there it was. It came at me in a sudden surge of realization, and a piece of this complex jigsaw I was trying to put together fitted and fitted tight. So that's what Dan Benson couldn't remember. Lucas James had mentioned seeing Caitlin Dexter holding hands with a boy as they were walking into town.

My voice was low and urgent. "You think the body in the creek is that young boy?"

Amory shrugged. "Maybe yes, maybe no. As I said, I been wondering on it all day."

"Could be this Donald Averly made it up?" I said.

"Could be but I don't think so. I think you need to check it out for yourself."

"Why don't you?"

He recoiled as if I'd slapped him hard across the face. "Oh no, Mr. Bale. Not my business, not my place. Someone less connected with this town would make more sense. Sheriff wouldn't listen to me."

Too scared of what the consequences might be, I thought. "OK, Amory, I get what you're saying. Tell me how to get there and I'll go take a look tomorrow."

Viola came over and sat down. "Music's gonna be starting soon. You gentlemen finished?"

"Not quite," Amory said. "There's something else."

"Go on," I said.

Amory took another sip of beer, breathed in and then relaxed. "Folks around here appreciate what you done for Ellie-Mae, finding Alice and all."

"Thanks. I did what I could."

"But there's more gone missing over the years and relying on the system to help, you might as well piss in the wind."

"Amory Nesbitt," Viola snapped. "Where you getting off talking like that?"

Amory looked at his wife, his eyes softened. "Sorry, just got a little carried away."

"Well, just don't be getting carried away any more."

Amory held up his hands in apology. "Another thing."

I waited.

"Go see a guy called Sam Cooper, lives over on Dale Street. Used to work alongside Carl at the mill. Maybe he can help?"

I held back about the specifics of my conversation with Cooper but said that I'd already spoken to him.

"He give you much?"

"Some."

"Well, go talk to him again, he know more than he let on."

"Like what?" I asked, wondering if Coop really had any more information to give.

Amory finished his beer, got up, and went over to the bar. The conversation appeared to be over. I looked at Viola and threw my hands in the air.

253

"No good asking me, Mr. Bale. Just do as Amory says, go see Sam Cooper."

I was about to say something but was drowned out by Louis Shine's voice over the microphone. Feedback squealed through the PA system and someone unseen adjusted the levels.

Louis Shine had a cigarette in his left hand. He put it to his mouth and then blew smoke into the microphone. "OK, OK," he said. "For your pleasure, we got some old friends come back pay us a visit."

The door with the star on it opened and a black man of medium height, with hunched shoulders stepped out, his right arm held aloft, hand gripping a pair of drumsticks.

"Will you please welcome all the way from Jackson, Mississippi, Mr. Sticks Smith on the skins."

The man was about sixty years old I guessed but mounted the small stage with a speed and agility that belied his age. He wore light-brown pants, a white shirt, and a creased pork-pie hat just like Amory's. He sat behind the drum kit, tapped out a quick rhythm and bowed his head slightly to the applause and the cheers that greeted him.

"Thank you," he said into his microphone.

Louis Shine faced the crowd again, blew another cloud of smoke over the front row. "From Lafayette, Louisiana, Mr. Toots Moyelle on the bass guitar."

Another man, younger this time but no less than fifty, stepped out into the spotlights, climbed the stage and stood over to the left of Sticks. He had a Fender bass around his neck, picked up the curly guitar lead draped over his combo and plugged it in. To much cheering and applause he said, "Uh-huh," through his microphone.

"Listen up now," Louis Shine said. "Back by popular demand, we got Mr. Amory Nesbitt on the blues harp." Amory came forward, grinning his wide grin, waving his harmonica at the crowd.

"Back by popular demand?" someone shouted from over by the door. "He ain't ever left." Laughter and cheering filled the room.

Louis Shine batted down the laughter. "Dropping by while on his latest tour and paying his respects to the good people down here in the Bottoms…Mr. Clarence King on lead guitar."

The room erupted as an immensely proportioned man, aged somewhere between forty and fifty stepped over to his microphone and bowed to the audience. He had close-cropped black hair, wide brown eyes, skin the color of coffee beans and a fat cheerful face. He was dressed in an immaculate white two-piece suit with a matching bow tie. Resting at an angle against his ample stomach was a cherry-red colored double cutaway Gibson 335 guitar.

"And finally," Louis Shine shouted over the riotous applause. "From La Grange, Georgia, our very own Ms. Honey, Peach-Pie De-Souza."

A tall strikingly handsome black woman in her late thirties walked up to Louis Shine with the slow grace of a leopard. The men in the audience cheered and blew wolf whistles while the women clapped respectfully and attempted to disguise their obvious envy. Ms. De-Souza wore a blood-red, knee length satin dress that did nothing to hide her physical attributes. Her jet-black hair had been straightened and cut into the Jackie Kennedy style. Her long, brown legs tapered down into matching blood-red high-heels.

I leaned toward Viola. "That's quite a name," I said. "Peach-Pie."

"You really interested in the name, or you concentrating on the body?" Viola said, with a 'typical man' expression on her face.

I prodded my chest, smiling all innocence. "Me?" I said.

"Yeah, you. You men are all the same. I even have to remind Amory that he's a married man when Honey De-Souza's in town."

I laughed. "Where does the Peach-Pie come from?"

"You'll know it when she sings. Honey ain't her real name but she's called that cause her voice is as thick and rich as Honey and Georgia peach pie. Any case, thought you had the eye for Charlotte."

I swept the audience, couldn't see her anywhere. "Know where she is?" I said.

Viola's face cracked into a smile. "Around."

I looked some more but there was no sign of her. I studied the audience. Some were dressed conspicuously better than others, but mostly the folks wore the same style of clothing; men in bland, gray or brown pants with open-necked shirts or T-shirts, women with flower-print dresses and maybe a string of artificial pearls around their necks.

"These people all from around here?" I asked.

"Some. Others from neighboring towns, 'cept those folk on the stage of course."

"Yeah, I wondered about that. They've come hundreds of miles just to play at this juke joint? Doesn't make any sense."

"Used to be a famous place way back. People would come from all over just to be seen and heard here. Times change though. The depression, war, people die, people move on. Still, some are happy to come back."

Louis Shine started up with another announcement. "Now all these good people behind me," he said, waving a hand in their direction, "are staying over for the church service tomorrow. I know you folks ain't got much, but I'm gonna pass Amory's hat around and I wanna see you dig as deep as you can for Jessie Robard and the twins."

I fished my wallet out, opened it, and counted out forty dollars. I gave it to Viola.

"I best be going, I'm absolutely bushed. Put it in the hat will you?"

Viola took the money. "I will, thank you, Mr. Bale."

"It's not much, but…"

"It's fine. It's more than most folks around here earn in a week. Now you be sure to heed what Amory told you." She nodded over to a door set deep in the back wall of the 'L'. "Probably best if you go out that way." She turned before I could say any more, picked up her drink and went back to her table.

I watched my money disappear into Amory's hat, walked over to the door, and back out into the humid summer night. I stood at the rear of the juke joint, breathing in sweet air and thinking how dark it was. The stars and moon seemed to have vanished from the night sky, replaced by a gigantic veil of total blackness. I focused my eyes and stepped forward. A breeze came up and brushed my face, an owl hooted in the distance.

And that was the last I saw of Saturday night.

CHAPTER 31

I came awake disoriented, dizzy. I shook my head several times trying to draw focus on the shapes around me, but all was a blur. It felt like I was swimming in a sea of molasses, my arms drawing back, legs kicking, fighting for breath, fingers clawing for the surface but getting nowhere. The struggle seemed immense.

Time passed in a strange dream in which an earthenware bowl was pushed between my lips, forced upward by an unseen hand, urging me to swallow the warm, bitter tasting liquid. I retched, wanted to bend over and be sick but more hands held me steady. And slowly, as the seconds passed, the feeling of nausea evaporated and my head cleared. The hands that held me fell away, shapes melted into dark, and mist rose like devil's fingers from the marshes, clutching at the overhanging branches of gum and cypress trees. Flames and gray smoke rose from a large bonfire some thirty feet away, dead tree branches cracked and spit, and the brackish odor of the swamp mixed with the smell of burning wood played with my senses. The moon was high, its incandescent light reflecting on the black swamp water.

I shook my head some more, noticed that my jacket had been removed and my shirt was open to the waist. My chest and stomach were streaked in red, and I deftly felt for wounds thinking I'd been injured. I couldn't feel any cuts and I wasn't in pain but when I drew my hands away my fingertips were coated in what looked and felt like blood.

An old woman came toward me, small, her movement filled with intent. Silver hair blew back from the face; the eyes were deep and as black as coal. Something metallic rattled and a bony hand gripped my chin, long fingernails scratched my flesh. The hand was strong, the face inches from mine. Fire reflected in her eyes, liquor and tobacco on the breath, gaps between the rotting teeth. The bony fingers dug into my skin, the black eyes bored into my own.

"I see good intentions," the old woman said, her voice rough, the throat cauterized by years of bourbon and cigars.

She held my face in her grip for several moments, released me and stepped back. I automatically raised a hand and felt along my jawline. The strength of her grip had been astonishing, and my jaw hurt as though it had been clamped in a vise. I studied her in the firelight, the long robes, bracelets hanging from her wrists, a cigar burning in her left hand, wooden beads, pendants, and charms around her neck. I caught the texture of her skin, the structure of her face. Her flesh was taut and leathery, the color of burnished copper in the fire. She was most definitely of African descent however the shape of her nose was most certainly not of Negro design. Somewhere in her history, there was Indian blood.

"Cherokee," she said as if reading my mind. "Some came south from the Appalachians and mixed with the Muskogee before they were driven out of their homes and forced to resettle. My great grandfather had a daughter by a Cherokee squaw. The daughter stayed but his woman was taken from him. She died like many others on the 'trail of tears'. You know what that is, you know your history, Mr. Bale?"

I nodded, recalling with instant clarity. Tens of thousands of Indians died from exposure, disease, and starvation, as they were forcibly removed from their homelands and resettled in Oklahoma. All-in-all 25 million acres of land had been forcibly given up to help settlement of Whites. Sometimes this country's history appalled me.

"I can see you are not taken with what happened?"

"A terrible time," I said.

The old woman drew on her cigar. Smoke engulfed her face, but she appeared not to notice. She said, "Even the Cherokee had black slaves."

Now I saw her history. Her great grandfather was a Negro. I let the thought dissolve and took in my surroundings. There were several dark shapes molded with the shadows. The shapes were human, men and women, but I couldn't see their faces. My eyes traced a complete semi-circle. We were in a clearing about fifty feet across and surrounded by oak and cypress. An old tarpaper shack with a bottle tree next to it stood over to my left. The bonfire danced, smoke plumed and swirled, flames reflected off the bottles in spots of red and yellow.

"Where am I? Why am I here? What did you do to me?"

The old woman spread her hands. A breeze fanned her hair and flapped her robes. Sounds of owls on the night air. But they were not owl hoots, there were too many.

"You're on my island, Mr. Bale," the old woman said.

"Where?"

"Somewhere," she said. "You'd never find it, long as you lived. Ask you something. Do you believe in magic, Chicago Man? In voodoo magic?"

I turned back to the woman. "No," I said firmly. She threw back her head and laughed. It was a laugh that seemed to reach into my very soul.

"Of course you don't. You are blind like all the rest." She lowered her head and fixed her gaze on me again. "Those sounds you can hear on the wind are the sounds of evil spirits. The bottles catch and contain them."

I thought about what Charlotte had told me. Didn't believe it then, didn't believe it now. "No," I said. "No such…"

The old woman broke in, "There are some who think they are God, Mr. Bale, but in truth they are evil. Their spirits are not on the wind as yet, but you need to drive them to me."

I shook my head again. "Voodoo, spirits, bottles, my ass," I said.

"You unbelievers are all the same. Your minds are closed. And this is why we brought you to this place, to begin the healing." Her voice lowered to a whisper. "I ask you. Does your mind not feel less cluttered than before? Do your eyes not see clearer, sharper?"

The truth of it was that I did feel like that. It was like I had been born again and was seeing and hearing things for the first time. Everything seemed to be in sharp focus, details uncluttered, there was order. But I refused to believe it was because of some voodoo spell.

262

More like that bitter tasting liquid was a drug of some kind designed to give that effect.

"You on the road, Chicago Man. You starting your healing journey. You gotta take what's been told to you and do good with it. Don't let your mind close down again. Expand it and accept what you know to be the truth."

I was angry. "This is just too much." I swept a hand wildly in the air. "All this voodoo, the fire, the crazy dream, and...and whatever it was you made me drink. It's just nonsense."

"That was no dream," she said. "You now on the path. You changed. But heed this." The old woman raised her right hand, stretched out her forefinger, the tip of a long fingernail, a witch's fingernail touched my chest. "There is someone close to you who is also blind and refuses to hear. You will have to deal with that, regardless of the sacrifice it will mean."

She turned away from me and moved noiselessly into the shadows, cigar smoke floating around her in the shape of long fingers which seemed to claw at her body, pulling her deeper into the dark until she was gone.

The bottles moaned in the wind.

Hands grabbed me again. More liquid was forced between my lips, different this time, sweeter.

Seconds later I was gone.

Burning sunlight had bleached everything to a pale yellow-white. I had to shield my eyes, thought I'd died and entered heaven, but a shadow fell across me and a hand came forward holding a cup of strong smelling coffee. I doubted they served coffee in heaven. The hand most definitely belonged to a female. I blinked several times, focused. It was Charlotte. My heart danced while my head ached.

"Good morning," she said, her chocolate voice soft, welcoming.

I sat up, felt a little nauseous, and my head swam for a second or two then it passed. I took the coffee, put the mug to my lips, hesitated, but I couldn't think why.

She laughed and it was the sweetest sound. "Don't worry, it's just coffee."

"Where am I?"

"My house."

"How did I get here?" I asked, confused.

"I drove you."

"From where, was I drunk?"

"A little. Did you have a party in your car?"

"What?" I rubbed my forehead. What in God's name had happened to me?

"Your car smells like you had a party in it. Broken glass on the floor."

I remembered then. "Yeah, Sam Cooper. Met up with him at Nat's Bar. He was way too drunk to drive, gave him a lift home. Had to brake hard to miss a truck, a bottle of bourbon got smashed."

I sipped coffee, felt a little better. Dust motes swirled in manic confusion, caught in hot blades of sunshine. The room was comfortable, sofas, tables, lamps, rugs, framed drawings and paintings of Negro slaves working the fields, musicians playing in the juke joints. There were various sculptures dotted around, one in particular about eight inches high of a naked man with a grotesque misshapen face and an erect penis that was way out of proportion for the size of body. Charlotte caught me looking at it and smiled.

"Fertility," she said.

"Right," I said. "Big guy. Puts me to shame. But in my defense he's a real ugly bastard."

She laughed and I turned to her. I saw for the first time how truly beautiful she was. Coffee-cream colored skin, thick wavy black hair, eyes so dark you could drown in them, an angular line to her jaw, and full lips that seemed to be fixed into a perfectly shaped 'O'.

"They all have their place," she said. "I will tell you about them sometime. More coffee?"

I handed over the cup. She smiled again, turned away and went through to the back of the house where I assumed the kitchen to be. I stayed rooted to the spot with my heart beating fast and my stomach doing loops. Last time I felt like this was when Jenny and I first met. Jenny, my beautiful Jenny. Sorry, but I think I'm falling in love all over again.

Charlotte came back a minute later with fresh coffee and we sat opposite each other. "You look sad," she said.

I attempted a smile. "No, no. It's OK," I lied. "Just confused about what happened to me last night."

Her eyes drifted down to the floor for a moment as she considered her answer, turning her coffee cup around in her hands. When she finally spoke her voice was measured, serious. "Several young girls…black girls have gone missing over the years. Some have been officially reported, mostly not. The people down here don't trust the sheriff's office to do anything. They say they'll look into it but after a couple of days they just let it go."

"There's only so much they can do and…" She held up a hand stopping me and shook her head, her dark hair shimmering.

"No. They don't even try. People have given up asking. Ellie-Mae was the first in a long time."

"From what I've been told four girls have gone missing."

"They're the official ones. In total there's nine."

"Jesus," I said. "Over how long?"

"Twelve years or so."

"None found?"

"Only one was Alice, thanks to you."

That was crazy and I said so. "What about your own community, surely they searched?"

"Always, but somehow these children just disappear, like they walk into the forest or the swamp and never come out again."

"You'll be telling me next that it's some kind of voodoo thing. I mean, what in hell was that about last night."

She smiled. "So you remember."

I rubbed my forehead again, sipped some more coffee. "I remember this old crone telling me I was on the path or some such shit."

"Miss Veronique. She's very old and very wise."

"Wise my ass. Just a lot of nonsense."

She gave me a wry smile. "You'll see."

"See what?"

"When it's time, you'll see. Just don't ignore what you've been told."

"Feels like I'm the one everybody's suddenly relying on."

She took my cup and placed it on a table then held both my hands. Her skin was warm, softer than I expected. She gave me a penetrating look of such intensity, I thought she was seeing into my very soul.

"I have to be honest with you, Tom. The reason for you being here is far more deliberate than it seems."

"What are you talking about?"

"For a long time we had been thinking about what to do, who could we turn to, who would help us find the missing girls. We had completely dismissed the sheriff, considered the FBI, but eventually decided on a complete outsider. Someone who could see things with a fresh perspective, someone not perhaps constrained by legal procedure. Someone with a heart, with a conscience. That someone was you."

I leaned back in my chair, she released my hands and it felt like I was slipping away from things. "You're saying me being here was deliberate?"

"Yes."

"So how do you explain Alice Jackson?"

"Little Joe had spoken about you before to Ellie-Mae, told her what an honest guy you were, how you approached things not from just the motivation of money or that it was your job, but with a conscience. Somebody with honesty and decency as their code."

"It was Joe who saved my life not the other way around."

"Yes, but you became friends and he got to know you real well. Ellie-Mae would call him from Dan Benson's store, and he would talk about you a lot. We asked Joe to sound you out about what was going on down here, but he died and then there was the funeral and other things. Ellie-Mae found your business card and decided to call you, but Alice disappeared. That was just a tragic and dreadful coincidence."

I closed my eyes felt the sun on my lids. As each day passed, I was discovering remarkable and shocking things. Suddenly I was the Lone Ranger. I doubted Clayton Burke would fit the role of Tonto and I didn't have a white stallion. I laughed.

Charlotte's mouth formed into that perfect 'O' and squeezed her eyebrows together. "What's so funny?"

"Nothing, Charlotte. Nothing at all."

Fire leapt in her eyes. "It's no laughing matter."

"You're right, it isn't. Forgive me. I don't mean to offend."

The flames reduced to embers. "When you went back to Chicago, we didn't know what to do. All we did know was that it would happen again."

"And then the white girl, Caitlin Dexter, was murdered."

"Yes."

"And I came back, my conscience telling me I had to find Alice's killer, and I discover that Carl Robard is on trial for murder."

"You didn't know?" she said surprised.

"No. Found out Friday morning from Dan Benson and Lucas James."

"Oh," she said. "We all thought Ellie-Mae had called you again."

"No," I said and shook my head. "I needed closure on Alice."

Charlotte's whole expression softened completely. "Thank goodness you came back."

"Glad I did," I said, my eyes searching into hers, leaving Charlotte in no doubt about the meaning.

After a moment we both averted our eyes, embarrassed. Charlotte was first to speak. "There's a lot to be done, Tom. All the information you've learned so far, been given by Donald, Amory, Sam Cooper, Miss Veronique, as much as it may seem complete nonsense to you, you must follow it. Otherwise more girls will go missing, more families will be devastated."

As I left, I kissed her on the cheek, my mouth lingering there a little longer than was probably appropriate. Charlotte backed away after a moment and the taste of her flesh dissolved on my lips. I was lost.

I had been manipulated. To a degree. I didn't like not being in control, made to act like a puppet. Still, other factors conspired to turn this from a missing person case into something much worse. People dead, innocent young lives brutalized, taken forever. I needed to put an end to it, and soon. I would check out Donald Avery's story a little later. But now, right now, I needed to go to church, and it would be the first time in a very long time.

CHAPTER 32

The mid-morning sun hung bright and powerful against a backdrop of pure blue sky, made you feel everything was OK with the world. Moved by a gentle breeze, the leaves of cherry and magnolia trees clacked against each other, and ancient oaks threw shadows across the graves and headstones.

I was in the grounds of Towers Hill Church, leaning against a live oak and watching two men standing in respectful silence, looking down at the well-tended grave of Caitlin Dexter. Both men were of similar height and age, one dressed in an expensive smart summer-weight blue suit, the other in priests' robes clutching an open bible.

A handful of people strolled through the cemetery, pausing now and then to read the headstone inscriptions or to place fresh flowers at a loved one's grave. I noted that a fresh grave had been dug over to the far left of the cemetery, I assumed for Deputy Torrence. Carl and Jason's bodies would be interred at the chapel graveyard in the Bottoms. With Jason gone I wondered who would be the minister presiding over the burials.

I had caught the last fifteen minutes of the service in a church full of people; all white. I had to stand at the back as all the pews were occupied. I listened but didn't take part. My religious beliefs were nonexistent. I couldn't believe in something I couldn't see, hear, touch that was apparently watching over us all, guiding us down the chosen path and welcoming us into heaven when our time came. I'd read somewhere that most of the biblical stories were copied and embellished from tales told thousands of years before the man who walked on water: Moses in a reed basket, Noah, ten commandments. All stories previously told in ancient Egypt and Greece. Still, if people felt comforted by doctrine, then that was fine by me. Each to their own. Jenny's parents had insisted on a burial and church service, and I didn't argue. Did that make me a hypocrite? Probably. In my book, though, when you're dead you're dead. Just dry bones in the earth. I carried the memory of Jenny in my heart and head. And that was enough for me.

At the end of the service, I was first outside, the intention being to casually talk to people as they wandered the cemetery, see if there was any nugget of information, no matter how small, that would add to what I already knew. However, I became intrigued by the behavior of the reverend. He didn't wait at the church doors, as was customary to thank people for coming as they filed out. Instead, he went and joined the other man at Caitlin's grave, a move that the townsfolk seemed to appreciate.

The man in the expensive blue suit, swept a hand through his thick, and obviously dyed, dark-brown hair and they both uttered an 'Amen' before turning and making their way back to the church. They embraced at the doors.

"Goodbye, brother," the reverend said. "Thank you for coming, thank you for your support."

The other man left with a wave and a thank you, as his brother chatted with the churchgoers. Henry and the Reverend Alvin Towers.

Henry: tall, confident, charismatic, stopped when he saw me. He flashed a wide, bright, thousand-dollar smile, held out his hand. "Henry Towers," he said. "Mayor. Don't think we've met."

I shook his hand, the grip strong, purposeful. "Tom Bale," I said. "No, we've never met but I saw you on the courthouse steps Friday, with Clayton Burke. After the trial."

The smile lost some of its shine. "Ah yes, a most tragic and terrible day."

His words had about as much sincerity as a starving shark's promise not to have you for lunch. "I was in court when it happened," I said. "And it truly was a terrible experience." More than just the innocent lives taken, I thought.

He looked at me quizzically. "Wait a minute, I know your name. Of course I do. You're the private detective from Chicago who found that Negro girl…what was her name?"

"Alice Jackson. And yes, I am he."

"Well, it's good to meet you." He shook my hand again.

"You too, Mr. Mayor," I lied. I'd taken an instant dislike to this man, this scion of Paradise Creek. I never liked flash. I liked people with something about them, people you could scratch the surface of and find substance underneath. This guy was as shallow as a puddle of rainwater. I'm sure his nephews Larry Swales and Floyd Tibbett had told him all about me.

"So, you're back down here. Did you come for the trial?"

"Pure coincidence," I said. "Came back…" I stopped myself then. Carl Robard had already been convicted of Alice's murder. The mayor would be more than satisfied with that result. No sense in rocking his boat. "…because I wanted to pay my respects to Mrs. Jackson."

"That's very commendable, Mr. Bale. You've done the family and this town a great service. Long way to come, though."

"It is, but I gave my word to Mrs. Jackson that I would find Alice and now her killer has been tried and convicted, my conscience is clear. But I aim to stay around for a while, I like it down here. Made some friends last time. Pace of life is slower. Chicago can be a nightmare."

A worried look spread across his face, serious. "You be careful then, Mr. Bale. Small town gossip and our ways down here are a whole lot different to big city life. It'd be wise not to get caught up in it all."

"Appreciate your concern, Mr. Mayor." Wondered at exactly what he meant by that. Small town communities are very reluctant to welcome strangers into their midst, I knew that and maybe that's what he meant. Maybe?

The false smile again. "Henry, please, no need to be so formal."

"Thank you, Henry." We shook hands again. "Just going to spend a few moments with your brother, see if he can help in any way."

He looked a little surprised. "Alvin? He's got church matters to attend to. I shouldn't bother him if I were you. Help with what exactly?"

"Got something bothering me, on a personal level. I appreciate he's busy, but I'll ask him, see if he can give me a minute. If not, I'll come back another time. Nice to meet you, Henry." I walked away before he could protest further and could feel his eyes on me every step to the church doors. I didn't look back as I let myself in.

All the townsfolk had left by now and I caught Reverend Alvin standing in front of the altar, back to me as I approached. Sunlight came in through the high arched windows and washed everything to a pale-orange sheen. Dust circled in the rays. He turned at the sound of my footsteps, let out a small gasp of surprise.

"Excuse me, Reverend," I said. "Don't mean to disturb you, just wondered if I might have a moment of your time?"

"The service is over," he said, voice polite, but strong, resonant, not unlike Jacob Robard.

"I know," I said. "It'll just take a minute. Would like your help."

Reluctance on his face, but he agreed and indicated that we should sit on one of the pews. "What can I do for you, Mr....?"

"Bale," I said. If he'd heard my name before he didn't show it.

"Yes, Mr. Bale."

Up this close, the similarities between the reverend and his brother were obvious. Same noble facial structure, same build, the reverend a little heavier. And I guessed maybe three-four years younger, early fifties perhaps. "I met your brother outside, and we chatted for a while. Good to finally meet the mayor."

He nodded sagely. "Ah yes, Henry. Good man, served this town for several years. Plans to run for governor next term."

"Really?" I said, wondering if Clayton Burke was aware of the competition. "Well, I wish him good luck."

"Thank you, I'll pass that on. Now, you needed help with something?"

"Yeah, I do," I said thoughtfully. "You may not have heard my name, but I'm a private investigator. I was the one who found Alice Jackson back in May."

He tilted his head. "Ah, so that was you?"

"It was."

"That poor girl. Terrible what happened to her. I cannot believe that such men exist who could do something like that."

"That's what I'm here about. I'm a friend of the Jacksons and I thought I'd go pay my respects. But I was surprised about Carl Robard. I knew his family too and feel I need to see Mrs. Robard. After all, it wasn't her that committed any crime, Jason neither, and I'm having difficulty with believing it was Carl that murdered those two girls."

He looked shocked at my inference. "Carl was tried, convicted."

"It's just playing on my mind. I should see Mrs. Robard, but don't know how to handle the situation. Looking for guidance I guess."

He was a little flustered when he spoke. "I…don't see how…I can help you with that, Mr. Bale. You just got to show kindness and a willingness to help and support. There's little else you can do."

"Just doesn't seem enough." I leveled my eyes with his, boring into those dark pupils. "I wonder if, now their own minister is no longer with us…if you might consider holding a service for them, either here in your fine church or at their chapel in the Bottoms, it would go a long way to help bring the communities together, and it would make me feel like I had made something positive happen."

I wished I had a camera at that moment, the look on his face was priceless, like God had personally come down and smote him. The very idea of offering his services to the black community had such a profound effect that he took a good half minute to recover. It amused me, this playing around with people's heads, the mind games. But one day, it would come back and bite me on the ass. Ass, was I allowed to even think that word that in church? I smiled inwardly.

"That's…err…quite an undertaking, Mr. Bale. Church duties take up…err…a lot of my time. Don't think I could accommodate that request. And it may not be seen as appropriate."

No. Of course it wouldn't. You would rather shake hands with the devil himself. Did I want to push the point, play with his head a little more? "In what way do you mean, not appropriate?"

"Well…they are Baptist, and here we are Presbyterian. Slightly different ways of doing things."

"I understand," I said. "But you are all men of God, are you not?"

He was really struggling now, so I put him out of his misery. "It's OK though, I hear what you're saying. You've got your hands full supporting the townsfolk, and there's Deputy Torrence's service you have to prepare for."

Relief did not go anywhere near to describing the change in his countenance. It was like a great, cleansing wave had swept over him and the caring reverend had returned.

"You do seem very troubled, Mr. Bale. There's sadness in your heart, and I understand your reluctance to believe that Carl Robard committed those heinous crimes, given that you are friends with the family. But you must learn to accept what has been decided in a court of law. It is truly shocking how it all ended, and as God is my judge, I will pray for the souls of those three men. It will take time, but you will be able to move on. I don't run a confessional. We are not of that religious bent, shall we say. However, you can always seek my counsel if you feel the need to talk things through." He gave me a smile then and I could see the spit of his brother.

I laughed. "Confession would be good, Reverend. Expunge my sins at the same time." I looked at him with as much sincerity as I could muster. "Thank you. These few minutes we've spent together have helped enormously."

That smile again, and his warm priestly hands on mine offering comfort to the downhearted. "Anytime," he said. "My church is always open."

"You're very kind," I said.

"I expect you'll be heading back home soon," he said.

"No, Reverend. I plan to stick around for a while. Got some things I need to do."

"Such as?" His tone light, chatty, almost deliberately so.

"Stupid I know, but I have to satisfy in my own mind about Carl Robard's conviction." I got up, headed for the doors. I looked back. "Thanks, Reverend, I'll be sure to take up your generous offer if I need to."

I left with that 'God has come down and smote him look,' etched into my memory. Nothing like rattling a few feathers here and there, and to be honest, the reverend Alvin was only guilty of not having the courage of conviction to help the black community. Was that a crime? Yes, in my book, but not in the great scheme of things. You rattle innocent people sometimes, and they in turn pass that to someone else, and so the gossip and rumor machine kicks in, spreads eventually to the person that counts, and then you find the killer. What may seem like time-wasting game playing, actually had a far more serious intent.

I could be such an asshole at times.

There was a sudden crack, like a bullet fired from a gun. It made my heart flutter and I looked up at the sky to see if lightning was about to strike me down. No. God was not seeking to punish me this day.

Just a car backfiring as it went past the church.

CHAPTER 33

Swales was at the front desk when I entered the sheriff's office. He briefly looked up at me, sighed, and carried on with his paperwork.

"Morning, deputy," I said.

"Can I help you?" he said, eyes still focused on paperwork.

"Shame about Deputy Torrance," I said.

"He was a good man."

"Tragic what happened to Carl and his father."

He looked up this time, put down his pen, annoyed. "Is there something I can help you with? Because I'm pretty busy right now."

Wasn't this turning out to be a day for unsettling people. I was about to say I'd wait for the sheriff when a little voice inside my head told me to press on, see if Swales knew anything about the boy who had been seen with Caitlin Dexter.

"Well, maybe there is, Larry," I said, smiling, friendly.

He shot me a hard look. "It's Deputy Swales, if you don't mind."

I held up a hand in apology, "Sure," I said. "Deputy Swales it is."

Swales eased back in his chair and spread his hands. "Shoot."

"You've lived in this town all your life?"

"Yeah, whole family has, why?"

279

"So, you'd pretty much know everyone around, give or take a few faces here and there?"

"Sure."

"Because of your...familiarity, shall we say, a stranger would stand out, yes?"

"Absolutely. Like a sore thumb. Much like you do." Swales drew himself up in his chair, rested his elbows on the arms. He turned his head just slightly to one side. "Excuse me, but is there a point to all of this?"

"Maybe something, maybe nothing," I said. "But I heard a rumor that Caitlin Dexter might, and I do stress that it is only, might, have had a male companion on the night of her murder. Someone not from this town, and I wondered whether you'd heard or seen something, especially with your knowledge of the town and the folk around here."

The deputy's face grew into one of incredulity. It was a good show of surprise but it didn't fool me. If ever there was an Oscar for overacting, Swales would be first in line. "Where in God's name did you hear that one?"

I let out a heavy breath. "To be honest, the source of the rumor is not exactly reliable, an old man went by the name of Lucas James."

"Isn't he the one died outside the hardware store Friday morning?"

I nodded. "Apparently, he'd seen Caitlin with a boy about two-three years older walking together along the road when Lucas and a friend were headed back from Waresboro."

"What friend?"

I didn't want to drag Corey into this, so I lied. "Travis, I think Lucas said. Don't know the last name."

Swales tugged at his right ear. "Well, I ain't seen or heard nothing about that, and I don't know any Travis. The old Negra, he weren't none too bright, or could have been drunk, you know what they're like, so I wouldn't hold too much on what he tells you. Any case, if there had been a boy with her, don't you think he would've done something or reported her disappearance?"

"What I thought. As I said, probably nothing to it, just the ramblings of an old man."

"So, you getting close to heading back home? Must be done with all that snooping around and getting under everyone's skin."

I went to open the door. "Not really, Larry," I said, giving him my best smile.

His eyes hardened again and credit where credit is due, he somehow maintained a genial countenance. "That's fine, always welcome. I'll let the sheriff know you called in."

"You take care now, deputy. Oh, and by the way. Lucas James was a well-read man, and he didn't touch alcohol."

Even though I'd left the windows open, when I got back in the Dodge the heat had cooked up the bourbon soaked into the floor and seats so much I was going to get drunk just smelling it.

Swales knew nothing about the missper report. Swales knew nothing about Caitlin Dexter's boyfriend. Swales found the evidence that ultimately convicted Frank Delaney. Swales took charge of the evidence found on Caitlin Dexter. Was this just a mix of incompetence and circumstance, or was my head telling me that my earlier suspicions, the ones I'd so readily dismissed after I found Alice, were now coming back to haunt me? My world seemed skewed, off-kilter, my focal point just a shadow on a tilted horizon. I needed to regain my direction. I needed to finish this.

I headed off to the creek, windows down, air blowing bourbon through the car. The sawmill would have been the easiest way to get to where Donald Avery had described the location of the rocky overhang, but as the mill was closed and the gates locked, I couldn't be seen to have trespassed for what I was about to do. I had to drive about five miles out of my way and circle back to a point where I could leave the car and investigate on foot.

I crossed the old Indian burial grounds, then up through Jacobs Cutting, a disused railway line once used to transport timber from the mill. The summer heat was exhausting and sweat fell of my face as I carefully tracked along the marshes and ditches to where they fed off the creek.

There was an unsteady looking bridge spanning the creek, which took you to where the bank sloped into the water at a much kinder angle than the steep sided fissure I would have to negotiate from the side where I was standing. The bridge was just a couple of cables strung across the creek and secured to rusty metal poles on either side, which were buried deep in the ground. Wooden slats were fastened to the cables with rotting rope, and several of the boards were missing and others rotten and cracked. It didn't look anywhere near safe for a child, let alone an adult, so I elected to climb across an overhang of rock covered in dense thicket and dogrose and then down the fissure.

Two months of burning sun had caused the water to fall back at this point, enough to expose a smattering of rusty beer cans, a couple of fish picked to the bone by birds and animals, a bicycle wheel, and a rusted cantilever toolbox with its padlock looped and secured through two eyeholes in the toolbox lids.

I clambered up the dry bed and crouched down, poking my head into the gloom. A rank, fetid stench greeted me and I immediately recoiled, covering my mouth and nose. I sat back on my haunches for a minute, letting my eyes get used to the dark. Then I saw what at first looked like a pile of red rags, but as my vision adjusted and settled, I saw the rags were in fact a red plaid shirt. A shirt with a body in it. Donald's dead communist. Could this be the kid that Lucas James spoke about? I had no choice but to get the sheriff involved.

I drove back into town, informed the sheriff. He got Floyd Tibbett out to unlock the mill gates, the road through giving us much easier access to the creek. Three hours later, the body, or what was left of it, had been removed and dispatched to the morgue. The sheriff told me not to leave town, and I told him I had no intention of doing so. Once he'd dealt with the body, he was going to call me in for questioning. He wanted to know what made me go looking for it. I assured him I would be more than pleased to give a formal statement.

CHAPTER 34

I persuaded Clayton Burke out of his house, much to the chagrin of his wife, who, from her customary position on the davenport, emphasized her displeasure in very colorful language.

We drove in separate cars to his office. Climbing the stairs, he badgered me for information, but I kept quiet until we were sitting, windows open, ceiling fan whirring overhead, a stack of files on one corner of his desk.

He spread his hands wide, as if to say, 'come on I'm waiting'. So I told him about Lucas James and Donald Averly and my finding the dead body at the creek.

"So everything points to it being the man that Lucas James said he saw with Caitlin Dexter on the evening she was murdered?"

I nodded slowly. "Body needs to be identified, examined, and we can't be absolutely certain, but for it not to be and just a coincidence is highly unlikely. And you know what that means don't you, Clayton?"

He thumped his arms down on one of the files, raked his hair. "Yes dammit. But it could be that Carl Robard also murdered the boy and hid the body down at the creek."

"You honestly believe that?"

He stood up, started pacing. Seemed to be his favorite thing to do when under pressure. "I honestly don't know what to believe."

"You know Carl didn't do it."

He turned to me and threw up his hands. "Why the hell not? You've seen the evidence. He could have murdered the boy first then hid his body after he strangled the Dexter girl."

"Christ's sake, Clayton, listen to what you're saying. Carl supposedly abducts Alice Jackson, ties her up in a shack out in the swamp, rapes and kills her. Then, weeks later, he kills Caitlin Dexter's boyfriend, and we're not talking about just a kid here, a young man, about twenty, six feet tall, not a lightweight. Carl's truck is being fixed, so does he carry the body all the way to the creek? And how did he get Alice Jackson's body to the swamp? I've been there and trust me, you would need two men to pull that off. He rapes and strangles Caitlin Dexter but doesn't hide her, just leaves her in the long grass to be discovered. Now that's just fucking stupid, Clayton, and you know it. You'll be telling me he has an accomplice next."

"He didn't actually rape her. No evidence was found during examination to prove that. Molestation, yes. And how many times have we been through this, Tom? There is nothing, no link to anything or anyone else being involved or who might have a motive." Burke swept a hand across the files, like a dealer spreading his cards on a table. "I mean what have we got here: a minor theft, possession of marijuana, a drunk-in-charge? There's a whole bunch of them, some more serious than others, but nothing so major that in any way, shape, or form demonstrates that anyone on record has the motivation or inclination to do such things. And why couldn't Carl have had an accomplice, someone with a vehicle? That would explain how the bodies were moved."

"Oh, give me a break, Clayton. That's just clutching at straws and complete horse shit. You're searching for ways to justify the trial and the outcome. Just stop and think for a minute."

He rounded on me then, and I saw his fists bunch, knuckles white through the tanned flesh. He leaned across his desk and for the second time asked if I was accusing him of misdirection.

What is it they say about childhood? I thought. That it forms us, maps the geography of our being, shapes us for adulthood. When was it exactly that Burke's desire for glory, acceptance, and recognition came into being? At what point in his life did that eat its way into his very soul?

I stood up and leaned toward him. "I know you have a desire to run for governor next term, Clayton. Is that why you're so blind to this?"

Fury leapt into his eyes and his fists bunched tighter. Before he could say anything, I told him to sit down and listen. It took him a moment, and he did as I'd asked. The fury left him in graduations, but he was still on the edge.

"My opinion," I said, "is that Carl was framed. Evidence planted as a cover up, something more than just the murders of Caitlin Dexter and Alice Jackson. Maybe Carl saw or heard something that could make life really bad for someone."

"Like what? You've seen all these files. The evidence against Carl is watertight. And what could he have seen and heard, eh? Just what? Tell me."

I sat back down, composed myself. Outside, the daylight was slipping away. "Truth is, I don't know. But what we do know is that the murders of Alice Jackson and Caitlin Dexter are linked in some ways and not in others."

He threw his head back, briefly laughed. "What in God's name do you mean by that?"

"Because Caitlin Dexter was arranged. And I believe she was killed someplace else and her body moved to where it was eventually found."

"Moved...from where?"

"Don't know, but not somewhere Carl Robard would ever be seen, that's for sure. Caitlin's body was then put, conveniently, close to where Carl would be walking home from the mill, and then arranged."

"What do you mean 'arranged'?"

"The evidence: Carl's crucifix in her hair, his blood on her skin, her scarf in his locker like some kind of trophy."

"Undeniable evidence."

"Then why nothing on Alice Jackson?"

"We got a fingerprint on a billycan found in the hunter's cabin."

"Which was missed when the sheriff investigated after I found her. But surprise, surprise after Caitlin's murder, with all that evidence pointing at Carl, the billycan was retested, and a print found. How do you explain that?"

"Happens. Things get missed. We haven't got a whole department dedicated to finding forensic evidence like up in Chicago. Sometimes you have to go back and review if there is a suspicion."

"OK, I'll grant you that. I'm aware of the procedure. But answer me this. Were there any traces of sperm found on Caitlin Dexter?"

"No, only the blood match. It was assumed that Carl couldn't actually perform the act and, in his frustration, he choked the life out of her."

"So, no indication of actual penetration?"

"No. That's what I said a moment ago."

"And if Carl was the type of murderer to take a trophy, then why nothing from Alice Jackson? The Robard house was searched. Zip."

"Maybe he hid it?"

"Like he hid the Lawrence girl's scarf?"

"Yeah, in his work locker."

"Right, where anyone could have seen it. Not very secure."

Clayton merely shrugged. He had no answer for that. Then something came to me about a previous trial he'd told me about only the day before. The open file on his desk.

"In fact, Clayton, the trophy idea isn't so far from that Delaney case you told me about. Didn't he have trophies? Items of the missing girl's clothing, a bow from her hair or something? Things he said he must have collected. He was a hoarder, could have picked the items up from anywhere. Delaney had junk all over his house, didn't he?"

"So, are you saying that evidence was planted as well?"

"Why not? Another missing girl, body never found."

"Then you've just contradicted yourself?"

"How so?"

"Delaney's victim was black, and he took trophies. Alice Jackson was black, no trophies. If your theory is correct, then…"

"Yeah, yeah," I interrupted. "I hear you. But what about Cooper, who was never brought forward as a witness, swears that Carl lost his crucifix the day before Caitlin's murder?"

"We only have his word for that, and it's circumstantial at best. As I said before, Cranver obviously thought it a waste of time."

I sat for a moment, thinking on something that was turning over in my head, but I couldn't get to it, couldn't pull it into focus. It was something about Delaney and I asked Burke to quickly go over the case again. And then I got it. I asked Burke to give me an hour or so and I would bring Cooper back with me. He protested, saying that he and Maryanne were hosting a summer barbecue that evening. I told him to sit and wait.

Could I do what I wanted in an hour? Yes, if I used the sawmill's access road. Time to trespass.

As it turned out, I needn't have worried as the mill gates were still open. There was a black-and-white parked up near the shed, right next to Floyd Tibbett's truck. No surprises there. Floyd and Larry were no doubt up in the office doing whatever they did together; cousins poring over pornography magazines, probably. I didn't care if they saw me. I had returned with only one purpose in mind and all I needed was a few minutes.

I parked up about two hundred yards from the creek and made my way over, the sun starting to bleed through the trees. The dead fish and rusted cycle wheel were still there but someone had taken the toolbox, and assuming it had only been the sheriff, his deputies and the medical team on scene to remove the body, it had to be one of them. Of course it may not be the same cantilever toolbox that was discovered at Delaney's house with the missing girl's finger inside, there must be thousands of similar toolboxes in the county, but what if it was and why would someone have disposed of it in the creek? It was a long shot, but now it was missing only served to make me want to dig deeper. Julias Cranver and the Sheriff's Office, the link made perfect sense.

What were they hiding?

CHAPTER 35

The sun was low by the time I pulled up outside Cooper's house on Dale Street. The buckled Chevy was absent from the drive which told me he hadn't been back to Nat's to pick it up. Either that or he was out.

I knocked the screen door a few times and waited, my head scrambling together ideas when something hit me quite suddenly and instantly made so much sense, I couldn't help thinking that maybe Clayton Burke was right after all. Did Carl have an accomplice, and could that accomplice be Sam Cooper? They worked together at the mill, personal lockers next to each other, Cooper had a car and a desire for young girls. Maybe he talked Carl into it? Could he have framed Carl?

Getting no response, I went around back and peered through the windows, but the blinds were down. I tried the rear door, it was open. I stepped into a laundry room with stale smelling clothes piled up on a counter ready to be washed. I called out a couple of times but still no answer. I went into the kitchen just to be sure and saw his car keys and the note on the table where I'd left them. I called out again. Jesus, I thought, the guy could sleep through a war. Leaving the kitchen, I went down the hall and discovered why Cooper hadn't answered me.

He was sitting upright in bed, a single bullet hole center forehead. A dark ocean of blood had soaked into the pillows and half his brain was stuck to the wall behind him. Both arms were slumped to his sides and a .38 Smith and Wesson revolver, hung loosely from his right hand. There was a folded piece of paper on a side table. I flipped it open. It was a suicide note. Short, to the point.

I'm done. Goodbye

And then I found something else tucked down his left side partially obscured by a blood-soaked sheet.

An empty bottle of Wild Turkey.

I went back to the kitchen, picked up the phone, and called it in. I sat at the table thinking, waiting. Cooper was almost out when I'd brought him home last night. He wouldn't have been capable of opening another bottle let alone drinking it. Unless of course he woke up in the middle of the night, decided enough was enough and finished another bottle to make it go a little easier. Sick of his life, depressed, alcoholic, guilt. I'd been close a couple of times myself after Jenny was killed.

Everything rampaging around in my head was speculation, coincidence, and yet it all made perfect sense. So far, I didn't have one shred of proof that it was all connected, but connected it was. I was dragging Clayton Burke into something he was very reluctant to be involved in. Something, if proved incorrect, could damage his career irreparably and ruin his chances of running for governor; a huge price

292

to pay. And, if I dare admit it to myself, I was somehow trying to expunge whatever demons lurked in my soul out of guilt for not yet finding Jenny's killer. I just hoped that whatever it was possessing me didn't cloud my mind into making foolish decisions that would see me locked up or worse still, dead. And then there was Charlotte, another reason for me to remain in this town. I couldn't risk her getting caught up in all of this.

When you live with someone for several years, you come to know their geography, their patterns and rhythms in the same way you know your very own. The cadence of their speech, the way they walk, breathe, sleep, think, and eat. Over time, subtle changes take place along with shifting desires and needs. It's a form of communication and if you fail to notice those changes an almost imperceptible rift starts to appear until it widens into a gaping hole never to be repaired. Jenny and I never had that. We knew each other. And now, six years on from her death, I was starting to fall in love all over again and wondered if I might eventually understand Charlotte the way I understood my wife.

I'm sorry Jenny, I truly am. Forgive me.

Alban Somers arrived with his deputies, went to the bedroom, came back out, sat in front of me while his deputies secured the scene until Ferris Bewley, the county examiner arrived.

He removed his sweat ringed hat, perched it on the table, wiped moisture from his ribbed forehead.

"That's twice in one day, Mr. Bale. You trying to set some kind of record?"

"Not intentionally, Sheriff, can't help what I find."

"Well, since you been down here poking your dick where it ain't wanted, dead bodies have been turning up, so I think me and you need to have a talk. Official. Now."

"Wouldn't you rather do that at the office?"

"Here's as good a place as any. You wanna tell me what's going on?"

And so I did. I repeated the story I got from Donald Averly, tied that into what I'd heard from Lucas James and recounted my meeting up with Coop at Nat's bar and then bringing him home because he was too drunk to drive, pointed out my note and Coop's keys on the table. When I was done, he called out to Swales who was standing by the front door, listening in to our conversation.

"Larry."

Swales came over, hitching up his pants. "Sheriff?"

"Take one of the boys with you over to Nat's. Check out Mr. Bale's story."

Swales grinned at me and I guessed it was one of those grins that Dan Benson was going to wipe off his face someday. Hoped I would be around to watch that happen.

"On my way."

At that moment, Ferris Bewley turned up, hot and flustered. He came through the door, looked at me. "Making a habit of this ain't ya fella?"

Bewley was a tall man around sixty and not given to much in the line of conversation, which I guess suited most of his clients when you considered that they were usually deceased. He had a thick head of white hair combed straight back, held in place by the liberal use of Brylcreem, an imported and popular pomade from England. His aquiline nose jutted out from a thin liver-spotted face.

"He's in the back bedroom, Ferris," the sheriff said.

Five minutes later, Bewley returned. "Initial examination puts time of death sometime between ten last night and four this morning. I can be more accurate when he's on the table."

"Was it suicide?" Somers asked.

"Looks like it. Boys will be here in a minute to remove the body."

He shot one final glance at me and left.

"Well, I guess you're off the hook, Mr. Bale." Somers said. "For now."

"You didn't seriously think I had shot him?"

He shrugged his big beefy shoulders. "Who knows? We'll make sure your story checks out."

"It will," I said. "Nat saw me." And although I didn't believe it, I added, "The Doc's just confirmed suicide."

"Ain't official yet. Something else might turn up when Ferris gets to work."

When I got back to the office, I found Burke in the men's room, shirt off, splashing his face with water.

"Hey, Clayton. Surprised to find you still here."

He reached for a towel and began to dry his face. "Just about to leave. You took your time, and I'm late. Maryanne will kill me. Where's Cooper?"

"You haven't heard yet?"

Burke hung the towel on a peg, picked up his shirt and slipped it on. "Heard what?" he said fastening the buttons, checking his appearance in the mirror. "It's Sunday. News travels even slower on a Sunday."

"Cooper's dead. Shot himself."

Burke turned to me, eyebrows raised. "What?"

"I found him an hour ago. He was just sat up in bed, bullet through his skull, gun in his hand."

Clayton's eyes grew intense as he absorbed the weight of the news. "That's an extreme action for any man to take, Tom. What would have possessed him?"

"All the usual. Heavy drinker, a loner since his wife left him a few years back. He left a note. If you believe it, that is…"

"You're saying it wasn't suicide?"

"Not from where I was standing it wasn't."

"Tell me."

"I have my suspicions, but I'd rather wait for the official verdict."

Clayton scratched his chin. "I assume the body is with Ferris down at the morgue?"

"Along with the boy I found this morning. Ferris is going to examine the bodies tomorrow."

"OK. Not much more we can do here."

"And there's something else."

He looked at me despairingly. "Pray tell."

"The Delaney case. That toolbox found in his basement with the girl's finger?"

"What about it?"

"Found a cantilever toolbox in the creek this morning, not ten feet away from where the body was hidden."

Clayton raised his eyes to the ceiling, let out a long breath. "Let me guess, you think out of all the hundreds, maybe thousands, of cantilever toolboxes ever sold in this county, Delaney's is the very same one you found. Someone snuck it out of evidence storage and dumped it in the creek."

"Before I went to Cooper's house, I went back to the creek to get it and bring it here, but it was gone. Someone...and it could only have been someone from the sheriff's office or the medical team, had taken it. And my guess is Larry Swales."

"And you're saying that because Swales was the deputy who found the toolbox with the girl's finger in it..."

"Precisely. When I got back to the creek, there was a cruiser next to Floyd Tibbett's truck. I guess he and Larry were up in Floyd's office."

"Doing what, exactly?"

I shrugged. "Hiding the toolbox, looking at porno magazines."

"Porno magazines? How the hell would you know that?"

I looked off to one side, debating whether to tell him I'd broken into Floyd's office and found magazines in his desk drawer. To hell with it. I told him.

He stared at my reflection in the mirror, incredulous. "You did what?"

"Floyd's behavior when I first went to see him aroused my suspicion that he was hiding something. Wanted to know what it was."

Clayton tuned to me. "So you trespassed, broke in…and for what? To discover he has a thing for porno mags. Big fucking deal, Tom."

"Had to find out. Almost got caught. Almost."

He scratched his forehead, raked fingers through his hair. "This just gets better and better."

"But you got to admit, Clayton, the toolbox suddenly disappearing is a little odd, don't you think?"

"Yeah, it is," he said in one long sigh. "Look, why don't you come over to the house? You can freshen up and have a spot of something to eat. It's casual, a few guests, Chef is cooking up some shrimp and ribs on the barbecue."

I hesitated, thinking I should go back to the motel, work through all that had happened, but then it hit me that Charlotte might be there.

"Thanks, Clayton, be glad to."

He locked up the office, and we went outside to our cars. He offered me a lift, and I refused but he wouldn't have it. Told me I could stay overnight if the champagne took hold, and he would bring me back in the morning.

Dusk turned everything to a deep reddish orange with streaks of dark blue and gray. Clayton had put the top down and the summer air was warm and sweet and heavenly as it whipped through our hair. We drove in silence for a couple of miles.

"I'm thinking about something, want your opinion," he said.

"Go on," I said.

"Have you met our mayor, Henry Towers?"

"Yes, briefly this morning at church."

"You went to church?" he said, surprised.

"Why is that so surprising?" I asked.

"Didn't have you down as a churchgoer."

I thought about what Reverend Alvin had said and smiled at the personal joke. "I must confess, Clayton, I'm not. I went there just to ask the congregation a few questions hoping someone might know something. In the end, I didn't speak to anybody apart from the mayor, and then I had a short conversation with his brother."

"How did you find them both?"

"Honestly?"

"Yeah."

"The mayor: a bit too much, too self-possessed, too flash. Bit like a used car salesman, only wealthier."

He laughed. "Oh, he's wealthy all right. His family built this town on cotton production, then timber, and God knows what else. And that smile of his...great for the newspapers."

Not unlike your own, I thought rather unkindly. "You know he's running for governor next term."

"I'd heard a rumor. What of it?"

"Nothing really, except you also want to run, stiff competition."

"I'll have the town and the county behind me. Henry will have either run his powder keg dry by then or have moved on. Make way for a younger man."

Perhaps. But I didn't think for one minute that Henry Towers would run out of steam. In that short time when I met him, I saw a totally focused, ambitious man with power firmly on his agenda.

"Reverend Alvin is a spit of his brother," I said.

"Very much so. Not so shark-like, perhaps."

We both laughed at that.

"Now that wouldn't be right for a religious man."

"Indeed not, and Alvin he does have a softer side, not so ambitious."

We were heading along Braintree now, lights from the mansion houses set far back from the road, strobing through the trees.

"You know he came back to Paradise Creek about fifteen years ago."

"Back?" I said.

"Yes. He was a minister in another county for many years. But when his father got ill from the cancer, he came back to help Henry look after him. Not that they didn't have nurses and doctors on call, with their money that wasn't an issue. But Alvin wanted to comfort his father and support Henry, at least emotionally. Henry took it hard when his father died, and Alvin helped him through it."

Somehow, that made them seem more human to me. "Henry married?" I asked.

"No, never."

We drove through the gates, parked up. I saw Charlotte's pickup in its usual place, and my head and heart joined together in a waltz.

Clayton turned to me. "Before we go in…this thing I've been turning over in my head."

"Shoot."

"Given what we've discussed, I'm thinking I should approach Henry about it. Quietly, no fuss, just explain what you've told me and that you are still looking into things. It would be important for him to know that. It's his town, after all."

I shook my head. "I don't know, Clayton. I may have a lot of events all linking together, enough to place doubt on everything that has occurred, but I still don't have absolute proof. I think it best to wait until I…we, have that proof."

"Hmmm, you know my feelings on that, but I'm willing to go along and let's just say that some of what you've discovered so far is correct then Henry's influence could actually help."

"Don't do it, Clayton," I said. "Don't tell anyone yet. If you do, it could make the whole thing a lot worse for me and you, and others around us. Now is not the right time."

"All right," he said after a moment's consideration. "I'll leave it for now."

Maryanne Clayton was where I expected her to be, on the davenport.

She was dressed in summer pants and a pale green silk blouse, smoking a cigarette and sipping at a large measure of gin. Clayton told me to help myself to a drink, then took off upstairs to change.

Mrs. Clayton reached out to the side table, her hand casting a shadow over a book that lay in a pool of yellow beneath a single stemmed lamp topped by a pastel-green shade. She put down her drink and picked up the book, flipped to the marker, read four lines, and placed it back on the table, clearly irritated. I saw the title, *The Postman Always Rings Twice* by James M. Cain. She rose, ignored the fact that I had entered the room, and took her drink to the open French doors. She leaned against the door and blew smoke. I poured myself a generous measure of bourbon. Outside, the vast lawn was illuminated from lanterns strategically placed along footpaths and draped through the ancient trees. People were organizing tables and chairs, plates of food, ice buckets for the wine and champagne. It all looked rather too formal for something so apparently casual.

Maryanne Clayton was indeed a beautiful woman, almost a spit of Hedy Lamar, only more radiant. I could imagine wherever she and Clayton went every man would have their eyes on her. She surprised me further still by starting up a conversation. She had the southern drawl, but every word was perfectly enunciated.

"I expect you'll want to freshen up?"

"Yes, ma'am, straight after this drink."

"So, you're the man keeping my husband at the office?"

I stepped closer but allowed plenty of space between us just in case war broke out. "That would be me. Yes."

"And what's so pressing that takes the little time he has for me away further still?"

"The trial."

She turned her attention away from the activity out on the lawn and looked at me. "I thought it was over. He won didn't he?"

She said that with a hefty dose of sarcasm, strode back over to the davenport, crushed out her cigarette in the marble ashtray, and sat down. She indicated that I should sit opposite.

Her eyes were thoroughly absorbing, deep hazel replete with an energetic intensity and intelligence. It was hard not to die in them. I explained briefly what had occurred, left out the parts about how Clayton might have a made a terrible mistake with the evidence. And then she said something which surprised me even more. In fact, it almost took my breath away. It came unbidden and why she would choose to disclose it to me, a relative stranger, I had no idea. I crossed my legs, sipped and listened, and my respect for Maryanne Clayton grew with every sentence. She was far from the demanding, bitter shrew I had first imagined.

"Clayton's obsession with his job had, at first, been like an addiction to me. There he was, handsome and fresh out of university, the very top of his class. Idealistic, with morals, sound judgement, and a determination to be the best prosecuting attorney in Georgia State. And of course, later on, a decorated war hero. But there was something else I hadn't bargained for until much later, and that was his ambition to also be seen as the most successful prosecutor, an ambition that won him accolades, interviews with the press, invitations to the senator's parties, Judge Manning's select group of dinner guests, and the opportunity to rub shoulders with many wealthy businessmen. He'd become the county's golden boy. But I also knew his family history and eventually came to understand the true motivation behind the man. Clayton had been born into modest means and I, whether you consider it a blessing or otherwise, came from good old blue-blood stock."

She reached for her cigarettes, took one out, and lit it with a slim gold lighter. She blew a plume into the air and continued.

"There were times when I sympathized with his internal plight. My father is a wealthy businessman, granddaddy had sat in the upper house of representatives, and my great granddaddy held the governorship of Alabama for two terms." She swept a slender, toned arm across the room. "My father has generously supported us with this fine house among many other things, the sole purpose being to keep his only daughter in the style she had been accustomed to."

She stopped, and a complete change came about her. Her deep, fathomless eyes lost some of their radiance. Her whole face altered from iconic beauty to sad and ordinary, if such a description could ever be given to Maryanne Clayton.

"And while my husband continues to strive to achieve more, to become someone of standing, I yearn for less. All I actually want is the man, not the ambition."

She seemed to lose herself then, as if I wasn't there. Maybe in her head I hadn't been. Maybe she was just airing her thoughts and feelings to the room, and I was just a ghost.

"Why are you telling me this, Mrs. Clayton?"

She came out of it a little bit at a time. "Because you seem to be like someone I can talk to."

We left it there as Clayton came down the stairs dressed in fashionable but expensive casuals and looking like a fresh-faced poster-boy. I finished my drink and was invited to take one of the guest bedrooms at the back of the house where Ms. Nesbitt could run a bath for me. Given we were roughly the same size, Clayton offered a change of clothes. Maryanne looked me up and down, suggested I take up his offer. Ms. Nesbitt would gather clothes for me to choose from. It would be an hour before the guests arrived.

CHAPTER 36

When I came back down the staircase, fresh underwear, shirt, and pants, my own shoes spit-shined and looking half-way decent, I caught Henry Towers and Clayton shaking hands. I stopped, studied the scene. I could hear chatter from the living room, indicating that some of the guests had already arrived.

"Henry," Clayton said. "Glad you could make it."

"Apologies, Clayton. A little delayed at the office."

"Busy man. Office on a Sunday?"

"You too, I gather. Always things to attend to."

"Quite so, quite so."

Maryanne stepped forward, looking like a movie star. The mayor turned to her and wrapped both his hands around hers. "Maryanne. Always, a pleasure." He kissed both her cheeks then drew back, his eyes betraying just a hint of licentiousness as they flicked momentarily to the deep cut of her blouse. "Stunning as ever."

"Why thank you, Mr. Mayor," Maryanne said flirtatiously. "You are most kind, sir."

"And it's Henry," he said, pulling her right arm through his left and guiding her into the living room. "Now, let's get ourselves a little drink."

Clayton went off to the kitchens. I wondered where Charlotte might be.

I reached the foot of the staircase just as Viola came out of the kitchen with a tray of food in her hands. "Damn, don't you scrub up well," she said. Whatcha here for anyway?" She gave me that dark look again. "Run you a bath, fetch you clothes. I am not your slave."

"Clayton invited me, and I couldn't refuse."

"You ought to be out there, doing what you're supposed to be doing, what Amory and Charlotte told you. Didn't that meeting with Miss Veronique mean anything?"

"Let's please just not do the voodoo thing," I whispered. "And yes, I have been out there doing what I was supposed to. I found that body Donald Averly and Amory spoke about, down at the creek. That's how come I needed fresh clothes and a bath."

"So Donald wasn't just raving like he usually does. You think it's the boy Lucas saw with that girl?"

"I do, but we'll find out soon enough. And another thing. Sam Cooper, the guy worked the saw—"

"I know who he is," she said abruptly.

"Went to his house earlier this evening. Dead. Shot through the head."

Had it not been for the tray of food, Viola would have clasped her hands over her mouth she was so taken aback. "Oh my Lord," she said. "Murdered you think?"

"Yes, I think so. Sheriff is assuming suicide at the moment. There was a note."

At that moment, Clayton stepped into the hallway, munching on some edible delight. "There you are, Tom. Wondered where you'd got to. Come grab a drink and mingle. Ms. Nesbitt, you've done us proud again. The food is delicious." He placed a hand on my shoulder, guided me into the living room.

There were perhaps twenty couples, all drinking champagne and in good spirits. Clayton moved among them, pressing palms, smiling, enquiring after their health and introducing me as a family friend. I recognized not one of them. Waitresses busied themselves arranging silver platters of food on a long stretch of tables just beyond the French doors, and I could see more people milling around outside. I caught sight of Maryanne moving with easy grace through the crowd, her every action, touch, smile the personification of high society elegance. This was indeed her stage, and she molded to it like a second skin.

She was talking to a congressman Clayton had introduced me to who had come all the way down from Atlanta. "An influential man," Clayton whispered as we moved through the room, who had exerted his not inconsiderable political muscle in support of a new business venture of Maryanne's father. I asked him about it.

"Agriculture has become big business since the end of the Second World War. Maryanne's father saw an opportunity for smaller mom and pop farms to be consolidated into larger, single, more productive operations. Do you know how much farming output was worth after the war?"

"I have no idea, Clayton."

"Thirty billion dollars. That's a huge chunk of change, and Maryanne's father predicted it would double and wanted a slice of that change. Trouble was, the move for big corporations to control the agricultural business was highly controversial, resulting in hundreds of farms disappearing and thousands of people left without work. However, corporation power and money won the political debate. The family farms were bought out and closed down. And I have to say, not that I've voiced my opinion to Maryanne on this, but I've often wondered about how many pockets her father had to line to get political backing."

Everyone has their dark side.

Clayton excused himself and went to press more palms. I watched Henry Towers guide Maryanne out the French doors to a table brimming with flutes of champagne, light from the lanterns reflecting off the rising bubbles. Henry's right hand was pressed against the small of Maryanne's back. And then he let it slip down and deftly glide over 'her right buttock. She appeared not to notice.

I looked around for Charlotte. There was no sign of her anywhere, so I went back through to the hall and into the kitchens, where I saw her over at one of the counters, slicing tomatoes. She smiled as I went up to her and I grinned like a teenager on a first date.

"Wondered where you were," I said.

"Strictly backroom tonight."

"Why?"

"So much to do, and there are enough waitresses to cope with the drinks and food outside. Need someone to prepare it all, so that's me and Viola."

"I spoke to Viola a short while ago."

"Yes, she told me. Old Donald Duck not so stupid after all."

"What time do you get off tonight?"

"Around ten. Viola will supervise the clearing up. Why?"

"I'm not comfortable with all these people. Don't know anyone, and I don't move in their circles, so my conversation topics tend to be limited. Plus, I'm wearing Clayton's clothes…it's just not me."

"And you want me to give you a lift back to town?"

"So you know I came with Clayton tonight?"

"Viola told me."

"Yeah, he persuaded me, said I could stay overnight."

"I can take you back," she said. "And you can tell me what's really going on in this town, who's really behind the murders."

I placed my hands on her shoulders, turned her toward me. Charlotte put down the knife she was using. Her eyes were sad, and I wanted to hold her so much at that point my body was shaking inside.

I lowered my voice. "I'm not there yet," I said. "But I am close, and I promise you and all the people who've suffered over the years, all the missing girls, that I will find this man, these men, and bring him or them to their knees."

She leaned forward then and kissed me very lightly on the mouth, and before I could say or feel anything, we heard a voice behind us say, "Huh."

We turned to see Viola marching back out the door into the hallway. We looked at each other and laughed, embarrassed, both stuck for something to say. Charlotte picked up the knife and went back to chopping tomatoes and I just stood there watching her. A little boy lost.

Viola returned a minute later, bag in hand, which she dumped at my feet, the expression on her face disapproving, thunder in her eyes. "Guess you'll need these, as you won't be staying here tonight."

I looked in the bag, saw my dirty clothes. "Thanks, Viola," I said, smiling.

"It's Ms. Nesbitt to you," she said, ploughing her way through the kitchen to the refrigerators.

Charlotte and I grinned at each other. "She's very protective," she whispered.

"I'd better go show my face," I said.

"See you at ten."

Walking on air, that overused cliché, was exactly how I felt stepping out of the kitchen.

I returned to mix with all the luminaries, wandered into the garden, and saw Henry Towers and another man off to one side, illuminated under lamps draped through the branches of a live oak. I couldn't hear what they were saying, but their exchange looked a little heated, judging by their expressions and body language.

311

Clayton saw me, lifted two glasses of champagne off a table, and came over. "You know, Tom," he said quietly, his eyes beginning to take on a glazed, alcohol induced sheen.

"At the moment, Clayton, I'm beginning to think I don't know anything."

"I've been watching my wife being the perfect hostess all evening. She's radiant, beautiful, draws everyone to her like she has this…magnetism."

I wondered where he was heading with this. "She's a beautiful woman all right," I said.

He clumsily waved his glass around. "All these people, they're nothing really."

Alcohol. Brings out the truth in everyone. "You seem to get on fine with them."

"Nah, it's all a sham. I want to get on in this world, so I need to be seen. Grease the wheels, so to speak. Maryanne, she comes from a different world. She's part of all this nonsense, this charade, and I need to show her I can be part of it too."

"You ever thought you might be looking at this the wrong way?"

He stared at me with those glazed eyes. "I don't understand?"

"You're not seeing the real Maryanne. You're missing the subtle differences between the show and the reality. Look at her closely. See how she reacts when she's talking? Smiles, a little flirting with the men, gracious with the women, charming, complimentary. You see all of that?"

"Yeah, she's always the same at these events."

"Look closer when she turns away. Her eyes lose that sparkle, her smile vanishes, like she's turning off a switch only to suddenly flick it back on again when she meets the next person. It only happens for a second or two, but it's there. She doesn't want to be here among this gathering of vacuous so-called important people, preening and shaping themselves, any more than you do."

"I don't see it," he said after a moment. "There's a dozen men here who would gladly lick the shit off her shoes just to spend more than ten minutes alone with her. And she encourages it."

"Clayton, don't you see? She's doing it for you, not for her. You've grown apart, and I think you've missed her changing personality. It's like a woodsman who doesn't continually hone the cutting edge of his axe. The edge becomes dulled, and the effectiveness of his blows becomes duller still. You need to talk to her, get to know her again. I think she wants you, the man she married, and not all of this." My turn to wave my glass around.

"You see that in her?"

"Yes."

"You know my wife better than I do."

"I just see what I see." I decided not to mention mine and Maryanne's earlier conversation.

The bulky shape of Randall McKinley, a prosecutor from the neighboring Pierce County, who Clayton had earlier introduced me to, strode toward us. "Clayton," he said. "Here you are, been looking everywhere."

"Shit," Clayton whispered. "We'll be here for hours."

313

He touched glasses with Clayton, ignored mine. "Mr. Star Prosecutor," he said. "How is life at the top?"

Clayton was instantly all smiles and false bonhomie. "I wouldn't say that, Randall."

The big face broke into a wide smile, displaying a row of crooked teeth that, like the goatee wrapped around the lawyer's alcohol fueled red lips, were stained yellow from cigar smoke. "Don't be so damn modest," he said. "That was some case you pulled off, though I heard it got a little messy at the end."

"It did," Clayton said. "Shouldn't have happened. It was a bad end to a sad day."

"Oh dear me," McKinley said a little too sarcastically. "Do I detect a sense of regret?"

Clayton let out a heavy sigh as McKinley drew on his cigar, finished his champagne, and grabbed another off a passing waitress. He took a swallow, wavered slightly then adjusted himself to the moment.

"No, Randall," Clayton said wearily. "Not regret. It's just that innocent people lost their lives and that can't be right, not for their families, this town, or for justice. It all went terribly wrong."

McKinley waved a fat finger at him, cigar smoke forming a zigzag shape in the air. "Not as wrong as our dear president. That Kennedy fella's not been in office a year and he's already up shit creek without a paddle. I mean, what about that Bay of Pigs fiasco? What do the Spanish call it, Bahia de Conchinos, or something like that? Castro got an army of bandits trained by eastern bloc commies and they wipe the damn floor with us, and we got the biggest army and navy in the world. Tell you, Clayton, there's gonna be another fucking crisis soon, you mark my words."

The look on Clayton's face said it all. He'd had more than enough of Randall McKinley with his expensive suit, silk tie, graying mousey-brown hair, and small piggy eyes.

Smiling, Clayton said, "Anyway, good to see you, Randall. Better go mix or people will think I'm deliberately ignoring them."

And with that, he left us. McKinley turned to me. "I need the bathroom," I said, and went out to the hall, leaving him standing there, looking around to see who he could bore to death next.

My thoughts turned to Charlotte, and I almost flew up the stairs. Halfway along the carpeted landing, opposite a walnut occasional table with a telephone on it, was one of three bathrooms. I went in and locked the door. A couple of minutes later, I was drying my hands on a fluffy cream-colored towel that smelled of roses, when I heard someone outside on the landing. I was about to unlock the door when I recognized the mayor's voice. I'd managed to avoid him all evening, but our eyes had met across the living room and we raised glasses to each other. Now he was on the phone and I pressed my ear to the door. His voice was urgent, angry. No doubt why he'd chosen to use the phone up here on the landing and not the one in the hall.

"Yes, he's here," he snapped.

Silence as the person on the other end of the line spoke.

Then. "Well, you'd better goddam well do something about it. This can't go on."

Silence.

Then the mayor again. "Just fuckin' do it and do it soon."

He slammed down the receiver, and I heard him marching along the landing. I gave it a moment, unlocked the door and followed him. I saw him reach the bottom of the staircase and immediately switch to that million-dollar smile.

"Bill," he said to Congressman William Rawlings. "How are things with you and Audrey?"

Towers was like no other small-town mayor I'd ever met. He just didn't fit in this town. He was too big a personality. So why was he still in Paradise Creek? He should have run for governor years ago. Was the death of his father the reason? Clayton had said he was devastated by it. It could be reason enough. And who did he mean on the telephone when he said, 'he's here'? He was remonstrating with someone, probably about the man I saw him talking to outside. Still, none of my business who he was pissed at.

I went back into the living room. Most of the guests were outside, sitting at tables or standing and feasting on plates full of shrimp, chicken and ribs, salad and potatoes. The chef Clayton had employed for the barbecue was clearly doing something miraculous behind all that hickory smoke wafting around him, because it smelled delicious and I was tempted to stay, but the idea of spending more time with Charlotte far outweighed anything any chef could create. I sought out Clayton who was outside with Maryanne and Henry Towers.

"Great party," I said.

"Thank you, Tom," Maryanne said.

316

"Always puts on a terrific spread," Henry said.

"Chef is working miracles, judging by all the satisfied faces," I said.

"We always hire him for these occasions," Maryanne said. "Viola and Charlotte do a great job in preparing the food for Chef, and of course they make the hors d'oeuvres themselves."

"Well, you've got a great team," I said. "First class."

"You haven't got a plate yourself, Tom," Clayton said.

"Yeah, I came to say good night and thank you for inviting me. I'm completely bushed and not good company."

"Oh," Maryanne said, genuinely disappointed. "Surely you can stay for one more drink, Tom? That bedroom is yours if you want to stay over."

"My my," Henry said. "You three seem to have gotten real close real quick." He nudged Clayton in the ribs and his face grew deadly serious. "Tom's a Chicago man, and down here we don't accept outsiders so readily."

Maryanne looked at him, shocked. Clayton just smiled, knowing it was a joke. Henry's face burst into laughter. "Just joshing with you, Tom." Clayton and Maryanne laughed with him.

"Oh you, Henry," she said, scalding him, slapping him on the arm.

Henry gave me the shark smile. "Welcome any time, Tom. You're almost part of the community anyway, you being down here so much."

"Thanks, Henry," I said, knowing exactly what he meant by that remark. "But I need to go. Charlotte's gonna give me a ride into town.

I'll pick up my car and head to the motel. I'll get these clothes back to you sometime tomorrow, Clayton."

Clayton looked at his watch. "Charlotte doesn't leave for another fifteen minutes. Stay and have another drink."

"No, I'm really on my last legs tonight. Thank you, but I'll go wait in her pickup. Probably be asleep by the time she's finished. Thanks again for everything. Goodnight, Clayton, Maryanne…Henry."

They bade me goodnight in return and I went around to the side of the house where Charlotte's truck was parked, let myself in the passenger side and breathed an enormous sigh of relief as I sat back and closed my eyes.

CHAPTER 37

I was completely out of it when Charlotte got in the truck. She was later than expected, only by fifteen minutes, and I'd been asleep since the moment my head hit the restraint.

I shot up in my seat as the pickup moved forward, looked around, wondering where I was. Charlotte laughed, and I relaxed. She negotiated her way through the phalanx of cars filling the driveway and turned onto Braintree.

"Sorry," I said.

"What for?"

"Being asleep."

"That's OK," she said. "You were snoring."

"Oh shit, was I? How embarrassing."

"It wasn't loud, don't worry. More like a gentle humming."

"Humming?"

"Yes…humming."

"Sorry again."

"Don't have to be. I can handle humming. Snoring not so well."

We sat in silence for a minute or two, and then I updated her on everything. She was surprised at the conversations with Clayton Burke and didn't think for one minute he'd be so cooperative.

"Not so much cooperative," I said. "More willing to listen rather than take any action. I need to get proof."

"How will you do that?"

"Ferris Bewley is carrying out examinations on the body I found at the creek and on Sam Cooper tomorrow. Then, perhaps we can ascertain the identity of the body and whether Sam committed suicide or was murdered. I'm pretty certain he was murdered for what he knew or what someone assumed he knew. And then there's Julias Cranver. He's the key, the link. I think he's manipulating evidence, along with the sheriff's office."

"What, Sheriff Somers has a part in this? I don't believe it."

"Why not?"

"Just doesn't seem like something he'd do."

I thought about that for a moment. He came across as a pretty straight guy to me as well. "Probably right, it's more Larry Swales I have a concern with."

"That would make sense. I don't like him. He's a nasty, sly little man."

Couldn't agree more, I thought. I still hadn't told anyone about that note under my motel room door, and I hadn't said anything about the night I got warned off and hit on the head with the pipe, or the damage I did to Weaver's arm the next day. I was keeping that all to myself, ready just to slot it into place at the right moment. I knew it would. I just didn't know when.

We were about two miles from the turnoff to Charlotte's house when I caught movement at the extremity of the headlight beam, up ahead in the bushes to our left. A perfectly still night, no wind, sudden movement. A deer perhaps?

Wrong.

The driver's window exploded, and she screamed, instinctively throwing her hands up to protect her face as glass showered into the cab. The bullet sliced across my forehead and blew out the passenger window. The pickup veered off the road and she grabbed the steering wheel, fighting for control as we pitched and yawed over the rough ground. Another shot slammed into the metal behind us and she floored the gas pedal. We heard two more shots, but no contact, so they must have gone wild.

The old Ford wasn't exactly a fast machine, and it seemed like forever before we hit seventy and were far enough ahead to breathe. Charlotte's chest was heaving, and her thick mane of hair was covered in broken glass. Her hands gripped the steering wheel so tightly, I could see her knuckles, bone-white and proud through her skin, and her eyes were so fixed on the road ahead she almost went past the turning to her house in the woods. At the last minute, she looked up into the rear-view mirror, braked hard and swung the steering wheel to the right. No mean feat given our speed and no power steering. We bounced down the old farm track, the pickup rattling, throwing up stones so fast it felt like a machine gun going off underneath us. Tree branches whipped at the cab, and smaller ones snapped off and fell inside through our windowless doors. She hauled the pickup to a stop outside her house, got out, and threw up.

I ran round and put a hand on her back, but she twisted away and threw up again until there was nothing left to give. She leaned back against the driver's door, drawing in deep breaths.

"Come on," I said, "let me help you inside." I extended a hand again, but she ignored it and left me standing there.

"I can do it myself," she said.

I followed behind her and the first thing she did inside was head to the bathroom, run the faucet and splash cold water over her face. She furiously brushed her teeth, the brush clacking against the enamel so much I thought she would be toothless by the time she finished. After, she consumed six glasses of water, stood there holding on to the basin, shaking. She'd been very lucky. There were no cuts that I could see on her face from the glass. Her left hand had taken most of that, and those wounds had been cleaned while she was splashing her face. Even so, I checked just to make sure there was nothing hidden that needed urgent attention. I picked pieces of glass out of her hair. She let me do all this without complaint.

When I was done, the most important thing was to get her calm, so I gently pulled her away and she let me take her to the sofa in the den. I sat her down, told her to wait a moment. I lit a couple of hurricane lamps, using matches I found next to some batteries in a kitchen drawer. Then I got two glass tumblers and a bottle of bourbon I found in a cupboard, half-filled the tumblers, sat down next to her and passed one over. She threw half of it back, coughed a couple of times, and put the tumbler down on the table in front of us. I wrapped an arm around her shoulders and she snuggled into me, gently shaking, crying softly. We stayed that way for a good hour, not speaking, just letting the shock ease down gently. I kept my senses tuned for any sudden noise or movement from outside, but I doubted anybody would have followed us. Charlotte's place was deep into the woods and unless you knew the old farm track, you wouldn't know her house existed.

I got up after a while. She sat there sipping bourbon, the shakes gone, as I went around the house, locking doors, pulling blinds and curtains. I grabbed pillows and a blanket off her bed, took them over, made her lay down and covered her with the blanket. She instantly drew it tight around her like a cocoon, closed her eyes. I brushed her hair back and pieces of glass I hadn't spotted in the bathroom fell onto the floor. Then I kissed her forehead.

"Please don't leave me," she whispered.

"I'm here," I said quietly. "I'm not leaving."

And that was as much as we said to each other from the moment we got into her house.

Within a minute, she was asleep. Adrenalin rush can be exhausting. I went to the bathroom, looked in the mirror and saw world-weary eyes stare right back at me. I too had glass in my hair for the second time. Hoped it wasn't habit forming.

There was a thin red line about two inches long where the bullet had grazed my forehead. Blood had seeped from the wound but had congealed about halfway down my head. I cleaned it up, took another tour around Charlotte's house, and unlocked the rear kitchen door. I went outside just to make sure, wishing I had my Smith and Wesson with me. I stayed out there a good ten minutes, staring into the dark, searching for signs of sudden movement or noise. But there was none. I looked over at the bottle tree. The spirits were quiet tonight. Three inches further forward, and that bullet would have blown Charlotte's head apart. Maybe there was something in what she'd said the other night about feeling protected.

Satisfied that I alone stood out there in the darkness, I went back inside, locked the door again. I picked up my tumbler and the bottle of bourbon, sat at the kitchen table, sipped bourbon until dawn gathered and spread its glorious wings across the tops of the trees, and light crept through the slits in the blinds and bled through the curtains.

CHAPTER 38

Having finished the bourbon and with dawn's light making our world a safe place once more, I got up from the table and sat my weary body down in the chair opposite Charlotte. I let my mind drift and my eyes were starting to close when she came awake with a heaving gasp. She sat up, breathing hard.

I went over to her, knelt down. "It's OK," I said gently, calming her. "You're safe."

She instantly threw her arms around my neck and hugged me so tight I could hardly breathe. It took her a full minute to relax and compose herself. When she was ready, I went through it all.

"So, you think that was just a warning?" she said.

"Yeah. I think the gunman got closer to killing us than he intended to, but I'm sure it was a warning. To me, not to you. He...they...whoever they are, know I'm getting close."

She thought for a long hard moment, her eyes troubled. "I hate to say this...but why don't they just...kill you?"

It was a fair question. "They can't."

She shrugged. "Why not? You'd be out of the way, and..."

"Because," I said, interrupting, "they know if they kill me then Clayton Burke would start an official investigation. He could easily get the FBI involved, make it a federal matter. They cannot risk that happening, so I need to be warned off, made to go away, made to think if I carried on I would be killed."

She shook her head and another sliver of glass fell into her lap. She picked it up, turned it around in her fingers. "I don't know," she said, eyes glistening. "Maybe it's best we do let it go. It's too dangerous. I'd hate to see anyone...you get hurt."

I took the piece of glass from her fingers, placed it on the table then clasped her hands in mine. "I can take care of myself," I said. "And you, and everyone else."

"You're not a one-man army."

"No, but I'm not a coward either, and I don't give up." I let go of her hands then held up my right forefinger and thumb barely apart. "I'm this close, and I can't let it go."

I made us a pot of fresh coffee, some toast and eggs, and by the time we'd finished, the sun was up, high and proud and we'd agreed on a plan for the day. We'd clean up her truck, drive into town to pick up my car, and then I would follow her out to Corey's yard and get her windows fixed. Charlotte would go stay with Viola and Amory for the day, as it was Viola's day off. I would go with Clayton to see Ferris Bewley, maybe visit Julias Cranver. I promised I'd be back over to her house by early evening. We could have supper together and I could bring her up to speed.

326

I left Charlotte at Corey's and on my way back to the motel, I passed Towers Hill Church. A black Lincoln Town Car was parked out front of the gates, assumed it was Henry Towers visiting his brother.

The church was very different to most small-town churches I'd seen. Not so much because of its grandeur, built with Towers family money like the courthouse and municipal buildings, but more for how untypical it was. Most town churches were bland-looking gray or red-brown brick buildings stuck on the corner of a soulless street with a cemetery out back or away from the church in a different part of town. Towers Hill was none of that. It stood, majestic and proud in a prominent raised position set back from the road a good hundred feet with maybe two or three acres of cemetery and gardens around and studded with ancient trees. Neatly manicured grass with shingle pathways intersected the lines of gravestones and monuments, wooden benches with brass remembrance plates screwed to their backs were set at strategic points. Summer flowers cascaded over raised borders. It was, I had to admit, a very peaceful and beautiful place.

And then I got to thinking that surely if Alvin had come back to Paradise Creek all those years ago, to help support his dying father and his brother through that difficult time, then it would be safe to also assume that he lived with Henry in their father's mansion house. So why visit him at the church? Anything they needed to discuss could be done at the house.

Come on, I said to myself, you're over thinking things again. What does it matter where Henry decides to meet with his brother? Maybe

Henry was a religious man, but somehow I doubted that, despite his presence at Caitlin Dexter's graveside the day before.

I drove on to the motel to shower and change. I'd get the clothes I borrowed from Clayton laundered with my own and give them back tomorrow. No surprises when I entered my cabin. Fresh pillowcases and sheets, room cleaned, fresh towels.

The prosecutors' office was busy with secretaries scurrying around, typewriters clacking, legal assistants with armfuls of case files.

A woman came over to me, tall in her heels, blond, powder-blue eyes, cute button nose and pouty lips. Her figure was displayed to maximum effect under a cream-colored silk blouse and hip-hugging, blood-red pencil skirt. A string of pink-gray pearls hung from her neck and her lips matched the color of her skirt. Standing next to each other, she and Norma Jean Mortensen could be twins. I guessed this was Donna Benjamin, the secretary Clayton was supposedly having an affair with. Had to admit, it'd be tempting.

"Can I help you, sir?"

Damn, she even had the same voice but southern style.

"Name's Tom Bale. I need to have a word with Mr. Burke."

"Regarding?"

"If you could just tell him I'm here, he'll know what it's about."

Clayton came out of his office. "Hey, Tom. Thought I heard your voice, difficult to hide among us southerners. Come on in. Thanks, Donna. Oh, Tom, you want a coffee?"

"I'm good thanks," I said.

I smiled at the secretary and she went over to her desk, seams of her stockings a perfect vertical line down her shapely legs.

Clayton caught me looking at her and when I got into his office, he closed the door, looked at me with a wry smile. "Thought you had a thing for Charlotte?"

"I do, but you can't exactly ignore your secretary. She's Marilyn Monroe and then some."

"Likes to think she is. Personally, not my type. Damn good secretary though, and a lovely lady, but that's as far as it goes."

I sat down, noted the dark circles under his eyes. "How you feeling?" I asked. "You were starting to tip over the edge a little by the time I left."

"Had a headache when I woke up, but it's gone now, thanks."

"It was quite some party."

He sat down at his desk. "Indeed. Got to bed around two, got up not long after six." He looked at me as if I were the one to blame for his lack of sleep. Turned out I was. "This fucking case is driving me nuts. It circles around in my head. It woke me up this morning when I should have been sleeping like a baby until nine. And it's your damn fault."

I huffed. "Think you had a rough night. I didn't get any sleep at all."

"I'm not interested in what you and Charlotte got up to."

I shook my head. "Sadly, no," I said. "Nothing even remotely like that. Last night, someone took a potshot at us with a rifle."

He jerked his head forward. "What?"

329

I told him and after I'd finished, he got up, did his pacing thing for a minute, then stood by the open window, staring out across the square.

"I'm so sorry, Tom. For you and Charlotte. I don't know what to say."

"You don't have to be sorry, Clayton. We're OK. Charlotte's safe with friends down in the Bottoms and I'm going to meet her later back at her house in the woods."

He turned away from the window, sat down again, and rubbed his forehead. "This is maddening," was all he said.

"Someone is trying to warn me off and I intend to find out who that someone is."

On his desk was a single file. He pulled it into the center, opened it. A breeze drifted through the office window, ruffled the papers a little then faded. He turned it towards me and I read the typed label on the front top right-hand corner: POLICE EVIDENCE. VICTIM: C. DEXTER.

He flipped over several typed pages until he came across a dozen photographs, which he spread across his desk. He pushed the file to one side, selected a photograph at random and studied the detail. "This is all I've been able to think about since I woke up," he said. "Since you first came to see me, it's all I've been able to think about."

Caitlin Dexter lay among trampled grass, head twisted to her right, eyes wide and frozen in the moment of her last breath on this earth. The tip of her tongue protruded between her full lips. Her white cotton shirt had been ripped apart, exposing her breasts; her skirt raised to her waist and her panties torn so they hung midway down her left thigh.

I tried to imagine the girl's fear, hear the futile screams in my head, and feel the girl's arms as they battled uselessly against Carl Robards, his superior strength and power pressing down her, one hand on her neck crushing her windpipe the other tearing at her clothes as the seconds fell away. I could not begin to imagine the horror. And I could not imagine Carl Robard doing this to Caitlin Dexter, nor Alice Walker.

"Let's go see Ferris Bewley," I said.

CHAPTER 39

Ferris Bewley was making notes at his desk when we entered the morgue. Although the chill atmosphere was a welcome relief from the stifling afternoon heat, there was something about being among the dead, the stainless-steel tables, the chemical smell that made me want to turn around and head straight back out into the sunlight. A morgue, despite the very nature of its purpose, was not a peaceful place.

Ferris looked up. "Clayton...Mr. Bale. What brings you down here?"

"Morning Ferris," Clayton said, extending a hand as the examiner stood up. "Wanted to see how you were progressing with the two bodies you currently have in residence."

Ferris offered us a mechanical smile, which vanished a second after it was made. "You shouldn't make fun of the dead, Clayton."

"I know. Sorry, Ferris. Just my way of dealing with this place."

"Hmmm," Ferris muttered, nodding as if he understood man's distinct inability to function around matters of an uncomfortable nature. "Guess you'll be wanting to see the bodies?"

"Not necessarily, Ferris," Clayton said. "Just wanted to ask you if there was anything you found untoward, assuming you've completed your examinations that is."

Ferris nodded, walked over to the refrigerators, and pulled the first drawer. He turned back the cover, folded it across the chest area. It was Coop, face a ghostly greenish-white, head with the puckered bullet hole almost dead center. "Can't be absolutely exact on time of death, but blood lividity directs me to thinking it was sometime between midnight and five a.m. yesterday morning."

He beckoned us over, handed a magnifying glass to Clayton. "Now, here's something else. Take a look at the flesh around the bullet wound."

Clayton did so, then stepped away and made to hand the glass back, but Ferris declined. "What did you see?" Ferris asked.

Clayton shrugged. "Bullet wound?"

Ferris said, "Initial examination at scene yesterday evening suggested suicide. Examination this morning told me something else." He nodded at the corpse. "Go on Clayton, take another look. What would you expect to find in a suicide, when a man puts a gun to his head?"

Clayton bent over the corpse for a second time, taking in the magnified image of the creased and furrowed flesh of Coop's forehead. He backed away. "Sorry," he said, "don't know what I'm looking for."

"Powder burns," I said. "There are no powder burns. And probably no powder residue on his right hand."

"That's right," Ferris said, relieving Clayton of the magnifying glass. "No powder burns or residue which you would expect to find on the skin if a man had put a gun to his head, or at least very close to his head, and then pulled the trigger. Cooper here was shot from at least a distance of five feet away. He couldn't have shot himself. Someone did it for him."

"Murder," Clayton said, stating the obvious.

"Either that," Ferris said, "or Cooper had very long arms, and having looked at them I can confirm he doesn't." He covered Coop's face and slid him back into the refrigerator. "This one has proved a little trickier."

He pulled out the body I'd found at the creek, threw back the cover so that most of the corpse was revealed. Clayton turned away, hand over mouth, trying to compose himself. Most of the flesh had gone, rotted and picked away by animals and birds. The skull was almost completely exposed, and I noticed a wide crack about an inch, inch and a half long over where the left eye would have been.

"Dead approximately fourteen to eighteen days," Ferris said. "And he didn't die well."

"That cracking on the skull," I said, pointing to the wound. "He was hit and hit very hard by something."

"Yes, indeed," Ferris said. "Can't determine what it was that hit him, but it was one helluva blow."

Clayton turned back, right elbow crooked in his left hand, right hand covering his mouth. He was struggling to hold everything in.

I looked over the body. There were several broken bones, ribs, arms, upper thigh. "Jesus," I said.

"Jesus didn't do much to save this guy," Ferris said, his dry, mechanical humor a product of everything he'd seen over many years. Too much for too long. "He was savagely, brutally beaten to death."

"Have you been able to identify him?" I asked.

"No. Nothing on him. Sheriff was here earlier, told him the same. He's looking into it. One thing I did discover though was a ring." He covered the body, much to Clayton's relief, sent it back into the refrigerator and went over to his desk. He picked up a silver signet ring, handed it over.

"Can only make out two of the initials," he said. "C, D. And what looks like a heart."

I used the magnifying glass and Ferris was correct. Something, something, then a partial heart shape, then C, D. I couldn't make out the first two initials at all they were so scratched and worn. I handed it to Clayton. "Could the C, D be Caitlin Dexter?" I asked.

"Could be," Ferris said. "Could be anybody with those same initials. Nothing to say for certain."

Too much of a coincidence, way too much. Here was the boy Lucas James had seen. "Can you put an age on the body?" I asked.

"Nineteen or twenty. Twenty-one at the oldest."

Had to be, I thought. Caitlin was about seventeen. Couldn't be anybody else.

Ferris said, "Number of dead people we've had over these past days and weeks town should rename itself. More like Dead Man's

Creek than Paradise. Anyway, gentlemen, got to finish my report and write up the death certificates. I wish you good day."

Back outside, breathing in hot late morning air, the color having returned to Clayton's face, we looked at each other and without saying a word knew what had to be done.

"I've been a fool," Clayton said. "Carl didn't murder those girls, did he? Or that boy."

"No, Clayton, he didn't. You're no fool, but what you have been is misdirected all along. That kid laying in the morgue was about our height, give or take an inch. He could have probably handled himself against one man, but you saw those broken bones. I'm guessing two men at least. As Ferris said, it was savage. That was pure rage, nothing short of it."

"But why not just shoot him or use a knife?"

"Fair point," I said. "Maybe a gun would have made too much noise at the location where he was killed." So why not use a knife? I considered that for a few seconds. "Maybe the killer is not comfortable with weapons. Or they couldn't risk getting blood on their clothing. I don't know, could be a hundred reasons."

"I'm going back to the office," Clayton said. "Got a ton of things to do and I want to look over those files once more."

"Sure," I said. "I've got a few things I need to be doing too, and I'm heading over to Charlotte's later."

"You like her a lot, don't you?"

"A lot." So much more than a lot, I thought.

"Keep her safe."

336

"You can be assured that I will."

I headed out on Towers Hill Road, the blacktop rising no more than a hundred feet up from the flat plain of town. Towers Hill Church stood almost at the summit and as I got closer something made me pull over. I sat there for a full minute, engine running, wondering why I suddenly needed to visit Caitlin Dexter's grave. I certainly hadn't planned to and couldn't think of any reason why I needed to. But certain things presented themselves to me sometimes without any knowledge of where they came from or the intent behind their arrival. And this was one of those occasions. Something was tugging at me, urging me to get out of the car.

I switched the engine off, got out, and went up the steps into the cemetery. I walked along a shingle path, stones crunching under my shoes, turned left along an intersecting path and found myself standing at Caitlin's grave, easily identified as it was so recent. Fresh flowers in the stone pot, a gleaming red marble effect headstone with gold lettering. Eighteen years old, just. A week before she was murdered.

"Why am I here, Caitlin?" I said quietly. "What made me stop and come see you?"

I didn't expect an answer, but something drew me here. Some notion, feeling, hunch. What was I expecting to find, or was it just guilt that I had gone back to Chicago? If I'd stayed and found Alice's killer, would you still be alive?

Yes, probably, was the answer to that question. "I'm sorry, Caitlin. I truly am."

I glanced across at the grave next to Caitlin's and my heart leapt into my mouth. Caitlin had been buried next to her mother, Emily Dexter who had been laid to rest fifteen years before. The headstone had turned from white to gray over the years and wasn't anywhere near as expensive as her daughter's. There was a dirty-brown stain where a small part of the top edge had been chipped off. Falling tree branch during the storm back in May I guessed, remembering the havoc it caused. It wasn't a large stain, no more than an inch in length and half an inch wide, but it bothered me, so I thought I would clean it off. When I bent down for closer inspection, I saw a small piece of headstone had fallen and lodged itself between the stone flower vase and the base of the headstone itself. I tried to get it out, thinking that I could perhaps hand it to the reverend, and he could get it cemented back in place. It was stuck tight, so I used my car key, and sure enough I managed to prize it free. I married it up to the damaged section of the headstone and it fitted almost perfectly. I stood up, turning it over in my fingers. Like the damaged area of the headstone, it too was stained a dirty-brown, and I felt something else scrape very lightly against my thumb. The outer face of the stone chip had a tiny piece of what felt like a thin sliver of plastic stuck to it.

"Surely not," I said out loud.

CHAPTER 40

I caught Ferris Bewley closing down for the day.

"Mr. Bale," he said, slightly irritated. "Another dead body, is it?"

"I need to ask a favor," I said. "A big favor."

"About to head home. Come back tomorrow."

"Seriously, Doc, this is important. Literally life and death."

He gave me a cold, hard stare. "Try me. You've got thirty seconds."

I withdrew my handkerchief and carefully unfolded it. "I need you to analyze this piece of stone for blood and skin tissue."

"You're not serious, surely?"

"Never been more serious." I pointed to the stone chip. "The red-brown stain, I think is blood and there's a small piece of dead skin stuck to it. Feels like a tiny flap of plastic."

"Where'd you get it?"

"From…look, I'll explain in a minute. Can you test it? It's vitally important."

"Everything is important. Can you rush this, do that, and make this a priority? Frankly, I can't wait to retire." He unlocked the door to his lab. "Come on, let's see what you've got."

He removed his jacket, sat at a bench, and examined the piece of stone under a microscope. After a minute or two, he sat up. "Blood and skin tissue, no doubt about it."

I felt the rush. "Can you tell the blood type?"

"Don't want much, do you?"

"I wouldn't be asking if it wasn't important."

"It'll take about ten minutes."

"Fine," I said. "Whatever you have to do."

He did things while I waited, silently urging him along, not listening at all to his running commentary about the process he was going through. Finally, he had it.

"A-positive," he said. "Thirty-four percent of Americans have that blood type, so matching it is gonna be quite a task."

I thought about the size of the piece of stone and something else I'd seen earlier. "I need to see the body of the young man I found at the creek."

"For God's sake, Mr. Bale, you are really starting to try my patience."

"I'm sorry, Doc, I really am. But I need to see that body."

He went over to the refrigerators, pulled the drawer as he had done this morning, folded the sheet back. I placed the stone chip against the crack in the skull and it was almost the same length.

"Well, I'll be damned," Ferris said.

"Could the sharp edge of this stone cause that fracture in the skull?"

"Well…yes, but I don't see how…"

340

"Imagine someone slamming the victim's head against a heavy, solid piece of stone, the top of which has a sharp edge. Slamming the head with such force that a piece chips off." I held it up. "This piece."

He nodded furiously. "Yes, yes indeed. That would do it."

"What's the victim's blood type?" I asked.

Ferris almost ran to his desk, picked up a report, scanned it, looked at me.

"A-positive," he said, eyes wide.

"Want to know where this piece of stone comes from?"

"Where?"

"Towers Hill Church. It's part of Emily Dexter's headstone."

"Caitlin's mother?"

"The very same."

Ferris gave me an evidence bag, and I was in Clayton's office ten minutes later. I placed the bag containing the piece of stone carefully on his desk.

"Know what that is," I said.

He picked up the bag, turned it around a few times. "A piece of stone?"

"Correct."

"What of it?"

"It came off a headstone in Towers Hill Church. The headstone belonged to Caitlin Dexter's mother who died about fifteen years ago. Caitlin is buried next to her."

"Wasn't aware of that."

"No reason you should be. But. And this is the interesting part. I visited Caitlin's grave earlier, after I left you. And I found this piece of stone. That reddish-brown staining is blood."

"How do you know that?"

"Went back to see Ferris, got him to test it. Blood type A-positive."

"And this is significant, why," Clayton said, turning the bag around some more.

"It also has a small piece of skin attached to it. Not only that, the blood type matches that of the body I found at the creek. And that sharp edge on the stone, that matches the crack on the skull above the victim's left eye socket."

The significance of the facts sank in, and Clayton's jaw dropped. He started to say something, but stopped as all the pieces of a convoluted puzzle started to make sense in his head.

"Yes," I said, leaning over his desk. "Caitlin Dexter's boyfriend was murdered in the cemetery. Someone smashed his head against Emily Dexter's gravestone with such force, it cracked his skull and broke a piece of stone off. I found it by complete accident. My thinking is that he and Caitlin were visiting her mother's grave. And it tells you one other thing."

Clayton looked up at me. "Carl Robard would never have set foot in Towers Hill Church. He's…was, Baptist and black. Most townsfolk are Presbyterian and all of them white. Lot of immigrants from Scotland came to fight in the Civil War, some for the North, some the

South. Many stayed, set up homes. Hell, I might even be Scottish myself."

I sat down. "And there we have it, Clayton, actual proof that Carl could not have murdered Caitlin Dexter."

"Have you told the sheriff about this?"

I shook my head. "Oh no, and I don't intend to. It's the one thing we have that the killer doesn't know about, and we can't risk anyone in the sheriff's office leaking that information to whoever is behind it."

"You're talking about Deputy Swales."

"Yes. I don't think the sheriff's involved. I get the idea that he's too decent a guy to be wrapped up in all of this. I think he, you, and a lot of other people have been misled all along."

"So, how are we gonna take it from here?"

"I'm going over to Charlotte's. She should be back from Viola's by now. I'll think it through, you do the same. Tomorrow, we come together and agree on what to do next."

He nodded. "OK, we'll do that." He held my gaze, smiling. "Fuck me, Tom, you've opened a big can of worms."

"Well, let's see how many hooks we can bait with them. And you hang on to that evidence, put in the safe for now."

CHAPTER 41

I got to Charlotte's house, and she was already there, but only by a couple of minutes ahead of me. We sat at the kitchen table, cups of coffee in front of us. I told her about the piece of headstone I'd found, my visit to see Clayton, and the fact that he now completely agreed with me that Carl could not have murdered Caitlin Dexter. Jury was still out on Alice Jackson, but it was too ludicrous an idea to give more than a second's thought to.

"Thank God," she said. "Finally, our community, Ellie-Mae, Alice, Jessie Robard…all of them are going to see justice."

"I'm not there yet, Charlotte. There's still a lot to be done, and I may not get to the end of it at all."

She reached across the table, touched my arm, looked at me with such intensity and emotion in her eyes. "I know you will, Tom. I have every faith in you."

Charlotte pulled her hand away and suggested we go sit in the den with a bottle of Wild Turkey to keep us company while I told her about my life. We got ourselves comfortable, sipping bourbon, feeling at ease with each other.

"So what made you give up your shield and become an investigator?" she asked.

I gave Charlotte a half smile. "It's a long story," I said.

"That's just a cliché," she said. "Stories are never that long."

I finished the bourbon, set down the glass and stared out the window at the orange sun dipping behind the live oaks and pines that bordered her land. "Not mine," I said.

"Try me."

And so I told the story, and she was correct. It wasn't a lengthy tale and done in three minutes.

A long silence passed between us before Charlotte asked the question. A question I've been asking myself ever since, and each time I feel the heat of the bourbon on my tongue and at the back of my throat I find the answer has drifted further away from me. Charlotte's voice was barely a breath when she spoke.

"And the driver?"

I shrugged. "To this day I don't know. We had the whole weight of the Chicago police department behind it. We investigated every possible lead, every suspect. We tore apart people's alibis, pushed potential witnesses until they were almost ready to file complaints against us for harassment. But we got nothing."

"Nothing at all?"

I sat there, head bowed, eyes fixed on a knot in the wooden flooring. I rubbed my forehead to ease away the growing tension.

"Is that why you became an investigator?"

345

"Maybe, subconsciously. As a plain old citizen, I wasn't bound by police procedure. And there was the fact that I found my soul in the bottom of a bottle every night and then every day until I couldn't function as a detective any more. So I got out before I was asked to take a very long leave of absence."

"You're still drinking but I don't catch you grabbing the bottle like your life depended on it. Did you get help?"

"Two years of my life went by in a blur. Every bar, every hour of the night and day. Some nights I didn't get home, found myself in a doorway, on a park bench. I was pissing away what money Jenny and I had saved. One morning I woke up in a friend's bar to the sound of Art Tatum playing "Tiger Rag". It was on the radio, and they were doing a special tribute two years after his death. It was November, freezing cold, and I got to thinking about the legacy Art left behind. He was a great piano player, probably the best. Virtually blind from birth he somehow had magic in those fingers, made them do things on the keys that other players could only dream about. There are some people who make their mark on this earth, who plant their flag. Like Blind Lemon Jefferson and Robert Johnson. Their names will forever be associated with the blues. Like Art, they were unique. They planted their flags for everyone else to look up to."

"And how did that change anything? Did you know Art?"

I shook my head. "Never had the pleasure, but it just made me think about what legacy I was leaving. What would people think of me? Art was revered. He'd taken piano playing to a higher level, and he's still talked about today. I was a drunk, wasting away two years, an ex-cop with nothing anybody wanted. Jenny deserved much more from me and from that moment I started to get my shit together."

"Did you go to AA meetings? Heard they can be tough going."

"Didn't go, didn't want someone preaching about steps and God and being on the program. I knew if I had to rely on a program and regular meetings then I'd always be one step away from falling over again. I had to do it by myself, had to show Jenny that I was man enough and strong enough to do it alone. And, with the help of a handful of real close friends like Little Joe, I climbed out from the bad place."

"But you still drink."

"Yeah, and occasionally I have a few too many. But it's a balance, not a need. I drink because I get pleasure out of it. I like the taste of good bourbon. Sometimes it gets me a little morose and I lose myself, but on the whole I do OK, and it doesn't cloud my vision when it matters."

Charlotte took my hands in hers and I felt the warmth of her skin radiate through mine. Something shifted within me, some unfamiliar emotion seemed to click into place, and I suddenly felt as though I'd known her for years. She must have felt the same because of what happened next.

"You been with anyone since?" she asked softly.

"Just one, only lasted a couple of months."

"Why so short? Didn't get along?"

I hesitated. This wasn't something I was keen to dwell on. "Not really..." I searched for the words. "We...let's just say we weren't...compatible."

She stood up but kept hold of my hand so I had to stand with her. She looked into my eyes and knew exactly what I meant, but was too embarrassed to say. I couldn't believe I had opened up to someone after all this time. I thought I had locked it all deep within me and thrown away the key.

"I understand," she said. "Trauma you went through, make it impossible for a man to get close to another woman, especially when his wife meant so much."

She drew me closer until I could smell the scent she wore. Then I touched her face, her skin soft as a baby's, her dark hair silk smooth.

"I haven't done this in a very long time," I said.

"It's OK," she whispered. "You'll know what to do."

We were real close now, close enough for me to feel the pressure of her breasts against my chest, close enough for me to feel the flicker of her eyelashes against my face, close enough for me to feel the heat of her body. "And what if I don't?"

"It will come back to you," she said, her voice soft in my ear. "And if not, then we will just have to make it up as we go."

She kissed my face and then I felt the fullness of her lips on my own. Her fingers reached for me, and my breath caught in my throat.

She stepped back after a moment, reached behind herself, and released the buttons on her cotton dress. She shrugged it off her shoulders, and it whispered as it fell to the floor.

I stood there breathless, and she laughed.

After, we lay together for a while in the stillness of early evening, and for the first time in six years I didn't feel the need to be anywhere else. A half-hour passed, and we made love again and it was every bit as intense and satisfying as the first time. A while later, we got up and made dinner together, ate it under the shade of the porch, relaxed and felt good in each other's company. I told her what it was like to live in a big city. She countered with stories of rural south. We found our rhythm around each other and it felt natural, as if we had spent years together. Around nine, I got up, carried the dishes into the kitchen. Charlotte followed me and as I was about to start the washing up, she took my hand and led me back to the bedroom.

It was around midnight when they came for me.

I'd woken up and pushed the covers off completely, letting the air in the room cool the sweat on my body. Charlotte slept on, undisturbed by the shift in balance as I rose from the bed. Slipping on my pants, I went through to the kitchen and poured a long shot of Wild Turkey, took it out onto the porch. The moon danced behind a cloud as I drew in the summer night, sweet-scented with honeysuckle, jasmine, swamp magnolia. A pair of white-tailed deer came out of the trees, nuzzled the grass and looked up at me, the moon bold and bright in their eyes. I held their gaze for a moment, tilted my glass to them. They turned and were gone, lost in the darkness like ghosts.

I stayed that way for a while, savoring the night, looking up at the rich panoply of stars and listening to the chatter of nocturnal creatures. The amber heat in my glass was a good burn at the back of my throat. I had come to a midpoint in my life, like a bridge spanning journeys past and a speculative future on the road ahead. Perhaps Charlotte was my future.

I heard the creak of wooden boards to my left and I turned around to look. It was nothing, just the old bones of Charlotte's cabin in the woods, adjusting and settling itself. I turned and raised a toast to the moon, just in time to take a blow to the head.

I jerked back and was suddenly falling, my weight carrying me down the porch steps. The glass tumbler flew from my hand and bourbon spattered my face. It seemed to be happening in slow motion. I could hear, over the spreading pain, a voice deep and strained calling me a 'nigger lover'. My shoulders hit the ground first, and red dust exploded into the air. My head fell back hard and pain burst behind my eyes. All the breath was hammered out of me as a foot drove into my side with enough force to roll me over. I tumbled over again, tried to get to my hands and knees. My entire body was thrumming from shock and adrenalin rush. Breath ragged, harsh, my eyes couldn't focus. All I could think about was getting to Charlotte.

I was kicked again. I had no idea how many there were; three, four maybe, but it was too dark and had happened too quickly for me to get a look at them. There was nothing I could do except instinctively curl up for safety as the blows kept coming. I started shivering, couldn't catch my breath. Pain screamed from every inch of my body. I raised my hands to protect my face and head. I thought, my God, they're going to kill me and then they'll do the same to Charlotte.

And then it stopped. A voice was in my ear, breathing hard. I could smell the stench of his aggression and his whiskey breath. He left me in no doubt of their intention.

"Carry on snooping around and you're a fucking dead man. But before we kill you, we're gonna take your nigger bitch slow and hard while you watch."

And just as suddenly as they had come they were gone. Like the white-tailed deer, just ghosts in the trees.

I took a deep breath, sucking down the warm night air. Something bubbled in the back of my throat, and I coughed, bringing up blood. I leaned over and was violently sick. My body screamed some more.

I was done.

I don't know how long I lay there unconscious, but it could only have been moments.

I came back to reality, body aching, ears ringing. Charlotte was beside me, her voice frantic.

"My God, Tom. Oh my God, what happened?"

I rolled over onto my back, my arms and legs protesting, joints telling me it was a bad idea to move them. Somehow, I managed to push myself into a seated position. I felt dizzy for a moment and nausea cramped my stomach, but I willed myself to get to my knees and with Charlotte's help, stood up. I ran my hands carefully over my body, feeling for damage. My ribs ached. More than anything, I was relieved to know that Charlotte was unharmed.

"Three men, maybe four," I said and spat blood. "Whoever it was is long gone." I ran my tongue along the inside of my teeth. They were all still there. I licked my lips, tasted dirt and blood.

I gritted my teeth as Charlotte helped me stagger up the porch steps to her front door. Despite the pain coming from various points of my body, we made it inside.

"You need the Doc," she said. "Come on, I'll take you in the truck."

"I'll live," I said. "He won't be too pleased about being woken up this time of the morning for a few cuts and bruises."

"Don't be stupid. You need to get checked over."

"Forget it," I snapped rather unkindly. "Just get me to the bathroom and I'll sort myself out."

We got to the bathroom, and I shrugged her off. Without a word, she walked away.

The mirror told the story in graphic detail. I had a puffy eye that would be black by morning and an ugly bruise across the left side of my face. My lips were cut and swollen. I cautiously examined the back of my head—bruised, painful to the touch. When I took my hand away, it was slicked with blood. I ran the faucet, splashed cold water on my face, dabbed at the back of my head with a hand towel and got the dried blood off my skin.

I pulled my ruined vest up over my head and the effort brought tears to my eyes. There were ugly bruises all over my chest and abdomen. I washed the red dust off my arms, undid my pants, and eased them down. My legs were as bad as the rest of me.

More than the physical damage, I was ashamed. I hadn't even managed to put up a fight. Didn't matter that a group of men came at me from nowhere, I still didn't feel good about myself and had taken my frustration out on Charlotte. She hadn't deserved that.

When I got out of the bathroom, Charlotte was back in bed and had drawn her knees and the sheet up to her chin.

"Sorry," I said.

"I was only trying to help."

"I know."

"You should really get a doctor to check you over."

"It's just a few cuts and bruises. Nothing's broken."

"A few cuts and bruises. You're like the walking dead."

I smiled best as I could. "I'll live."

"What did they want?"

"Another warning...told me to back off."

"You gonna walk away?"

"No."

"Those men tried to kill you."

I shook my head, and it felt like my brain was rattling in my skull. "They could have killed me if they had the mind to."

"Maybe you should just let it all go. Head back to Chicago."

I said nothing. I found my pants and slowly tried to pull them on again. I got about as far as mid-thigh and felt a little dizzy, so I slid them off and laid on the bed. The room turned for a few seconds, then righted itself. Charlotte leaned over me, careful not to press too hard on my bruised, aching body. Her voice was soft, concerned, tinged with sadness.

"It would be better if you left."

Turning, I looked into her dark eyes, saw she didn't really mean it. She was just protecting me. "You want me to?"

"No…I just don't want to see you hurt again or worse still, killed."

I stroked her face, drew her down to me so that her full weight was pressing on my body. My bruises told me no, and I sucked in my breath sharply. Instinctively Charlotte tried to pull away, but I held her, feeling more comforted by having her close, having her warm flesh marry with my own. She rested her head gently on my chest.

"I'll lie low for a couple of days," I said. "Let things settle. But I'm not leaving. Best if I stay at the motel, make them think their message has hit home. They'll assume I've distanced myself from you and I'm planning to leave. But you need protection, and I'm not happy with you being here alone, so I would suggest staying with Viola and Amory for a while."

Charlotte rose up and the relief on my aching ribs was sheer bliss, but I didn't let on. She looked at me as though I was the only thing that ever mattered to her. "I would rather you stay with me, Tom. I mean it. I couldn't bear the thought of you getting hurt again."

"It's OK," I said. "They'll be watching me more than you, and in a way that's good."

"How so?"

"Because they will make a mistake. They always do and I need to watch out for them with no other distractions."

"By distractions, I'm guessing you mean me?"

"Yes, but not in a bad way. I can't be in two places at once and worrying about those men, whoever they were, threatening you when I'm not here. I'd rather you stayed with someone you know and trust while I try to find out exactly what's going on in this town."

Charlotte kissed me then. Kissed me, not with the passion and fire she had done during our love making, she kissed me with tenderness, warmth, love. My heart was soaring.

"OK," she said. "I'll arrange something with Viola. But promise me you'll be careful."

I smiled at her. "I will. Those men came here on the orders of someone else. Someone with a lot to lose. I'm getting close, but damned if I know what I'm getting close to."

We lay there until dawn clawed its way over the horizon. We both slept fitfully, but even so by the time dawn had sucked the darkness away, I felt a little better. Charlotte got up first, made us a light breakfast and packed an over-night bag for herself then helped me into the Dodge, told me to take it steady. She would be going to work with Viola later and I felt happier knowing that she would be safer at Clayton's house. She got in her pickup and headed off.

By the time I got back to my motel room, the day looked set to be another blindingly hot one. I just managed to get through the door when this surge of nausea flooded my stomach and I dived into the bathroom just in time to throw up. It was painful, stomach muscles protesting. When I was done heaving, the bathroom circled around me and I had to cling to the washbasin for support. I was most definitely concussed, albeit only slightly, and I should have gone to the doc as Charlotte suggested. Instead, I stumbled over to the bed, lay down, closed my eyes and allowed sleep to take me.

I came awake sometime late afternoon, every inch of me hurting. Even the hairs on my skin hurt. I'd taken a hell of a beating, and I knew I had to finish this before the warnings stopped and serious violence took over. I couldn't let anything happen to Charlotte or Clayton, and if I died as a consequence and they remained unharmed then at least I would have died with a clear conscience, and I would have fulfilled my promise to Ellie-Mae.

Fuck lying low for a couple of days.

CHAPTER 42

I picked up the phone, got through to the manager's office, and spoke to Mrs. Trenton. I asked for an outside line. The line buzzed, clicked, and I dialed the operator, and she put me through to the prosecuting attorney's office. It rang half-a-dozen times before a familiar husky voice answered. I asked for Clayton and was told he was just finishing a meeting and would then be leaving for the day. I told Donna Benjamin who I was and gave her a message to pass on, and that it was urgent.

Clayton turned up at the motel an hour later. He knocked on the door, and I let him in. He threw his jacket on a chair, hardly noticing me. He turned. "So what's so damn urgent...good God, what the fuck happened to you?"

I told him.

"Sonofabitch," he said. "Let me take you to county."

"No," I said. "We...I need to end this. I'm not wasting any more time."

"You can't stay here. It's not safe. We'll go to mine. Viola and Charlotte will be there by now, and between us we can patch you up and you can rest. You'll be safe there."

Seemed like a sensible idea. I could make plans from there just as well as I could from here. "All right," I said. "Thank you. But first I've got to rattle some people."

"Who exactly?"

"Larry Swales and Julias Cranver."

"What are you intending to do?"

"You just wait in the car. Leave the rest to me."

I gathered some things together, and we drove into town. I had to have the soft top down, the windows closed and air conditioning off, as wind and cold air buffeting my face hurt like hell.

We stopped at the bandstand. I got out, legs stiff, hurting like crazy, and made my way over to Cranver's office. I was greeted by his secretary, hand over mouth, shocked at my appearance, and was informed that Cranver hadn't been at his office all day and she had no idea where he was. I thanked her and left, headed across the square, turning heads, made my way to the sheriff's office. Inside, I found Deputy Swales right where I wanted him to be, sitting at the front desk, grinning stupidly at my appearance. He wasn't even surprised and that in itself told me all I needed to know.

"See this, Larry," I said, pointing to my face.

"You been in a bar fight?" he said, almost laughing.

I leaned over the desk, placed both hands down, and got so close he had to move back, fear in his eyes. "I'm going to find the bastards that did this to me and make them pay, and pay dearly. And I'm going to find out who really murdered Caitlin Dexter and Alice Jackson and fuck their lives so badly they'll wish they'd never been born."

I left before he could say a word. Christ only knew where Cranver was, but at least one line of communication might start a panic. I was almost smiling when I got into Clayton's car.

"What the hell have you done, Tom?" he asked.

"Had a word with Larry Swales. Cranver's not been in today. Secretary doesn't know where he is."

"What did you say to Swales?"

"Enough to get him worried. I'm sure it will get to whoever is pulling his strings."

"You're playing with fire, Tom."

I turned to him. "I know. I lit the fucking match."

As we drove, a black Lincoln Town Car came toward us and flashed its headlights. Clayton did the same back. "The mayor?" I asked.

As we passed each other, Clayton waved and the Reverend Alvin waved back. "They share Henry's car," Clayton said.

We arrived at Clayton's house a little after six. Viola was at home, sick with a summer cold, and Charlotte had come early on her own to cover Viola's chores. Maryanne had let her in then left immediately for a friend's house other end of Braintree.

Charlotte hugged me the moment I stepped through the door. There was a lot of pain, but the hug was worth it just to feel her so close and smell her scent.

Between us, we patched me up some more, and I threw a couple of Tylenol down, hoping it would ease the pain a little. Charlotte left me and Clayton to talk through everything in his study while she busied herself around the house. Clayton poured bourbon into two crystal tumblers. Mixed with the drugs, it took the edge off.

"What are you planning to do, Tom?" he asked.

"Got to pay a visit to Cranver's house. My guess is he's had a weekend of hitting the booze hard after Friday. And that would explain his absence from the office today. Probably out of it, but I'm going to confront him, anyway."

"What if he denies any wrong doing?"

"What if he does? I'm going to get it out of him one way or another."

"Careful," Clayton said. "You don't want to start accusing him of something illegal if you can't prove it. That's a lawsuit waiting to happen right there."

"Clayton," I said. "I'm beyond caring. If I'm wrong, he can sue the ass off me. But I know I'm not."

Clayton thought about it for a moment. "Look, maybe I should go along with you. That way I can step in if I think things are bordering on slanderous."

"No need to, Clayton. You've done enough already. I can take Charlotte's pickup. You stay here. I'm not going to risk you getting a beating as well."

He snorted. "Doubt Cranver's capable of that."

"Agreed, but we don't know who else might be there; could be the same guys that came for me."

"It's possible, but at least there'll be two of us."

"I'll go on my own."

He stared at me, an incredulous expression on his face. "You're a piece of work, you know that?"

"What do you mean?"

"Since Friday, you've done nothing but push and push me until I finally begin to accept what you're saying. You asked for my help and I'm giving as best I can within the constraints of the law. You brought firm evidence to me yesterday, so I'm in. And now you want to handle it on your own."

"You want to know why," I said, voice raised.

"Damn right I do."

We faced each other, swords drawn like two gladiators. I was first to back down, mainly because of my injuries. It hurt to stand for too long and I didn't have the strength to argue. I had my head bowed to the table, spread my hands and thumped them down, rattling both glasses, making the bourbon in them ripple.

"Because…" I began. "Because I'm at the point of no return and I could not live with myself if you were killed. It's not your fight. As I said earlier, I lit the match. I dragged you into this because someone needed to know what was going on. When we spoke Friday night, I felt you were somebody I could begin to trust, even though I didn't really know you. And you came through. Shit, you even invited me to your party. I still don't know why. I was a stranger."

"Yes, I did come through, Tom. And even though your theories are sound, a lot of holes remain, so legally we have to tread carefully."

I looked up at him then. "Has anybody trod carefully around me, Clayton? My injuries say otherwise."

He took a very deep breath, let it out slowly. "I guess what I'm trying to say in a roundabout way is…that I can't let you do it alone. I would not be able to live with myself if you got yourself killed and I could have prevented that from happening. That's why I'm being careful."

Charlotte stepped into the study. "You boys kissed and made up yet?" she said, a smile playing on her face.

"I guess we have," I said, smiling at Clayton.

"What time is Maryanne getting back?" Clayton asked, sitting down at the table and scooping up his glass.

"Eight, I think," Charlotte said.

"Perfect," Clayton said. "Tom and I are going to Julias Cranver's house tonight. Will you be OK, just you and Maryanne?"

"Sure," Charlotte said, a little too chipper I thought. "I can handle a gun, and I know where you keep them."

"You do?" Clayton said.

Charlotte screwed her face up. "Of course. I clean your house remember? I know where everything is."

Clayton finished his bourbon, held his head in his hands. "I don't even know what's going on in my own house."

Despite the circumstances that had brought us together, we laughed. But the laughter died in Charlotte's eyes too quickly, and she turned away. I wanted to go after her, tell her it was going to be OK, but Clayton was talking, suggesting we freshen up. The sun was almost down and Maryanne would be home any minute.

When Maryanne got back, she expressed genuine concern for how I looked. I thanked her, told her it looked worse than it was, which was a lie because every part of me felt as bad as it looked, and then we left it for Charlotte to explain.

We'd gone about a mile in Clayton's car, using Chester Avenue as a shortcut across the north side of town to Cumberland, when he asked what the plan was if Cranver wasn't at home.

"We break in," I said.

CHAPTER 43

If Clayton could have got up and paced around his car, he would have. "Oh, come on, Tom. We're pushing the boundaries as it is. He won't just sue your ass if we do that and get caught. We'll both be behind bars."

"You got a flashlight?"

"Yes, but…"

"You can stay in the car. Park up where it can't be seen and we'll go on foot. If he's not there, you can go back to the car and wait."

"God, what am I getting into?" Clayton said.

We were driving along Cumberland when Clayton suddenly pulled over and tucked the Lincoln into a space under a live oak, killed the lights and the engine.

"Cranver's place is up ahead on the left," Clayton said, reaching into the glove box and withdrawing a small flashlight. He looked anxiously out the windshield. "You sure we're doing the right thing?"

"Gotta be done," I said. "We're so close. I'm sure of it."

Clayton made to open the driver's door then stopped, looked back at me. "I don't know what's waiting for us," he said. "But I've got the feeling it's going to be bad."

I gave him a half smile that was probably lost in the darkness. "Let's go," I said.

We got out, scanned the road. The next nearest house was a quarter mile back of us, so there was no fear of neighbors taking an interest. Stars glittered above, cicadas chatted, the smell of summer blooms invaded our senses.

Cranver's house was large, elegant, late colonial; two floors with white columns supporting a balcony that ran around the whole of the top floor. There was a mass of shuttered windows with a couple hanging awkwardly by a single hinge. The exterior looked in reasonable shape as far as I could tell, but the gardens had lost every vestige of grass and formality that they may have once had. There was a large oak out front, a couple of ancient maples, and a path that wound through the lawn and around to the back of the property.

The house was in darkness, so we went around to the rear and stepped up onto the porch. I peered through the French windows into the lounge. Weak moonlight came in through the front windows, silhouetting the furniture. I tried the doors, but they were locked.

Further along there was another door. Clayton stood there gripping the handle. "I could get disbarred for this," he said.

"We're beyond that," I said. "Two teenage girls and a boy have been murdered. Innocent people have lost their lives. You worry about disbarment?"

He held my gaze for a moment, then nodded. "You're right. Time to put things straight."

He turned the handle and pushed. There was a loud screech as the door swung inwards. It had probably been left unlocked for years, never used and forgotten given the sound those hinges made. Made us catch our breaths for a second, half expecting to see someone standing there exercising their rights under the Second Amendment.

Moments passed without any guns appearing, so I switched on the flashlight, shone it around. We were in the laundry room. There was another door at the far end.

"Probably the kitchen," Clayton said.

Sure enough, it was.

I pulled the laundry room door shut behind me. Did it slow to try and eliminate the noise, but I might as well have stood there singing Dixie at the top of my voice for all the difference it made. Still, no guns appeared.

The atmosphere in the kitchen was rank with the smell of rotting food and whiskey. I swung the flashlight around illuminating ancient cupboards, a sink full of dirty dishes, shelves stacked with pots and pans, a small table with a single chair set at an angle and a huge fireplace you could have held a July 4th parade in, and finally the source of the unpleasant odor. A large cardboard box sat over in one corner, full to bursting with discarded TV dinner trays and empty Jim Beam bottles.

"Jesus H," Burke said, covering his nose and mouth with a handkerchief.

I did the same. "Place hasn't been cleaned for months. Man lives like an animal. Doesn't he employ a housekeeper?"

"No idea."

We exited through the kitchen door, coughing to expel the smell that had settled in our throats, and into a long, wide hallway. The flashlight beam picked out a semi-circular mahogany table against the left wall. On top of this was a glass vase full of dead flowers, a telephone, and a well-thumbed directory.

We stood on a threadbare rug in the center of the hall for a moment, looking around at the drab, dark brown wooden paneling, staircase and doors. Above us, a huge, dusty chandelier wrapped in a million spider webs hung from the cracked ceiling.

"What exactly are we here for?" Clayton asked.

"Not sure," I said. "But we'll know when we find it."

The lounge was a treasure trove of dust covered tables, cabinets, framed photos of Cranver's parents, ornaments, more threadbare rugs and two ancient davenports with matching side chairs and covered in a fabric so worn and faded that the original pattern was indistinguishable.

Back across the hall the dining room revealed a large sixteen seat table, a huge ornately carved dresser and several portraits of obscure heritage. Again, every surface was coated in a thin film of dust.

The next door along the hall led us to a gentleman's smoking room. There was a floor to ceiling bookcase covering the entire back wall and in the center of the room four high-backed leather chairs were arranged around a low circular table. More portraits adorned the walls, and under one of them, which I took to be of Cranver's grandfather, a walnut writing desk stood in dusty slumber. We opened drawers, examined the bookcase, and threw the flashlight beam into dark corners. Still nothing.

"Where the hell does he keep his papers?" I said.

"Let's try upstairs," Clayton suggested. "Nothing's been touched or moved down here in a while. The dust is too evenly settled. Cranver had to live somewhere other than the kitchen."

Standing at the foot of the wide sweeping staircase, I shone the flashlight along the handrail. There were handprints in the dust. We looked at each other, began our ascent.

There were a dozen doors leading off the upper landing, one of them slightly ajar. Seemed like the obvious first choice. I pushed it all the way, and we stepped into the main bedroom. Moonlight spilled in through the double sash windows.

The room was a mess and reeked of stale sweat and soiled clothing. Several pairs of shoes had been kicked into a corner. Empty bottles of bourbon and sticky glass tumblers stood or lay at various points around the room. Even in the partial light, I could see ingrained dirt and stains on the carpet. The double bed was a mess of crumpled, grubby sheets. The room stank of corruption and sleaze.

To either side of the chimney breast stood matching military armoire cupboards, each with two large doors over four drawers. I pulled open the doors to the one on the right of the chimney breast while Clayton investigated the bedside cabinets. A pile of clothes tumbled out onto the floor, sending wafts of unpleasant odors into my nostrils. I waved a hand in front of my face, kicked the clothes out of the way, and opened the drawers. More clothes, more smells.

"How could anyone live like this?" I said.

"Beats me," said Clayton.

I tried the other armoire and found a dinner jacket and two suits on hangers, one a grubby off-white the other charcoal gray. Then I tried the drawers and got what we came for.

In the two right hand drawers I found boxes of the size that would normally contain dress shirts. In one of the left-hand drawers there was a buff colored folder and Cranver's battered brown leather briefcase, the one I'd seen him with in court on Friday. "Well, well," I said. "What do we have here?"

Clayton came across, peered over my shoulder. "What have you got?" he said.

I took out one of the shirt boxes and flipped off the lid, let it tumble to the floor. I shone the flashlight into the box. There was no mistaking the contents, and I felt instant and absolute revulsion.

"My God," Clayton said.

CHAPTER 44

We stared at the photographs for a long moment. I was afraid to touch them, thinking that in doing so I might become contaminated by their content. Instead, I shook them out of the box onto the filthy carpet, played the flashlight over them.

They were all black and white, various sizes, some grainy, some focused. Cranver was naked in all the shots. In one, he was standing up, held tilted back and eyes closed in the ecstasy of the moment. His fat hands were clamped firmly around the head of a naked black boy who was kneeling in front of the lawyer, forehead pressed against the enormous white belly. The boy was erect and looked to be no more than twelve or thirteen years old. The same boy featured in another shot, this time lying face down on a bed with his hands tied to the headboard. Cranver was on top of him, crushing him with his great weight. Both faces were turned toward the camera, the boy's screwed up in agony, Cranver's leering stupidly.

There were more of the same in the second box: different poses, different partners. Some even featured young girls, but the majority were of Cranver and young, male Negros. Underneath the boxes, we found several magazines, all illegal and of highly graphic child

370

pornography. Clayton picked up one of the photos from the edge of Cranver's bed and stared at it for a few seconds. Then he suddenly threw it to the floor and wiped his hands on his pants, almost as if his flesh had become tainted by the image.

"The evil, sick bastard," he said.

I looked at the photos of Cranver and the boy lying on the bed. Decided that they weren't taken in the room we now occupied. "Wonder where these shots were taken?" I said.

As if he hadn't considered it before, Clayton suddenly leapt off the bed, turned back and stared at it, shocked. "Jesus Christ."

"Calm down," I said. "They weren't taken here in this room."

"How do you know for sure?"

"Different bed and you can just make out different furniture in the background."

"Where then?"

"Brothel, hotel, another house. Who knows? You don't have a brothel in Paradise Creek that's for sure."

"We don't? I mean, I don't think so."

"It wasn't a question. Trust me, you don't."

"Never even occurred to me that we might have, that such an establishment could exist in this town."

"You know, for a guy who's lived here all his life, you haven't got the first idea of what goes on, do you?"

In the long silence that followed, an almost unearthly chill seemed to creep into the room and merge with the ice-blue wash of moonlight.

Clayton eventually asked the inevitable question that had played around in my head for the past five minutes. "Do you think Cranver murdered Caitlin Dexter and Alice Jackson?"

"My first thought," I said. "But now I'm thinking no, not Cranver."

"But what about the photographs? I know they're mainly of boys, but young girls feature in some of them. It must be him."

I shook my head and pointed to one such photograph. "See this?" Clayton squatted down next to me. "This girl is young, barely teenage. Look at her body."

Clayton shifted his gaze away. "I'd rather not."

"Come on," I said, irritated. "Hold it together will you? We've come so far, we're close to ending it. Look at her body. What do you see?"

Slowly, he turned back to the photo. "Err...a young girl."

"Yes, and..."

He threw his hands in the air. "How the hell do I know?"

I stared at him, wondering where he'd got his reputation as a fastidious trial lawyer from. He'd completely missed the obvious. "She's got no breasts."

"What?"

"Her breasts have hardly begun to develop. She's so young. In Cranver's eyes, she looks like a boy, just hasn't got a penis. Cranver's not into females." I shone the flashlight onto shots of Cranver with other girls. They were all about the same age with bodies yet to develop. "See."

372

"Fuck yes."

"Know what I think?" I said.

"No, I don't. I don't know what to think."

"I think that someone had knowledge of this and was blackmailing him. Perhaps that's why Cranver deliberately throws cases. Cases that if the defendant was to be found innocent, that would make life very hard for whoever is doing this."

"That's only assumption. You don't know that for certain."

I hefted Cranver's briefcase and the buff-colored file out of the other drawers, laid them on the carpet.

"You think Floyd and Larry are mixed up in this...this...pornographic stuff?" Clayton said.

"No," I said, flipping open the catch on the briefcase. "The murders, yes, but what Cranver got up to in his private life I'd say was a secret shared between him and maybe only one other person. Sure, Tibbett likes his porn, but it's straight adult material, not kiddie porn."

I hauled a bunch of papers out of the briefcase, sat cross-legged with my back against the bed, and laid the papers on my lap.

Clayton reached for the buff folder, withdrew the contents, let out a tiny gasp. "Jesus H...what in God's name is Cranver doing with this."

I looked across, read the front page: TESTIMONY OF CARL J. ROBARD. Clayton flipped through the file. There were pages of witness testimony from Sam Cooper and two other names I didn't know.

Clayton read through it. "None of this was presented at the trial," he said, disbelief on his face and in his voice. "It's all here: when Carl lost the crucifix, the scarf, Carl cutting his hands on the steel blades...what a damn fool I've been, Tom. Three innocent men have lost their lives because of me."

I was quick to step in. "No. Not because of you, Clayton. Because of other evil men. Men that will do anything to anyone in order to protect themselves."

We opened files and quickly read through them. Clayton was shocked at how much there was, including pertinent information about Frank Delaney that should have been presented as defense testimony but had never seen the light of day. In the end, he angrily swept it off his lap onto the floor. "Fuck."

I searched the briefcase once more and pulled out Cranver's diary, flicked through it, stopped at certain points when something caught my eye: names already on my radar. No detail, just names, and the final entry for that very night. There it was in capital letters underlined several times:

KILLING GOD TONIGHT.

Something jolted in the back of my memory and came rushing to the forefront. Mabel Watt's husband sitting under the bandstand one night and Julias Cranver out of his face on booze being dragged into a cruiser by Larry Swales and Floyd Tibbett. And Cranver shouting out about going to church and killing God.

"Clayton. If I asked you, who considers himself above everyone else in this town, this county…who would you say?"

He gave me an odd look. "Strange question."

"Indulge me. Who considers themselves almost God-like?"

"Given his ambition, status, way the townsfolk see him…throw in a huge streak of arrogance…then our mayor is your man. Why?"

And it all came together in that moment. I could see how it all played out. Henry's power, ambition, the fact he'd never married, his black Lincoln, Swales, and Tibbett covering for their uncle and probably having sloppy seconds after he'd finished with his victim. And he would stop at nothing to become governor, and onwards to the senate. His brother, the Reverend Alvin, had to know. How could he not? Had he returned to this town fifteen years ago, not only to care for his dying father but also to support, and more importantly protect, his brother?

"Clayton, we need to go to Towers Hill Church."

"At this time of night, whatever for?"

"I'll explain on the way."

Chapter 45

We parked up about a quarter mile from the church and came in through the woods. It was close to midnight when we entered the cemetery from a stand of cypress and live oaks; the moon casting its baleful glow across the gravestones.

"Have you any idea what we're supposed to find here?" Clayton asked.

"I don't know. Something. I'm not sure what. Could be in the church itself, a clue leading us to the names, maybe. Cranver could already be here. There are several cars parked close by."

I stopped, searched in my pockets for the diary. I was sure I had it in my hand when we went back downstairs in Cranver's house, couldn't think where I'd left it. Had I dropped it somewhere in the woods or left it in the house? There was too much bouncing around in my head for me to get a fix on it.

I looked up and saw that Clayton had already reached the church doors. "Clayton," I yelled, pulling the Smith and Wesson from my pocket as he stepped inside. "Clayton." He paused at the sound of my voice, but it was too late. He was already across the threshold.

I ran toward the doors, weaving through the gravestones, flicking off my flashlight. My body let me know that it didn't like what I was doing to my injuries. I got to the doors just in time to hear a dull thump and then a heavier sound, like a body hitting the floor. I should have stopped then, taken stock of the situation, allowed my eyes to adjust to the dark before stepping fully inside the church. I was breathing heavily as pain stabbed viciously at every breath. I should have stopped to think, but something had happened to Clayton. He could be injured, or worse, dead. I had to get to him.

Something moved on my right. My head exploded. Red mist in my eyes. And then, nothing.

When I opened my eyes, all I could see was a haze of flickering yellow and dark shapes moving in the background. I shook my head to clear my vision, wished I hadn't. A searing pain tore through the base of my skull. I groaned, squeezed my eyes shut, and instinctively reached up to massage the pain away.

I couldn't move my hands.

I opened my eyes again and my vision cleared enough for me to realize that I was sitting upright on a wooden chair, my arms tied behind my back and my feet bound together. And that's when I registered the additional aches in my shoulders and at the points where the rope pressed into my wrists and ankles. Along with the beating I had suffered, it now felt as though every inch of my body, each tiny nerve ending was sending a message to my brain that it hurt and hurt badly.

I struggled uselessly for a moment or two, trying to free my hands and legs, but all that did was make me cry. I shut my eyes again.

"Wasting your time," a voice said.

I looked up, discovered I had an audience. They hadn't been dancing after all, just moving around in the candlelight waiting for me. My eyes pulled them into focus. "Why am I not surprised," I said.

Henry Towers was standing at the altar between and Larry Swales and Floyd Tibbett. Even in the candlelight, I could see hatred and anger in his eyes. Swales was holding a Colt .45 Peacemaker in his right hand and had that shit stupid grin on his face. Tibbett was crooked over to one side, looking nervous, tongue playing at the corner of his mouth. Much like Clayton didn't look happy to be with Henry Towers on the courthouse steps on Friday, Tibbett didn't look at all happy to be where he was at the moment. I looked around, saw Clayton a few feet away, tied up like me but still out of it. Thankfully, he was breathing.

"You don't look too good, Tom," Henry said. "Boys worked you over pretty hard."

"A couple of scratches," I said. "Nothing more. I'll live."

"Hmmm, debatable point. Shouldn't have busted Weaver's arm. He took real pleasure in kicking the shit out of you."

"I'll wager not half as much as I got when I busted his arm."

"Couldn't leave it alone, could you, Bale? Couldn't just fuck off back to Chicago and stay there."

"Your brother wouldn't want to hear you talking like that in his church, Henry."

378

"Fuck you," he snapped.

"Profanity. God will strike you down."

"Fuck him too."

"Oh, yeah," I said. "There's only one God in this town, and that's you. Isn't that right, Henry?"

"Yeah, and don't you fucking forget it."

I shook my head very slowly, and even then it hurt to do so. "That attitude won't serve your case for election next term. Townsfolk heard you swearing like that, might not be so keen to get behind you."

The mayor fought to control himself and in less than half a minute he was calm, affable even, back on first-name terms. "You should have left it alone, Tom," he said. "I mean, just how many warnings does a man need? But now it's come too far and you've gotta go. No way around it."

"What about Clayton?" I asked. "You can't kill him."

"Correct. He'll come around, though. You dragged him into this. It's not his fight. He doesn't want to be here. He's got the same motivations as I do, cut from the same cloth, so to speak. He'll take some persuading but when I mention to him that I know something about his father-in-law's…shall we say, less than legitimate business dealings, and one phone call could bring everything crashing down around his head…well, I don't think he'd want to put his wife through that, and he certainly won't want to give up the lifestyle he's become so accustom to."

"You really believe Clayton will just roll over?"

Henry nodded. "Yes, I do."

I stared at him, incredulous. "After all the lies, deceit, the cover-ups, the planted evidence, the manipulated trials. The shame and embarrassment that would bring to him. You think he will just carry on like nothing happened?"

"He will."

"And you think blackmailing him about his father-in-law, just like you've done to Julias Cranver, is going to make him an obedient slave forever more? Your self-aggrandizing, Mr. Mayor, is far greater than I thought it was when we first met. You struck me as an egotistical sonofabitch then, but now…jeez."

"Enough," he snarled. He pulled my Smith and Wesson out from his jacket, pointed it at me. "You're gonna die, so is your black whore."

"Let me do it, Henry," Swales said, grinning, holding up the Peacemaker, the candlelight playing on its nickel-plated barrel.

"Shut up, Larry," Henry said.

"This has gone too far, Uncle Henry," Floyd said, his voice shaking. "Way too far."

"You too, Floyd," Henry said.

All the time we'd been talking I was moving my hands as best I could without them noticing, trying to stretch the rope enough to free myself, but I was getting nowhere. Looked like this was it. The end. Henry thought that Clayton could be blackmailed into accepting the situation. But Clayton was too far into this just to back away. Henry didn't know that Clayton had all the details. Henry didn't know Clayton had that piece of headstone with the blood and tissue match.

Even if I died tonight, I felt I could trust Clayton to use all he had at the appropriate time.

"Where's your other sidekick, Julias Cranver?" I asked.

"He was being a pain in the ass," Henry said. "Told him to make himself scarce for a few days while we considered what action to take. Probably down in Tallahassee, feeding his fantasy, sick sonofabitch."

I laughed. "You're really something, Henry. You call Cranver sick. What do you call what you do, acceptable behavior? You're just as sick as he is."

Candlelight flickered in his dark eyes as he stared at me. "OK, time to end it. I'm gonna get Clayton awake first. I want him to see me put an end to your fucking worthless, shitty little life...you know, reinforce the message."

I glanced over at Clayton who surprisingly still looked unconscious. Concussed probably, but his breathing was too even, too controlled, despite his head being flopped over the one side. And then I saw it and realized he wasn't out of it at all, just pretending. He had somehow managed to work that small, pearl-handled fruit knife he carried out of his rear pocket. He'd opened the blade and was gradually slicing through the rope binding his hands, his movements deft, imperceptible. He literally had a couple of strands to get through.

"Yeah, Clayton and me, we're gonna have a long conversation after Floyd and Larry here put you in the swamp. Let the gators have their fill."

I looked at him. "What?"

"You not listening to me, Tom?"

"I'm done listening to you, Henry. Just do what you have to do."

He went over to Clayton, tapped the side of his face with his free hand. "Clayton, come on now, wakey, wakey." He tapped his face a little harder. Still no reaction. "Jesus, Larry, you crack his skull or something?"

I prepared myself. There wasn't much I could do. Tibbett was too far away, but he wasn't holding a weapon of any kind, just nervously shuffling where he stood, wanting to be away from this nightmare. Swales, however, was only a few feet away, gun at his side, stupid grin on his face, watching his uncle. I pushed my feet down as hard as I could, found purchase, and launched myself at him at the very same moment Clayton cut through the remaining strands and swung his right hand around in an arc, plunging the blade into Henry's left side. Henry screamed out and staggered backwards across the altar, dropping the gun.

Caught off guard, Swales didn't see me until it was too late, and my head connected with his diaphragm, knocking the wind out of him and sending him sprawling backwards, his own gun clattering to the floor. I crashed to one side, felt wood cracking under me as the chair came apart. There was a sharp pain in the small of my back as a piece of splintered wood went through my jacket and shirt and pierced my skin. It triggered all the other injuries I'd received, and it seemed like my body was protesting from a thousand different places as I fought to get my hands free.

The mayor was clutching his side, screaming obscenities as Clayton cut through the rope binding his feet, came over, and freed me from the tangle of ropes and splintered wood. We stood up, ready to face anyone and anything. But in those few moments of confusion, the three of them had disappeared. We looked around, swiveling our heads this way and that. Nothing. The Colt Peacemaker was gone, so Swales had obviously retrieved it, but my Smith and Wesson was still on the altar steps. I picked it up, feeling comfort from its familiar grip.

"Look," Clayton whispered. He nodded over at the vestry door. It was open. "Henry must be in there hiding."

I nodded. Unarmed, the mayor wouldn't be a major threat, so Clayton, with the fruit knife still held firmly in his right hand, quietly stepped over toward the door. Tibbett was nowhere to be seen, and I didn't feel threatened by him, anyway. Instead, I focused on Swales, wondering where he could be hiding. I crouched down as best I could, every muscle and joint in my body arguing against the movement. I made my way carefully through the rows of pews, peering into dark corners, the candlelight making the places in shadow much darker than they ordinarily would have been without any light at all.

A weird kind of juxtaposition.

Then I saw movement in my peripheral vision. It was Swales edging along the far wall, making his way silently to the church doors. Either that or trying to come up behind me, shoot me in the back. I turned to face him and for an instant I hesitated, thinking he may be unarmed. It was one of those split-second hesitations that proved to be wrong. His gun came out of nowhere. My shot was half a second behind his, but he was moving, and his shot was a little off. I felt a searing hot stab in my left side, which threw me around but I managed to stop myself from falling by hanging on to the back of a pew. My head registered pain racing through torn nerve endings, my left hand registered blood as I clamped it over the wound. I pulled myself up. Swales was slumped against the wall. I made my way over to him, my .38 still extended, but my hand was shaking.

I'd shot him an inch or two above the heart. I could hear a faint whistling sound as I crouched next to him, the wound in my side protesting angrily. Blood was bubbling out from the hole in his chest. And then a moment later, it all stopped, and I heard someone cry out. Sounded like Clayton.

I stood up, using the wall as support, my left hand covered in blood, sweat pouring down my face. The bullet wound howled at me. I was losing blood fast.

I got to the vestry, saw Clayton slumped on the floor. He was unconscious, and I had no idea how badly he'd been hurt. Standing over him was Henry Towers, gun in his right hand, left nursing the stab wound. He looked up at me and I leveled the Smith & Wesson.

"It's over, Henry. Put the gun down."

Even in the gloom, I could see his eyes, hollow and expressionless, the eyes of a man devoid of any emotion. I was beginning to feel a little faint from the loss of blood and leaned against the doorframe to stop myself from falling, my breathing labored. "So many…lives," I managed to say. "There is nothing…that gives you…the right"—I could feel myself slipping, the gun a huge weight in my hand—"to play God. If your brother was here…he'd hate you for…what you've done."

"Good thing my brother keeps a gun in his desk drawer," he said, the shark smile back in place.

So that's why he'd headed straight for this room. It wasn't to escape as there was no door leading outside. It was to get the gun. I think I even smiled as I heard my own gun clatter on the floor. My eyes flickered, and the last thing I saw was Henry Towers raising his gun toward me then someone pushing me down and the ferocious sound of gunshots exploding in my ears.

PART THREE

August

CHAPTER 46

I drifted in and out of consciousness. Faces and shapes appeared and disappeared in the milky-gray fog which seemed permanently suspended in front of my eyes. Some I thought I recognized: Charlotte, Viola. Clayton, Dan Benson, Sheriff Somers. Doctors and nurses came and went.

By midday the following day, three days after Larry Swales shot me, I was sitting up in bed, half my body wrapped in bandages, head rested against freshly laundered pillows, eyes closed, and face turned towards the sunlight cascading through the window. The sunlight was warm on my face, the color of dusky pink behind my eyelids.

I turned away from the window and opened my eyes. Charlotte smiled gently, and I smiled back at her, appreciating her being at my side and admiring her beautiful face and how the light played against her slender neck and cheekbones.

"How are you feeling?" she said softly.

"Like my insides are on fire."

Her smile broadened, and she squeezed my hand a little tighter. A single tear escaped her right eye, travelled without resistance over her cheek, and pooled at the corner of her mouth.

"Thought I was going to lose you," she said in a tremulous whisper. "Doc said there were intra-abdominal injuries…whatever that means…and potential infection. It was touch and go…"

I raised my left hand and lightly brushed the tear away. She closed her eyes, bent her head over, and held my hand there for a long moment.

"But I'm here," I said.

We talked for a time, then Clayton stepped into the room, his left arm in a sling, hand bandaged so that it resembled a heavy club. He had a large plaster on one side of his forehead and looked exhausted, in pain. "Hey," he said, trying to sound cheery.

"Hey," I said back to him.

Charlotte bent over and kissed my forehead. "I'll leave you two to catch up," she said, then whispered, "I love you."

"You too," I whispered back.

She kissed Clayton on the cheek as she left, something she would not have done a few days ago when their places in this world were perceived differently. Now she was his equal, and it had taken all of this to make it so.

Clayton sat down next to me. "How are you, Tom?"

"Sore, stomach doesn't like me much and my ribs ache like a bitch, but otherwise blood is flowing through my veins, so I guess I'm alive."

"It was close."

"So I hear. You look as though you're suffering. What happened to your arm?"

He held it up, wincing as he moved it beyond his injury would allow. "Doc's given me painkillers, but they're not having much effect. Henry caught me by surprise in the vestry, knocked me out with his gun then stomped on my arm and hand. Arm's not going to be a problem, but fingers are so badly broken, Doc reckons I'll never recover full use."

I felt truly awful at hearing that. I should never have dragged him into this and said so. "I'm sorry, Clayton. I am so sorry. My fault. I shouldn't have involved you."

"It's OK," he said. "You were right to involve me. I was blinded by many things. All that corruption going on around me and I never suspected a thing until you started putting questions into my head. If I had acted sooner, all of this may never have happened. So don't blame yourself. If anyone's to blame, it's me."

"You're a good man, Clayton. Your heart's in the right place. We all get blinded sometimes, it's unavoidable. I've been where you are on so many occasions, I've lost count. But I am truly sorry about your hand."

He gave me a withering smile. "Well, let's see what happens when the bandages come off."

"Good thing you had that fruit knife with you."

"Told you. Never know when you might need it."

"So explain to me what happened," I said. "Last thing I remember was you on the floor out cold, Henry Towers standing over you, maybe someone next to me, and then I dropped my gun and heard shots as I passed out."

"Of course, you don't know what went down."

"Not as yet. Charlotte didn't say anything, apart from to tell me that Henry Towers was dead and that you were alive. I guess she doesn't know the rest."

Clayton gave out a little laugh. "Oh, she knows everything believe me."

I stared at him, confused. "I don't understand."

"She and Maryanne played a larger part in this. In fact, they probably saved both our lives. Sort of."

I was suddenly wide awake and propped myself up on the pillows, stomach and ribs reminding me that they did not appreciate the sudden movement. "Charlotte...and Maryanne? What the hell did they do?"

"Charlotte will fill you in on all the details, but cutting a long story short, she told Maryanne everything. They went and got the sheriff out of bed, insisted he helped. That would be about the same time we left Cranver's house."

"Thank God he listened," I said.

"Maryanne can be a very persuasive woman. She threatened to get her father involved, the governor, you name it."

Sometimes, wealth and power does have its upsides, I thought. Should I remind him about what Henry had said in the church, about his father-in-law's supposed dodgy business deals? No. Dodgy they may be, and Clayton already suspected that, anyway. Enough was enough.

"But how did they make the connection with the church?" I asked. "What made the sheriff go there?"

390

He tapped me on the arm with his good hand, smiled. "Think I'll leave that one to Charlotte. I'll let you rest. I've got to go, Maryanne is waiting for me."

"Sure. You take good care, Clayton. See you when I get out, and...thank you for sticking by me."

His expression changed then, grew deadly serious. "No, Tom. Thank you," he said.

"Why? You've nothing to thank me for. Look at your goddamn hand."

"For making me see," he said, and left.

CHAPTER 47

I spent that night and the following day in hospital. The doc was happy with my progress. X-rays completely clear, no signs of infection or internal bleeding, blood pressure good. I was discharged into the care of Charlotte.

It was good to be out of hospital and breathing in the summer evening, though getting into her truck proved difficult. My stitches and ribs didn't like that one bit. We drove in silence for a few minutes, my head back, just watching the pine trees whipping by.

"Can I ask you something?" I said eventually.

"You can ask me anything," she said.

"What happened that night in the church?"

"Clayton didn't tell you?"

"No, he left all the details for you. I didn't realize you and Maryanne had gotten involved. Clayton said you dragged the sheriff out of bed."

She let out a long sigh. "I just had a feeling something really bad was going to happen. It was so…final…this feeling. I really can't describe it, you and Clayton going off like that." She turned to me, fear and sadness in her eyes. "Just felt like the end was coming."

The pickup caught the edge of the road and the steering wheel juddered as the tires plowed into rough ground and the back end fishtailed. Pain shot through me. "Jesus," I said out loud.

Charlotte instinctively slowed and eased the truck back onto the blacktop. "Sorry, Tom. You OK?"

"I'll live," I said, wincing, clutching my stomach.

She looked at me again, a playful smile on her face. "I'm glad about that."

"Just keep your eyes on the road."

She turned back, concentrating.

"So…Maryanne…?"

"Yes, of course, sorry. This feeling I had was so strong, but I knew the sheriff wouldn't listen to me, so I told her all about it. I'd overheard you talking to Clayton, that you were going to Julias Cranver's house. I thought if anyone could influence the sheriff Maryanne could. I explained as best I could. She listened, and we went over to his house, woke him up, and gave him the details."

"I understand from Clayton that Maryanne threatened the sheriff."

"Oh, yes. Didn't know she could be like that. She gave him both barrels and then some. She's quite a formidable woman."

"How did the sheriff know to come to the church? You couldn't have told him because you had no idea."

"It was something you said about the night he was seen outside his offices, drunk and screaming out 'killing God'. I told the sheriff you and Clayton were headed to Cranver's so we went there first. He found a diary on the kitchen table…"

"So that's where I left it," I said, resting my head back and closing my eyes. "I meant to take it with me." It was that simple, I thought. "So the sheriff saw the entry for that night…and just put two and two together."

"That's it. If you hadn't left that diary behind…you might not be sitting here…with…me."

I opened my eyes again and saw Charlotte was crying. I wanted to hold her then, hold her and never let go. My injuries prevented me from doing so, but I held her hand tight, just so she knew. Her actions had saved my life.

"We got to the church and heard shooting. Sheriff told us to wait in the car…"

"What? Wait a minute. You went with him. What were you thinking?"

"He had no choice. We insisted."

"My God," I said. "What if it hadn't turned out the way it did? You could have both been killed."

"Nothing he could do about it."

I shook my head and laughed. "I guess not. Still, I'm glad you came when you did. So the sheriff finally got his act together and ended it for the mayor."

She slipped her hand from mine and wiped the tears away. "You think the sheriff shot him?"

"It was the sheriff who shot Henry…yes?"

Charlotte was shaking her head. "Maryanne and me, we followed the sheriff into the church a half minute later. He'd radioed for backup then told us to wait in the car, keep the engine running, and if we felt a threat of any kind, even the smallest sense of danger, we should just take off. But we couldn't just sit there. We crept into the church, saw him in that doorway next to you. You were completely gone."

"Yes," I said. "I remember. I dropped my gun, felt someone behind me…heard shots…after that…nothing."

"Sheriff had his gun raised, but at that same moment Floyd Tibbett came out of nowhere, pushed past you both, and shot Henry with Larry's gun."

"Floyd Tibbett shot Henry, his uncle?" How many more surprises awaited me? I wondered.

"Told the sheriff he couldn't stand it any longer. Sick of the lies, corruption, his family, and what they'd done…the young girls, the murder of Cooper, and he and Larry having to clean up after them."

"Swales was a willing servant, deserved what he got in the end."

"Floyd's in one of the holding cells for the moment. He'll be tried for murder. Add all the other things he was involved with, he'll get the chair or life at the very least. He'll spend those at Georgia State Pen over in Reidsville. Thank God that's the end of it all."

If only it were, I thought. "It's never over, Charlotte. There's always something or someone else. Cranver was being blackmailed by Henry Towers. Swales and Tibbett covered up, planted evidence, made files disappear. They even murdered an innocent young man, hid his body down at the creek then set up the whole scene so that Carl Robard took the blame. And all because Henry Towers couldn't keep away from young girls. When he strangled Caitlin Dexter in his brother's church, they saw that as an opportunity to explain Alice Jackson's abduction and murder by framing Carl. Why they chose Carl, I don't know. They would have been better off framing Cooper instead of killing him. Especially with it being common knowledge that he liked young girls, particularly Caitlin Dexter."

"Stands to reason. Black girls gone missing, murdered, black man gotta take the blame."

"Caitlin wasn't black."

"Don't matter. Coop was white."

With a heavy heart, I said, "You're probably right. Still, there's more to this, I'm certain of it."

"You really don't think it's over?"

"There's more. I just don't know what. It doesn't seem conceivable that only Henry, Floyd, and Larry were involved."

"Henry's brother was arrested and questioned by the sheriff, but he swore he had no idea. He's been released."

"I don't think the reverend Alvin is quite as innocent as he makes out. The two of them lived together, for Christ's sake. He must have known something. But I don't think he had any involvement with the murders or the evidence. He may have protected his brother, but beyond that, no."

We got to Charlotte's house in the woods, and I was still in one piece despite the farm track's best efforts to tear my stomach apart. She helped me inside, and after lighting up a couple of lamps and getting me settled on the sofa with a bottle of Wild Turkey to keep me company—despite the doc's strict instructions to leave the alcohol alone—she headed off in her truck to see Viola, for what reason she didn't say. I didn't like the troubled look on her face, didn't like it one bit.

Charlotte had an old TR-1 transistor radio in a faded ruby-red plastic which she'd left on the side table. I reached for it, switched it on, twisted the dial a little until most of the interference disappeared and found a news station. It was broadcasting a repeat of President Kennedy's nationwide address, which I'd caught part of earlier on the TV in my hospital room, but with visitors and everything else going on around me, I'd missed most of it.

I sat, sipping bourbon and catching snippets in between crackles, whistles, and buzzes. The TR-1 was a great invention, but the quality left a lot to be desired.

The Soviet Union was preparing to take control of West Berlin, and Kennedy was giving an impassioned speech, saying that the United States would be prepared to go to war. He was planning to increase US Armed forces to one million men, and we should all recognize the possibilities of a nuclear attack. My God, I thought. Nuclear war. Surely it wouldn't come to that?

The radio started to fade, and I missed what came next. I twisted the dial some more to retune the station, but the signal weakened to the point I couldn't hear it. The battery had died. I knew Charlotte kept a spare 22.5 volt Ever Ready in one of the drawers in the kitchen, so I carefully eased myself up from the sofa and padded over. Light from the hurricane lamps barely extended beyond the den, but I knew my way around and found the battery straight away. I headed back to the sofa.

"Bale."

CHAPTER 48

I sucked in my breath and stood there for a moment. The desire to turn immense, but any sudden movement might trigger a reaction that I did not want from whoever was standing behind me. I took a moment to compose myself and turned slowly, hands away from my sides to show I was unarmed. The voice wasn't one I recognized, and whoever it was hiding in the shadows wasn't here to wish me well.

I faced the direction of the voice and could just make out a figure shrouded in darkness about fifteen feet away, far back in a corner of the kitchen. He must have come through the side door after Charlotte had left. I noticed through the kitchen window that she had lit some of the hurricane lamps strung through the trees outside.

"Who are you?" I said. "What do you want?"

The figure stepped forward. I got a good look at the gun first as it came out of the black and into the partial footprint of light from the lamps in the den.

"You, Bale," the figure said. "And then your buddy Clayton Burke."

As he came closer, I recognized the face. In many ways, it didn't surprise me. He was dressed casually, free from the constraints of his formal uniform.

"You?" I said.

"That's right," he said. "Me. I guess you think it's all over with Henry gone, and now you're free to get all settled down and cozy with that mulatto woman. She is pretty, I'll give you that. Wouldn't mind taking her myself…before I kill her."

"You touch her," I said, "and I'll tear out your throat."

"And how are you going to do that exactly, when you'll already be dead?"

"You've got to kill me first."

"Exactly what I intend to do. Now drop that battery."

I did as I was told, threw it on the sofa. It was hardly going to make an effective weapon. At best, all I could do was throw it at him, but he wasn't going to take any chances.

Sweat started to ease out of every pore in my skin; not just from fear of dying or from pain, but also from the fear of what might happen to Charlotte. I needed more time, time to work up some plan.

"So what's your involvement in all of this?" I asked.

"You really want to know?"

"Yes, I do," I said, thinking about where the hell I'd left my gun.

He came a couple of feet closer, but far enough away to easily deal with any sudden movement I might make.

"OK," he said. "Here's something I bet you've been thinking on since the first time you showed up looking for Alice Jackson."

"And what might that be?"

"Who put that note under your motel room door? Right?"

"Yeah, I always wondered about that."

"Floyd," he said.

"Floyd? I don't get it. Why would he do that?"

"Figured he'd try to stop what was going on. He bitched and whined about it forever. We tried to warn you off the first time. Pity Weaver didn't crack open your skull. Then all the problems would have gone away. But you were getting nowhere trying to find that Jackson girl and so Floyd thought you could use a helping hand. He and Larry had taken her out of the way to the swamp, somewhere Henry thought you'd never find her."

"And so Floyd slipped that note under my door, knowing I would find her, and that would be it. I'd head back to Chicago, and it would all fade to black, everything would stop, the missing girls, murder, blackmail, corruption. Finally, it would all go away. I know Floyd hated being involved, and he thought me finding Alice Jackson would put the fear of God into everyone, and that would be it."

That seemed to amuse him. "Fear of God, I like it. Anyway, after you found that Negro bitch, we wondered how you did it. She was moved there for convenience but got it out of him. Floyd doesn't handle confrontation too well."

"And then Henry murdered Caitlin Dexter. Couldn't keep his dick in his pants. Got Floyd and Larry to hide her boyfriend's body down at the creek. Plant evidence on the girl, and with Henry blackmailing

Craver, Carl Robard's fate was well and truly sealed. And you knew all along."

His eyes closed for just a moment and when he opened them, there was a distant smile on his face.

"Shame about Cooper," he said, "but that was down to you. You brought him into this, and we couldn't risk him getting drunk down at that bar and blabbing about what he knew."

"He didn't know who was involved. He didn't have to be killed."

"Perhaps not, but you got him involved. So he had to go. After that, we decided to stay on the sidelines, keep quiet, watch from a distance."

"So who's been following me around all this time?"

"Henry paid a couple of local guys to keep an eye on you as well. Couldn't be in two places at once."

"Did they know what was going on?"

"No. They couldn't care less. When someone offers you good money for an easy job with no strings attached, who would refuse? Weaver packs a pretty good punch now his arm's fixed."

The car I'd spotted on half-a-dozen occasions, waiting in the shadows. The red glow of a cigarette burning. "Was it Weaver who also took a shot at me and Charlotte?" I asked.

He nodded. "Just to scare you off."

"And the beating?"

"Same, but he had help for that one. Still, it didn't stop you."

"I have a conscience," I said. "Innocent people, children were being murdered. I could not let it continue."

"And now you're going to die for what you did," he said, so matter-of-factly that I wanted to go for him, wipe that smug expression off his face for good. But I held myself in check. He would be expecting me to do something, and I would be next to useless anyway with my injuries.

"So, what are you here for, revenge? Tell me, when did all this start?"

An amused look spread across his face. "Oh no. I ain't going to give you that."

"Why not?" I said. "There's nothing to lose. You're the guy with the gun pointed at me. I need to know."

He scratched his chin with his left hand, as if considering whether to tell me or not. And it was at that very moment when it all fell into place, and I'd got it all wrong. It felt like clouds parting to let the sun come through, and it all made perfect sense. It was the wrong way around all this time.

"You were the one who smashed that young boy's head against the gravestone."

"Yes, that was me. He and that white bitch of a girlfriend were arranging flowers at her mother's grave. I saw a perfect opportunity."

Sweat was beginning to sting my eyes and my injuries were telling me that I urgently needed to lie down. I could feel the stitches pulling against my wound.

"You don't look too well," he said. "Got to be careful. Don't want to break those stitches or get an infection." He stepped a foot closer and fixed his aim at the center of my chest. "But I was forgetting, you're going to die, anyway."

When you look down the barrel of a gun, even from a few feet away, that's all you see. It looms at you, takes over your vision; becomes a gigantic black tunnel. Think, I said to myself. Think. But my brain wouldn't focus. All I could do was stall.

"I have to know," I said. "You can at least grant me that. When did it all start? How many?"

"You don't need to know anything more where you're going."

I saw it through the kitchen window, just a flash of something outside, caught for the briefest of moments in the light from the hurricane lamps. I shifted my balance, ready. My stitches pulled, my stomach and ribs said no. He steadied his gun. From where he was standing, it would be impossible to miss. Another flash of movement outside. Whoever or whatever you are, I thought, and whatever you're going to do, do it now.

The window suddenly blew inwards, and glass rained over him, the force of the shot sending razor-sharp fragments across the kitchen as I threw myself to one side. He pitched forward, bumping his head against the table. His gun clattered to the floor and spun toward me. I grabbed it and aimed at his head. He was barely breathing.

"Go on," I hissed at him. "Make a move. Give me an excuse."

CHAPTER 49

I propped myself up against one of the kitchen cabinets, breathing hard. My stitches had torn, and pain was beginning to spread across my body; blood soaked through my shirt. I had the gun resting on my knee, still aimed at his head. He hadn't moved, but he was still breathing. I guessed a combination of pain from the gunshot and hitting his head on the table and then the floor had knocked him out. I held myself upright with my other hand feeling broken glass cutting into my skin as I pressed my hand against the floor. I almost laughed. This was the third time I'd been sitting in a sea of glass.

I didn't notice someone coming through the door until I felt movement at my side, heard the crunch of glass and a voice say. "Want me to finish it?"

I looked up, shook my head, saw my .38. "There's more I need to know." The pain was intensifying. "We need to get him and me to the hospital."

Charlotte crouched down beside me. "Oh my God, Tom...I...I didn't think. Your injuries, I'm so sorry."

"It's OK," I said breathlessly. "I'm glad you did what you did, but my stitches have torn and I'm bleeding. Need to get it fixed."

She looked desperate, helpless. "But I can't get you both in my truck."

"I know. Just get something to tie his hands and feet. He's not going anywhere. He's losing blood, but I think he'll make it. try to stem the flow as much as you can, then go get the sheriff and the doc."

She hesitated. "But I can't leave you alone with him." She almost spat the last word out.

"Just tie him up and go...quick."

"I've got duct tape and twine."

"Perfect," I said.

Charlotte used both, and five minutes later she was gone. While she was tying him up, she told me how she knew someone was waiting for us to return from the hospital.

Coming down the track about a quarter mile from her cabin, she'd caught a glimpse of a car backed into the bushes, a big town car but couldn't be certain. Once she'd got me settled, she took my gun and went to investigate. The car was still there when she drove past it, giving the impression she was off somewhere, but she stopped a few hundred yards further and made her way back on foot. She had no intention of seeing Viola, she just didn't want to worry me. When she got to the car, the driver had gone, so she made her way back and that's when she saw him through the kitchen window.

Brave, clever girl. That was twice in one week she'd saved my life.

He was starting to come round. He groaned, turned his head toward me still propped up against the cabinet. I didn't know how much longer I could take the pain before passing out.

"She's gone for the sheriff and the doc," I said.

"What...who?" he said, voice groggy from pain and disorientation.

"You know, that mulatto woman you wanted to kill."

"Oh...fuck," he said, realization flooding back.

"Now there's a word I would never have imagined coming from your mouth. Sheriff will be here very soon...so you might as well tell it to me now."

"Fuck you." He tried to move and shouted out. "Jesus, that fucking hurts."

From the position of the wound, I guessed the bullet may have lodged close to his left lung. Charlotte had probably aimed for the center of his back, the largest area. You always aim for the largest area. But the bullet's trajectory would have diverted slightly because of the window, and it would have also slowed down. I very much doubted it had punctured a lung because his breathing, although shallow, was not erratic or strained. However, the bullet would have fragmented after penetration and that could cause significant injury.

"I wouldn't try to do that," I said. "That bullet's got to be close to a major organ. You don't want it moving. Now, tell me."

"I'll wait for the sheriff," he said defiantly.

"OK. Suit yourself," I said. "But I'm going to get it out of you one way or another."

My injuries were really getting to me now, but I managed to push myself away from the cabinet, fighting with everything I had not to pass out. I shuffled over to him, knees and left hand bleeding from the fragments of glass. It took me about a minute to get to him. I aimed the gun right into his face, pressed it against his forehead.

"Tell me," I said, fighting for breath.

I could see his dark eyes filled with pain as they strained to look up at me, sweat falling down his face. "Fuck you," he said again.

The screams both he and I let out when I fell on top of him could have woken the dead. The bullet fragments would be straining inside him, tearing nerves and ready to pierce through into his lung.

"Tell me," I screamed at him. But he had passed out again.

Somehow, I managed to get off him and back to the cabinet. My left hand and knees were studded with tiny pieces of glass. I was hanging in there, but for how much longer I couldn't guess.

The sheriff, two deputies, and the doc arrived in a blaze of lights and noise ten minutes later. It had felt like an eternity. Charlotte got me a drink of water, which I sipped in between breaths. Deputy Carson got me up and with Charlotte's help, to her truck. We left the others to deal with the Reverend Alvin while we headed for the hospital.

He had better not die, I thought. Don't you fucking dare die.

CHAPTER 50

I was back in county again, same room, recovering once more. How my body was managing to cope with all the injuries I couldn't even begin to guess. What a marvelous invention we are, I thought. Most of us.

Deputy Carson came in to see me, and couldn't apologize enough, thinking it was that missing person file he'd failed to action; the missing person file Clayton and I found in Julias Cranver's bedroom. We shook hands as he left, with my assurance that he had nothing to apologize for. What happened, happened. Even his dad came in to see me, offered to repair and service my car for free and whenever I needed it.

Reverend Alvin had survived and confessed under questioning. He and Floyd would be heading for the chair. Clayton was angry that he couldn't represent the prosecution. As he'd been directly involved, it would class as a conflict of interest. As for Cranver, nobody has seen or heard from him since. He'd be found, I felt sure of it. Man of his size, his incompetence, his...needs; couldn't stay out of the way for long.

So, there we were in hospital again with Charlotte, Clayton, Maryanne at my bedside, watching the news on TV. It was dusk now and I could see through the window the stars just starting to come out, beautiful and bright hanging there in a cloudless night sky.

Bud Trevin, fifty-years-old, anchorman for *JNBK Atlanta*, face purposefully set into a mask of practiced sincerity, dyed hair immaculately groomed, faced the camera. People were moving around behind him in the fading dusk, and as the camera drew back and panned to the left, Bud went out of frame for a few moments. We could see arc lights had been set up and more people were bending down and examining items on the floor. We couldn't make out where they were or what specifically they were doing.

Bud was back in frame and speaking into his microphone again. *"I'm reporting from the town of Paradise Creek, Marston County, Georgia. Behind me"*—he turned and pointed as the camera drew back—*"is the Towers Hill Church and we are standing in the grounds of the cemetery."*

We gasped collectively and my heart started to pump a little harder.

"What the hell…?" Clayton said.

"Shush," said Maryanne.

We were silent once more.

"The church was the scene of Monday's bloodbath"—Hardly a bloodbath, I thought. But that was media sensationalism for you—*"And I would like to point out that some viewers might find this interview distressing."* He paused just long enough for his words to

410

create effect. *"With me is Ferris Bewley, the county's chief medical examiner."* Ferris nodded to the camera and gave us that same cold, dead smile that he'd given me and Clayton down in the morgue.

"Mr. Bewley," Bud said, turning to him. *"We understand that Judge William Thomas issued an order this morning to exhume several of the graves here at the church."*

Bud shoved the microphone under Ferris's chin. Ferris bent forward a little, mouth almost touching the mic, so much so that when he spoke his words were too distorted. Bud pulled the microphone back and asked him to comment again.

"Yes, that is correct," Ferris said.

"And I believe you had a vacation planned this week. Is that correct?"

"Uh-huh," Ferris said. *"Had to cancel 'cause of what's been taking place."*

"Tell us about that," Bud urged.

"I was called to the cemetery here earlier this evening in an official capacity to oversee the exhumations. All the families who have loved ones buried here have been informed...err not all, of course, only those whose graves have to be exhumed."

Bud was back, looking serious, looking sincere. *"And what have you found so far?"*

"Seven coffins have been exhumed so far. Buried further down in the graves underneath about a foot of earth, we discovered skeletons and rotted clothing."

We all looked at each other, stunned.

411

"*And...?*" Bud prompted.

"*Difficult to tell at this time, as we need to examine the remains properly. But judging by the size of the bones, length, weight, and so on, we're looking at seven young girls so far. We've got two more graves to exhume.*"

"*Anything else you can tell us at this time?*"

"*Well, it looks as though some of the remains are several years old, back as much as fourteen or fifteen years. Again, hard to say without proper examination.*"

"Fifteen years," I said quietly.

"What?" Clayton said. "You know about this?"

They all looked at me speechless. "No," I said. "I just remembered what you told me, Clayton, that night we headed up to yours for the barbecue. Fifteen years ago the reverend Alvin returned to Paradise Creek to look after his dying father and support Henry."

"Oh my good God," Maryanne said.

"Henry's been covering for him ever since," I said.

"All this time," Charlotte said. "All...this...time."

We turned back to the TV, wondering how many more revelations awaited us.

Bud was commenting on the discoveries and asking Ferris more questions. Ferris scratched his chin and a deep frown creased his forehead. "*It's a little strange,*" he said, "*but all the skeletal remains are intact apart from one.*"

"*And why might that be?*" Bud asked.

"*I don't really know, but one of them has the proximal, intermediate, and distal phalanges...*" He stopped, considered that might be too technical for some viewers. "*Part of the little finger of a right hand missing.*"

CHAPTER 51

I took an early walk through town as dawn eased out of a gray-black sky and unfurled itself over the horizon, interweaving light with shade through the buildings, across the streets and avenues. A pair of swifts rose shrieking into the sky, greeting the morning, and the final remains of a chill mist lifted off the pine and cypress trees and became absorbed into the new day.

My work was done. My suitcase already packed.

An hour later, I'd handed the cabin key in to the manager's office and was outside the Paradise Creek Motel, biding my time loading the Dodge, thinking through what had taken place over the past weeks, what had come and gone; lost and found.

I'd found myself.

More importantly, justice had been served. Evil men had been caught and punished. There would be others of course. There would always be others. I hoped Alice would be looking down on me with a measure of forgiveness. Not that the other girls and Caitlin Dexter deserved any less of my consideration, it was just that I couldn't connect with them like I could Alice. I am a man and it was a man…men who did those terrible things, and that at the very least made me guilty by connection. There are those who are evil, and thankfully there are the rest of us.

I placed my suitcase in the trunk, got in, and turned the engine over. I had come to a decision.

Just as I was heading out of the lot, the Chevy BelAir with the white walls drove in, Scarface in the driver's seat. Another time, I thought.

Another time.

CHAPTER 52

I was sitting on the glider in the dark, toying with an unlit cigarette, listening to the night sounds. I picked up the tumbler of Wild Turkey and held it aloft so the moon could dance in its amber heat. I raised a toast to the good people of Paradise Creek. I thought about Jenny, how much I missed her, how there would always be a place in my heart for her.

She would never leave me, and one day I would find her killer.

I stayed like that a while, lost in time and space, until my thoughts drifted to wondering if Kennedy would fulfill his dream of landing a man on the moon before the end of the decade. Didn't seem possible.

Perhaps a whole five minutes passed before I sensed a sudden shift in the air. Fingers lightly brushed across my shoulders. A kiss, more delicate than a feather, touched my head.

"So," she said. "How long will you be gone?"

Charlotte sat down next to me, stared out into the purple-black night.

"You assume I'm leaving."

"There are things still left undone, Tom. I assume you'd want to go back."

"I will when it's ready. I can't leave Jenny's killer out there, wouldn't be right."

"It wouldn't. You owe it to her."

"I do."

A long beat of silence passed between us and then it came, the question she'd being dying to ask me. Her voice faltered as she spoke.

"Will you…will you come…back?"

I put the cigarette in its pack, snaked my arm around her shoulders, and drew her to me. My injuries didn't like that one bit, but I really didn't care.

"Chicago doesn't need me anymore, Charlotte. I am home."

Author's Note

I have taken great liberties with the accuracy of location in creating the fictional town of Paradise Creek and Marston County, Georgia. Those of you with intimate knowledge of the Okefenokee Swamp and its breathtaking beauty, and the real towns surrounding it, might be drawn to thinking that Paradise Creek's location is currently occupied by the town of Waycross, Ware County. I can assure you that Paradise Creek is not based on Waycross, but the location…?

All I can do is apologize for any inaccuracies relating to the swamp, surrounding countryside, the Satilla River, and other locations between Paradise Creek and Chicago. What happened in my head to create this story is my fault alone.

You can be assured though, that Tom Bale has made Paradise Creek his home.

Brian W. Caves
@bwcaves

Printed in Great Britain
by Amazon